A WORLD BENEATH THE STARS

EXPANDED EDITION

by

G. David Nordley

A WORLD BENEATH THE STARS

EXPANDED EDITION

Brief Candle
Press

Previous versions of these stories were originally published as follows:
"P. C. Software," Analog Science Fiction/Science Fact, November 1992
"Hunting the Space Whale," Tomorrow, #4 1993
"Tin Angel," with H. G. Stratmann, Analog Science Fiction/Science Fact, July 1994
"His Father's Voice," Analog Science Fiction/Science Fact, September 1994
"Karl's Marine and Spacecraft Repair," Analog Science Fiction/Science Fact, Dec. 1994
"Of Fire and Ice," Mindsprings, March 1995
"The Kubota Effect," Analog Science Fiction/Science Fact, May 1996
"Democritus' Violin," Analog Science Fiction/Science Fact, April 1999
"Harpoon" Analog Science Fiction/Science Fact, February 2005
"Voice of Ages" Golden Age SF, Eric Reynolds, ed., 2006
"A Wartime Draught" How Beer Saved the World, Irene Radford, ed., 2013
"The Off Switch" in Horseshoes, Hand Grenates and Magic, M. Frishberg, ed. 2016
"Last Call" How Beer Saved the World II, Irene Radford, ed., 2016
"100 Miles from Reno," Uncertain Stars, Valerie Frankel, ed. 2016
"Flight of the Steam Dragon," *Steam and Dragons,* Knotted Road, 2017
"Run Lagomorph," *Pulling Up Stakes,* Joyce Reynolds Ward, ed, Knotted Road, 2018

All other material is original to this work and is printed with perssion of the author and publisher.

Cover design: Brief Candle Press

First Brief Candle Press edition published 2017
Expanded Edition published 2021
www.briefcandlepress.com

ISBN: 978-1-942319-63-4

DEDICATION
To
Stan Schmidt

ACKNOWLEDGEMENTS

My thanks to Dawn Minnette Hurley, of Boron, CA, the initial reader for some of my earliest stories, and to members of the Whensday People writers group, for their gift of time as first readers of many of these stories. Special thanks is owed to John Bray for advice on things British. When I have gotten something wrong despite their best efforts, the fault is mine, not theirs. Thanks also go to editors Gardner Dozois, Sheila Williams, Stan Schmidt, Algis Budrys, Phyllis Radford, Valerie Frankel and Catherine Asaro for purchasing these stories originally. Thanks especially to Deb Houdek Rule for getting started the project of making my backlist available in print and electronic format and last but not least to Lars Hedbor for keeping it going.

PREFACE

A *World Beneath the Stars* covers my stories that take place almost entirely on the planet Earth. This collection is quite different in many respects. There's only one spaceship tor readers to fly along in, with mention of a couple others. These stories mostly do not fit into the future timeline of my other works, and some are clearly stories that did not happen in that or any timeline. They were written with other things in mind, such as my fascination with Winston Churchill, or my memories of family summers spent on Gull Lake, Minnesota. There are four stories not written in my own authorial voice, but are rather conscious homages to other writers I admire.

Nonetheless, most of them have some real science at their core and may send readers to Google or textbooks (or whatever, dear readers, in times far from now, are their equivalent). In two instances, the technological anticipations have actually come to pass, though in different ways than I imagined. "Democritus' Violin" and "Of Fire and Ice" were early anticipations of what we now call 3D printers, a technology which I think will be transformative of society in the way that personal computing has been, but do not represent anything that is likely to be done very soon, nor necessarily in the way described. It is impossible to predict the future in any detail, of course. What I try to do is place most of my stories in a future that plausible enough that they may have some continuing relevance.

Following the stories are "Story Notes" with some additional background information on each story.

G. David Nordley, February 2015

TABLE OF CONTENTS

THE STONE HEART

After a moon of darkness, the fires, at last, burned themselves out and the rain of hot stones lessened. But then winter attacked in the middle of summer. Frost seeped into Gelich, even at noon of the longest days. Yet they had to eat.

He gazed at the pale Sun, so dimmed and reddened by the grayness in the sky that he could look directly at it. Still, its return was welcome, a sign of life among the stench of ash and death all around.

He took a spear, left the mouth of the cave, and followed his nostrils. Nothing stirred but the birds, and those seemed strangely lethargic, preferring to stand rather than fly, most of the time.

It stank most in one direction; Gelich headed that way. He also kept his eyes open for furrythings. Now that every tree was a blackened ghost of itself, they would be easier to spot, and their burrows were often full of good-tasting nuts.

About a hundred strides left from where the stream reached the seashore, Gelich found the source of the smell—a longneck carcass, only slightly scorched. He thumped his tail on the ground and licked his cutting teeth; at least there would be meat, he thought, for a while.

The climb back to the cave mouth tired him, as if he were an elder, or labored in the high western hills where they found black glass and hard stone for their tools. He was not that old, but he'd not eaten in days. Perhaps that was the reason. He stopped for breath.

A double boom and a crackling noise came from above, so he

started up again and hurried himself as much as possible. The sky still had some falling to do.

A flash from far to the East lit the mouth of the cave as he entered. He folded himself down to catch his breath and rest as the others emerged from the depths of their cave. "We have food," he told them, between gasps "about five hundred strides toward the shore and north a bit."

A deep boom shook the world around them, but they did no more than glance up. Such things became commonplace months ago.

Buuk, Matriarch and mate of Gelich, came forward and touched his beak with hers. "I knew you would find some."

The clicking of falling stone began, but they were safe inside.

Buuk had taken charge when the ground shook and the cave-in had trapped twenty-two of them deep inside where they'd gone to look for sharp stones and a place to camp safe from the long-teeth. Moving carefully in the blackness, they'd found a pool of water deep in the cave. Surprisingly, it had a few fish.

In weeks, the rain of stones lessened. It had taken them five days after the thunderclaps lessened to dig out by feel, their eyes almost useless in the gloom. When Buuk led them out of the cave, they found the world had burned, the sky had turned black and it still rained red-hot stones. They'd found grazer carcasses, some only partly burned, near the cave mouth.

After a Moon passed, the sky lightened and grayed without a tinge of red. Despite a near constant rain, of water now instead of rock, Buuk led teams to recover unburned driftwood from the river mud and seashore and carcasses of animals cooked by the fire and strangely untouched by scavengers.

Gelich depended on her now, bonded by far more than her mating choice. She always seemed to make the right choice at the right time; they'd emerged in time to find food, but avoid most of the falling sky. Only one had been injured, and not seriously. Who else could have led them through this? As their bills touched, he felt himself the luckiest being alive.

Gelich, Platek and Gogor returned to his find in the morning; the long-neck carcass was still untouched by anything but the curiously torpid birds. They butchered it with black glass knives, using part of its hide as a tent to shelter them from the rain. It took many trips and several days to haul the meat and skin to their cave, but no predator challenged their spears.

At the mouth of the cave, sheltered from rain, wind, and now snow, they scraped the hide and cut the meat into strips. This they dried and smoked, that it might last a long time.

Gelich and the others then cut the hide into capes to keep them warm. Fires did not seem to burn as hot any more, but the wood lasted longer. That, he thought, was a good thing, as they rapidly exhausted nearby supplies of unburnt wood and had to make ever longer journeys to collect it.

This could not go on forever, he thought. If nothing else lived, they were as good as dead, too.

* ✶ *

In the paleontology lab, amidst rocks, bones, and dust, the tenured professor and the dean circled each other like a triceratops and a *T. rex*. Peter and his fellow student, Lilly, tried to make themselves small, like ancestral mammals watching dinosaurs fight. The discussion, as almost always, concerned money.

"It's been there a billion years, Sandra. It will be there a few more," Dean of Sciences Michael Burkton said, jowls wiggling. His manner was polite, but dismissive, as if an irrevocable decision had already been made and the only chore left was to deal, politely and professionally, of course, with the complaints of those affected.

"This could be an historic find, Michael," replied Dr. Sandra Wright, sweetly, and touched his arm as her long blond hair rippled down a magenta silk shirt that emphasized her curves, with perhaps one fewer button buttoned than usual. She had the figure of an athlete, but her brown and prematurely wrinkled skin testified to the better part of two decades in the field. "Think of what that might mean in grants, alumni donations, and magazine interviews."

Lilly got Peter's attention, with difficulty, and whispered, "It's sixty-six million years, not a billion."

Peter shook his head and put a finger to his lips. Dr. Wright had enough sense not to argue with a *T. rex* over details. Not with so much at stake.

Burkton harrumphed. "I have to make a ten percent cut. Either e everyone shares the pain, or I cut something completely. So don't go over ninety percent of last year's budget." He glanced down momentarily and his bald pate sent a momentary reflection of overhead fluorescent light to the two students. "You should prepare for shutting down the dig."

"Dr. Burkton, we have theses that depend on that dig; student's degrees and our publication output. We need to keep up with WSU! The school's reputation is at stake, too."

"That's what they all say." He looked around, down at Dr. Wright, and harrumphed again. "Well, I don't suppose it would matter if you stretched what you have out to the end of the summer. But next fiscal year, ten percent less. Do you understand? Ten percent."

Dr. Wright visibly relaxed. "Yes, Dean. Can I show you some things?" she asked.

Dean Burkton rolled his eyes up

"You have five minutes. Then I have to . . . to talk to archeology."

"Lilly," Dr. Wright looked at her. "Would you show him 180522-47-3-5?"

Why Lilly, Peter thought? Then, after a moment of reflection, he knew why. He bit his lip and thought about Dr. Wright's shirt: desperate measures for desperate times. He glanced at Lilly, who rolled her eyes up and pasted a silly false smile on her pretty brown face.

"Thanks for caring," she whispered.

Did he care? About more than just the sleaziness of the situation? He shuddered involuntarily. Lilly's boyfriend was almost two meters tall and not very skinny. He would have to be careful about caring.

"This way, Dean Burkton," she said, and led the man around the big central lab table adorned with large sandstone rocks that entrapped the as-yet unliberated skeleton of *Troodon megacephalus burktonsis*.

Lilly pulled open a wooden drawer labeled "18 May 2022 #47" that revealed a five by five grid of cells separated by thin boards. The one on the end of the third row down held a teardrop shaped rock with some bumps on the top. Lilly picked it up carefully and held it for Dean Burkton to examine.

Burkton grunted. "It looks biological. A fossilized internal organ?"

"We don't thinks so, sir. The rock is Cambrian granite, probably from an uplifted area west of the site. Our site used to be a river delta. Erosional sand buried it as the west uplifted, so today we have a Paleocene sandstone bed on top of late Cretaceous mudstone. Dr. Stone found it."

Burkton frowned. "Is that a joke?"

"He is one of my postdocs," Dr. Wright interjected. "That is his name."

"Harrumph. So it rolled downhill and got smoothed in the process? Maybe during the ice age? I realize that's somewhat simplistic."

Somewhat? Peter thought.

"The sandstone formed around it just above the K-Pg boundary area. It was probably transported to the site, but not by ice."

Burkton looked confused. "K-Pg?"

"K-Pg used to be called K-T, sir," Lilly offered.

"When the dinosaurs died out . . . "

"Yes, sir. The stone is about the size and shape of a Troodon heart, and appears associated with the fossil. It almost appears to have been deliberately worked."

Burkton was silent for a while, then he pursed his lips and said, "And the Face of Mars looks like a sculpture in certain lighting. I wouldn't make too much of this." He turned to Dr. Wright and Peter. "We especially don't need any sensationalist press releases. Not that

I think you would do such a thing, Sandra, but there have been some embarrassing attempts to do a public end-run around the budget process of late. Tenure review boards do not look kindly on such things."

Dr. Wright's smile didn't waver, but there was a hint of steel in her voice as she answered, "Of course they don't."

Peter winced. Burkton's brother's foundation gave the college millions in grants, including the one for this dig, but getting them was like pulling teeth. Also, one did not mention big brother's contributions to the endowment in Dean Burkton's presence, lest there be any intimation that something other than the Dean's academic merit had contributed to his elevation.

★ ✳ ★

Gelich and the other scavengers found two more longnecks in the next eight-day. They treated them in the way of the first. So fortified, he estimated the group now had several seasons of food and time enough to find another way to survive. It would take many journeys, he thought. If only he didn't get so tired all the time! But that bothered him less each day, it seemed, and his coughs subsided.

He even found time for his drawing. On thin slabs of white stone he'd found in the hills west of the seashore, he drew crude images of what he remembered from before the sky fell, huge longnecks and thundering herds of horned-faces. He discovered that if he ground the charcoal into dust and mixed it with unripe berry juice, he could dip a chewed twig in it and make a fine line that ate its way slightly into the stone and left a long-lasting mark. His line images didn't look much like the real thing, but he got better with each try. Also, his efforts made him more observant.

Buuk came to him one afternoon and pointed to a scene he'd drawn. "That looks like when the great-tooth tried to take our long-neck kill." She traced with her claw a line he'd painted between a stick figure and the two-legged great-tooth.

"Is that the spear I threw to take it down?"

Gelich placed his beak against Buuk's. "It is. I was afraid we might lose the kill, or become snacks for the great-tooth ourselves. But you saved us."

"I was afraid of that too, but even more angry at what it had done to our eggs. I never threw a spear so hard."

Gelich sighed. Because of that incident, they had no hatchlings of their own among their survivors. Two earlier ones had gone east, on rafts across the sea before the sky fell. Did they still live? How many other people survived?

"We need more eggs," she said. "I need to make more eggs."

"What would we feed the hatchlings, dearest?"

"An answer will present itself. We won't last forever. If we don't have more eggs and more hatchlings, everything comes to an end. Then, everything our ancestors strove for, every sacrifice they made, will prove worthless, and everything we have done will be for naught."

"Perhaps later."

"My beloved. I need. This has all been very hard and I feel empty of hope. I need. Please."

She raised her tail, and Gelich felt the call of ages fight for possession of his body. He gave into it and made his mate happy, if only for a few minutes.

★ ❀ ★

To save funds, Lilly had borrowed her family's camper; her father could deduct its mileage as a contribution. Maybe Dr. Wright would let them name something for him, Peter thought. Lilly's father was a very tall, dignified, African-American gentleman. For some reason, he'd been quite friendly with Peter and had been happy to help out.

There were four of them in the van and its air conditioning was inadequate. Dr. Wright knew the trail well and drove. Dr. Stone, a tall skinny young sandy-haired fellow with a scruffy beard, sat in the right seat. This left Peter and Lilly scrunched together with bags of gear on a back seat that could be made up into a bed.

This forced intimacy seemed to bother Peter more than Lilly. She had a boyfriend, he knew, on the basketball team, who might not like to see the way she and he were just now. Peter had no thoughts of poaching. He'd had maybe two dates all the way through high school, one of them an old friend he'd asked to the senior prom at the last minute so neither of them would miss this event of a lifetime. To his complete surprise, she'd said yes. Then she'd spent the night chatting with her friends, leaving Peter to chat with Mr. Hooper, the physics teacher and designated chaperone. It was his accepted lot in life.

Lilly, however, wasn't the least bit shy about her thigh pressed next to his for the ten-hour ride across dusty summer Nebraska. She even fell asleep with her head on his shoulder. Wow!

A thunderstorm broke as they rolled up to the site and served notice that the site wouldn't last another billion years, sixty-six million, or even one, exposed as it was. A shelter would have been too expensive. Torrents of water sluiced over and through their diggings and excavated more in minutes than the crew could have done in an hour. They sat in the van and waited for it to stop.

The "stone heart" wasn't the only rock whose isotope analysis put much older than the bulk of the sandstone and mudstone. Their *T. m. burktonsis* lay in a sort of ramshackle box of Silurian limestone slabs, stuff that might have washed down from the hills to the west in an ancient flash flood to take its place in the Paleocene sand. The arrangement of slabs had protected the fossil, they thought, to the point where a slab on the east side of the box would have completely enclosed it. But, if there had been one, it must have tumbled down slope years before the road cut was made, and left the present arrangement open like a proscenium stage. Dr. Wright had spotted dark bones in light rock—a tooth, a vertebra—along the road on a trip to somewhere else, and traced them back up the hill.

The rain let up and they surveyed the damage. Dr. Wright pointed out rocks in a newly formed gully that she thought might contain bones. Peter couldn't see it.

"Here," she said. "Look at this knobbly thing." She showed Peter and Lilly the end of the rock. "Rocks don't do that; it just looks biological. It's probably a joint. Maybe the end of a Troodon metatarsal, from the size of it." She surveyed the "box" and saw where the water had cut through. "That's probably the foot end of the fossil. The question is, do we preserve as much as we can of that, or go for the head, presumably near that slab to the left?"

Peter thought about the stone heart. If it was an artifact, *T. m. g.* had to have been very bright. Really bright omnivores wouldn't need toe claws, just like human beings didn't need big canine teeth—they'd use spears. "Did *megacephalus* have a claw on its foot, like *formosus*?"

Dr. Wright looked at him in a way that told him she'd gotten the implication immediately. Then she looked down at the wash where the suspected metatarsal had shown up. "Maybe not. If we can collect a complete foot, we'd know.

"Okay. Stretch it out, the man said. So, we'll to do the wash, the feet and both ends of the fossil and we'll stay here until we've got it all done."

"Dean Burkton . . . " Dr. Stone began.

"I'll take care of Dean Burkton," Dr. Wright snapped, with a certain wintry edge in her voice. "I know what he wants. But we really do have to economize. No expenditures for anything but fossil preservation supplies. No hotels; we can sleep in the van, bathe in the river, whatever. We get it done!"

Lilly smiled mischievously at Peter. "Have you ever been skinny dipping?"

Peter's heart raced. He tried to push images of being naked with Lilly out of his mind; those kinds of things were not for him, not ever. Well, maybe when he was older, graduated, had a job, some money, and some self-confidence. But by then every girl he cared about would be taken. Lilly was already taken, of course.

★ ❋ ★

A year after the sky fell, the ground started to turn green again. Some trees Gelich had thought were dead sprouted new leaves.

He wondered if it was in time. They'd reached the end of their dried longneck meat—that which the furrythings had not sneaked in and eaten—but ceaseless efforts to find and raid their burrows and collect the occasional ground-bound tired bird almost closed the gap. Still, his people were mostly tired skin and bones. Three of them had passed and their flesh was not wasted.

Buuk laid a clutch of eggs, as did one of other women. The latter, famished beyond recovery died soon after laying, and Buuk only just survived herself. None of the eggs hatched, and when they were at last opened, for need, none of them contained more than a tiny, stunted, prehatchling.

But grass was now plentiful, and its roots were nourished. They brought water up from the river to help it grow and pushed up long banks of ash to shelter the sprouts from the cold northwest wind. They made meal of its seeds.

The sea still teemed with life. No more water people or sea-longnecks came to their shore, but fish, if anything, were even more abundant than before. They seldom saw the dragons that hunted fish, though a rare shadow might still cross the ground from time to time. Perhaps their eggs did not hatch well, either.

Gotuk, mate of Buuk's brother, became gravid later that summer, and they all made great celebrations. As her time came closer, however, she became thin and weak. At long last, Gotuk laid a clutch of four eggs and, with Buuk's help, placed each of them on a bed of straw inside a box of earth the men had built to keep the furrythings out. Then she turned to her mate, took two steps toward him and wavered. Buuk's brother rushed forward to hold her up. Their beaks touched for a moment, and she was no more. Her body was light as a feather.

They could not waste what remained, and laid her cleaned bones among the spring flowers where the long-neck carcass had been.

★ ❄ ★

Dr. Wright led by example, and the dig team worked and worked as long as there was light, and then some, under the Coleman lantern on the flimsy camping table. When they were too tired, they slept on cots in the open, often in the same clothes they'd worked in, and when the sun rose, they went to work again.

They bathed on Saturdays, in the river in shifts. So much for romantic notions—though Peter, by chance, caught an eyeful of a very skinny Dr. Wright, who seemed not to notice, or care.

Lilly drove into town, now and then, to get supplies. She had a credit card that her father paid. She was frugal, but they were fed, and it was deductible. He'd been a professional basketball player and had made good investments.

"But he doesn't like me dating men who are likely to be professional basketball players," Lilly said to Peter, one evening before the campfire. "I do anyway, but maybe not for the right reason." She gave him a kind of a half smile.

Dr. Stone laughed and Dr. Wright suppressed a chuckle.

Lilly's father had also secured the loan of an imaging radar scanner that could see through as much as a foot of sandstone, and delivered it himself, along with lots of deep dish pizza and beer.

In a couple of days they found that the "head block," indeed, contained a head. The foot, indeed, had no ripping claw. Every one knew what that implied, but nobody dared say anything. It was too astounding to be true. Everyone's spirits were sky high.

But the next day, Lilly came back from her trip into town, parked the van, and headed up over the hill without speaking to anyone, tears in her eyes. Peter looked up from the half cleared ravine and caught Dr. Wright's glance from the "head" end of the fossil.

"Go to her," Dr. Wright called.

He did, and as soon as Lilly saw him, she threw herself into his arms, sobbing. Finally, she released him.

"Dwight?" Peter asked. Dwight was her boyfriend's name.

She nodded. "He got drafted. Going to Minnesota."

"Isn't that good news? You'll be a millionaire."

She shook her head. "He's got other options now. Like, he's probably always had other options. That little white girl that's an assistant coach on the woman's team. Apparently all the time we've been digging out here . . . "

Peter avoided mentioning that he was every bit as white as the assistant basketball coach. Then he looked at his arm. On the other hand, after all summer on the dig, maybe not so white.

"You want to put up a fight? I'll drive you back, right now."

Lilly shook her head. "The dinosaur. We gotta keep working on it, long as we can. Besides." She grabbed him again and sobbed on his shoulder. "Besides, it's too late. He's gone and married her. Just like that—no phone call, no text, no email, nothing. Married her just like that."

"Oh my god! Does your dad know?"

Lilly backed off and looked Peter in they eye. "Don't know. If he knew and didn't say nothin' . . . anything. I'm going to kill him. I'll kill him."

Then she threw herself into his arms again and sobbed uncontrollably. An hour later, with her face dry, they came back over the hill and went back to work.

Dr. Wright came down the gulch a bit later.

"I think we're ready to take the head block out. Can you give Dr. Stone a hand, Peter? Some brawn may be called for." She smiled at him, winked, and nodded her head toward Lilly.

The message finally got through Peter's thick head block. "Oh, yes, Dr. Wright. I'm on it," he said as he scurried away.

Actually, most of the "brawn" involved was in clearing the way for their miniature electric forklift to ascend the ramp to the fossil. Very gently, with wood chisels and ropes, an inch at time, Stone and Peter slid the sandstone block out of the cut and onto the plate bolted to the fork. Thus secured, Dr. Stone told it to back down the hill. It moved about a foot, tilted precipitously, then stopped.

"Unstable," it said, lowering the block down to the ground.

Peter could see where one the rear wheels had sunk into the soft mudstone soil, a return to kind of sorts.

Okay, he thought, maybe they could work with nature instead of against it.

"Dr. Stone, we could put rope around the block and slide it down. Like those slabs slid down the hill."

Dr. Stone got a surprised look on his face. "Dr. Wright," he called out, "Come look at this! Lilly, you too!"

When the women arrived, Dr. Stone turned to Peter. "You figured this out, didn't you?"

Peter hadn't, not until that moment. So when it hit him, he couldn't hide his surprise. "Those slabs . . . maybe they didn't just slide down hill. Maybe they were slid down. Deliberately."

"Ohmegod," Lilly said.

It was a minute before anyone said anything. Then Dr. Wright nodded slowly. "Okay folks, if you are right . . . if we are right, and this is not just a chance collection of slabs, it's a tomb. An intentional tomb."

★ ❄ ★

The next warm season, Gelich thought sun somehow seemed hotter than he remembered it before the sky fell. Nights felt colder, days felt hotter. But it may have been age or failed memory. The forest had returned; the trees were nothing like the giants of the past, but there were some tall enough to provide shade now. And the wood was now rife with furry game that knew no predator, save them. They reconstructed the village, mostly. The stockade of skinny saplings would not keep out a long-tooth, but there were no more long-teeth.

Only eight of them remained and all but one were male.

Buuk came to him again, in need. "I do not get any younger," she said.

"I cannot bear to lose you."

"I survived this once, in much worse circumstances. If we have no hatchlings, we are gone. Even if I do not survive, the eggs may hatch. One of them may be female."

"We can wait another season."

"I don't think so. I am as old, if not older, than any woman who has laid a successful egg."

"I will not do it."

"You must. Please don't make me go to one of the others. You are my mate. I need you. Together we will repopulate this world. My love, we will make our people so strong that not even the sky can destroy us." She put her beak next to his. "Remember when we were young and the trees were tall and great juicy long-necks and fearsome horned-faces, and even the great-tooth roamed the land? Remember when there were villages up and down the seashore, and people ventured across the sea in rafts? Must it all end as if nobody had lived here? As if all our lives and all our ancestors' lives were pointless? Come, be young again with me."

Gelich could refuse her nothing.

The next day, as he looked at the nest with its four earth walls, he thought of a larger nest. Something that would last, that would be there whatever happened, that would protect his mate and their eggs. He knew that the walls could not be made of earth, which the rain would wash away.

He discussed his idea with Buuk.

"There are big, flat, white stones on the way up to the quarry," she said. "They would make long-lasting walls."

She touched her beak to his. You could draw on them inside, so our hatchlings could learn our story even if . . . "

"You will be here," he said. "The gods cannot be that cruel."

"If they are, they are not worthy of believers." She clicked her beak. "Gods, like ticks, need hosts to survive."

He found some stones in a place where they could be slid down a silt-filled ravine, and with the help of others and under Buuk's guidance, they dug, slid, levered, wedged and pushed the stones into a box.

"It needs a top," Buuk said.

"Logs?"

"They will rot."

Gelich looked at the box. The slabs were much to heavy to lift. But, of course, they had slid down the hill to get here. The answer jumped at him like a slicer from behind a bush. "I could fill it full of sand and fill in behind it, then slide a big stone down over and arrange it, then take the sand out again!"

"That will be much work," Buuk said, but she was clearly happy with his idea.

With easy hunting to keep their gizzards full, the box was ready in a couple of moons. It opened to the east to warm with the morning sun but the cool stone slabs shaded the inside the rest of the day. .

When they took the sand away again, he painted. He got good enough that one could tell his great-teeth from his longnecks and horned-faces.

At first, Buuk looked very well. Everyone saw that she had plenty of food, plenty of rest, and did no heavy work. Everyone hoped that she would succeed in this, where all the others had not, because she had succeeded in everything else.

But the gravidness began to take much out of her. Gelich had her lie in the box, where the rain and pests could not get at her. He fed her and talked to her as he drew on the walls the story of their village: Her choice of him as a hatchling from his mother, his first hunt with his father, his father's death in a fight with a great-tooth, the flood that swept half the village into the sea, their first brood, the group that voyaged into the sea on a platform of logs—inspired by those logs that floated away in the flood. He painted their second nest and her killing the great-tooth (much better rendered now). He painted, as best he could, the day the sky fell, but it was too big. Nonetheless, people got the idea. At last, he painted how they made the box.

Buuk urged him on, though she grew weaker day by bay. He could not draw well enough to distinguish one person from another, so to indicate Buuk, he put a dot over her head.

"I'm getting near," she told him. "I will live."

But when her time came, she was too weak to push the eggs out, barely conscious. Gelich was with her at the last.

She rallied a bit before the end and spoke to him. "Take the eggs, when I am gone. They may still hatch. I am very near term. Survive, my mate. Live . . . "

And then she was gone. Almost in a trance, he went for the knife. She barely bled; her hide was like paper. Everything had gone to the eggs.

Three of the eggs looked good and one was underdeveloped, unsymmetrical, shaped like a heart.

They left her in the box.

"Let's put a stone in front and fill it with sand again, my friends," Gelich asked, "so nothing will feast on her. The drawings, I can do those again." And this they did, filling the stone box and all around it with sand.

The eggs did not hatch.

The other males built a raft next year, with large evergreen branches to catch the westering wind, and set out across the sea in hopes that their predecessors had survived and had females.

Gelich stayed, and tired of painting, tried his hands at sculpture. But the best he was able to do was to make a rock look like the little, misshapen egg, that might have been his and Buuk's hatchling. It helped him remember, even if the memories were sad. Some days he would imagine that it hatched and saved the world. If only such magic could exist!

Eventually he became too old and feeble to feed himself, and so perished in front of the stone box on the land of his ancestors. The furrythings cleaned his bones.

★ ❋ ★

From the hillside, Peter saw Lilly lead the truck to the site with her van. It could carry all the blocks they had excavated and then some. Her father had donated the funds for it. Besides the driver, the truck carried a passenger, one Dean Michael Burkton—one very angry Dean Burkton—from Lilly's surreptitious cell phone report.

He had reason to be angry, Peter reflected. Dr. Wright had pretty much ignored his cease and desist orders, overstayed her time, and wild rumors were circulating. Dr. Stone's absence-abused girlfriend was possibly the source of some of them.

So Burkton was in a state. This was to be it—absolutely, positively, irrevocably, *IT*! The site would be shut down indefinitely. There would be no tenure renewal for Dr. Wright. Indeed, Burkton was going to recommend suspension. Dr. Stone would be assigned elsewhere. Peter and Lilly would have to find other thesis advisors and topics, and probably should consider transfer to another institution.

Lilly parked the van and ran up to Peter. Her hug was more than friendly, a frequent and not unpleasant experience over the last few weeks. Peter was partly embarrassed on one hand, but felt that he belonged with her in a way that he'd never felt before. Who knew what the future would bring? But right now he wanted to spend as little time separated from Lilly as possible. With her around, he could look nowhere else; and it seemed she was always looking back.

"I'm so sorry, Dr. Wright," Lilly said after their embrace, as if it was all her fault.

"Be calm," Dr. Wright told them, unreasonably calm herself. "Dean Burkton can't have his pound of flesh and eat it, too. Besides, he was a scientist. There might still be some of that in him. Let's see if we can't rekindle his sense of discovery."

When Burkton got out of the truck, Dr. Wright greeted him like a long lost lover, not someone in the process of destroying her career. His confusion was almost comical.

"This is really the most amazing thing, Michael. We haven't put out any rumors; they wouldn't do it justice."

"This dinosaur tomb business? Whose idea was that? Animals don't have tombs, at least not on their own."

"Just look at it, Michael. It's just a short walk."

Dean Burkton groaned, then sighed. "I've come this far, Sandra, so I may as well. But no pictures. Absolutely no pictures." He shot a look at Peter and Lilly. "I don't have to confiscate your phones, do I?"

Peter and Lilly shook their heads.

"We're being very careful with the bone blocks. The fossils need the matrix; they are very thin and bent, as if the creature was very old when they buried it."

"Buried? Bullshit." He looked at Dr. Wright, shook his head and snapped. "I'm no bull in a china shop." Then he stared at her as her words sank in. "You're serious, aren't you? Sandra, have you gone mad? Stark raving mad? What will you do next, call the National Exposer? The Fortean File?"

"Michael," she said, putting her hand on his arm.

No, Peter realized, more than her hand.

"Michael, just come take a look. The stone placement: that can't be natural. Doesn't it look like something from Egypt, or maybe Skara Brae?"

He harrumphed, but pushed his bulk up to the front of the site.

Dr. Wright point out the cracks where the stones joined. The roof slab had broken, and they'd propped it up with timbers, but the other joins still seemed to be at something resembling right angles. He squinted and frowned. "How deep into this have you gotten?" he asked.

"Not very. We've been busy with the fossil and resources are . . . "

"Tight. You don't have to tell me that. Okay, it certainly doesn't look very natural, but it could be a fake."

Dr. Wright shook her head. "Michael, it was in solid rock exposed by a road cut. I found it by complete accident. It's sixty-six million years old. We have isotope data."

"Yes, yes." He turned back to her. "Okay. Just an amazing coincidence, then; that's what we'll have to say." He turned back to the end slab. "Now let's get ready to close this place . . . "

Peter had never seen a man stop in mid sentence like that.

"What the . . . Sandra, do you have one of those brushes?"

Dr. Wright, it so happened, had one on her equipment belt. She flashed a cat-who-got-the-canary look back at Peter, Lilly and Dr. Stone, before handing the brush to Dean Burkton. He whisked some at the sand covering the exposed lower right slab. Then whisked a bit more.

"Is this some kind of a joke?"

"What have you found?" Dr. Wright asked, sounding totally sincere.

"Hmmm. It looks like someone's drawn a sort of plan of the . . . "

"Tomb, Michael. It's a tomb."

Dean Burkton whisked harder as sand yielded to sandstone.

Peter gulped and started forward, but Dr. Wright raised a hand to stop him. It was, Peter belatedly realized, a calculated risk.

Burkton put the brush down. "Are you sure this wasn't done by one of your staff?"

"They wouldn't. But let's check." She bent down to examine the writing, then, with a dental scraping tool, slowly uncovered another few square centimeters. "The images appear to extend back behind the undisturbed matrix."

"Careful with that word 'images.' We need more analysis. Mass spec on those linear discolorations." Dean Burkton was, or had been, a chemist. "Redo all the dates on the stone and the grooves in it . . . ."

"Expensive," Dr. Stone said.

"I'll find the money. Can we pry a little more of the sandstone off? Just to be sure?" He reached out his hand and Dr. Wright, after just a little hesitation, handed him the scraping tool.

"Very carefully."

He grunted. An hour's worth of gentle prying and brushing showed that the line drawings did, indeed, extend along the white sandstone beneath the Paleogene matrix.

At last Burkton pushed himself up and grinned. "This changes everything, you know. This changes everything." He turned to Dr. Wright and patted her butt. "We can celebrate tonight."

"Oh, I'm looking forward to it, Michael."

"Like hell she is," Lilly whispered.

All they had from him was promises so far, Peter realized. Dr. Wright still had work to do.

A couple of hours later, they'd exposed a full tomb plan. As it was late, Burkton stayed the night, with Dr. Wright, in Lilly's van. Lilly, Peter, and Dr. Stone slept under the stars—Lilly with her arms around Peter and Dr. Stone some distance away, speaking softly into his tablet.

★ ※ ★

The next year, rain came to the village ruins with abnormal frequency; the world still sought a new balance. Mud rolled down the hill and poured over the tomb again and again. Millennia passed and the land to the east rose; Buuk's resting place was now near the bottom of a valley. Glacial lakes came, silted, and left. The weight of eons pressed down. New tribes roamed the land. Then one of them cut a road.

★ ※ ★

The "Burkton Graphics" were totally revealed three years later, just in time for Peter and Lilly's wedding, which was held a safe distance in front of the tomb by special permission of Dean Wright—Dr. Burkton having been promoted to a safe university vice presidency.

Dean Wright caught the bridal bouquet and gave it to Dr. Stone's new girlfriend.

After a few drinks at the reception dinner, Peter asked Dr. Wright the question he'd wanted to for three years. After all, as a graduate student now and his name on one of the most important scientific papers in history, one could be a little more collegial.

"Dr. Wright," he began.

"Dean Wright, now, Peter, I like the sound of it. Do you know I'm the youngest one at the college since 1892?" She smiled.

"Yes, ma'am. That was loose sand covering the tomb plan. But the rest was hard sandstone. You found the graphics first, and covered them up again!"

She raised an eyebrow, but said nothing, turned and walked up the hill to the tomb.

"You knew," Lilly said, running after her, "you saw them first and you let him take the credit!"

She turned and shook her head, with a wintry smile. "I took time and date stamped imagery first, and I imagine that someday when both the Burktons and their money have passed on, more of the story will be revealed. In the meantime, I have what I need, and so do you. So please keep quiet. After all, his change in heart was essential to the project." She smiled, "Now, Peter and Lilly, I wonder who sealed this tomb?"

"The female with the dot over its head?" Peter asked. "But if that was the fossil in the tomb, it couldn't have sealed it."

"Probably not. But perhaps the one who decorated the walls? We'll never know. But whatever did, it must have loved her very much, don't you think? Maybe as much as you two love each other?"

Peter reached for Lilly's hand. "Impossible!"

STORY NOTES:

This was a Valentine's day story that didn't find a niche for a number of years.

It was inspired, as were a number of other stories, in part by articles about the "Troodon" (the terminology is evolving), a gracile two-legged dinosaur with a large (for a dinosaur) brain, and an encounter with Irene Pepperberg and Alex the Parrot, which hinted that bird (and maybe dinosaur) brains could do a lot more per unit volume than we do with smaller neurons, closer together. I imagined a tribe of evolved Troodon, not too much different outwardly than the ones we've found, on the brink of doing cave pictures and stone shelters when the dinosaur killer hits.

In our day, what the did is found by a college paleontology team beset by budget issues and sexism of the kind which that we read about all too often. What we read about, of course, is the tip of an iceberg—this story goes down below that public surface to what I imagine is the more usual result of such things (educated by some stories told at college reunions). It is also inspired, both in the Cretaceous and modern times by the title of a book I read years ago by Rollo May: *Love and Will.*

VOICE OF AGES

ST. PETERSBURG, 24 AUGUST 2040

The North Atlantic Treaty Organization committee on collective security was called to order by V. M. Petrov amid the gilded splendor of the old palace. As the occasion was the centennial of Churchill's ascension to the prime ministry of the United Kingdom, the British delegate, Sir Spencer Payne-Shelton, was recognized first. That, instead of the expected platitudes, he launched into something totally unexpected would have delighted Sir Winston. Delighted, but not surprised: for Sir Winston himself was the apparent cause of such irregularity.

At Sir Spencer's signal, robotic aides passed to each of the seated delegates a few sheets of paper, bound by a ribbon passing through a hole punched in the corner, while Sir Spencer explained that the papers were replicas of a document which Barclay's Bank had delivered to them as being addressed to "those responsible for the collective security of Europe and the Western World in the year 2036." The handwritten document, he told them, had been subjected to the appropriate tests over the last four years and appeared to be authentic. The delegates followed along as Sir Spencer cleared his throat and began to read aloud:

KENT, ENGLAND, DECEMBER, 1936

I trust this letter has reached its intended time and audience. If so, I address those with responsibility for maintaining a balance of military and economic affairs so to preclude the grievous troubles of my century from ever again blighting the face of history. It is well you do so, and even better if your responsibilities now encompass the world and perhaps more.

I write these words with some worry — and with less art than I wish — since, by their nature I cannot commit to typists and revisions. Nor can I leave them lying around. This letter shall be sealed, with instructions for its opening after 100 years, as soon as it is completed. Then I shall do my best to forget. For I shall be long gone when these words come to light, and if the experience related here is real, I must do nothing more to bring question to my judgment and the dregs of my political career — too much lies in the balance. Europe wanders toward a stygian hell like a blind man walking down hill because it is easier. But you will know all that.

I have three tasks, or as it were, the same task three times: now, against Hitler; in a time and place wh I shall explain, against the inexplicable; and to you against the belief that there may be nothing to be against. I pray I shall be successful at least once, or all is utterly lost.

A week ago, I sought refuge in my painting from a most vehement London; the press vehement in their squalid rejection of their King, the Commons vehement in rejecting his defence. While it may astonish from yr view of all that shall happen hence, this is an age that confounds honour and its defence - no, even the *threat* of defence - with folly. It shall learn better, at great cost. But you know that.

I was painting a somber landscape roughed earlier in France when I heard softly, but distinctly, my name, accompanied by the so far unbestowed honourific of "sir." Since the voice was unannounced, I took mental note of my pistol — my livelihood involves giving offence to barbarians. Irritation replacing momentary concern, I turned and grumbled, "Who? . . . "

But the door was empty. My chairs and tables in their dust sheets stood like ghosts of offices past and I thought for a moment that the Dickens Christmas tale might be less inventive than on its face. Returning to my painting I mumbled, "Indeed." And that was the key, for immediately I heard:

"You do hear us then, sir. Please do not be alarmed . . . "

I continued painting as if to deny the masters of this prank any satisfaction of disturbing me and, without turning my head issued a simple command. "Show yourself!"

The disembodied voice proceeded to explain that would be

impossible, because it spoke from a millennium in the future. It claimed to speak for a group of a dozen future historians, and told me that when I wished to answer, I had only to paint along a line as I spoke, the bristles of my brush acting upon the paint as the needle in a dictation machine. From that, the art of their science could pluck my voice.

My habit is to leave the explanation of such things to the Professor and his colleagues, not possible in this instance. Because the credibility of this must be an issue with you, I will attempt an explanation myself. Pray don't be too harsh.

Their speech was accomplished, as best I can remember, by "modification of subnuclear probability fields with nu-tachyon beams" emitted by particles traveling at a precise fraction of the speed of light focused to a point several billion miles outside the solar system in their time, where the Planet Earth is in ours. The beam's position with respect to me was governed by monitoring their image of the painting itself. I am to understand that electrons spinning about their atoms react to these tachyons in an unbalanced fashion — "parity" was mentioned — wh affects in some small way how atoms in my inner ear go about colliding with each other. A compression and rarefaction, hence sound, so comes into being where only random motion was before, and this can be modulated as with a radio beam. The process invokes no change in overall energy, as the minute energy of the sound waves comes from equally minute quanta of thermal energy in the area modified. The ear, then, grows cold at the sound of this.

"What of entropy?" I asked.

I was told that that is a matter for philosophers. This scientific discussion engaged and mollified me and I pray it is intelligible to you a century more advanced than I. During it my landscape was not neglected. Nor, I imagine, did Hitler neglect building his Reich.

ST. PETERSBURG, 2040

"The 'Professor' was Dr. F. A. Lindemann," explained Sir Spencer. "Tachyons are theoretical particles that move faster than the speed of light, Their existence also implies an ability to transmit information backward in time, provided there is significant space and velocity separation between the transmitter and the receiver, a standard result of relativity theory. No such tachyon has been found; but for those who do not find causality an insurmountable barrier, they are possible. Naturally, we are not overlooking the military implications for high speed computers and communications, but that is not the point of the Churchill letter."

"Alleged Churchill letter," The French *delegate said with a superior smile.*

Sir Spencer raised an eyebrow. "We did not spend four years working on this to create an 'allegation.' It is much more certain than that." He continued reading.

KENT, ENGLAND, DECEMBER, 1936

The speaker gave me his name, but asked me not to divulge it, wh request I shall honour, lest it affect his personal history with no need. About ten centuries hence our descendants had been happy with their lot until an emergency occasioned their effort to contact me (I pray your forgiveness about grammatical tense in such discourse - it confounds me as well.). These historians welcomed me as a colleague. I told them I am not an historian, but a writer of history, and that their true colleagues in my day do not let the difference between myself and an historian go unremarked.

I asked what had transpired, and if they hoped to somehow alter such events by contacting me. Did this not present a grave risk?

They thought not, for, while what they would tell me of future events would give me some comfort, there was no serious concern that I would thereby act differently. Indeed, such analysis was an overreaching consideration in their decision to contact me. My writings of late, they said, show that the broad outlines of the future were apparently known to me already. Since telling me would change nothing, they were safe to do it.

Perhaps. In my lifetime, I have seen where a very small deviation in the flight of a bullet, or a train schedule, would have changed everything; but I have also seen the entire careers and fortunes of great statesmen, resolutely and competently applied to a cause, have little effect on the onrush of destiny.

Their news of our immediate future is not good news; for what I foresee is the futility of my present labours followed by unchecked slaughter.

The paradox of this communication with the future still escaped me. They hear my answers in microscopic variations in the brushstrokes as I paint. Did (does? will ?) this painting, and thus their whole past, change as they watch? They say this must be so, but as far as they could tell, everything has always been that way. They ask if I had noticed any discontinuity in their line of speech wh might result from changes to their past, as they, necessarily, would not notice.

"I have not," I told them. "But I would rejoice to have more details on Hitler's machinery of war. Can you give me bullets of truth to riddle the hides of the irresolute?"

Not now, they told me. Their time was short and they have a problem wh demands my attention.

But I had one last short question, of more import to me than even the glory of the Empire, which they answered. I am relieved to know that I shall have, through my dark toil and to my ultimate triumph, that wh Baldwin and duty have denied my King: the support and companionship of the woman I love, my Clementine.

What was this immense problem of the future? Nothing less, I fear, than the survival of Earth and all that goes with it!

In their time there is a research colony on the north pole of a small airless planetoid wh circles the dimmer component of the brightest star in the constellation of the Centaur. Said colony, a self-sufficient outpost, has received non-human refugees from yet another star. Communication established, the refugees' tale was one of sudden threat, failed negotiations, implacable aggression, surrender and genocide, wh only a few escaped. The doers of this evil wr headed, in their opinion, toward our solar system.

Their civilization has only a few years to prepare to fight or flee this impending calamity, and they have no military capability, judging as minimal the chance of encountering a race so close to humanity, so like it in technological achievement and capacity for war, but also lacking a sense of reciprocity and unwilling to treat with honour.

The irony does not escape me. Baldwin must be immortal.

What, in the future, have they done about the threat? My historian correspondents are aware of the general principals of war and reason a defence at the solar system would involve short lines of supply, but vy great risk.

So the historians asked me to change not their past, but their future: to advise and convince their leadership to take a stand before it is too late. Could I help rally them?

At this point communication ceased for the day, and I was left with the problem. But I had almost no information, and so set to work.

Did I know of the star, wh astronomers call Alpha Centauri? From a distance. It was my constant companion, to the east of the Southern Cross, on nights spent in the Veldt during the Boer War, and is said to be the closest to our solar system, light needing only four years and four months to bridge the gap. This, indeed, confirms their urgency.

My ill ease with this spooky conversation was not helped by this announcement of a colony at another star, even the nearest one. The Prof and his friends would hold it fantasy. Stars are too distant; not even Verne or Wells went so far in wild imagining. Yet I am aware that their successors, particularly in the less reputable parts of the American press, do.

My daughter Sarah described such a fantasy wh she read in a magazine left to her by an American studying economics in London who had taken an interest in my efforts. I dismissed it quickly and can't now research the question, but vaguely remember it as authored by a Scottish-American physicist and mighty machines were thus involved.

One of these was supposed to manipulate probability fields.

Perhaps that is not so unlike Mr. Watson-Watt's radio efforts, to wh I cannot write much here lest this be discovered too early. But the gist is that radio transmissions can cause metals to betray their location at a great distance. Such developments promise astounding capabilities, and give pause to those who would limit their considerations of future science to current practice.

I queried the Professor on the subject of voyages between stars, not revealing my purpose. The short of his answer was that the energy required to accomplish such a trip in a lifetime was beyond anything known except, perhaps, the energy source of the sun itself; and that the means to use such energy on a large scale were well beyond current knowledge. But he would not quite say it impossible.

So unease did not deter me from this exercise. Indeed, the distraction was welcome, and I resolved to help if I could. Besides, I had so far risked nothing more than mumbles while painting. My man tolerates my eccentricities; no one else is here. I fear my black mood has driven them all out, even Clem!

ST. PETERSBURG, 2040

"My ancestor's acceptance of the concept of star travel a century before even the first unmanned probes were launched may seem overly precocious." Sir Spencer signaled a serving robot for a drink *of water before resuming. It soundlessly complied in seconds, and he took a drink.* "But if there was part of Sir Winston that seemed stuck *in the 19th Century, there was also part that would not be out of place in ours. Also, the romance of it may have appealed to him."*

KENT, ENGLAND, DECEMBER 1936

Having thus confirmed what I could, I attempted to renew contact by speaking while painting, and after several attempts was rewarded. I asked for more information about the situation—the politics, the industrial power, and the threat.

The politics of their future is in a quandary. In their assembly, a rough equivalent of our League of Nations, several views are put forth. Should not communications be established with the raiders and reason attempted, or at least intelligence gained? Should not the colony be withdrawn, allowing more years for preparation? Does mankind flee, abandoning heritage for some dark corner of the universe to cower in? Or are the arts of war to be relearned? But if war, when and where?

The curious argument, they relate, is raised that the moral destruction of reviving the terrible arts of war would be the equivalent of the physical destruction wh might accompany invasion.

"Nonsense," I told them. "Lose, and all that survives *is* War wh its evil arts in the victor's strengthened hands!"

Those who contacted me whispered in reply, "That kind of rhetoric is what we need!"

"Could words but win a War!" I answered. "What is yr potential for manufacture of military equipments?"

I found the industrial might of the future rests on the almost limitless supply of material in the planetoids wh orbit between the planets and on great spaceborne factories wh run themselves, and even reproduce themselves. (Among those things wh I hope you in yr day comprehend better than I in mine are machines wh build themselves.)

But *time* is needed for the design of weapons and the reschedule of these self-made factories, and *time* is needed to deploy such forces far enough from Earth to save it, and *time* may be insufficient. They reported that light from the great enemy fleet had already been received at Alpha Centauri.

Pray call your more immediate ancestors, I suggest.

"Causality would surely wipe us from existence," they protested.

What, again, was the number of their group? I asked.

There were eleven, the voice related.

It did not pass my notice that this was one less than on the first instance. Whatever minute effect their communication with me would have on their future, it was at the cost of the effect it had on their past. Where there had been twelve there were but eleven. How many lives, once *lived* and now/then *not lived* did that represent, I wondered. But I held that from them. With so much at stake, that would be the inevitable result whatever would be done.

"Vy well," I said. Now what knew they of this oncoming horde?

They gave me what intelligence came with the refugees: it speaks of ominous force. After months of radio communications, robot projectiles cruise into a planetary system ahead of the invader's fleet. Their speed was that of Rutherford's and Thompson's bits of atoms, vy nearly that of light itself, and their mass was that of ships. Though easily evaded by more agile spacecraft, such weapons are intended for continents and artificial moons wh cannot evade, and so are destroyed completely.

Negotiations had been in progress when these projectiles of death entered the refugees' solar system. The refugees' race had but eight hours warning, as useless in that time and place as here and now.

An army of tiny machines then occupied the outer reaches of the invaded planetary system. Those built more machines which in turn built devices for reducing the velocity of the van of the main invasion fleet.

While this occurred in the refugees system, what remained of their race made one last supreme effort and sent forth a ship toward a distant refuge. Along the way, by chance, it encountered signals sent between the colony at Alpha Centauri and the Earth.

As for the invaders, when their main force arrived, they fed on the remains of the shattered civilization, reorganizing and reconstituting themselves to set off again.

In this case, toward the Earth.

Why is unknowable. Perhaps they, as well, flee something.

Pray understand my problem. What could an eccentric, aging, out of favour British politician possibly do about all of this that he could not do for his own nation?

I asked for a few more days to consider what I had been told.

They were singularly busy days. I produced, for my King, some prose with wh he has executed his folly as gracefully as might be done. I pray it will be quickly forgotten.

I made progress on my neglected history of English speaking peoples, and, in so doing, firmed its lessons in my mind.

Holiday cheer then invaded Chartwell with smiles, treats and good brandy. So fortified, and with black moods banished, I roused my mind to battle.

In our next conversation we discussed the broad outlines of what might be done. The concealment of the Earth is not mentioned. Radio and its descendants have for a millennium, at the historians' time, proclaimed the location and all the weaknesses of man, to an incredible volume of space and cannot be called back.

There is one stroke of luck in all this, the position of the Alpha Centauri colony between the solar system and the marauding fleet.

"By all means engage them there with whatever can be marshaled," I told the historians. "Throw rocks at them if you have nothing else. You have nothing to lose that will not be lost anyway, and much to gain; time and perhaps respect. Given what the refugees reported, you must not flinch to risk the lives of the colonists: they are at risk in any event. Courage and resolution there just may save the situation.

"Should their numbers be reduced more than resources scrounged from the sparse Centauri system can replenish, that is to the good, even at the cost of blood. Use the advantage in speed of communications. The result of negotiation with no defence is known, so learn, if possible, the result of negotiation combined *with* a defence, however feeble, that draws at least some blood."

I could not resist some tactical advice as well: "If there are time and resource, send a force from the colony toward the Solar System, to be passed by the invaders in the darkness of space and hence to observe their disposition and, if possible, fall on their rear."

But time shrank. Their link could be maintained only so long for the mass of the Earth was starting to interfere with their beam. My endurance that day waned as well. I had missed my afternoon nap.

Though, as a pariah, I would have no dinner guests for which to prepare today, a quiet meal with family and an evening bath awaited. After that and perhaps a brief rest, I would commence the writing by wh I support this household.

I promised in two days' time to prepare suitable remarks for their assembly and for the military forces wh they must assemble, and mutter those words into this painting.

I did all that: the rhetoric was some of my best, for I may need to use it myself in the more immediate future, modified for the occasion. I gave these speeches the marshaled argument, repeated points, evocative analogy and mounting tone of such work. Though I was vy careful about analogy as the clarity of my language to them must be as that of Shakespeare to me. The delivery remains to them, though even our wrong-headed former monarch did not do badly with my text.

ST. PETERSBURG, 2040

"I am perplexed," the Canadian delegate, a military historian himself, stated. "Are we to trace some of his wartime speeches back that far? The whole thing strikes me as someone's romantic fraud, concocted to maintain a military establishment in the absence of any genuine threat."

"Some go back even further," Sir Spencer replied. "He saw the whole bloody business coming and was well prepared. He had only to be unchained. As far as the document's authenticity is concerned, a complete report is being prepared and you are all welcome to inspect the original, though we must, of course, constrain removal of analytical samples from such an historic document. Moving along —"

KENT, ENGLAND, DECEMBER, 1936

We talked for the last time the following afternoon. They thanked me for my efforts and thought to recompense by feeding me dear morsels of my own future. As they tell it, Hitler shall be defeated, though with far more blood and confusion than needed. Stalin and his successors shall be outlasted and by indefatigable show of force by the great democracies. My role, it seems, shall be demonstrative in the first instance and advisory in the second, the bloody lesson having been learned by those who then rise to power. Shall I tremble at the labor ahead, or rejoice of its ultimate success? It does not escape me that the confidence I have gained from this revelation might well be instrumental in making it come true!

But I shall not know the outcome of my efforts on behalf of those who contacted me from the future: that was their final message to me, at my suggestion. When we first talked they told me there were twelve people involved in their project. That afternoon I asked again and they told me that there had always been only eight.

I apprised them of this, whereupon they thanked me for my efforts and immediately ceased communication.

Unfortunately, to that time, after a passage of days for me, but months for them, their league had taken no action, and the first missiles of the invaders were only eight months from the Alpha Centauri colony. If these invaders are as practised in their vile art as I suspect, then no strategy or tactics my colleagues from the future can devise in so short a time will be of any use. They shall die as cowards or die as heroes, but die they shall.

My efforts to save them may fail, but I must try to save our legacy — that of mankind, western civilization, and not in the least the English speaking peoples. These people are, were, our heirs. Their disaster is ultimately our own — for what is the ultimate meaning of our lives here if it all comes to naught then?

ST. PETERSBURG, 2040

The British delegate paused, whereupon the chairman reminded him of their agenda.

"Comrade, I am almost done," he said, "and I apologize for going overtime on a ostensibly non-substantive item. However , the writer of this document , whether Sir Winston or not, certainly believed he had a substantive contribution to make, and one which is consistent with the views of His Majesty's government on the next agenda items. I will therefore yield five minutes of my time on those to the author of this document, who makes the same points with perhaps greater force."

The Russian agreed and the Briton took a sip of water. Tired but determined, he spread his feet for greater balance and hooked his thumb in his belt to support his arm. He continued reading:

KENT, ENGLAND, JANUARY, 1937

So I have written these pages. If I have judged the times right, in about the hundredth anniversary of the cataclysm to come, our victory might inspire you to remember how it was achieved, what I stood for and what I stood against. I will write to some length to ensure this. Also, by yr time, science shall have advanced enough make these words plausible. Perhaps more so to you than they are to me even now.

There is great evil in the universe. Consider the number of stars. Consider our rapid accumulation of scientific advance through these last two centuries. Consider how close Hitler and Stalin came to having all of it. How often are such awful beings generated among the denizens of the scattered stars? Pray be warned: some will succeed.

Make your grand alliances. Search for them even beyond this world if possible, but use discretion in yr search. Make covenants. And pray keep their spirit, even to much unhappiness. Even at the expense of their letter, keep their spirit. Even in the face of public apathy, let every dictator and would be dictator or conqueror know his limits. Do not neglect the ability, nor will, to enforce those limits against those who test them. In this way, mankind shall live with itself in as much peace as it can, but still grow strong enough to face the challenge that is sure to come.

Do not neglect yr heritage of courage in arms, from the blackamoor spearmen of Africa, from the samurai of Japan, from the steadfast poilus and doughboys, from the knights of the airplane, from the riflemen of the Outback, and from every heroic tradition. And do not neglect the arms themselves, without wh the heritage perishes.

Secure the high ground; it hangs over yr heads. The air bombardment doctrines of Douhet in my day are but a shadow of what awaits you if you do not. Do this, and when evil comes, as it always does, you can face it resolutely with hope of vy great success.

But do this and that defenceless culture of the well-meaning historians who contacted me will perish quietly, painted over in time like the somewhat different landscape to wh they first put their instruments.

Still, you must do your duty. I suspect they knew their fate. This, then, is their heroism — to stand, in their own way, with Nelson, Moore, and Gordon. And so I honour them.

ST. PETERSBURG, 2040

The committee was silent, and the British delegate, having nothing more to say, sat down. After a pause, the delegate from the United States of America requested that action on the next two agenda items be postponed until the authenticity of the British documents could be independently verified by the various governments.

The man shook is head in wonderment. "Are we supposed to think that he took it on himself to wipe out billions of lives and a millennium of history on his own judgment that it would end anyway? How could he be so confident his ends justified such means? Do we really believe he was such a bastard?"

The Russian, possibly brooding over his own nation's history, simply nodded. "Da. But where would we all be now if he had not been such a bastard?"

STORY NOTES

While based on an historical person, this is a work of fiction. No offence is intended to the surviving relations or estate of Sir Winston Leonard Spencer Churchill. Some terms of Churchill's (I did not invent them) may irritate the politically sensitive ear — but they were part and parcel of the spirit of his times. What is remarkable about Churchill to this author is not how much he was an imperial politician, but how much broader his vision reached.

I have many thousand words of polished Churchill prose in my library and very little of rough notes or scribbled letters, such as this one would have been. I imagine the difference might be less than one would think; Churchill dictated much of his writing.

This is also one of the very few stories in which I've used any form of time travel and one of the very few times where I've intentionally leaned on something that I suspect is not physically possible, though proving that would be beyond me. I have imagined that to communicate backward in time, the future is somehow able to alter the probability distribution of molecular scattering in the air near Churchill's eardrum. There is a change in the organization of the molecules though no change in their bulk energy, but perhaps there is a change in the entropy, since one might be able to extract energy from the resulting compressions and rarefactions. Logical consistency is preserved by wiping out the entire future past the point of communication and letting another future develop; if one does this and stays in the future, one commits a form of suicide, but perhaps one hopes that the changes are sufficiently minor that the future that develops still includes the time meddler.

Another, less parsimonious scenario is where the time meddling creates another whole set of universes, but the meddling has no effect on the meddler's universe. One's mind boggles at the number of universe so created, but is this any more weird than, say, the many-worlds interpretation of quantum mechanics wherein every random event creates near-infinities of separate universes?

At any rate, unlike anything else of mine save the jest vignette, "Attraction," which is a not-serious tongue-in-cheek probability zero tale, this story exists in that arguable gray area of causality and the meaning of time. It exists because I wanted to do a science fiction story with Winston Churchill in it, had a time-limited anthology opportunity for it, and came up with this. Or it exists because it always has.

GDN January 2016

A WARTIME DRAUGHT

I'm not going to describe where the White Horse is; one American finding the place, despite the jukebox the owners mistakenly placed in the public bar in hope of attracting them, was quite enough. He was an American military man who liked real ale. And, in retrospect, that was our first clue.

I was a bit late for getting a couple of pints in before closing, and trotting down to the Embankment from Fleet had left me a bit breathless. In spite of my haste, Mr. D. was getting a pint of Fuller's London Pride ready for me by the time I'd gotten from the door to the Saloon bar.

He was standing there, in his American Army Major's uniform, his long dirty-blond hair almost reaching his eyebrows, looking critically at what was likely a pint of Young's stout.

"We don't get Dunkel like this in Ulm," he said.

A dozen eyes turned his way. There was a war on, of course. And he pronounced "Dunkel" as if it were spelled doon-kil.

"Oh. New Ulm, Minnesota. We sometimes drop the 'new.' I'm Wally, Wally Petersen." He stuck out a beefy palm toward me as the most convenient British victim. "The place was settled by Germans, but I come from Minneapolis now. I'm an engineer. Valves, current, that kind of thing."

Arthur's head came up at the mention of valves. He and his brother Fred sat near the dartboard — but not too near, given that Harry was there and had a tendency to mix darts and draughts. Wally happened to be looking in Arthur's direction, and his eyes narrowed at Arthur's reaction. A couple of other heads turned and the chatter faded away.

We generally knew what Arthur was working on, and generally did not discuss it aloud, in public, ever. But high power amplification valves were an important part of it.

"Hydraulics, pumps, that kind of thing," Wally said, as if he had to divert attention from electrical valves.

"You like the Young's?" Mr. D. asked into the silence.

"Ah, it's not quite Hamm's," he said, "but good, very good."

That brought a quick smile from John Sims, our occasional Sunday Times astronomy columnist. John had actually been to Minnesota before the war.

"Greetings, Wally," John said. "I know a man in Minneapolis. Bill Luyten, astronomer, science writer. Ever run into him?"

Wally pursed his lips and looked up as if trying to remember. "No, don't recall the name. Is he involved in the war effort?"

A brief frown passed over John's face. "Not that I know of. He's more the academic type."

Wally nodded and looked over to Arthur. "You're interested in valves."

Arthur smiled nervously. "Not that I'm free to discuss now, am I?"

Wally grinned. "Of course not. You barely know me. Barkeep . . . "

"Our barman is Mr. D," John said.

"Yes, of course. Mr. D., I would like to purchase a round for the group. Are there any rules for that here?"

"There are tonight. It must be consumed in the next fifteen minutes. Then out the door. Closing time approaches."

Nonetheless, pints were passed around, not the first such ritual as last orders approached.

I took the barstool next to Wally. "Arthur is into spaceships, you know."

"Spaceships?" asked Wally.

Harry nodded. "Rockets, except with people inside of them."

"That would hurt coming down."

"Spaceships don't come down. Or rather, they come down softly, on their tails, wherever you want them to. There are some engineering details to work out, of course, but the main thing is propulsion."

Wally looked interested. "Could they come down in America, or Germany, for instance?"

"I think Arthur is more interested in the Moon. But yes, in Germany, if one wanted."

Wally's smile flicked off for an instant. "Very interesting," he said. Then the smile was back on. "You betcha."

★ ❄ ★

Mr. D turned the light off, then on again, as Wally waddled along the Embankment into the mist. After he was gone, we all re-entered, guarded by the "closed" sign. Should anyone have asked, we were the volunteer cleanup crew; many places depended on such with all the help off on the war effort.

"German," Mr. D said. "Or I've not been doing this for thirty years."

"He hasn't been to Minnesota, I should think," John added. "Hamm's, indeed. That gave him away."

"I rather thought that was an American beer of that region," Harry said.

John nodded. "Indeed. And nobody who likes real beer will drink it."

"What's he doing in an American uniform? All this talk about pumps and the like," Harry asked. "We're building the . . . "

I put a hand on his arm. "There's not a little mingling of forces; Yanks in the RAF, RAF chaps flying Yank bombers, and so on. I imagine someone with credible looking papers could get himself involved as an exchange officer, and as such, he could be a little different without being too obvious."

"He'd be in on the whole bloody thing," Mr. D said. "We should talk to someone."

"Or he could be what he says he is," Fred said.

"An American wouldn't connect valves with electronics," Harry said, now quite sober, "and then correct himself so clumsily."

"An American who likes beer wouldn't have a good word for Hamm's," John added.

"If he is a spy," Arthur said, "he would need to communicate with his handlers. Perhaps a clandestine radio."

"I hazard certain parties could pick that up rather quickly," John said.

Harry nodded. "Yes. And other things. We are being watched."

Arthur got a faraway look in his eyes. At twenty-seven, his imagination was a little less hindered than ours, and we were a not unimaginative group. "Watched. Hmmm. Yes, well, I imagine such a transmission would have to be a one-shot sort of thing. Send it, then get out if you can."

I nodded, with a slight feeling of compassion. In all likelihood, we were going to trick Wally into sacrificing his life for the wrong reason. On the other hand, he was going to sacrifice it anyway.

"Perhaps we could get him to use that one shot for something other than my work or whatever else is a-building. I may, inadvertently, have already laid the groundwork. John, you have a fairly large telescope."

He nodded. Rooted firmly in his garden, John had made a half-scale working model of Herschel's largest telescope, which he took delight in showing off to the occasional grammar school class.

"It would work in reverse, would it not? If one were to replace the eyepiece with a powerful lamp and place an aircraft-shaped mask at the prime focus . . . "

★ ❋ ★

A couple of weeks later, we were ready to spring our trap.

Wally came into the bar at his now-usual time and Mr. D. started pouring his now-usual stout. Once he was with beer, he turned to Arthur.

"How fast does your rocket go?" he asked. "As fast as sound?"

"I don't recall saying that I had a rocket," Arthur said. "But if I were to design one to travel through space, it would go many times the speed of sound here on Earth. Of course, it would not be proper to say that it went faster than sound in space, where there is no air to carry the sound."

"Yeah, yeah. Okay. It could get to Berlin, or Washington, in a few minutes."

Arthur stared across the room, saying nothing, which I knew to mean his mind was elsewhere. Then he came back. "At orbital speed, it would be about three minutes to Berlin."

"Or the Moon in a couple of days," John said.

"I'd like to see something like that," Fred said.

"Me too," Wally added.

"Perhaps something can be arranged," Harry said, then took a long slow drink of his Pride.

Arthur looked upset. "Really, we shouldn't be talking about something that could get someone to one of Dr. Luyten's stars in a lifetime. If someone wanted to weaponize that . . . "

"Wally's okay," Harry said. "The Yanks are on our side, this century."

Everyone chuckled at that.

"Now, I've talked to Mr. Bray at the Met Office . . . "

"Group Captain Stagg's aide?" Wally interjected.

"The very man, yes. You do get around, Wally," Harry said.

"Ike expects his exchange officers to be up on stuff."

"Ah, quite. Well, Bray thinks conditions should be just about right tomorrow night for, shall we say, an unusual event."

"Are you sure, Harry?" Fred asked, alarm written on his face.

"I think we can trust Wally to do the right thing."

Mr. D quickly put a bar rag in front of his mouth and coughed slightly. Wally, with a big grin on his face, appeared not to notice.

I didn't smirk. Everything had gone smoothly so far, but if we made a mess of this, it could be at best very embarrassing. At worst, lives would be lost.

★ ❋ ★

As expected, there was a dark low cloud deck over clear air that night. We arrived early in Fred's car on the south side of Albany Road near the end of Bagshot Street, where one could get a relatively unobstructed view over the lake. It was not far from where John lived on St. Georges; though, of course, John had sent his regrets for this expedition. Trouble struck immediately.

"You're here early, Wally," Fred remarked.

"Yeah, your British cabs are efficient."

I had an essential piece of setup to do, that we didn't want Wally to see. While I was trying to think of a diversion, Fred took charge.

"Quite. Now, Wally, what we are looking for should show up over there," Fred pointed toward the western side of the lake, "and proceed east, rather rapidly. You see the oaks across the lake? It should pass . . ."

While Fred had Wally's attention, I pulled a big box from the boot and lugged it over a few yards right of our vantage point. I came back unobtrusively trailing a wire, attached to a button.

"Look carefully. It will be very subtle," I said. "There will be a glow, somewhat like a searchlight beam. Something to do with ionizing the air to lower friction, I should think. Mind you, I don't know anything about this. Nor does anyone else here."

Wally bobbed his head.

We waited, and waited. Half an hour passed. Conditions were just right now, but might not be in another hour. John was having fun with us, I thought, or maybe playing a psychological trick; information gained too easily might not feel as important to a spy.

"There!" Fred said.

It was very subtle, only a patch of distant searchlit cloud scudding rapidly over the lake. I looked through my binoculars and smiled. A deep black triangle lay in the center of the glowing spot, wavering slightly as the clouds whipped by. And then it was gone. I had almost forgotten my button, which I then pressed, only microseconds after the tardy thought had entered my mind.

A soft distant-sounding boom echoed from our right, long after the triangle had passed.

"Much faster than sound," Harry covered. "Like lightning. It takes the sound a while to catch up."

"Yeah, yeah," Wally said.

I could detect no suspicion in his voice.

"Mind you, this didn't happen," Fred added.

"I saw nothing," Wally said, and I imagined the "o" in his nothing had more of an "oh" sound to it than an "uh," but I might have been mistaken.

"Two minutes 48 seconds," Arthur said. From the look on Wally's face, he didn't have to add "to Berlin."

We had played our roles to perfection. The hook was set. The only question now was whether he would run with it and Section 5 could reel him in. But that was out of our hands.

★ ※ ★

Wally wasn't with us on the fifth of June.

I arrived last and got my pint from Mr. D. Harry already had a nice cluster around the bullseye, and Fred, in his usual place, had an eye on him. Arthur had his head in a book, not totally unusual.

John was at a side table staring at the foam of an as-yet untouched stout.

"Anything from five?" I asked Harry, pint in hand. He frowned at my use of the number, but one had to call those people something.

Harry nodded, and the room fell silent.

"They homed right in on him. Walter Petersohn." He pronounced the "W" as a "V" and dragged it out into a buzz. "They waited until he got off everything about Arthur's supersonic spaceship, then nicked him right proper, clean as a whistle. "He didn't get a word out about the invasion."

"German! I knew it. Cut it a wee bit fine, if you ask me," Mr. D. said with just the hint of a smile.

Harry shook his head. "Bray says it's all up to the weather, and the weather isn't talking very clearly to us or the Gerries right now. Wally couldn't have compromised anything. And their intelligence should now be thoroughly confused as to Arthur's activities."

Arthur looked up from his book and gave a quick smile.

John also looked up, as if confused about something. "It worked, then?"

"Perfectly. Exactly as planned. You know, if you had whipped that beam across the face of the moon in a hundredth of a second, its apparent velocity would have been roughly the speed of light."

"Do you think we'll ever go that fast for real, Arthur?" John asked.

"Given enough time. Given we don't kill ourselves in wars. Or maybe something else will find us that already goes nearer light speed."

"In this case, faster than sound was more than sufficient," Harry said. "Another pint. Mr. D. Make it the Young's Stout; as it betrayed Wally and helped secure our invasion's success. Is something wrong, John?"

John looked around, with the oddest sort of look on his face. "I was going to apologize. The operation was all a complete flop on my end. The power supply for the lamp burned out and I couldn't get the light on at all. There was no projection."

Then what was there?

After a decent interval, Harry said, "To reiterate, we are being watched. Another pint, Mr. D." He lifted his glass with the kind of manic smile with which a man greets his dentist. "Cheers. Shouldn't be long now, should it?"

STORY NOTES

This was written for the anthology *How Beer Saved the World*, put together by Phyllis Irene Radford. I had long admired Arthur C. Clarke's *Tales of the White Hart*, and wanted to do something similar, so a story about beer saving the world gave me an excuse. The setting is the same real London bar Clarke used as a model for his White Hart stories and I've used the first names of some of those characters as well as that of Dr. Clarke and his brother; however, that is pretty much where any resemblance stops. The Clarkes were elsewhere at the time of this story and had significantly different personalities, if my sources are to be believed. Any resemblance is, as they say, coincidental. Harry, however, should remind you of Clarke's character Harry Purvis; that is a very intentional allusion. Also, I hope the style of the story reminds one of the White Hart tales, including a Clarkeian twist at the end. As to what they saw, well, perhaps it was a meteor of the natural or RAF variety. And the watchers? Well they may have had someone with an "M" designation leading them. But in science fiction, there are other possibilities.

GDN March 2015

KARL'S MARINE AND SPACECRAFT REPAIR

"Mr. Karlsson, we need your help."

It was a crisp, cultured, vaguely British accent and I looked around, hoping to find some source of the voice other than the frog Ellie was holding up to me.

"Sir?" It was the frog. Something about how the sun had come up red this morning told me it was going to be a different kind of day. The frog seemed a quite ordinary, if large, green spotted leopard frog. It wasn't quite large enough to catch the attention of Marie at the Allouette Grill and French Kitchen, who was known to skulk the shore reeds of this chain of ponds and channels leading from Gull Lake up to Nisswa searching for fresher fare than she could get from her Duluth suppliers, but it was a largish frog. Maybe the size of a man's hand. Pretty natural looking; seamless, no sign of any buttons or anything electrical, but they're pretty good at disguising that kind of thing today.

"Grand*pa*," Ellie stomped her ten-year-old foot on the oil darkened floor of the shop, "the frog wants to talk to you and my arms are getting tired."

"Uh, pardon me, Frog." I humored her and addressed the frog; Ellie got her way with me pretty easily, but had some sort of common sense not to take advantage of it too much, the way some kids who have to grow up too fast do — like they have a kid part and a small adult part.

Ellie had to grow up fast about her ninth birthday; she moved in with me after Tad and Ellen got killed in a car wreck. It was a bad time. Six months earlier, my Terri Ann had got what was going around, except she got it a lot worse than anyone else did. All they could do at Brainerd was to keep her comfortable enough to die in her sleep. So, in less than a year, Ellie had lost her parents and her grandmother.

It snowed early June that year, too, which cut a couple weeks off the tourist season. A real stinker. Trying to keep Ellie on an even keel was all that kept me from going to Minneapolis or something. So now, Ellie had a talking Frog — well, she could have had a lot worse. I didn't see how playing along would hurt.

"You know," I drawled at Ellie's talking toy, "it's been a while since I've run into an English frog. Some people wouldn't use that accent on the Fourth of July, however."

"Grand*pa*,"

Had some condescension crept into my voice? Have to work on that. "OK, OK, Ellie, maybe the, er, frog would be more comfortable on the workbench." I indicated an open spot between the cowling of an old Evinrude and a cracked prop off a Chris Craft which I had better get fixed or replaced by tomorrow noon.

Ellie nodded seriously and held her hands up to the edge of the bench and the frog waddled off her fingers with the grace and dignity of a miniature sumo wrestler. An expensively realistic toy, I thought. More than my Ellie ought to be spending, but I pretty much let her spend her allowance as she saw fit. The frog turned, faced me, and opened its mouth very slightly.

"Please don't be alarmed by the form of this motile. It is a rather convenient shape to be going about in this area with little notice, don't you think?"

I had to concede that point. "Whatever. You look like you belong around here, OK."

"Of course he does, Grandpa; he's a *frog*!"

"Uh, sure Ellie, have you taken the trash out yet? The truck comes by at noon, you know."

"Oh . . . " Ellie's eyes got large and she scampered out without a further word. Score one for Grandpa.

She forgot to take the frog.

"We really do need your help," it said.

Who the hell was controlling it, I wondered.

I looked quickly around to make sure no one else was looking at this and turned to Frog again. "OK, you've had your fun; now I got work to do."

"Perhaps, motile was the wrong word. I am linked to our cybersystem, but am quite capable of independent action. More of a robot, really. And I do have work for you."

I groaned. Some days start out better than others. The shop door looked out on the marina where most of my regular customers kept their boats. One of them was probably sitting out there on a boat with binoculars, a microphone, and a radio control get up. I decided to call whoever's bluff and grabbed a piece of oil-smeared newspaper and held it up to the frog. "What's this say?"

"The headline reads 'Good Wild Rice Harvest This Year, Tribe Says' and it goes on to talk about how much sun . . . "

"OK," I interrupted. So those eyes weren't glass. I grabbed the Evinrude housing and slapped it down over the frog. It was an old style metal housing which should have made any radio link with the frog pretty difficult. "Now turn the scrap of paper over and read the other side."

There was a rustle, then the frog read: "Alice Jensen, 93, Crow Wing County librarian for sixty years. Drowned in a boating accident when her jet ski . . . "

Damn, it was an autonomous, multi-sensored, talking frog robot like something out of a Popular Science dream — or nightmare. I wasn't ready to guess just where Frog might be from, but it clearly wasn't out of the Target toy department. "OK, uh, Frog. Whatever you are, I'll have to admit you seem to be on your own."

"Very much so here, unfortunately. I had to come a long way to find someone open today."

"Now let me get this right. You are something that someone, er, *made*, and you need my help?"

"Quite so," Frog replied. "I represent a pair of astronauts and the cybernetic mind of their excursion craft, which unfortunately suffered a most inconvenient encounter with a jet ski down in Steamboat Bay last night. I'm afraid I've come to regard those vehicles as a significant nuisance."

"You bet," I agreed sympathetically and removed the Evinrude housing. If you ignored his shape and his accent, old Frog began to make a certain amount of sense. "Astronauts, you say. I suppose you don't mean human astronauts?" Not too likely, but one could always hope.

"Our biological progenitors originated in the Small Magellanic Cloud about seven million years ago, but we are from a relatively local colony in Proxima Centauri's asteroid belt."

"Uh, have you folks checked in with NASA or the UN or the Chamber of Commerce or anyone?"

Whatever else he was, Frog was probably some kind of what we used to call, um, a wetback. "That might not be very wise for us or you. We've been observing the emergence of your race since the advent of wireless telegraphy. It's a rare event of great scientific interest, as you can imagine. I can assure you that your extreme discretion will be well rewarded."

"Some folks around here might call that a bribe, trying to keep me from my civic duty."

"Quite a noble sentiment! Very well, then, we shall simply ask for the favor and ask that you contemplate what complexities might result from your report of a conversation with a frog."

The thing you don't need in Nisswa, Minnesota, is complexities. We've got weather and tourists and that pretty much takes care of complicating life by itself. I backed off a mite. A talking frog had a repair job for me? Whatever, I could use the work.

"Then again, some folks might consider it common sense to keep quiet about something like you. You have a repair job in mind? I do good work but I gotta charge for my time."

The frog turned and stuck its tongue out and into the crack in the Chris Craft prop. A kind of fuzzy gray foam appeared over the crack and the prop moved ever so slightly. Then the foam vanished and the tongue flipped back into Frog's mouth. The prop looked good as new.

"I trust we have a few hours in the bank, so to speak?"

"Maybe four or five," I replied with the poker face I reserved for negotiations, but it was clear that Frog wouldn't be a total loss in my kind of business. "Fine. We can barter. But if you can do that, what is it you think I can do for you?"

"We could fix any simple damage with our nanomotiles, but we cannot quickly regenerate material which is utterly gone. I regret to say that the aeroshroud which protects the propellant tank of our landing craft and stabilizes the mechanical interface with the life support module under max Q conditions was impulsively detached in the Jet Ski collision and lies somewhere in the aqueous sediment of Steamboat Bay. The boat activity in that area made any recovery effort most impractical. I fear we shall have to ask you to fabricate a new one."

I nodded slowly as if I'd understood all this. A shroud was likely a thin shell of something, and I'd guess it was lost in the bottom muck. "I've got some sheet steel."

"Too massive for its strength, we fear. What is required is a ten-mill aluminum-laminated graphene sheet."

I should have guessed something like that. I shrugged my shoulders. "Maybe you need to go somewhere they can pronounce whateveritwas you said."

"We've taken the liberty of accessing your supply net."

I looked sharply at Frog. How the hell had he done that? Then again, how the hell did he do anything he did. Seven million years, he'd said.

"The nearest vendor," Frog continued, "is Olsen's Roofing in Brainerd. The Japanese are exporting it as a substitute for corrugated iron. It is three times as dear, but lasts indefinitely."

I knew Thor Olsen; he liked to open early, seven thirty as I remembered, and he'd give me wholesale if I picked up enough to cover the boat shed as well. Pricey, but it would likely be the last time I'd have to do it. At fifty-five, I was beginning to feel that my roof climbing days might not last through another set of tin. Brainerd was anywhere from a thirty to fifty minute round trip down 371, depending on how many tourists were in town. I guessed I could go after breakfast tomorrow and be back in time to open. I nodded to Frog.

"A four-foot, three point five six two-inch diameter circle would do nicely. I'll cut a twenty-seven point oh eight three circle in the center and a point seven two eight nine three radian wedge, then we bend it into a cone. I or one of the other motiles can nano-meld the seam after installation."

I nodded again. "That might be a good idea: your doing it. My, uh, nano-melding is a little rusty."

"We can count on your assistance, then?"

I shook my head. "Whatever. I'll pick it up tomorrow morning." I wasn't contemplating leaving the shop on the Fourth. All sorts of emergency repairs turn up, and at doubletime holiday labor rates, it was one of my bigger days.

"Grandpa!" Ellie shouted, "someone's outside and they broke their outboard and they need it fixed right away."

See? All I had to do was think the thought. "Be right back," I told Frog and walked out to the front office.

It turned out to be a couple of young ladies, both about medium height and build, one a short-haired full figured blonde and the other more lithe and boyish, with long black hair falling free to her tight rear end. She looked familiar, sort of. They were barefoot, wearing utilitarian walking shorts and barely legal swim halters that showed lots of tan. We don't see a whole lot of that in Nisswa and Ellie was staring, about as wide eyed as I probably was. They didn't seem to mind, or even notice. A Winnebago trailing a twenty foot outboard runabout with a cabin was parked in front.

"I'm Kim, she's Kate," the blond said, so businesslike it almost pulled my mind off her chest. "We got a Johnson fifty-five that won't start and we've got to get down to Bar Harbor. Business."

I wasn't about to ask *what* business, but suspected I'd make some people happy if I could get them on their way. They seemed sane enough, and my libertarian instincts weren't displeased.

"We'll pay cash," Kim added.

Kate looked me up and down with the kind of smile a kid has when she's got a surprise she just can't quite hold in. My hair's still all there though it's been white since my early thirties. My skin's not too loose and I don't have much fat on me, courtesy of the annual Nisswa County senior ten-K and my winter season cross country business. The wart next to my nose was removed last winter, so, for fifty-five, I probably passed muster, if that's what she was thinking.

"Or barter," Kate said in a very quiet sincere voice, staring into my eyes in a way that promised more than simple fun.

It was a strange thought that something like that might actually happen to me now, even as part of a transaction. I'd met Terri Ann my first day at Bemidji State, and while we'd both had special friends and experimented with life styles a bit in those loose and heady days, we'd settled down by the mid seventies, and there'd been no one else for me for thirty years. God, I missed her and there was something about this girl that brought it all back, instantly.

"Whatever. I'm Karl." My real name was Anthony, courtesy of my mother. It didn't stick past first grade, but I remember every time I introduce myself. "Battery okay?"

"Full charge, cranks fine," Kim replied. "Engine pops, smokes, won't catch. Bad symptoms."

"The smoke was black," Kate added, "and the plug fouled. It's my uncle's boat, and we have to get it back by the weekend. Don't you remember me, Grandpa?"

Kathy Alquist! The name came suddenly and with it the face of the tomboy that used to babysit Ellie maybe five years ago. No relation, but Grandpa was what everyone had called me in that family, and she'd been pretty much part of it for three or four summers. Damned if she hadn't been a bit of a flirt back then, if I remembered. My mouth must have gaped like a walleye in a stagnant pond, the way she giggled. "So it's Kate now? You've grown up a bit; your face looks like your mother's."

Kim groaned. A hint of a frown passed over the subject face, to be replaced by a determined grin.

"So they say. Just a summer job, Grandpa. Kim, he's a good guy. We can trust him."

Oh? Exactly what was I supposed to say to Kate's family if and when it got out what she was doing and it got out that I knew what she was doing and didn't tell anyone that she was doing it?

Well, she was too pretty not to smile at. "Kathy, er Kate, It lays a bit of a burden on a person when you say flat out that you can trust him like that without asking permission. But your business is your business. We'll get your motor fixed, don't you worry about that."

Kim looked relieved and tossed her head toward the stern of the boat.

I nodded. "Let's take a look now. Ellie, could you roll the hoist out?" Pushing that big thing around made her feel important. She scampered off.

We had the engine disconnected and off the runabout in ten minutes and soon on my test stand on the side of a big oval cow-watering trough. I hooked up my DC and hit the starter button. It popped, smoked, and didn't catch. I took the cowling off, pulled a plug, stuck in the gauge, and cranked. Hardly moved the needle.

"What's the diagnosis?" Kim asked, frowning.

"She's pre med," Kate interjected with a smile.

Probably thought she was invulnerable to disease. But I nodded sympathetically. Our state rep had voted to increase tuition again, and I was beginning to feel guilty about voting for her. "It could be better, " I drawled. "Rings, or maybe a crack in the block. Happen all of a sudden?"

"Kinda," Kate sighed. "Wouldn't plane coming back in last night, though with six people on board I thought maybe it was just out of adjustment."

Kim looked impatient. "Mr. Karlsson, a good night tonight might mean a whole class next semester, if you understand."

"What do you do?" Ellie asked and I winced.

Kim rolled her eyes up but Kate knelt down to look Ellie in the eye and smiled. "I dance."

"You're very pretty. If I want to look like you when I grow up, do I have to take dancing lessons?"

Kate laughed lightly, "It wouldn't hurt."

Meanwhile, I had the starter and carb off, exposing the block. It had a crack. "I've got good news and bad news."

"Hit me," Kim groaned.

I nodded. "The bad news is that it looks like you'll need a new block and that'll be three hundred seventy-five plus labor and two days before I can get it because it's the Fourth of July. The good news is that Dick's Rentals is open 'till noon. He should have something to get you around for the next couple of days."

"We gotta get back to Minneapolis tomorrow. Business."

Ellie tugged on my trousers and pointed to Frog, maybe thinking Frog could fix the cracked block. For all I knew, he probably could, but I wasn't about to count on it just yet.

"Oh! That's a *big frog*," Kate gasped. Kim rolled her eyes again. Kate sidled up to me, pressing herself into my bare arm and demonstrating that there was even less to those net tops than met the eye. "I could drive back up Friday morning, pay and pick it up if you can't fix it today. Will you take it, please, Grandpa? The rig belongs to my Uncle and Aunt."

"Please, Grandpa, I like Kate," Ellie added.

I disengaged myself, perhaps a little abruptly in my embarrassment, and nodded curtly. "Can't promise anything, but I've got to go into Brainerd tomorrow morning anyway. If Northstar Marine Supply has something on hand, I can have it ready for you by noon." It's a two and a half hour drive back to the Twin Cites and I didn't figure their kind of business started much before five in the afternoon. "Meantime, you'd better get over to Dick's."

Kim shrugged and nodded. Kate touched my arm again, her eyes saying: "You don't fool me."

"I'll show them where it is!" Ellie offered.

Kim cracked the first hint of a smile I'd seen on her. "OK, then let's move our rears. We'll have her right back, Mr. Karlsson."

I thought a minute, then nodded. I used to know Kate, but If Kim hadn't smiled, I don't think I would have nodded. Dancers my eye, I thought, but they seemed nice enough and Kate wouldn't let anything happen to Ellie.

"There's a slight problem with tomorrow, I fear," Frog said as soon as they left.

"Oh?"

"We really have to be on our way tonight."

"It's the Fourth of July; Olsen's closed today. Why do you have to go tonight?"

"Otherwise the beings I represent will experience significant difficulty."

"Difficulty?" Damn it, was this a mater of life or death, or being late for dinner?

"You must be very discreet."

"I won't tell another human being."

"More discreet than that."

I should have guessed. It was that kind of day.

"Won't tell any other frogs either," I promised. "Now, what's up?"

"They need to return to the base spacecraft before their — the closest English words would seem to be guardian, or perhaps godparents, but the emotional relationship is closer to that of a human parent. The literal translation would be 'Egg Tender.' At any rate, they need to return before they are missed."

"Uh-huh," I said with a smile, having been at both ends of that circumstance in my life. "Is there more to it than that? I wouldn't want to get too far on the wrong side of the, er, egg-tenders by helping the little Huck Finns."

"Romeo and Juliet might, perhaps, be a more apt analogy, though I might concede a bit of Tom and Becky in the characters of these two. The salient feature is that their respective Egg Tenders are not good friends and the two lack the necessary approvals for spawning. The spawning pools of the observation ship were thus unavailable to them. Also, the eggs would not survive in your waters, and this saves the inconvenience of unregistered larva. So this was a convenient place. Their respective Egg Tenders are doing research at Lake Baikal, and will return to the observation ship very early tomorrow morning, by your local time."

"And they left Romeo and Juliet home alone. Uh-huh." I tried to explain to myself why I should care, and gave up. I did — maybe the Romeo and Juliet analogy was some very sophisticated psychological manipulation on Frog's part. He certainly was very well informed. They probably watched a lot of Masterpiece theater and what not up there.

"Frog, you seem to be taking Romeo and Juliet's side of this, rather than the authorities."

"A complex situation, I agree, particularly when unauthorized use of a vehicle is involved. However, the authority involved in Egg Tending is personal, not societal, and the vehicle and its motiles have primary loyalty to the vehicle passengers and must try to avoid their harm. Should they return undetected, no harm will have been done."

So our societies had that much in common — one could do whatever one wanted as long as one did it undetected. "Whatever," I answered.

OK, Olsen had the stuff, he wasn't open, but this was an emergency — for someone anyway — and a challenge for me. That had to be it: the challenge of fixing an authentic spaceship. I could leave that problem alone about as well as an itch.

"Well, we could try to reach Olsen at home. Wouldn't get your hopes up, though. Mac," I called out to my computer. "Call Thor Olsen at home."

My ancient computer lived on an oil-blackened wood shelf next to my coffee maker, with a good enough mic and speaker hanging beneath the shelf on hooks. Between the voice interface software and my interactive parts catalog, there wasn't room for a lot else. But I didn't need a lot else. Pretty soon, I heard a dial tone, then Mrs. Olsen's voice came on line to tell me they were taking the kids to Paul Bunyan Land and to please leave a message.

"Paul Bunyan Land?" Frog asked.

"Big amusement park outside Brainerd. Gotta big huge talking robot of Paul Bunyan and all sorts of north woods stuff around him, some legendary, some historical. We'll probably have to go there and try to find him. Shouldn't be too hard; Thor Olsen is almost seven feet tall."

"Is this, perhaps, the same Thor Olsen who played center for the University of Minnesota basketball teem fifteen years ago?"

I nodded. "You bet. NBA wouldn't take him though; too slow."

"I remember an image from one of your television programs," Frog replied, "and can update the apparent age of the image to his current age. Observe your computer monitor."

There was Thor, all right. I nodded. "Add a full beard to that; he had one almost down to his chest, last I saw." The beard seemed to grow in a second, and I was looking at Thor Olsen the way he looked last week at the Sons of Norway barbecue at East Gull Lake. I nodded.

"So, we are off to Paul Bunyan Land," Frog announced.

"I wanna go too!" Ellie squealed, followed by the sound of the front office screen door slamming. I made another mental note to turn the air screw out a bit — the darn thing closed so slowly now that a customer could pretty much come in, get a candy bar out of my machine, read a magazine, pick up a repair job, and be on the way out again before it finally slammed shut. Well, maybe I exaggerate, but an early warning system, it was not.

"You were talking to that frog," Kate observed, trying, not quite successfully to stifle a giggle.

"That's because it's a talking frog," Ellie explained, impatiently. "Can I go to Paul Bunyan Land with, please."

"Uh, later Ellie. Hi, Kate. I've got another job that's going to take me into town today — won't wait, so I might get a head start on your engine if I can find the right block."

Kate wasn't paying attention. She walked over to the frog, and stuck out her hand. "I'm Kate, and you are?"

"Frog seems to do nicely." Frog rocked back a bit and reached Kate's index finger with its own little five fingered hand. Except for a little webbing, leopard frog hands look quite human, I found myself thinking. Finger and hand moved up and down in a dignified simulation of a handshake.

"Glad to make your acquaintance." Then she bent over and kissed Frog's head, and laughed. "I've always wanted to do that. I wish I could stay to talk, but I have business. Kim's waiting."

"Another time, perhaps," Frog replied.

"My pleasure." Kate gave me that sincere, open, look again. "Ellie told me about your family; she's got a lot of grit. We'll be in and out of Bar Harbor tonight. You know the boat."

I gave it my best noncommittal "whatever" and she gave me a quick smile and bounced out through the front office door. It closed so slowly that a momma mosquito could fly in, brood in my test tank, and her children fly out before it locked them in. I stared until the sound of it crashing shut brought me back to my senses.

"Could I come and watch Kate dance?" Ellie asked.

"That," I chuckled, "I think, would be after your bedtime."

✦ ✵ ✦

We didn't head out for Brainerd and Paul Bunyan until two. An Evinrude came in with a carburetor problem; I replaced the fuel filter, and ran Gumout through it until the problem went away. A family limped in to dock with a methane-air fuel cell Merc Electric which had cracked the cork on its liquid methane dewar. I was able to match the threads with an LPG plug I had lying around, drill holes to fit the rest of the hardware and got them on their way. Next, against my better judgment, I patched the hull on a teenager's jet ski with some superfiber and heat-dried it solid — the customer was in too much of a hurry for a fifteen minute sand-and-glaze, so he took it as-was on a discount.

Then the front office was empty, so I consulted my internal Worst Case Scenarios service and set my "back-at" clock to five p.m. Then Frog, Ellie, and I were off in my old jeep Cherokee down the highway, window open, our hands diverting as much of the eighty-eighty degree slipstream to our sweating bodies as possible. They want too damn much to fix the air on it. Off the lake, it was a scorcher with that kind of heavy before-the-storm feel. The forecast for the Fourth had been hot, muggy, and partly cloudy last I looked, but I began to get a feeling . . .

Ellie carried one of Terri Ann's old bags that was big enough for Frog to hide in. It made her look older and that made me notice the way she was starting to fill out her T shirt, which started me thinking that I should ask Marie to talk to her about wearing something underneath the next time we stopped in crepes. Ellie was still a month short of her eleventh birthday and I thought I'd had another couple of years before I had to really start worrying about that kind of thing. But she was about five two already, and clearly running a little ahead of her age in all respects. It could be worse; the Bradley kid had managed to get pregnant at twelve.

"Grandpa, did you hear what I was saying?"

"No, Ellie, sorry. I was lost in thought."

"I just told Frog about all the Paul Bunyan legends, digging the grand canyon and everything, and he said if Paul's a real robot, he might be able to do things like that. That would explain a lot, wouldn't it, if Paul Bunyan were a big robot?"

I laughed. "Yes, if he were a real robot, it just might explain a lot. You betcha."

Paul Bunyan land was a zoo when we got there. We checked with the Olsen's answering machine from a pay phone, and it said they were still out, so we started wandering around the central square looking for a seven-foot guy with a beard. Turned out, there were a lot of big people around. The biggest, of course, was Paul, a twenty-foot animated giant sitting in a huge log-framed stage next to a monstrous blue ox.

I lifted Ellie up on a big fence post so Frog could peek out of the hand bag and get a good view without attracting too much attention.

"Possible target entering the lumber museum," Frog announced.

He had better eyes than any human-made robot I'd ever heard of. I spun my head around and caught a glimpse of a big guy in a lumberjack shirt disappearing into the entrance of the huge log shed that housed the old-time lumberjack exhibits. So I lifted Ellie and Frog down and headed through the crowd toward the entrance. It took us a couple of minutes, and I thought I saw someone who looked like Olsen outside the museum two or three times, but I wasn't sure.

The museum was crowded. In addition to all the nineteenth century logging equipment, there were all sorts of cheerfully unecological murals concerning Paul Bunyan and his Blue Ox laying waste to the forests of North America, and various cheap ceramic sculptures of this or that having to do with Paul's mythical entourage.

"Ahem," Frog said softly, peeking out of Ellie's bag. "Could you set me up on the shelf next to that china blue ox where I can get a view? I can pretend to be ceramic and fit right in."

One of the people next to me looked around, puzzled. I smiled at him, he nodded and went about his business. I sidled back to the wall near the shelf, and when I thought no one was looking, I put Frog up on the shelf.

After a minute or two, Frog told us, as softly as he could, "It looks like he's not here."

"Momma! A talking frog!" shouted a sun-bleached blond boy who looked to be about six. "Who are you, Frog?" A curly haired woman in a bright orange mumu, who might have missed a session or two with Jenny Craig, turned and stared at Frog.

"I *heard*," Momma answered. "Isn't that *cute*?" She waddled up to Frog's perch and poked at it with the red lacquered nail of her index finger. "Ugh, it feels real. What is it?"

"Ahem," said Frog. "I am one of the frogs that got caught in the lumberjacks' throats in the winter of seventy-eight."

The woman stepped back, and a couple of other people turned around. There was no chance to grab Frog and run.

"It got so cold and miserable," Frog continued, "that everyone had a frog in their throat because it was much too cold for us frogs to be *outside* of peoples throats. Paul saw that all this difficulty in speaking was getting in the way of cutting down trees, so he took his big kettle, the one that could make a thousand cups of coffee for a thousand men, and filled it full of snow. Then he chopped down a hundred trees to fire it, shoveled in more snow as it melted, and boiled a ton of water."

"I get it," the boy said. "It's got a switch under its skin; you poke it and it talks!"

"Then," Frog resumed in a stentorian voice that made interruption unthinkable, "Paul poured the hot water into a big frog pond near the camp, and it melted the ice and made the water so warm, that all the frogs forgot it was winter and almost all of the frogs hopped out of peoples throats and into the nice warm pond.

"Of course, the pond froze again, freezing all those frogs before they could hop back into peoples throats again. But it turned out that when spring came and everything got unfrozen, the frogs thawed and didn't mind having been frozen that much. After all, encased in ice, there was no danger that they would be swallowed and eaten, which is the sad fate of many a frog-in-the-throat. So that's how we frogs learned how to hibernate."

"How charming!" the little boy's mother exclaimed. "Even if it is icky."

Frog got poked again, and had to repeat the story over and over, trapped in its cover role. In the meantime, we weren't getting any closer to finding Thor Olsen, and my worst case scenario estimated return time of five p.m. was beginning to look a little shaky. I had visions of a some family whose outboard wouldn't start and had to get down to an island in Wilson's bay before sunset or lose a three hundred-dollar deposit on a cabin waiting desperately at my door watching their vacation tick away and getting madder and madder.

Finally, I pushed my way back through people, intending to reach up and take Frog in mid sentence and risk the consequences. I'd just raised my arms when the big robot Paul Bunyan called "Hello, everyone," in a clear deep bass that penetrated through walls like the woofer on a boom box and everyone fell silent, including Frog. Paul's vocal equipment had been upgraded, I thought, since I was a kid.

"The Paul Bunyan Look-Alike contest will begin in three minutes. Everyone that thinks they look like me should gather in the roped-off area just below Babe here. Again, everyone . . . "

Come to think of it, Thor Olsen would look a little like Paul Bunyan, especially if he wore a red lumberjack shirt. I didn't know Thor so well that I thought I could pick him out of a crowd of big, full bearded, guys in lumberjack shirts, however.

People were streaming out, and since Frog stopped talking, no one was hanging around. I held out my hands, Frog jumped down into them, and quickly slipped off into Ellie's bag. We joined the crowd heading to the Paul Bunyan Look-Alike contest. I spotted Thor, with his wife and the kids, about halfway there. Elsa Olsen is six-five herself and that's what clinched it.

"Thor, Thor!" I yelled. He turned his head, waved at me and kept on going toward the contest.

"Pagan!" a woman snapped at me.

I gave her a look and fought my way through the crowd toward Thor, hoping vainly that Ellie was able to trail along in my wake.

"Thor," I huffed as I finally got close to him. "I need your help."

"Oh, hello, Karl," he greeted me, then took a look at his watch. "I'm due at the contest. It'll have to be quick."

I nodded. He really meant it, or he would have mentioned the weather. So I ignored the preliminaries too and just laid it on directly. "I've got an emergency hull job that needs some of that new diamond-aluminum composite Japanese stuff."

"Graphene-aluminum"

"Whatever. I need a four foot square of the stuff, right away."

When a seven-foot three hundred pound giant frowns down on you, something happens to your self confidence. I began to feel like I could probably explain things to that imaginary family who's vacation I was going to ruin by being late back to the shop.

"I, I need to replace the roof on my boat shed, too, so I'll be needing about a thousand square feet. May as well pick that up, too."

A twinkle came to the corner of Thor's eye and he reached into his pocket and came up with a key.

"Go on over and start loading. I should be around in about an hour. Run you a little over three grand, I'd guess. But you'll never need to roof again."

"Whatever."

We shook. I took Ellie's hand and we started to work our way out of the crowd. We were almost out of the gate when someone hooked the handle of Ellie's bag and dumped Frog and assorted things on the walk. Ellie was down in a flash, scooping stuff up, but not quite fast enough.

"Look!" cried a kid, "They're stealing the talking frog!"

"Hey he's right. Hey you, stop!"

Someone grabbed my arms, someone else grabbed Ellie, and the kid's mother grabbed Frog.

"RRRRibbit!" said Frog, and hopped out of the startled woman's hand and toward the gate.

"Yuk, It's real," she screeched.

"Geeze it's a big one!"

"I'll catch it," shouted half a dozen small boys, who ran off in hot pursuit of Frog.

The hands disappeared from my arms and melted anonymously into the crowd. The woman holding Ellie let go, backed away, and soon disappeared. I grabbed Ellie and headed for the parking lot. Somewhere in my head a small voice was telling me I was missing out on a major lawsuit.

The parking lot was swarming with frog-chasing small boys when we got there. We climbed in the jeep and in a quick moment of instant Grandpa-granddaughter eye communication, didn't shut the doors. It needed to air-out anyway.

"Oh!" Ellie squealed as a green missile landed in her lap. "Am I glad to see you!"

"There it is!" shouted a young hunter, but we had the doors closed and were on our way before the disappointed frog posse reached us.

"We are becoming somewhat pressed for time," Frog remarked.

"Especially if I have to load the roofing part of the buy. We'll have to strap it to the roll bars, overhead." I was not looking forward to lifting all that myself. But I shouldn't have worried. When we got there, Frog was an amphibious dynamo. He located some angle iron and tongue-welded a couple uprights to the jeep's roll bars to keep the graphene-aluminum panels from sliding off. Then he hot wired the forklift somehow. It was one of these new computer driven models, so I guess he just cybernetically talked the thing into helping us. Anyway, by the time Thor Olsen got there we had her about all finished. The forklift was back where it had been parked, Frog was back in Ellie's bag, and I was just tightening up the final tie down.

"In a bit of a hurry, huh?" Thor remarked, looking very impressed. "That's some heavy work."

"I've seen worse. Got customers waiting."

"Here's the receipt. I'll send a bill. And let me know how the roofing works out — I haven't figured out how a good way to fasten it yet. It treats drill bits like they were made of plastic."

Now he tells me. How the devil was I going to be able to cut the stuff?

"Thanks for the warning."

"No problem. You might keep an eye on the weather."

"You bet." I waved and he waved and we were off.

The trip back to Nisswa was a bit cooler with cloud shadows taking some sting out of the sun. A shower or two would sure be welcome.

"Grandpa, it smells like rain," Ellie said.

"Wouldn't surprise me."

"Conditions *are* quite unstable," Frog added. "Our models indicate the front has strengthened."

I glanced at Frog in surprise. I'd kind of gotten used to him, but now this reminded me that Frog really was connected to, well, something bigger than the U.S. weather service anyway. Driving gives a person time to contemplate a lot of worst case scenarios, and the rest of the trip was filled with a dark, juicy, suitably depressing worry. Just exactly what was I getting into?

We pulled up to the shop ten minutes late, and my worst case scenario didn't have it exactly right. But it wasn't to far off. The irate family waiting for me to open turned out to be a black mother and daughter from St. Paul, and their boat was tied up by the boathouse with a broken spark plug wire. They'd actually rowed all the way in from Gull. Frog did something to the wire with his tongue while I had them looking the other direction and we got them on their way in fifteen minutes, in plenty of time to catch the fireworks at their resort. So they left all smiles.

It took another half hour for me to mark, Frog to cut, and Ellie and I to bend the shroud into shape. I figured we were starting down the home stretch; it was just a thirty minute drive down to Steamboat bay and we could rent a boat from Cragun's or someone to take us out to the spaceship. From what Frog said he could do, installation would be maybe a ten minute job in the water, so we'd be back by Ellie's bedtime. I pulled on some swim trunks and threw a clean pair of work pants in my athletic bag.

Then I started calling around Steamboat bay for a boat rental and discovered a flaw in my thinking. A last minute rental on the Fourth of July? With everyone and their uncle out on the bay fishing or getting ready to watch the resort fireworks display?

It could be worse. At least I hadn't rented my wrecker out to someone. The "Gull-Able" was a flat bottom barge, gunwales lined with segments of old tires, with a square deckhouse and a winch crane. It could do maybe ten knots on its little diesel inboard-outboard drive. Gull Lake bends about fifteen miles north to south and Steamboat bay is as far south as it goes and we are as far north, with thirty minutes of speed restricted channel between us and the lake. Almost three hours, I figured. So we loaded up some extra gas and Ellie, Frog and I putt-putted out of my service slip at about seven.

Frog said we were cutting it real close. I nodded, but told him I couldn't get anything more out of this engine and still get there. Ellie would miss some sleep tonight, but then it wasn't every day that one got a chance to play good Samaritan to some stranded extraterrestrials.

There was a bit of a breeze, but it was still hot as all get out. Ellie wanted to take her shirt off, but I told her no, she was getting too old for that. We should have had almost two hours of daylight left, but it was dark as dusk so I put my running lights on. We were just under the bridge when I noticed all sorts of commotion at Bar Harbor. Flash lights and County Sheriff cars.

"Grandpa!" Ellie shouted, "There's Kim and Kate's boat."

That was it, all right, anchored just a ways offshore and rocking a little more than the waves seemed to justify, I imagined.

"No, it probably just looks like theirs," I replied. All I needed was for Ellie to see Kate at work.

"I beg to differ," Frog offered. "I am sure that boat is identical to the one on Kim and Kate's trailer this morning. I suspect that it is considerably faster than this vessel, and that it could be hired with sufficient monetary inducement."

"You got that part right, Frog." I croaked, wondering if Frog understood irony.

"I will make good whatever it costs," Frog added.

"Are Kim and Kate dancing on the boat?" Ellie asked.

A drop of rain hit me in the face. The runabout would be much more comfortable for what I thought we were in for. Ellie, I decided, was probably old enough to find out a few things. I headed for Kim and Kate's boat.

"Ellie, about Kim and Kate. I think they're done dancing tonight." For the first time I could remember, I wished Ellie had gone to a big city high school; the kind where kids learn this stuff in the locker rooms and don't have to embarrass their parents. Education at Nisswa Junior High kind of hits the high points and leaves the low points to the imagination. "Uh, you know some people have boy friends and girlfriends and wives and husbands to hug and kiss? But not everybody."

"You haven't had anyone but me since grandma died. And you don't hug and kiss me that way."

"Uh, right. Well, what I'm getting at is like, you know when their motor got broken and Kim and Kate rented a new one. Well some people kind of rent themselves out to people who don't have anyone else to go out with. They aren't supposed to, and we've got laws against it, but they do it anyway, for money. Now I don't sit in judgment on the practice, but some people do and they can get very mean about it, so if you like Kim and Kate, you won't tell anyone, OK?"

"I promise," Ellie said, very seriously. "Its like going sixty-five on highway 371, right?"

Kids have big eyes. I should probably have come clean then and there about innumerable other sins and explained that "Big Problem, little law," wasn't really the way people should live, and Ellie should do as I say, not as I do, but what I said was: "Whatever."

We were near enough now for me to use the spotlight.

"Kim, Kate, it's Karl Karlsson. From the marine service. I have to talk to you."

"What the hell?" A male voice called out, followed by hushes.

It's amazing how sounds carry over the water sometimes. There were some thuds and bumps and finally Kim emerged wrapped in a beach towel.

"OK, Karlsson, this better be good."

"Bar Harbor looks like a Sheriff's convention."

She looked back at Bar Harbor and saw the flashing lights. At the same time I saw a Sheriff's boat start to untie from the dock. "Damn!" she said. "Kate, come up, we've got problems."

Kate came up and I doused the spotlight. Not quite immediately, I'm afraid.

"Karl? Can you help us?" She asked.

"She's not . . . " Ellie started.

"It's OK, Ellie, it's an emergency. Kate, I'd like to hire your boat to get us down to Steamboat bay fast. Your friends could take the wrecker back. I know a dock they can use, real quiet. But we gotta move now."

"I'll do it," she replied without any hesitation. "Come along side."

"Oh, God," Kim groaned.

I nursed the wrecker along side nice and easy, while Ellie and Kate handled the tie up and transferred equipment. Chores done, Kate smiled and shrugged. "I'll be right back up."

Ellie turned to Kim. "Grandpa told me about hiring dates. I think you're pretty enough that you wouldn't have to hire anyone if you just met people."

Kim looked like she was going to choke.

"Ellie!" I barked.

"Ellie," Kim said quietly. "We didn't hire them, they hired us. I don't happen to think it's wrong when you really need the money, but it's illegal and it's something you just don't talk about, OK?" Ellie nodded seriously. "One more thing I want you to remember, Kate is the best person in the whole world regardless of what anyone says about what she was doing with me, understand?" Another nod. "OK kid; I've got to go now." Kim vanished into the cabin.

The two men came up first, looking embarrassed and lost, while Kim and Kate were having some kind of animated discussion in low tones. I figured I'd better break the ice.

"Karl Karlsson, boys. Sorry to bother you, but it could be worse." I nodded to the Sheriff's boat, which had just turned its engine over and turned on its running lights. "Can you handle this rig?"

"I'm Bill," the taller one said and offered his hand after he scrambled aboard. He was really just a kid. "I grew up around here, I'll get her in safe for you."

"See that yellow light about ten degrees left of the Harbor parking lot?"

"Got it."

"Those people are in Minneapolis for the week. Just tie the Gull-Able up at their dock and you can walk back to Bar Harbor. I'll pick her up tomorrow. Toss the keys in the deckhouse and lock the door after, I've got a spare set."

"You bet. And thanks." He shook my hand and went to check out the controls.

Then a big duffel bag hit my deck. I looked up and Kim and Kate had their arms around each other, fully dressed such as it went for them: shorts and tank tops.

"Are you sure?" Kim asked.

"Take it." Kate insisted. "I want my amateur status back. You go get that M.D. I see what I want and I'm going to go for it."

"Oh god, just like that?" Kim stared at Kate until she nodded. "Well, take care, rookie."

Kate nodded, they kissed, then Kim jumped onto the wrecker and looked at me the way a suspicious mother-in-law might look.

"Make her write, OK?"

"You bet." Now wasn't the time to try and figure things out; the Sheriff's boat had its spotlight on and was heading for us in the gathering gloom. "We gotta get going. You guys just drift a bit lights off in the dark. They should follow us. Got the shroud, and Frog, Ellie?"

"All on board, Grandpa. Got the ties loose too, except the one I'm holding."

I could do worse in the Granddaughter department. "Good." I said and jumped over into Kate's boat, pushing the wrecker away, along with Kate's checkered past, I gathered. We let them drift about twenty yards in the freshening wind, then I pulled up the anchor and Kate started the engine. Dick had given them a Merc sixty, I saw. Ought to do twenty, twenty-five knots easy with that, maybe thirty.

"Turn on the running lights and head for that blinking light off the port bow," I told Kate. "Just fast enough to plane." Always keep something in reserve, I thought.

The engine roared and our nose went up, then settled down a bit, as we spanked the waves with our bottom in an irregular, surging rhythm. The lake was definitely getting rougher. I looked back and the Sheriff boat was following us.

"Kate, why don't you get below for a bit?"

She nodded and I took the wheel. The Sheriff boat hadn't turned on its siren or anything; it was just laying back and pacing us. I risked a little more RPM, and that did it; the rotating light and the two tone squawker came on, and the gendarmes rapidly closed the distance. I cut the throttle as they came alongside and gave the wheel to Ellie as we settled in. The spotlight played on us, and around like they weren't seeing what they expected.

"Who are you?" the bull horn blasted.

"Karl Karlsson, of Karl's Marine in Nisswa," I yelled. "I chartered the boat to get to a client with problems down south. The girl's my granddaughter, Ellie. What's up?"

Silence. Then:

"We got a storm warning. Have you got life preservers on board?"

"In the deck box," I yelled back, hoping the hell they were. On top of concealing space alien frogs, aiding and abetting ladies of the evening, and contributing to the delinquency of a minor, a boat safety violation would have just about done it. I recalled Garrison Keillor's tale about the circus elephant with its trunk in some poor guy's Volkswagen, getting food from his kids, and had visions of my headlines reading; "investigation reveals grandfather error."

More silence, then, out of the bullhorn: "Be careful. Lot's of drunks on the water tonight."

"You bet," I yelled, "Thanks for the warning."

And with that they killed the revolving light, revved up and headed back north.

"Can I gun it?" Ellie asked.

I nodded, said "whatever" and we were off. We found we could do twenty-eight knots, but I took over again and backed off to twenty-two to save the engine and fuel. The sun peeked out from under the clouds to the north west momentarily. It was still sticky hot, but the spray cooled us. With light to see again, I took us closer to the west shore, more in the lee of the wind, and our bumping backed down. It was an idyllic moment.

"Look, Grandpa, Kate, a rainbow!"

Kate was out of the cabin in a flash. "Oh, magnificent."

"Could be worse," I agreed. "Is there anything to eat around here?"

"Uh, a couple cans of tuna, some granola bars . . . "

"I'll take one!" Ellie shouted, having been reprieved from tuna.

"Okay. Frog, what keeps you going?"

"Anything that burns will be quite satisfactory. Perhaps a sip of your petrol?"

Kate and I had the tuna and we all cruised merrily along.

Then the rain started coming down on us.

"My shirt's getting wet," Ellie complained, and pulled it off and threw it into the cabin, daring me to say anything. Before I could say anything, Kate laughed, said "mine too," and did likewise.

Whatever, I figured. I pulled mine off and threw it in after theirs. We all laughed.

"Can Ellie take the wheel for a bit?" Kate asked.

"Yes!" Ellie said.

Who's to argue? "Keep well out from the shore now," I told her as she settled in.

Then I turned, and Kate had her arms around me, and her lips seeking mine. I kissed her back gently at first, then kind of let myself get into it. We cooled it before Ellie got too much of an eyeful and stepped away from each other, holding hands, eyes glistening. I don't get excited about very much anymore, but this had me pretty worked up. Chemistry I guess.

"You could use some help at the shop?" she hinted.

"Don't know if I can pay a living wage."

"Room and board will do for starters."

"Kate, it seems like yesterday you were twelve years old and off limits. We've only had twelve hours to get to know each other, as, well, adults."

"It beats twenty minutes," she laughed. "Look, here's what I know about you. You're a competent craftsman, too honest to ever get rich. You've got enough of a sense of humor to listen to a talking frog and enough imagination to go with it. You care about helping people you hardly know, enough to take crazy chances. You're loose enough to put up with a little girlish exuberance. You love the water and the wind the way I do. You're fit enough that you've got at least ten more years in you than the calendar says. And you come with a kid that's got my maternal instincts going crazy. "What you know about me is that I've got a damn good body and I'm not afraid to share it. I'm adventurous and curious enough to team up with Kim for money. I just gave up six thousand dollars and my junior year of college for the chance that you'll take me in. I really do take dance at the U, but I'm not that good, and it wasn't what I really wanted. *This*," she waved her arms around, "is."

I glanced down at deck. The rain had picked up to a bit more than a drizzle, the wind of our passage put a little chill into our passage, and I shivered. I looked out to the lake; the clouds above were lit from beneath by the lowering sun in a riot of orange, white, and grays that seemed almost green. The far shore was golden and the whitecaps sparkled.

I looked at Kate, hope all over her face, water running freely over her shoulders, arms, shaking free of her breasts as they rose and fell freely and naturally with every wave we hit, running over her firm stomach, past her small navel and soaking the white shorts clinging to her boyish hips to near transparency. Sharing. Was Kate an "Ado Annie" who was all heart and just couldn't say no? How would I handle that when other men became involved? Did she just want to be real good friends, or was she going for the rest of my life? Could I trust my business to Kate's impulses, however warm hearted? Just how many foolish decisions a man my age could make in one day?

I looked at Ellie, a miniature version of Kate in her intense concentration, her young chest seeming to develop before my very eyes. How unconventional should I let her be? Was that really my choice? Would Kate be good for her, or make her a social outcast? How much did I owe society, anyway? Was Ellie old enough to make her own decisions about these things? All she'd seen was the upside: the cheerfulness, the joking, the freeness. Ellie hadn't seen the downside of Kate: opening herself up to some fat, filthy, pig for a few bucks. Ellie hadn't been the target of schoolyard sniping and cruelty, which would happen as soon as Kate's history got around, and which was a given in a town like Nisswa. Ellie hadn't seen Kate turned away from jobs, get rejected by her family, told she could never run for office, or worrying about venereal disease because of a month of impetuous sophomoric wildness.

That made me mad to think about it, but I figured it would come, in a worst case scenario.

But Ellie had spunk. She'd seen the downside of losing her parents and her grandmother, and bounced back. She was already showing her independence from the crowd, keeping her hair simple and functional, nails short, playing with mechanical things, and getting good grades at school.

Damn, Terri Ann, I wish you were here. You'd know what was best. Watching the water run over Kate made me thing of that evening in Terri Ann's dorm at Wheatson College when half a dozen of us, fortified with Mogen David and Seven-up punch, decided to streak the frat house in the rain, misjudged the time, and had to crawl back in through a bemused Junior's first floor window to get back to our clothes. "I've never felt so fucking alive in my life," Terri Ann had gushed while catching her breath. They talked that way in girl's dorms in the late sixties. I kinda let myself go, knowing it would be a little hard for Ellie and Kate to tell the rain from the effects of nostalgia.

I don't believe in ghosts, but when you know someone real well, it's as if part of them lives on in your mind, like a little semi-autonomous subroutine, just to answer questions like that. I could hear Terri Ann saying, as clearly as if she were standing next to me, "let's go for it."

"Grandpa." Ellie had so shout over the spanking waves and the engine noise as the exhaust occasionally rose out of the water when the nose of the boat went down. We were all having to hold on a little tighter. "Can Kate stay with us, please?"

Whatever. "We'll see, Ellie. Kate, I like you. I like you a lot. But we've got a lot more to talk about and work out, before we do anything foolish."

She nodded seriously.

"Some of it could be easier."

She nodded.

"We could kinda feel our way through the rest of the summer, figure out if it's what we really want . . . "

"Yippeee!" Ellie yelled, about that or the big wave we just went crashing over, I wasn't really sure. Kate grabbed my hand and squeezed so hard I figured that she probably could help out in the shop.

"Excuse me," Frog announced in a surprisingly loud voice. It was sitting on the dashboard, hanging on to the center windshield brace with both of its little hands. "We are approaching a funnel cloud formation."

We looked up and there it was, underlit in the reds and oranges of the setting sun, probing down our side of what was probably Sloan Point.

"Ellie, let me take over. Go in the cabin and put anything loose away and lock the latches."

I tried to gauge the drift of the cloud. North, and maybe a bit east. I swung us over toward the west shore and poured on the gas. The boat leaped forward in a leaping rolling motion as it struck the storm waves at an oblique angle. I edged the heading back south after we rolled almost ninety degrees.

Hanging on tight to a dock cleat, Kate dug out the life preservers, which were right where I'd told the Sheriff they were. A squall hit us, wind whipping up to forty knots, I suspected, and my skin stung with hailstones. I couldn't see Kate four feet away from me, and my heart almost stopped. Then things cleared up a bit and she was pushing a life jacket into my hands. She steered while I put one arm through at a time, holding myself down with the other. When I was set, she opened the cabin door, and timing a roll just right, slipped in to give one to Ellie.

Boat sense speaks well of a woman.

I got a glimpse of the cabin layout as she went. Bed-benches in a V shape running forward into the bow under the foredeck, a tiny closet of a head midships left of the door to the aft deck across from an equally tiny galley. The floor was now about an inch deep in water. Ellie had a floorboard up and was bailing the bilge water into the six-inch galley sink. She had a gash on her head that she was ignoring. I looked for a bail pump switch, cursing myself for not getting checked out better. It had one, and a little tinny buzz added itself to the rest of the racket.

We rolled up in a trough that must have been fifteen feet high, and for a sickening moment, the lake looked like it was above me. Then we rolled back. I was too damn scared to get sick. By rights, we ought to be swimming for our lives right now.

On the crest, I could see the funnel cloud bearing down on us, just barely visible in the ruddy twilight. I think it touched the lake momentarily, throwing tons of water skyward, then shrunk back.

A downpour drenched me and the boat wallowed, far too heavy now. The engine vanished momentarily as a wave seemed to roll over us, coughed, and caught again, as the crest lifted us up and out, sending water streaming over the transom. The prop and exhaust screamed in open air and we lost momentum. Then the stern crashed down again and we leapt forward.

The rain let up a bit, but the wind turned ferocious. If we hadn't taken on so much water, I'd have expected that gust would have capsized us. Tornado or not, I turned directly into the wind and waves, barely making headway, south.

The funnel cloud did a ponderous dance off my port beam, between me and the band of gray over the east shore, a black thumb sticking out of glowing clouds down to the lake. It was, I thought, I hoped, going by us. After a heart-stopping minute it did.

The wind backed off, to maybe thirty knots, from the north now. We surged forward as it caught us, and I eased off the throttle. The door opened, and Kate was by my side again.

"We've got flotation tanks in the bow and on both sides," she screamed. "It's supposed to be unsinkable."

"Thanks," I yelled back. Now I knew why we weren't swimming. "Frog, are there any more of those ahead of us."

"No. In fact, it appears only partly cloudy behind the front. Not unpleasant, really."

Behind the front, it was cool, maybe seventy as opposed to ninety, and I felt cold from the wind chill. We straightened out, and I started looking for the buoy off Sloan point, signifying the entrance to

Steamboat Bay. I caught the strobe, eased to the right and backed off the throttle, managing to combine wind and thrust to head us toward it. We weren't going to make it.

"Kate!" I yelled. "Can you pull the engine up by yourself?"

She looked a question, then grasped the situation, shouted "Yes!" and headed back to the transom. I got as far west as I could, then cut the throttle as we brushed by the first reeds. "Now," I yelled. She struggled a bit, then rotated the prop up and out of the water. We crabbed sideways in the breakers, rose up, grounded on the bar, rose up on the next wave, grounded again, then floated gently in the lee of the bar into the bay. Despite the weather, the bay was starting to fill with running lights.

I pushed off the bar with the boat hook and Kate dropped the engine. In a minor miracle, it started. I got the running lights on again, gained headway, then put the stern to the wind and shifted to neutral as we drifted by the old Hunter Mansion. Did the family still own it, I wondered? I'd visited once as a kid and it was like going back to the previous century, servants, cooks and everything.

"Ellie," I called. "Want to trade for a bit? You steer and I'll bail."

She staggered up to the steps, but Kate stopped her and handed her shirt.

"Lot of strange people around, Ellie," she said. "Besides, it's chilly now."

Ellie gave a judicious nod, shrugged into the shirt, and climbed up to take the wheel. I slipped and sat down hard on the bunk bench opposite the little galley. I was exhausted.

"Me too," Kate sighed and bent down to continue bailing. I grabbed the pail. We had the interior waterline below the floorboards in another ten minutes; the pump could take care of the rest.

Done, she got out of her wet stuff, toweled off, snapped her net thing around her top, shrugged into a sweatshirt, and a dry bikini bottom all while grinning at me with the confidence of a bridge player that knew the only way to make the contract was to assume the unseen cards were in the right place. The last person that took me for granted like that paid for it with thirty years of marriage.

"Grandpa! Fireworks!" Ellie called. I heard a distant thump and a couple of bangs.

"I'll be right up. See if Frog can point you toward his spaceship."

"OK."

"I'd suggest a slight turn toward the left," Frog told her. Then "There, that should do nicely."

"Karl," Kate asked, "are you worried about a May-December thing? I'm not. I can handle it."

"Uh, let's not get ahead of things. Room, board, and work in the shop. If, and I say, if, things really develop in that direction, it might be a good idea if we take a trip to Ely, maybe in October after the first freeze, if things work out that long."

That seemed to unsettle her. "You aren't a deer hunter, are you. I mean it's OK, someone has to do it or they eat themselves into starvation, I know all that, it's just that it's not something I think we could share easily, but we don't have to share everything, just . . . "

I held up a hand. "Nothing like that. I just want you to meet my folks. They rent canoes."

"Your folks?"

"Yeah. Dad will be ninety-three in August, My stepmother is a couple years younger than I am, but she's got a bad hip. Dad's been taking care of her. Longevity, uh, runs in the family. Grandpa died when he got caught in convenience store robbery in Saint Paul and tried to stop it. He was a hundred and two."

So if Kate were having ideas of being a middling wealthy young widow with a boat repair business all her own in her late thirties or early forties, well, she could probably do better.

But she giggled and kissed me. "Sounds better and better."

The engine revved down and went into reverse, then idled.

"Grandpa, Frog says we're here."

We scrambled up to the deck. The night had changed dramatically; a fresh breeze was all there was left of the storm, and stars were peeking through billowing clouds, ghost lit by a setting crescent moon. We were about halfway to the island that splits Steamboat bay in two, some distance from the fireworks and the rest of the boat traffic. It was warm again near the water; the brief cold front hadn't done much to cool down the mid-summer-tepid lake shallows.

"They're on the port side," Frog said.

I got a flashlight and scanned the water, stopping at something that looked like a large propane tank floating on its side. But it had kind of a beach ball attached to one end by a lattice of open struts.

"I got it. The shroud is supposed to cover those struts, then?"

"Precisely."

So this was an alien spaceship. I shivered as all the implications of Frog hit home to me again. It was too ridiculous to start with; then it had been one silly thing after another, Kim and Kate, and the overall significance of this really hadn't sunk in.

"One would think you guys could do a lot for us." I said finally.

"If we started, where would we stop? Oh there've been a few individual exceptions, but an effective large scale intervention would destroy your cultures — removing the checks and balances of war, disease, and aging would require compensatory checks on population growth which would, I fear, be vigorously resisted. And that is but one example. There have been some very large scale dynamic simulations on this, I assure you, and much may happen in the not too distant future.

But for now, for most people, the cure would be assuredly worse than the disease. You have to come to understand the choices and make your own decisions. Not all members of all races we have encountered have wanted to accept the changes involved in easing even a harsh and brutal culture. It is not our choice, ethically."

"You give me a look at heaven, and snatch it away."

"To take your reference to heaven to mean eternal life, we cannot banish death; accidents and violence statistically limit biological life span even absent aging and disease. For snatching it away; as you are someone who risked so much for libertarian principle, I suspect you see the larger issue."

Yeah, he had me there. I could see it all too clearly. What the hell do we do when chimps kill other chimps' children, or tribal warfare, or superstition, breaks out among our fellow human beings? We sit back, take notes, and call it zoology, anthropology, peace and wisdom as long as we aren't involved ourselves. We've no right to complain about the ethics of others not helping us.

"We'd better get this thing fixed and on its way." I put the engine back in gear and edged us over to the spaceship and pulled it close with the boat hook. Kate tossed the anchor in.

It wasn't quite as long as Kate's boat. The upper part of the "beach ball" on the end of the tank was transparent. I saw immediately that it was a double sphere, the inner sphere freely rotating to keep down, down, no matter what else was happening. In this horizontal orientation, I could just see the edge of a platform in the transparent part, moving up and down with the waves. On that were what looked like two miniature army helmets side by side, each on four legs each with long skinny jointed arms sticking out from under the helmets, each ending in a delicate spidery four fingered hand. What looked like eyestalks protruded directly from the "helmet." The left eyestalk of the being on the right was entwined with the right eyestalk of the one on the left. I didn't need a degree to figure that out.

"Kate?"

"I'm here." She was right behind me. I put my arm around her so the aliens could see it.

"Let's wave."

The two free eyestalks waved back.

"They wish to tell you of their thanks and relief," Frog translated, "but they must hurry."

"Right. Can they rotate that thing so it's vertical, ball on top?" I asked.

"Certainly. They assumed their present attitude to reduce visibility and achieve some limited control over their movement."

As I watched, the ball rose out of the water as the tank submerged.

"Ellie, we need the shroud. Wrap a line around it before you give it to me." Didn't want another one lost down in the muck. "Frog, time to get wet." I was still wearing the life jacket, and I jumped in hoping it would keep me far enough up so I didn't have to tread water continuously. It did.

There were sharp pieces of the old shroud stuck in the grooved fitting around the end of the tank. I was about to ask for a pliers to try to pull them out when frog hopped up on the latticework and started apply his tongue to the problem. The shards fell away, leaving a clean groove.

"Nice work," I said. "Time for the shroud."

Ellie handed me the shroud. The line wasn't wrapped around it, but seemed to be fastened to it with a metal stud at a point opposite the open seam. I looked at Frog in the water next to me.

"What did you hold that with?" I asked.

"A rivet," Frog said, "One, ahem, which I can readily undo once we have the shroud attached."

"You bet. Let's do it."

Easier said than done. The shroud was a flapping, half bent piece of metal, and I quickly found I couldn't get it into place by myself. I needed four hands. Kate saw me struggling, stripped off her sweatshirt and jumped in with me. More agile than I, she managed to wrap her legs around the tank and hold. Together, we managed to open the shroud enough to fit it over the latticework.

Frog's measurements and cutting turned out to be almost too precise; it took quite a bit of bending and worrying to get both ends seated. The seam didn't quite come straight, overlapping a bit at the top and having a gap at the bottom, but Frog said it was close enough, and after he finished doing whatever he did with that fuzzy tongue, I couldn't see the seam.

I knocked on the transparent dome. "That about does it guys," I said, assuming Frog would translate. "Guess we'd all better be on our way."

Something that sounded like crickets chirping seemed to come from the dome, but it might have been from shore. Frog was no where to be seen. Must have gotten on board the spacecraft some how, I figured. But I didn't need a translation to tell me that, even if it was a very small rocket, we didn't want to be in the water next to it when it did its thing. Kate and I swam over to the ladder on the stern and climbed back in the boat. She got the engine going while I pulled in the anchor and we trolled out of there quietly enough not to draw too much attention to ourselves.

Ellie stayed in the back of the boat, looking wide-eyed at where we left the spaceship.

The fireworks display at the resort reached its climax then, and the sky to the south was filled with bursts, stars and streamers right on top of one another so lavishly that I wondered what percent of everyone's room bill went into it. Along the shore, various private cabin owners were lighting off their own rockets.

So when the one behind us took off, it didn't really look all that different from everything else going on. Except it just kept going and going, up and over us and off through a hole in the clouds to the north. Kate cuddled up against my arm and whispered goodbye. Last we saw of it was a spark moving right by Polaris, maybe half as bright. Then it was gone.

"Wow," Ellie said.

"Yeah, you don't see that everyday. I sure could use a cup of coffee for the trip back," I hinted. Events had left me a bit drained, and I realized I was hungry too.

"I think I can manage that, and some granola bars. But why don't we just anchor, stay here tonight and head back first thing in the morning? We've got a couple of sleeping bags."

"Yeah, I get to sleep in back, under the stars," Ellie chimed. "Please?"

Kate giggled and snuggled against me more.

"Whatever," I gave in. "You'll have to throw in the anchor, though."

Kate got Ellie settled and tucked in with a couple of granola bars, and we went below. Kate found the triangular piece that converted the bench beds on either side of the bow to one big, queen sized, roughly heart shaped platform.

"Uh, Kate. I'm kind of pooped and I suspect you've had about enough of you know what for the time being, and I wouldn't . . . "

She put a finger to my lip. "No hurry."

The last thing I remember was Kate snuggling up to me and saying "mmmm" or something like that. Then the sky was light in the east.

I found my bag, pulled on the work pants, went topside, and pulled in the anchor. It was a beautiful morning, but my thoughts had turned to more mundane things. I had a roofing bill of about three grand, another mouth to feed, and any promised payment from my erstwhile clients seemed beyond my powers to collect. I didn't even have an address for the bill.

Ellie woke up and was out stretching in the rising sun like some kind of Naiad. I frowned, but figured we were too early and too far from shore for it to bother anyone.

She caught my frown, and shrugged. "Grandpa, my clothes are still wet."

I gave up and smiled at her. "Whatever. Just be real careful about when and where you do that. Now it's a little chilly and Kate ought to have a beach towel or something below to keep you warm."

Kate came up just then wearing a big grin and carrying a couple towels. She joined Ellie in the stretching and arm waving. Then they gave each other a high five and wrapped up in the towels. Some kind of female sun ritual, I gathered. Could be worse.

"Ahem, I wasn't frowning about you, Ellie. I was just worried about the uncollectable bill we acquired yesterday. I've got to pay Thor for all that roofing, and I don't think I have the balance. Then we'll have to pay Dick for the motor rental because Kate gave all her money away, and she won't be able to pay us for fixing her engine, and I didn't collect from our last customers yesterday because I was so embarrassed about being late back to the shop."

Kate and Ellie nodded seriously, but blew it by giggling again. I shook my head, got the engine started after cranking a couple of times and playing with the choke. We'd need more gas, too; another thirty bucks. I left it on idle to warm up a bit. We'd asked a lot of it yesterday, and it was Dick's engine. Maybe I could barter an overhaul. I shook my head.

"It all adds up, you know," I groused. "The money situation could be better."

There was a splash that sounded like a fish jumping, and a wet slap on the deck. I looked around.

"I'm sure something can be arranged," Frog announced.

"Frog!" Ellie and Kate squealed.

I scratched my head. "Kinda surprised to see you Frog, not unhappy, understand — just didn't expect it. You sure you won't be missed?"

"There's little use for a robot of my unconventional configuration in space, and you do remember I mentioned that there are a few exceptions to the non-intervention policy? My talents might quietly increase the efficacy of your repair work, I should imagine. And a debt is a debt, is it not?"

"You bet. Welcome aboard then, Frog," I said, just as if I had something to do with my own destiny. "You'll start tomorrow morning. You too, Kate."

Ellie cleared her throat.

I sighed. "Whatever."

Okay, I do have to admit Karl's Marine Repair has been pretty prosperous ever since.

STORY NOTES

Growing up, I spent most of my summers at Gull Lake, near Brainerd, Minnesota, and this story takes place there, updated a little bit. As such things go, it turns out to be a bit of alternate history. The great white mansion on Steamboat Bay burned down several years ago but lives on in the story; it belonged at one time to Croil Hunter, an executive of what was once regarded as Minnesota's State Airline — the late Northwest Orient Airlines. My family's more modest cabin was about a quarter mile down a dirt road on property adjoining the mansion, and a boy named Sandy, who spent summers at the big estate, and I would play with his toy soldiers up there on occasion, or explore the woods, or go down to Floan's point and watch pretty young women play tennis.

When we first came to Gull Lake, before building the cabin, we stayed at Cragun's resort, which has expanded a bit since those days, and I've gone back there a couple of times and rented a boat to cruise around my childhood memories.

The alien robot frog is not to be taken too seriously, of course, but it does, in a way, stand for the possibility that we are being watched and studied, and while it seems very improbable that any contact would be allowed, it's not impossible that the watchers might be a little more relaxed; perhaps they are members of a more recent civilization who have not quite achieved godlike status, for whom the universe still has some wonder and mystery, who might yet have some nostalgia for their own distant origins. Perhaps they might even have a sense of humor.

This story is as much an homage to the works of Garrison Keillor as it is to my summers in Gull Lake. Gayle and I are fans of the Prairie Home Companion radio show. As the degrees of connection go, my late mother knew Mr. Keillor slightly; he once lived in another home that was once owned by Croil Hunter, and he owns a bookstore across from my alma mater, Macalester College. It is my sincere hope that one might be able to buy this book there, someday, completing a circle of sorts.

And yes we do talk that way up around Gull Lake, Brainerd, Nisswa, and so on. You bet.

GDN November 2014

HUNTING THE
SPACE WHALE

CODE 10S3 BIOGRAPHY MATERIAL.
EDITED VERSION:
DON'T RELEASE UNLESS I APPROVE, OR DIE.

My final hunt started when Cap's voice roared "Thar she blows!" down to the beach from the speakers across the runway. It was my watch. If NASA had gotten Endeavor off on time, it would have been Terry's mission. I hit the emergency quit, save and shut down key; shut the lid on my portable; grabbed my swimsuit top and sprinted for the runway. I waved bye to fellow whalers Kit and Terry; they could take care of the chair, books, and iced tea. I could catch up on the ET harpoon line dynamics study later, maybe with some real data.

Dead Kitten's shocking pink cat-whiskered C-5 had its APU's whining by the time I hit the tarmac. The cryo lines were already disconnected and the rear door was up. The band was rehearsing "Gonzo" from the tour pallet by the side of the runway as a farewell gift, and I pumped my legs to their beat. One of the dancers waved her top at me, swinging it around over her head like a lariat. I grinned and and waved mine back at her, getting a big good natured leer and a whistle from a bushy-bearded beer-bellied Jodo, the lead bass and chief stockholder of Dead Kitten, Inc. Definitely unbecoming behavior for

Captain Linda T. Stevenson, USAFR, I thought. Made me feel *good*.

The right engines were revving by the time I hit that little ladder you need to get up into *Dumbo's* belly. We were rolling before the door shut. Kathy, Dead Kitten's lead singer, had my insulated, female-plumbed flight suit ready to go, and I was more than ready to climb in it; it was *cold* in there with all that lox and methane loaded in the *Ahab*.

Brad whistled and I threw the swimsuit top at him. He snatched it out of the air. "This," he japed while I got my legs in the flight suit, "is an affectation for you." Kathy was breaking up. While she needed such objects for her comfort, my chest had problems keeping them in place.

Brad and I got along pretty well for three years of marriage, but this kind of banter usually left me feeling I needed to show him up to prove that I had more going for me than my ability to stick with a diet. "It's a matter of form," I retorted, "speaking of which, Brad Stevenson, you goggle eyed idiot, where's my checklist?" True to *his* form, he'd forgotten — it wasn't in my flightsuit.

Banter aside, I had the flight suit on by the time the C-5 got airborne. Kathy found my checklist where Brad had dropped it, and stuffed it in my breast pocket with a wink. Then I kissed my slim, steel-haired husband, popped Kathy good-naturedly right in her bovine splendor, grabbed my portable computer and scrambled up the steps on the nose wheel into the *Ahab's* tiny cockpit, holding on carefully as Cap upped the angle of attack. Cap Wilson had flown C-5's in the US Air Force until he failed to make a promotion. His sister, Shana Wilson, was a singer with Dead Kitten and got him a job — writing songs. He wrote "Gonzo," a platinum hit, for instance, and their new "Starstone," which might be the next one.

If all this airplane and platinum talk gives you the impression that Dead Kitten was just rolling in money, my apologies for the understatement.   But there's money and then there's the stuff governments throw around.   By *those* standards we were damn economical. Cap found *Dumbo* a couple of years ago on the used airplane mart; Uncle Sam had sold it to the Saudis, whose new king had traded it to Argentina for uranium, who listed it when the maintenance cost got too much. Well, the plane *did* spend time at the plant in Georgia. Anyway, Cap saw the listing and figured Dead Kitten could afford to move up in the tour bus area. It was a great gimmick: the band can fly into your local airport, off-load the tour pellet onto a flatbed, do the show right from the flatbed in your local fifty thousand seat stadium, reload, and fly away in three hours. One reason Dead Kitten is so successful is they don't have a counterculture attitude toward money. They love the stuff. They've done as many as three thirty-dollars-a-head shows in a day. And people pay to tour the big pink plane with the whiskers, too. A relic of the cold war, a C-5 looks too big to fly.

But it was flying now and we were getting close to a go for launch. Brad helped me close the *Ahab's* hatch, pulling while I pushed and hollered instructions. There was just enough room for me to bend over and rotate the latch. That seal was one place we didn't cut corners — no spacesuits on this hunt. Except for the relief valve, the hatch door was the only break in my little clear Duron tank of a cabin. No pipes or wires went through; we used commercial optical links. There was CO_2 absorbent and bottled oxygen for just over six hours — twice as much as we planned on using. I flipped down the tray, set my portable on it, connected the leads, and powered up the cockpit — my world for the next three hours. We gained two thousand meters while I was doing that, and my cabin pressure didn't change. Good seal. I'd done a precautionary preflight two hours before hitting the beach, so I didn't have any worries. *Ahab* was ready to go, all forty-one tons of her, including my own spare, flat, forty three kilograms.

"Everything looks okay here," Brad yelled. I gave him a thumbs up through the windshield and started *Ahab's* final prelaunch. My astronautical engineer husband and Cap had got the idea for *Ahab* and the whale hunt over a couple of afterburners about a year after Dead Kitten got the C-5. You see, a shuttle cost about two hundred million dollars to launch, depending on who's counting. Brad figured that, with a C-5 as the first stage, using composites and not carrying anything more than you had to carry, we ought to be able to reach orbit with forty-ton rocket plane for less than a million a shot. Dead Kitten was blowing that every month on publicity they didn't need anymore.

What was really brilliant was that NASA could provide the payload: that whale-sized external tank that they took ninety-nine percent of the way to orbit, and then threw away in what was almost a parody of government waste. If you just got the things up into a little higher orbit, there ought to be something you can do with them, Cap bet. With it costing well over a thousand dollars a kilogram to put *anything* in orbit, a few tones of construction material like that ought to be worth something to someone. All someone had to do was harpoon the things. We could sell them to Japan, if nothing else — an out-of-this-world retirement fund. Rockers start thinking about that when they hit forty. The composite airplane people in Mojave worked up a design for us on the back of a couple of concert flyers at Domingo's after the big desert bash in 'ninety seven. The weight margin was paper thin, but it seems Brad knew this pretty, competent, space-crazy, fighter pilot who couldn't weigh more than . . . So there I was, in the cargo deck of a C-5 sitting at the front of a spaceship that wasn't much more that a big lox and methane tank, good to go hunt whales in space.

The astrogation program kicked in: The map and horizon appeared on the LCD just as they should. The satellite position data looked good. Fuel state and other functions scrolled by below, all nominal.

I adjusted my piss cup, secured flip-books, smart pens, rations, spare memory chips, and such, then strapped into that strangely comfortable, half sitting, half standing posture the acceleration couch gave you in horizontal flight. All I had to do now was wait. We had reached ten kilometers and I was ready.

"*Dumbo, Ahab*, everything's go here," I sent, and waved through the window at Kathy.

"Roger," Kathy replied with a nod, her waist length, wavy, red hair rippling down the curves of her no-apologies bodysuit with every move. She was wild, loved everyone, and was super nice to me. And Brad. Brad was a fondler and she had something to fondle. Fine with me.

I double-checked the restraints on the portable — if it slipped it would fall on me with up to three times normal acceleration. Then Cap started the "vomit comet" maneuver: a shallow dive followed by a pull up into a parabolic trajectory. The noise level went *way* up as the back door opened and our minutes of weightlessness came.

Kathy fed the "Go down, come up" track to the intercom. She'd written the single — no guy would have had the nerve. I started nodding my head and tapping my feet. Getting psyched. Eyes wide. Mission lust — gonna go *do* something — gonna open up space for the whole human race.

"Get ready for separation — one red-orange space whale breaches in two minutes. Go get it, Linda!" Kathy cheered.

If I did, it would be our first success in three attempts.

Brad and Kathy, tethered to the front bulkhead, waved good bye while the now-weightless *Ahab* eased it off its support carriage and rolled out the rear on the wheel guide rails as Cap gunned *Dumbo's* jets. Don't try this in your Cessna, folks — Cap is a shit hot pilot.

Dumbo pulled away rapidly and I felt some buffeting as the *Ahab's* tail and side flaps struggled to keep my attitude right in the slipstream. Then the pumps whined and the engines cut in. I got nineteen out of twenty good chamber ignitions — no sweat; I just stifled the bad guy, pulled the gear in, and kept my hand off the chicken switch. Full thrust hit me and I went off to space thinking about how good Brad and Kathy looked together. Knew I was in the way. Deal with that later.

I lost one more engine on the way up — at least the vibe sensor went redline so I stifled it, too. No problem, we had plenty. Brad told me it costs a major company about twenty million dollars to design and develop a twenty-ton thrust rocket engine, and they charge more. He got a one-ton baby with the same thrust-to-mass ratio built at our local university for about the price of a home these days. Once we had the prototype designed and tested, we got someone in Taiwan to make a hundred of them cheap. Forty-two met our specs; twenty of those went on *Ahab* and we were saving the rest for the *Ned Land* or for spares. The pumps cost as much as the whole engine buy, but one set of pumps feeds all the engines.

The launch program cut the engines at just over seven and a half k.p.s. inertial and my weight went from almost one point three kilonewtons to nothing. Right on schedule, in the grove, *Ahab* was floating along just under the circular orbit velocity than our whale, waiting for it to come to us.

I pitched the *Ahab* with the track ball, RCS thrusters banging, and started scanning the sky for a moving, twinkling, red orange star. This had been our problem so far; twice before our pilots hadn't been able to find this spaceborne monster until too late. The rub was that our whale wouldn't show up anywhere near the cursor ring; there were just too many sensitive measurements required to get its relative position and we couldn't afford pricey SDI-type special electronics.

So, this time, I just used my eyes. I knew the general direction and what to look for now.

There! A pulsing orange and white speck drifting past the other stars. Now I selected the cursor and our el-cheapo heads up display, one glowing orange ring, appeared in front of me, twenty degrees left of my target. I rolled the ball, got, the ring over the tumbling whale and hit the enter key.

"*Dumbo, Ahab.* Contact and acquisition." This was the earliest we'd managed to date; might actually get a chance to shoot. Keeping the ring on the target, I enabled four of our main engines and waited. That was hard, the waiting. My mind went back to the years of being the runt of Mom's six-kid litter, the years of discouraging comments from my teachers when I was pushing for an aeronautical engineering degree, and all the condescension, and harassment I'd gone through to get to fly an ancient, third line fighter. I had something to prove — probably always would. I started humming the melody to Jodo's tonal rap signature tune. The computer must have taken less than a minute because I was just about to where you sing "exit the kitten and enter the cat" when the *Ahab* thrust sideways and pitched down. It was heart rending to see the target swing out of view, but we had to almost-match velocities with the whale by the time it reached us, and that meant pointing the rockets toward the whale and the cockpit away. *Come on Linda*, I thought, *trust the instruments!* The main engines came on and we executed a short powered dive toward the atmosphere. Then I looked overhead, expectantly.

No disappointment. When the whale showed up overhead again, it slid over me like something out of "Star Wars." Those things are *huge*! Its tumble was slow and seemed mostly in yaw; maybe the slight air drag up here at a hundred eighty kays was already affecting it. Harpoon ready, left hand on its trigger, right hand on the trackball. Only one shot at this.

First, a pitch up maneuver to point at the whale's center and then a pitch rate down maneuver to track it as it moved over and in front of me. I got the cursor on its approximate center of rotation and fired. By the time all this was done, its apparent size had shrunk from that of an oil storage tank to that of a VW across the street. But it looked like a good shot. Our modified black market TOW missile went off right like it was supposed to.

"Hang on!" I shouted to no one. This could put us over the hump. Dead Kitten owned *Dumbo* free and clear, and with real estate and video royalties, they had enough cash flow to keep going at this level indefinitely. But with a success, we could get some real financing. We had plans. Jodo swore that, before he played his last thirty hertz tenser thromb, there would be Dead Kittens on the Moon. They'd bought in for the long haul.

We'd kept our secret pretty well because we were sure someone would try to stop us, even if we couldn't figure out why. There had been a couple of unflattering articles asking why one of the few woman fighter pilots, and one who almost never listened to anything but Tchaikovsky at that, would all of a sudden quit the Air Force and walk away from everything to hang around half-naked with a rock band on a sandy island in the middle of the Indian ocean. But that sort of thing soon died away. "Hey, guys," I'd said, "I'm *free* and the island is *nice*." Life moved on. But they'd hear from me, oh yes.

Yeah! The harpoon set light flashed the news to me that the harpoon head had penetrated the whale's skin and the barbs had deployed. Hooked! The line whined as it unreeled from the rear of the ship over the top through its guides. Now everything would be done by feel. For the first time.

The reel brake control was a hand grip with a feedback force proportional to the harpoon line tension. It only took a few seconds to calibrate my grip, braking the reel gently with an occasional glance at the tension bar gauge on my portable's monitor screen to keep things in limits. I didn't want to break the line or tear up our whale. Acceleration pushed me back into the seat as I increased the tension. The whale tried to drag me down into the atmosphere with it. Thrusters clanged to keep the *Ahab* oriented correctly, and there were all sorts of jerks and torques as my tumbling prey set the harpoon line wobbling. I rode them out and pretty soon things started to damp down.

Finally, the unreeling stopped and cable tension went down to almost nothing. I started pulling in my catch with the reel motor to keep tension on the line and reduce its distance.

But time was going by too fast. The objective was to keep my space whale from burning-in and it would do that shortly if I didn't pull this baby from the shallows in the next ten minutes or so. We were already over Australia and perigee was just south of Hawaii.

Being attached, I didn't want to say 'hi, Mom' as a fireball.

I locked the reel, opened the front guide, and pitched down so that the line pulled away from the nose and released back to a guide near *Ahab's* center of gravity. Then I pulled the line tight with the reel motor, vectored *Ahab* at the local horizon, and ignited four main rockets. The cable tension went up to near the redline and fluctuated around it. Pitch down thrusters fought the torque. The whale, floundering at the end of the line, started swinging behind the *Ahab*, or, rather, the *Ahab* started swinging in front of it because the whale was much more massive.

So far, so good. I had steady thrust and there was no change in the tension for several seconds.

No change? I tried to click in another display. Nothing.

The computer had crashed. Hung up. Hung me out to dry.

No time to panic; first, cut an engine to keep tension under limits, then throw the attitude control system into backup mode: a dumb hardwired loop that Brad had rigged up to keep the spacecraft pointed in the same direction in an emergency. It even had a separate power supply.

"*Dumbo, Ahab,* Computer crashed but staying with it. Say perigee altitude, best fit from beacon."

"*Ahab, Dumbo.* Roger. We show you five kilometers, seven now; apogee, two-twenty."

"Thanks, Kathy. Repeat every ten seconds. I say again, repeat every ten seconds."

She rogered. Kathy had a music BA — and took to this stuff like she was born to it. Things were stable for the moment. I took a breath, hit the restart button on the portable and it didn't respond. So I powered down and powered up again. Bingo! I selected reload and waited for the program to get up to speed.

"*Ahab, Dumbo.* fifty-five, two eighty." Bless you, Kathy. "Roger." We needed four hundred each. The reason apogee was better than perigee was that Ahab was already near perigee. Too near. I weighed pushing that tension red line further.

Reaching a decision to do it, I turned control back to the computer, pitched down a little more and added another rocket, feeling the slight increase in acceleration. My harpoon line tension bar moved up to the redline limit again, then started dithering around it.

Line . . . I thought of the orange monstrosity wobbling far below me. If I were to just . . .

I felt my attitude starting to change, and without even looking at the portable, threw the ACS back into the backup mode.

Another computer lock-up.

As quickly and deliberately as possible, I took manual control of the pitch axis and pushed the nose back to where I felt it had been before. But we'd wasted a lot of fuel.

"*Dumbo, Ahab.* Lost the computer again. Must be the software.

I'm staying with it."

There was no answer. Below me: Cape York. *Ahab* was below their horizon, on its own.

NASA didn't even know we were up here, thanks to a friend of mine in Cheyenne mountain who I'd sweet talked into identifying us as part of the whale. Just as well; they'd only confuse things now. They'd be mad enough about everything later on.

Despite all the problems, *Ahab's* engines kept firing, and we were gaining velocity, altitude, and orbital lifetime. Trouble was, without the computer, I didn't know how much, didn't know my fuel state, perigee was awfully close and the whale was dragging. I had been in orbit less than twenty minutes, but it felt like either hours or seconds.

 I looked back at my catch again and smiled. *You aren't getting away that easily!* I reactivated the reel and felt the harpoon line tension rise and fall through the feedback grip. When it fell, I reeled in some line. It could get a lot closer to our mutual center of gravity before my rocket burned it.

The problem with my portable computer wasn't necessarily in its software, but that was the only thing there was a chance of fixing in real time. So the backup disk went in the slot, and the machine rebooted. A look showed that the harpoon line tension bar was still up around the red line.

Perigee was coming up, and there wasn't any visual sign of heating on the big orange whale; we weren't going to reenter this pass. That was worth a sigh of relief. Our whale had been saved for at least a revolution. We had proved that what we were trying to do could be done at least in principle. I could cut the rockets as soon as apogee was high enough, and do another burn fifty minutes later to raise perigee. It was just starting to look like we'd won the whole ball game when the portable crashed *again*.

Return to back-up mode. My fingers went to the bank of valve switches and stifled an engine. I should have stifled all of them, right then. I knew I was almost out of fuel and that if I succeeded in what I was trying to do, i.e. putting our space whale in a safe orbit, then there might not be any reentry, at least not in what would remain of my lifetime. But I don't think I was consciously trying to sacrifice my life, yet. Rather I was trying to do whatever it took to a mission I had long ago decided was worth the sacrifice. I concentrated on the computer problem.

 It must be a program error; some combination of things I was doing had not been anticipated. Maybe the problem was running that close to the tension red line without allowing the computer to reduce thrust. I could change the red line limit. Complicated and time consuming.

I spent more time working this problem than I realized. The lox ran out as I was rebooting.

We made sure the liquid oxygen ran out before the methane because if the methane fuel ran out first, the lox would use the red hot engine itself for fuel. Boom. Also, *Ahab* needed the vapor pressure of the residual methane for structural integrity — from now on it was, for all intents and purposes an overweight, hard skinned, methane blimp. In fact, the lox tank is just a flexible bladder inside the methane tank, and we have to lace the methane with hydrogen to keep it from freezing.

The folks in Mojave had really done a job for us. The old *Voyager* aircraft had carried almost five times its weight in fuel. On tubby *Ahab*, the surface to volume ratio was a lot lower, and it never had to support its full fueled mass on its wheels, so they'd pushed that ratio up to twelve.

If only that ratio could have been twelve point one.

The Ahab did have a liquid oxygen reserve: my fuel cell supply could be routed to the ACS thrusters for reentry control, but the main engines were out for the rest of the mission, so I'd have to be very sparing of *any* thrusting at all prior to reentry.

The computer came back up as if nothing had gone wrong. I was at perigee. Thirty minutes after launch, fifty minutes to apogee and a little over an hour before I could call *Dumbo* again. About a hundred minutes to the next perigee. Plenty of time to think about reentry.

And think about what I was trying to prove. It wasn't so much putting our space whales in a tank bank as it was giving this planet a way into space that it can afford, *if* people can accept taking a little more risk. Kip, Terry and I had told Jodo, Cap, and Brad right off that they were cutting enough corners off the way things were usually done that one or two of us might get ourselves killed before all the bugs were out. We made them all promise not to stop trying to get it right until either we were either all dead or someone physically stopped us by impounding *Dumbo* or something.

I guess that's when Brad started letting go a little and developing other relationships. What *Female Combat Pilot* implied must never have really sunk in to him, but it was about the same thing.

"You a strange bird," as Jodo says with wonder, but he accepts me like that. Death, as such, doesn't scare me — in fact it sort of fascinates me, like I was one of those old time poets or philosophers. When death happens, it happens. I look over high ledges and fantasize jumping; what *would* it feel like? You don't know what it's like close to the edge unless you go there.

Don't get me wrong, I like living. I think I get more out of life than most people. But to give up doing the things I want to do just to avoid risk? Well, foes and friends, that *would* bother me. And let's face it. You don't put yourself in a capsule at the end of a rocket with less technology aboard than John Glenn had forty years ago, less ground support, and no spacesuit if you're that scared of dying.

So I don't make it back. I had that option, in fact, having that option gave me an almost Faustian sense of power and freedom. If nothing else came of this, I'd *already* been part of something worth dying for. Our recurring costs for putting *Ahab* in orbit, *per kilogram*, were one one hundredth of what a shuttle launch cost. Those kind of economics would start moving industry off Earth and allow humanity to grow without fouling its cradle any further. Something to die for. But come to think of it, we all die for something — that something being whatever it is that we do with our lives.

Brad could have Kathy full time when I'm gone. It made me feel good to think of it. Everything Brad and I had was in this venture — Dead Kitten donated our room, and we slept on floor mats. The only thing in the world I could leave him was a good single friend like Kathy. I didn't have any insurance — I mean, who would insure *me*? So, Brad and Kathy, have a ball.

There was the Space Shuttle, of course. Same orbital plane. But calling on them for a rescue would spoil everything. See, they would say, you had to have a multibillion dollar government program up here to save you from your own foolishness. No, I would shout. I knew the risks.

I'll take death to that kind of humiliation any day. Besides, I didn't have a thing to wear in vacuum.

A chime reminded me that I was out of main tank liquid oxygen. I said 'thank you' and started recording this stuff for Kit and Terry, intending to dump it on the sideband next pass with *Dumbo*.

I felt like listening to my favorite composer's sixth symphony, or Berlioz' march to the scaffold, but we hadn't had enough weight margin to bring entertainment. My untrustworthy portable computer could listen to the global positioning receiver, though, and it told me that my apogee had risen to an acceptable three hundred sixty eight kilometers but my perigee had only reached two hundred forty. Marginal.

Might as well inspect my catch. The tension bar graph showed no tension in the harpoon line. I reeled some cable in to give it some. The space whale, of course, still had a lot of liquid oxygen in it, inaccessible for now. It came toward me. There we were, two big empty gas bags playing celestial chicken. It was tempting, but I slipped aside with yaw thrusters paired for translation.

Its red-orange color wasn't gold, but it might have been; at ten thousand dollars a kilogram *any* mass in orbit was worth owning, and this whale was ours by right of salvage now. It might take us a bit of time to realize that wealth, but the wealth was there. If we collected a bunch of them, well, that would be too much mass and volume to ignore. Someone would have to do something.

My whale bled a bit of gas from its harpoon wound as it floated by. Our next development . . . "Orbit Salvage's" next development, sans me . . . should be a harpoon that doesn't make leaks. That stuff is valuable out here.

★ ✳ ★

Dumbo would be over their horizon again in another ten minutes; maybe they would have an idea for me. I had enough power and breathing oxygen for another four orbits, if the time would help, though I wondered if I would use all of it if things were hopeless as they looked. No, I decided, I wouldn't. My life might be over, but I would get as much for it as I could. "Auguring in? — at least take the SAM site with you," type logic. Right.

"*Ahab, Dumbo.*"

"*Dumbo, Ahab.* Five by. Good to hear you, Kathy! We got one, folks. Don't know how long we get to keep it, though."

"Linda! We thought you were done for! Then when the tank didn't burn in over Hawaii like everyone thought it would, well, the you-know-what hit the international fan. Your ex-lover in the mountain spilled the beans and everyone in the world wants to talk to you. Thank God Dead Kitten's flacks knows how to handle this kind of thing."

"Roger that. Ah, I don't know how to break this to you, Kathy, so I'll just say it. I don't think I'm going to make it back. I'm almost out of lox; computer guidance problems. I kind of made a trade while I was fixing it."

Dead air. Come on, troops, I thought, I'll be below the horizon in ten minutes.

Finally Kathy said "Jesus, Linda. There's got to be something. We'll get the guys on it . . . "

"Roger, good luck, but I think I know the score. Anyway, I think I can get this job done. What I'll do is use what delta-vee I have left to pull perigee up a couple more notches. That ought to give us a couple months to do something more permanent, though I'll feel better about that when you run an integration. I'm just going on the King-Hele estimator we loaded in the portable."

"Linda!" That was Brad, getting sentimental on me. "We'll get you back, somehow . . . "

"Hey, I'm open to better ideas, believe me, but don't take too long. I'd rather not wait until the CO_2 gets me and I can't do the apogee maneuver right. I don't want to waste that shot. Look, is NASA screaming bloody murder like we thought they would?"

"Sort of," Kathy said. "They've figured out that you're in trouble and they're taking the high road, space-is-no-place-for-amateurs line. The real problem is in the Senate. Holmes wants NASA to rescue you and then bill Dead Kitten enough to put us out of business."

"No way! I'd burn in on purpose before I give him that kind of satisfaction."

That got some silence. Damn it, they had been considering it. Finally Brad spoke up.

"Okay, Linda. We said we'd do it your way, so I guess we have to. It hurts, love. Uh, we'll be in Perth next rev. Kathy's doing a solo. Help pay for the trip. Unless you . . . "

"No, don't cancel. If I don't make it back, use me. Do it *for* me. Wish I could stick around to see it. And one more thing. Kathy, take care of Brad. Will you do that for me? I know you guys like each other. It's okay." I tried to spot *Dumbo's* contrail below, but the Indian Ocean was full of cirrus.

"Linda, I will," she promised. But her voice cracked.

"Linda," Brad said. "I . . . I . . . ."

"Roger, Brad. Look, I love you guys, too. Both of you. Just don't let me down, understand?"

I was getting *me* to understand it too. Tell yourself something often enough and it has the echo, if not the ring of truth. Now that this was all out in the open, things wouldn't be the same even if I did get back. But the *last* thing I wanted was for anyone feeling guilty because of my supposed jealousy. That's *not* what I wanted to be remembered for.

"Roger," Brad said, the hurt in his voice making it through the radio. Whatever I lacked as a sex object, he still cared for me as a person, and that felt good.

"Okay. Now let's get back to business. I'm going out of range again. Have you got my data dump? Kit and Terry will need it."

"Roger, Linda, we've got it. What about NASA. Do you want to talk to them?"

"I'd rather fight the problem in peace, thank you. Talk to you next rev, if I'm still around. If not, it's been a blast. Just don't give up the hunt, understand? Love, Brad. Good-bye."

"We'll be listening. Love, Linda. *Dumbo* out."

"*Ahab* out."

Off went the transceiver, just in case NASA or someone else had my frequency. Then I realized that was the first part of letting go, shivered and looked at the stars. No problem, I can do this. And, just like anything else, do it well. The first good thing about deliberately letting go of life certainty. You start planning, accommodating yourself to it. Pretty soon, you start thinking, all right, let's do it. I'd never understood that about condemned prisoners until I faced it myself.

But there was work to do first. The *Ahab* jerked a bit, backward, which seemed odd since I hadn't fired any thrusters. Mental gears switched for a moment.

Of course — our whale had reached the end of its harpoon line. It would probably rebound and come back.

I settled back to think, going over options again. This was

important — I wanted people to know that if I bought the farm, it was a professional trade off, like the pilots that don't bail out to make sure the airplane doesn't hit a school. I didn't want people to think I bought it because I screwed up. So, I went over everything I could think of. I could split the remaining oxygen between a reentry burn and reentry control, hope perigee was low enough for reentry *and* hope for enough oxygen for the thrusters to keep things stable. But there wouldn't be any lox left for the fuel cells, so what would I do for power to control the lifting body surfaces? Then I could lose the whale and burn up anyway. Much rather get my catch safe in a higher orbit, then let my air out. Do it my way.

There was another tug on the harpoon line; almost like the whale was still trying to get away. I looked out the window. I hadn't used any gas and the *Ahab* was still pointing down at the Earth.

Down, of course. Tides. Gravity gradient. I knew about this, but we hadn't planned on using it, so it didn't connect at first. The whale and I were a tethered system . . .

Hope and uncertainty returned, along with a knot in my stomach. I almost resented the complication: but you can use a tethered system to change orbits. In principle, I could use my harpoon line to generate some de-orbit delta-V and help boost the whale into a higher orbit at the same time. Its like this . . .

My harpooned space whale was *higher* than the center of mass of the *Ahab*-whale system; at a larger radius but moving with the same angular velocity. So that end felt *more* centrifugal force, pulling it out, than our center of mass — and less gravitational force holding it in. So the whale tried to move into a higher orbit. But the *Ahab* was *lower* than the the orbit of the center of mass, and thus experienced *more* gravity and *less* centrifugal force. It was trying to fall into a lower orbit. That stretched the harpoon line between us. *That* was what was jerking the *Ahab*.

Ahab still had ten plus kilometers of half-ton test harpoon line on the reel. Just maybe . . .

My first perigee had been about at the international date line. In the next hour and a half, the Earth had moved twenty two and a half degrees east under my orbit so that my second perigee was over near where Amelia Earhart disappeared. Talk about birds of a feather! They might even end up looking for what's left of me in the same area where they found what was left of her. That was a kind of neat thought.

My third perigee, it so happened would occur when Western Australia was under my orbit, just after concert time. I started laughing. Couldn't stop for a while.

I let out all the cable as I coasted toward apogee, riding the cable brakes just enough to keep tension on it and used some cold methane, very sparingly, to take the swings out of the system and ease me into a mostly stable gravity gradient configuration. There were still some long period vertical oscillations; stretch in the cable. But, once things semi-settled down I had time to do the math: my space whale's orbit would still come closer to Earth than I wanted and my own not close enough. The whole thing was a low probability maybe. It was getting near decision time. I could use all my fuel to get the tank into a much better orbit, at the expense of any chance for a controlled reentry, or I could *hope* that the tether trick would keep it aloft long enough for our next mission to rescue and *hope* there was enough left in Ahab's tanks to get us down safely. I wasn't big on wishful thinking; it doesn't usually work with jets or in space. So, despite all the tether stuff, something inside me was proceeding with the letting go process. Once I'd gotten used to the idea, dying up here wasn't so scary. Taking the Kathy and Brad thing head on would be a lot more painful than just opening a valve and becoming a legend. There are all sorts of sacrifices, I reflected, and all sorts of cowardice. There were some real pluses. I'd achieve the kind of immortality that makes a point people never forget, and solve that personal situation back on Earth nice and clean. A sort of farewell present.

But, to be fair, getting back alive would make a pretty important point, too. All our bravado aside, the world might not let Kit or Terry take this risk if I bought it. Or even if I did, on the other hand. One whale was not the whole mission and the mission comes first. But if this was our only chance to show that the mission could be done . . . I like to think of myself as a winner. Back in officer training school, our Military history prof had told us the best way not to lose was not to get into fights you can't win. Select the battles you can win, and do what you have to do to win those. Easy enough to say. Salvaging the tank was the battle I knew I could win. This letting go really worked. I felt the exhilaration of the kamikaze, the joy of the martyr, the passion of an Ahab. I was grinning, released, ready. I'd come up here to catch a space whale; that first, then come what may. Below, it was dawn, blue, and clear. The plume of Kilauea stretched high and white to the southwest, almost to the shadow of night. I thought, in awe, that I was already in heaven, and had only to stay.

At apogee, my hand passed over the reel jettison switch and moved to the thrusters.

What happened then I never really understood. There was a sudden, unexpected, tug on the harpoon cable and my hand sort of fell down on the release switch. I saw the line snake up toward the big orange tank, which wobbled a bit, as if it were nodding at me. We all had fun calling that huge empty thing a "whale," but it was just a bunch of aluminum and stuff. No volition at all.

I think I sat paralyzed for a minute or so. The flag with our Logo and "Orbit Salvage, subsidiary of Dead Kitten, Inc." on it unfolded from the reel on its way up and waved farewell to me. I shook my head, laughing and crying at once. Can't be happening, I told myself. I'd made my choice, and then, somehow, the universe had said 'no.' Maybe I had something more important to do. Anyway, I'd damn well better find something more important, I thought.

"Okay, Moby," I said, in the privacy of my cockpit. "I sure hope you're right about this."

The decision had been made for me and now I had to implement it. When no single thing looks like it will work for sure, my motto is try all the compatible options at once. Since I wasn't going to try to make the fuel cells last another three orbits, I could steal a couple of meters per second push from the fuel cell allocation to make sure that I'd reenter this rev. I did it. I had the margin to sacrifice another couple of pascals of methane tank pressure for a cold gas delta-vee. I did that. Perigee at ten kilometers, the laptop told me. Right in the middle of the Columbo to Perth jet route.

That left about forty minutes until reentry, a little time to get some more of my thoughts into the computer, just in case I didn't make it anyway. Dear Brad . . . (sealed file). Thirty minutes later, I turned the ACS back on and released the spacecraft to the computer. Without the harpoon line tension messing things up, the software should be trustworthy; after all, it had worked perfectly on the two previous missions. *Ahab* wasn't in the nominal groove, but we can be a lot more relaxed about this than the space shuttle — *Ahab* is a lot lighter for its area, so its spray-on heat shield doesn't see as much friction, nor does it drop like a flying stone. The *Ahab* 's nose rose above a brilliant white horizon as the laptop adjusted the spacecraft's attitude for reentry.

I adjusted mine as well. After getting used to the idea of dying, some things didn't matter so much. This preparing yourself to die business wasn't like facing a danger that you probably would survive: I'd been in combat over the Balkans, and it wasn't like that at all. The certainty of what I had decided to do had been calming, releasing. I wasn't trying to hang on to anything except my own dreams and self image. It felt good. Now the whole mess was back again.

No, not the whole mess. It came to me that I didn't have to pick up everything I'd let go of up there, that I'd gotten a kind of disposition to leave some of it behind, and remake my life. *More opportunities,* I told myself, *Get with it, Linda.*

You can get busy flying a lifting body, second-guessing your computer about attitude, trim, and energy management. It gets your mind off your psychological navel. I was out of the ionization blackout, before I found myself wondering how long it had been since I talked to anyone, and then realized my radio was still off. Meaning no transponder either. I stared at it and started giggling — be a hell of a thing to go through all this and get cited for a near miss! I flipped the switch.

To avoid a mob scene, I used my maiden name with Perth RAPCOM and told them I was an experimental aircraft in trouble and had to make a dead stick landing. They bought it. So did I, buying the maiden name part, inside. I left Linda Stevenson up there, somewhere. Linda Takamuri would have the press conference.

The dead stick landing was no sweat, really. The *Ahab*, even though it doesn't have wings, has a lot of lift when empty, sort of like a stretched out and flattened beachball. It's heavier and wider at the tail than the nose because of the engines, so the canards and the nose rudder have a lot of leverage. I flared right on the program and we just glided in like a paper airplane, no sweat.

My radio patch call caught Brad and Kathy in a Perth Hotel, consoling themselves about my demise. Somehow, that didn't bother me a bit, like it was part of another life, in fact, I felt it was kind of neat that they enjoy each other. Let em be happy. Let everyone be happy. I wasn't dependent, and wouldn't be ever again.

Brad put a lot of innovations in the nose wheel. Besides using the wheel well as the hatch opening, he rigged a couple of lightweight rods and gears so that the motor which raises and lowers the wheel can also make the wheel spin, giving me some slow taxi capability with what was left of the fuel cells. Despite its size, *Ahab* only weighs about three metric tons empty and if its pilot isn't really careful, it sort of bounces along down the runway. The Perth tower controller was later quoted as saying I looked and sounded like I was high on something.

Well, in a way I was. After seriously contemplating the alternative, life is a blast.

PERSONAL FILE, LINDA TAKAMURI
CEO, ORBIT TRANSPORTATION INC.
CODE 1053

STORY NOTES

Life does go on, and for a science fiction writer that means that what one wrote as "future history" inevitably becomes some form of alternate history. Yes, some would quarrel with that, maintaining that "alternate history" should be reserved for tales deliberately intended as such. *Pace*. I don't classify the stuff, I just write it.

The Space Shuttle was mercifully retired at a body count of fourteen before, despite the best efforts of Gary Hudson and others, the first fully reusable air-launched spacecraft reached orbit in 2031. Well, this is a science fiction collection. Anyway, as I write, carrier aircraft exist, plans for orbiters exist, and stuff is being made by billionaires who dream like everyone else. I had anticipated some overlap, and it didn't happen.

Which brings up again the point that it is much easier to anticipate *what* sort of technology can come along than when it will come along, and even harder to anticipate in *what order* technologies will become significant to culture and history. Television was invented almost two decades before it began to dominate our living rooms. In the meantime, nuclear weapons made major wars virtually impossible. It was better than half a century between when a graduate student named Russell Hastings, later chairman of the Physics Department at Macalester College, worked on electric rocket propulsion (for Robert H. Goddard, no less) and when electric rockets began nudging NASA space exploration spacecraft through the solar system.

Meanwhile, Orbital Sciences Corporation did start launching orbital spacecraft, though not reusable ones, from an L1011. Virgin Galactic intends to do this with crewed spacecraft, eventually. XCOR had such dreams as well. The dreamers have moved on.

My future history took a twenty-year bump, but, at this writing, things seem more or less on track again and, because this happened in my lifetime, one can "retcon" some things and limp on. It really is all fiction, anyway. But, if, in 2020 or so, it's Gwynne Shotwell instead of Linda Takamuri running SpaceX and not Orbit Transportation, and space habitats are made out of Bigelow inflatables instead of discarded space shuttle tanks, I really don't feel too bad about that.

GDN April 2015

HIS FATHER'S VOICE

Scott caught himself staring at the bare wood and web-cluttered beams of his late aunt's attic instead of packing, but he found it hard to concentrate. Ten days ago, Scott hadn't even known who his biological parents were. Now, his search for his heritage had led to a dusty cardboard box in this dusty attic, filled with faded and broken moments of the long dead hopes of a father and mother he'd never known. Carlo Valdez had been a poor man with a little talent who had tried so hard to be more than a cog in the universal machine, and Theresa Rodriguez a plain girl who had once upon a time seen the light of his father's soul and been momentarily blinded.

Theresa, it turned out, had died years ago, but her sister Maria had lived on in this house they shared, increasingly frail, saving everything for "someone, someday, to make amends." Scott's arrival seemed to have completed something for her; he'd known her only a week, but in hours of talk, they'd begun to be friends.

Now Aunt Maria was gone too, her house was filled with strangers going through things trying to decide who would get what. Some were so closely related to him that he had the uncanny feeling of looking in a mirror when he talked to them.

Thank goodness it was a loving family; the arguments were all of the "here, you take this, she would have wanted you to have it," — "No, you take it, it meant so much to you . . . " variety. Then everyone had been too kind to even speculate that Scott's surprise appearance might have hastened Aunt Maria's heart attack.

The pictures in the album weren't faded, though some of them were black and white, they'd been treated well and, except for the quaint clothes and old cars, looked like they'd just come back from the photo lab. Some pictures were of the people downstairs in their younger days, some of strangers.

But a couple of them included a thin girl with long straight brown hair, thick glasses and buck teeth in an artfully sophisticated pose : his biological mother, Theresa Rodriguez. The house was full of her, too, but as an older, more accomplished woman, in whose eyes and face the world weariness was not affected. There was little of her counter-culture years here, a decade long flight from reality that, Aunt Maria said, really ended only when they heard of Carlo's death. Scott had two boxes full of Theresa Rodriguez: full of photos, clippings, school papers, and other things that kind people, trying to make up for what they'd done forty years ago, insisted he take.

Also, there was one precious picture, not one of the best, but good enough, of his father in an apron in front of a barber shop. He could see himself in his father; short but wide-shouldered and deep-chested. The same pattern of baldness, offset by a neat, well-trimmed moustache. If Carlo Valdez had been nearsighted like his son, he hadn't worn glasses; or hadn't been able to afford them. If so, Scott thought, that might explain some of his father's people problems.

Scott understood all about people problems. The person who had come up with the concept of the "alpha" male would probably have given Scott an "upsilon" or "phi." He'd been fourteen by the time the school had discovered he was mildly nearsighted; too late for all the unrecognized acquaintances, miscopied assignments, and athletic failures. With his build, Scott should have been a football player, but he was, as it worked out, an untalented but adequate and diligently informed keyboard musician who supplemented his "maintenance engineer's" income by fixing electronic and acoustic instruments, playing at weddings, and teaching. His one stroke of luck, a few years back now, had been to help compose and play the keyboard for the pop hit, "Rather be Blue," that had paid the mortgage and still produced a few hundred a year in royalties. But people in the business had got to know him, shunned him, and he'd had to fall back on janitorial jobs to support himself.

Carlo Valdez had been a barber to make ends meet. But the man had been a singer in his heart and in his spare time; a basso in the Tri-city Lyric Theater and chorus for years who had even changed the spelling of his first name to sound more Italian. Then, at the age of fifty-four, with no savings to speak of, after years of romantic failures painfully documented in the bundle of letters, Carlo had made love with the stage struck Theresa. It happened, the letters revealed, the night after his one and only performance as Don Giovanni as a last minute substitute for the Lyric Theater. A homely, artsy craftsy girl throwing caution to the wind and an over the hill want-to-be had tried, for one night, to be real people. In 1964, the pregnancy had been a major scandal.

"People were so stupid and cruel, back then," one of his new cousins had said. "Theresa really loved him. He only lived three blocks away, and they'd talk when she came home from school. He would have married her, but your grandfather wouldn't have any part of that. So he left town, she left town, and you went up for adoption. She found Carlo years later, when she was on her own. She was a secretary, you know, worked for Peabody and Cramer for thirty years."

And a street and commune hippie for ten years before that, but only Maria had told him that.

Scott had just nodded. "Yes, she found him. They wrote after that; the letters were in the box." "Theresa," the cousin added, "got that box in the attic after he died; it arrived UPS from his boarding house saying it was all there was left and that Carlo had wanted her to have it. Then she moved in with Maria, and the box came with her. They looked for you, did you know? If you'd only been a few years earlier — "

"I didn't know," he'd told them. "I didn't know."

He'd lost his concentration again. He looked down from the rafters, down at the cardboard box. Dust. A photo album. Old letters. Programs from various productions he'd been in. Discharge papers — Carlo had been in World War II. Some vinyl phonograph disks, heat warped, cracked, in cardboard dust jackets. Unplayable. Pinza, Callas, Tucker, Tabaldi and what was this? Tri-city Lyric Theater! Excerpts from "The Student Prince," "The Mikado," "The Merry Widow," and "Don Giovanni." Don Giovanni? It had been that live performance; Carlo was listed in the title role. Why had they recorded that one? Was it the only night they'd had first rate recording equipment? Or was it the best?

Impatient with excitement, Scott tried to pull the record from the dust jacket. But it was too warped to slide out easily, and before he thought to simply cut the dust jacket, it broke completely in two under the stress of his pull. He pulled out the pieces and looked at the simple inexpensive label.

Scott groaned aloud. Damn! Was there some kind curse running through his blood that decreed that his kind would get to touch the goal of their dreams once, then have it snatched away? Scott wanted to hit something, slam his hand into it and feel pain. But that would make too much noise, and then he'd have to explain and deal with the sympathy.

He took a deep breath instead and focused his attention on the fine grooves of the broken record; the music, his fathers's voice, were still there if he could think of some way to repair a record as broken and warped as the artist's life. He wrapped the pieces in an old newspaper so they wouldn't get further scratched, and fitted them gently, reverently, back into the jacket.

There must be something someone could do about that, he thought. Scott's inheritance, the one good thing in his father's life. Aunt Maria said Theresa had listened to that record over and over in her last month, dreaming of what might have been as her cancer consumed her drug-numbed body. Theresa had hung on until the turn of the century, but had not woken up on January first, 2002.

Scott carefully packed everything in the fresh book-pack moving box he'd brought, taped it up, addressed it to himself, and carried it downstairs.

There were polite good-byes all around and then, stuffed with fajitas and tacos, mellow with a Corona, he let his rental car drive him to the airport.

✦ ❀ ✦

He was still distracted and disconnected when Betty picked him up in their ancient Reliant and brought him home from San José airport to their two bedroom ranch house in a cheap part of Mountain View that had been built well over half a century ago, more for tight-budgeted junior officers from the old Navy field than for software executives. But even with the mortgage paid, the taxes were almost more than they could afford. The neighborhood was poor, but relaxed; people who had bought recently were poor from making payments, long term residents had always been poor. The streets were lined with old, dented, gas-engined pick-ups, and the air was multicultural with outdoor cooking from everywhere around the planet.

Scott took his precious box into the garage through the rear door to his shop. There was, he realized, the same sense of neatness and order to his workbench as in his father's photo album and the other things in that old cardboard box. Carlo Valdez had not had much, but as Scott's new relatives assured him, what he had was always in good order. So with his son.

Scott had taken two years of junior college physics, but didn't go on. He'd really been more interested in music. His adoptive father died drunk in a car wreck and he'd gone to work after school to help make ends meet. That had been the end of good grades. He got his AA and did band gigs.

In '95, the China War caught his reserve unit, and when he got back, Mom — she would always be Mom to him — had lost her job.

He'd gone to work full time for the school then and played for money at night. When Mom passed, Betty, a simple woman from a good family whom he had thought of only as a friend on the job, had offered to help with the inheritance taxes in exchange for the spare room.

That had lasted two weeks, Scott remembered with a smile. A simple, determined, woman. Who'd seen something in him no one else had seen.

Staring at walls again, he reproached himself. Somehow, he would do something to make her right, something for Theresa and Carlo, something to close a wound half a century old. Back to work.

He spread paper towels on the workbench, opened the box, placed the broken halves of Don Giovanni gently on them, and stared. Somewhere, in the neat rows of boxes that lined the garage, was an old Girard turntable. He searched, found it, found connecting wires, found their old amp, used alligator clips to attach the speakers from the old boom box he had for companionship in the shop, and ran the ridges of his thumb under the stylus. Nothing.

Three hours later, he'd found the broken wire, soldered it, tested again and was rewarded by a hollow grating sound. Very good. Betty called him in to go to bed.

After work the next day, he had disassembled, cleaned and lubed the turntable. Then he got it to play one of the unbroken records, after a fashion; it wowed as the needle went up and down the warped hills of the old disk. Nevertheless, progress.

Back to the recording of Don Giovanni. He blew the dust off and studied the broken edges again. With a dozen small clamps — you never have too many clamps, he thought — he managed to hold the edges back together. They fit. He got the super glue, carefully wet each edge and pressed them together, using large rubber bands around the clamp mounts to hold everything tight.

Two days later, he tried to play the record. But it broke again the first time the stylus hit the imperfect joint.

"What's the matter, hon?" Betty asked as he crawled into bed. She levered herself up on an arm and looked at him with that motherly concern that falls full on the husband in a childless family. She'd never made any pretense at beauty; too strong featured, too pear shaped. But she ate sensibly, did physical work all day, and exercised those muscles that didn't get what they needed that way. Her spare, big boned figure wasn't stylish; but it was pretty good for a woman in her forties.

"It broke again."

"There's got to be someone who can fix it."

He stroked her gently with the back of his hand and she smiled.

"Yeah. But they're expensive."

"It means a lot to you. I'd rather put money into recovering your Dad's voice than another dinner out."

Scott laughed. "I'll ask around." Then he slid over to her and they began to make love. She was the only one he'd ever been with, and he was too grateful to be curious about others. She was heaven. Afterward, they had the house turn the bedroom wall set on, and took a virtual trip over Pluto, courtesy of C-Span and NASA's latest probe. It had vast areas of rolling, washboard-like hills, blown up dramatically to ten times their real scale by hype-desperate NASA publicists. Various geologists tried, without too much success, to explain the hills, and Scott wondered what they really looked like. Betty giggled as his fingers mimicked their eye's virtual journey.

Scott's thoughts drifted from Pluto's valleys, to Clyde Tombaugh, and a meditation on persistence. When a chance to sing Don Giovanni had come along, his father, against all odds, had been ready for it. Never quit, Scott told himself. Never quit.

✳ ✻ ✳

"Hmmm," the Audion engineer muttered for the third time as he examined the broken record. Then finally, "yes, I think we can do that. We'll make rubber casts of each half, splice those together, and make a hard cast of that negative. That's going to lose a little fidelity, but not too much. Then we'll play it into the remastering system; you ought to get a pretty good CD out of it."

Scott nodded, then asked the hard question.

"How much?"

"Not that much, really. Less than ten thousand, I'd guess. Our business people do the estimating though, so you'll have to talk to them."

Scott nodded again. "Well, thanks for your help," he told the man with a confident sound in his voice, shook hands, and found his way out of the building.

He didn't stop by the business office and he didn't let them see him cry.

He saw a garage sale on Calderon on his way home, and stopped because he was in the mood to buy something at a reasonable price. He noted some technical books on the card table next to a dirty laser-toaster. He shook his head; facing arrays of high powered diode lasers, impossibly expensive twenty years ago, a top of the line consumer product a decade ago, a piece of five-dollar junk now.

"Doesn't work," the heavyset dark haired woman in the lawn chair told him. He nodded.

There was more stuff in the back of the garage. Whoever had died had owned a microscope; a real one, not an educational toy. He took it out into the sunlight, pulled a hair from his beard and put it where a slide would go.

"Doesn't work," the woman rasped again. "The old jerk was always fooling around with scientific stuff that doesn't work. He should have read his horoscope more; now I tell you that works! Predicted he was going to have a bad day the day he died, it did."

But the microscope worked just fine. It was just a little old fashioned; no built-in digital array. but the optics, the motion, the weight and steadiness spoke of a one time top-of-the line instrument.

"The little light doesn't go on," she added. That, he thought, would be the little light you used to backlight a sample slide. It probably needed a new bulb.

"How much?"

"Ten bucks."

He bit his lip. It might be worth a thousand. He ought to say something. Then he thought; she didn't give a damn about what the microscope meant, or she'd know what it was worth. The woman despised what it stood for. She had earned the fruits of her own carefully-nurtured ignorance, and he wouldn't do the world any favor by subsidizing that world-view. So he rationalized.

He looked at the hair again, and accidentally got his finger in the image and saw the loops and ridges as if they were the hills and valleys of another world, like those strange, periodically folded mountain ranges on Pluto.

He could sell the microscope for a tenth of what it would cost to recover his father's performance of Don Giovanni.

He gave the woman the ten bucks, his hands slippery with fear that she would change her mind and ask more. He only had eleven in his wallet.

"You can fix junk?" she asked as he handed it to her. "Take the toaster too. For you, one buck."

He shrugged. Spending habits: eleven bucks a day was three hundred thirty a month. Three years of that would recover the record. He smiled, gave her the buck, and took the toaster. He might indeed be able to fix it cheaply — but there were already many things that needed to be fixed in that garage.

Betty was waiting for him when he got home.

"Bad news. I can tell; you went shopping." She smiled.

"Bad news," he admitted. "Ten grand. They want ten grand."

"Your dad's important to you. We gotta know where we come from." She put her arm around him and squeezed. "Hon, we've got plenty of money in the house."

"We promised ourselves we wouldn't do that." The royalties and the dividends on what was left after they paid off the house were enough to eat on if they lost their jobs in another cutback cycle, if one ate ramen. Society had almost taken the house from him once for taxes — and the idea of giving the title to someone else, of giving the crooks, graspers, and cheats out there a chance at him, even though it made good financial sense, made him shiver. The house was what he had left of Mom's life, all her long hours at low pay, all her scrimping and discipline. He would not risk it. Mom, Carlo, Theresa, he vowed, someday I'm going to do something to make you all proud of me, something that makes it all meaningful. Something to make dad sing.

"Hon," Betty interrupted his thoughts, "we can't take it with us. You're obsessed with this; every night, every day we're not at work, you're in that workshop and we're not getting any younger, hon." She pressed her body against him, and murmured, throatily. "Let's make some hay while the sun shines. Go for it."

It lifted him out of his gloom a bit. "Hey, we gotta lot of years left, darling. We'll start saving more. Besides, maybe I can make some money off this junk I bought."

"Okay, hon. Whatever you think best. I love you."

He answered with the distracted kiss of a man running after a dream and running out of breath as it got further and further away. Perhaps some things were not meant to be.

★ ❀ ★

The day before the school's annual swap meet, Scott took the microscope and the now-working laser toaster out of their boxes for a last-minute polishing. The microscope tempted him again, reminding him of the days when he thought he might have a professional career ahead of him. A job in industry, or maybe even a professorship at some idyllic liberal arts college in a small midwestern town, far from want and tension; complete with fresh air, trees, and seasons.

The drawers of the plastic organizer that held his nuts and bolts had thin plastic dividers, that, he thought, might make good sample slides. He pulled one out, frowning and shrugging his shoulders as some number eights mixed with some number sixes.

★ ❀ ★

The now-working light could illuminate samples from above and below. The instrument worked perfectly, and he went on a microscopic odyssey, exploring nails, paint brush bristles, sawdust, bare wire ends and numerous other small objects.

Thinking back to the Pluto video, he took another look at the planet of his fingertip, and journeyed over its ridges. Then he remembered running the phonograph needle over that same fingertip. He reached for half of his father's record, stored on one of the neatly labeled "open projects" shelves over the workbench, blew the dust off of it, and placed it in the focal plane.

The grooves wavered from side to side; he thought of flying along those grooves; he'd be jerked from side to side and get airsick. That vibration, of course, was how these old records made sound. Now if he were flying along that groove, his radar altimeter would experience a doppler shift as the surface came in and out at him.

Could he build a little something to fly along those grooves? If it weren't in actual contact with the record, it wouldn't break when it hit the broken edge. And it wouldn't wear out the record — those old disks would last just as long as the CD's.

"Scott?"

"Oh, hi, darling."

"I brought you some soup. What are you thinking about?"

"I was thinking about building a sort of laser needle for these old records, that wouldn't touch the records so it wouldn't matter if they were cracked or warped."

"Sounds expensive. I mean it would have to be very precise, wouldn't it. And precise things cost a lot."

She had a point. He started thinking about the servos, tracking, doppler transducers . . . damn!

"You're right, I think. The way the Audion guys were going to do would cost a lot less, I guess."

The realistic professional in him could conceive of ten thousand dollars as being less. The boy reached out to the father he'd never known, and his hand closed on air. He couldn't give up, not now, not so close.

"Betty, I'm going to keep the microscope. If it's worth a grand now, it will be worth a grand next year. And by next year, maybe I'll think of something else."

"Sure, hon. Drink your soup."

★ ※ ★

But the next year was little different. He tried to make a tracking system, but it wouldn't stay on the groove. The stuff he needed to fix that was too expensive.

His latest idea was to guide the laser with a stiff teflon fiber to track the groove, using a resistive diaphragm and servo loop instead of physical force to guide it. But there was an interaction mode between the fiber and the servo control that caused it to hunt its way out of the groove.

He'd been trying a software damper when Betty came to the shop.

"Hon, they're releasing the Persephone encounter tapes tonight. Want to quit and watch?"

NASA had found a four-hundred kilometer iceball far out of the ecliptic for the Pluto probe to pass by. Some newspeople were calling it the tenth planet, causing a lot of astronomers to smile through clenched teeth. But it was probably the biggest event left in the saga of robot space exploration.

"Sure, why not? I give up. This isn't going to work either."

There. He'd admitted it. A broken idea depressed him even more than his broken record, and, uncharacteristically, he just left everything where it was. He turned as he left the shop, slapped the light switch off, said "Sorry, Dad" into the gloom, then followed Betty back to the house.

But instead of using the wall screen in the livingroom, she led him back to the bedroom.

"I know this sounds a little kinky, hon. But last time, well, it was kind of good."

Scott laughed. "Anything to please. We'll can it and play it back."

They did. They were making their fourth pass over Tombaugh ridge in deep afterglow when Betty suddenly gasped and her eyes snapped wide open. Then she laughed gently.

"Oh, Scott," she murmured, "did the probe actually fly down that valley, like this?" She took one of his fingers and used it to simulate the hypothesized probe trajectory in the folds of the bedding.

"No," he laughed, "they made a three dimensional model of Persephone in their computer and just transformed the coordinates of the pixels so that it looks that way, as if we were in a spaceship traveling right down that groove . . . "

She giggled as he was rendered speechless. Of course! He had lasers. He had a microscope. He had a turntable. A drill press to hold the microscope. He could track by hand, to prove the concept. He had his home computer and its optical floppy. As long as he had the *picture* of the groove, he didn't have to fly anything *physical* through it. His "needle" could be a purely software construct.

He threw his arms around his wife and kissed her a dozen times, then looked at her grinning, giggling face with the first hint of a suspicion. Exactly what *had* she been thinking while . . . ?

★ ※ ★

It was a rich, full organ of a basso voice, perhaps a little off key, perhaps with not enough breath left at the end. But it had an impressive volume, and with training, Carlo Valdez could have been good, very good.

It echoed through Scott's new house hidden on the wooded hill, a modest mansion as such things went, only thirteen rooms around a great, square Castillian courtyard, but it was unmortgaged. One wall was filled with old LP's; a collection purchased for peanuts before they became worth millions.

The programmers assured him that yes, Carlo sounded just like

Carlo had sounded, but that disappointed them because they could have made it sound much better than Carlo had sounded.

But Audion's new Research Consultant had politely told them where to go with that idea. If you could see me now, Dad, he thought.

"I should never have believed it . . . " his father sang

STORY NOTES

Every once in a while, you nail one. About ten years after this story was published, one of my writers group members emailed a link to a press release from Lawrence Berkeley National Laboratory:

```
PUBLIC RELEASE: 16-APR-2004
From top quarks to the blues
Berkeley Lab physicists develop a new way to digitally
restore and preserve audio recordings
DOE/LAWRENCE BERKELEY NATIONAL LABORATORY
   BERKELEY, CA — The 1995 discovery of the top quark
and singer Marian Anderson's 1947 rendition of "Nobody
Knows the Trouble I've Seen" may seem unrelated. But
through an interagency agreement with the Library of
Congress, the same technology used to study subatomic
particles is helping to restore and preserve the sounds
of yesteryear.
   "We developed a way to image the grooves in a recording
that is similar to measuring tracks in a particle detector,"
says Carl Haber, a senior scientist in Lawrence Berkeley
National Laboratory's Physics Division, who developed the
technology along with fellow Physics Division scientist
Vitaliy Fadeyev . . .
```

Of course, a national laboratory is a far cry from an inventor's garage, but things every bit as astounding have come out of the garages as well. This was my silicon valley inventors story. It was science fiction when it was written and published in 1993; it's an alternate history of a technology now. You'll also find references to the Pluto mission in the story; that's happened too. Otherwise my prophecy was so-so; there was no China War, there was an Afghanistan war, and we now have "dwarf planets" named for Hawaiian deities. I didn't get the name of the next discovered planet right in the original story; I called it Persephone, which was Arthur Clarke's (imagined) name for it. They didn't use it because an asteroid already had that name; After flirting with the name Xena, they called it Eris. A couple smaller ones were then found at average distances between Pluto and Eris; these have been named after Hawai'ian deities Haumea and Makemake, as they were discovered by a telescope on sacred Hawaiian ground. Who could have predicted those names?

So it goes. I had a technological idea and to make a story of it that people would relate to, chose a common emotional circumstance which also produced a recording to repair which suggested a back story for the recording. Thus I had a problem and the efforts to solve it make a story arc. This story has been anthologized at least twice before; once translated into French and just recently as part of a collection of Silicon Valley related tales by the Bay Area Library Electronic (BALE) publishing group. Being no longer science fiction, it is thus my first mainstream fiction publication!

GDN February 2017

P.C. SOFTWARE

"Mr. Prescott, I think the time has come for us to have a little talk."

George was concentrating, trying to figure out whether the October cover was showing just a little too much anatomy for current tastes, or not enough for current sales. So he first noticed that Brenda had said *something* to him, and only later managed to pull what it was out of his rapidly evaporating short term memory.

"Ahem. Ah, Ms. Steinherz, what is it we need to talk about?"

"I am uncomfortable with the atmosphere in this office."

"Me too. But breathing smog is one of the privileges of editing a magazine in Los Angeles." Immediately, he wished he hadn't said that. It just came out. Brenda's elephantine leg stomped and she shook her head so hard George feared for her short, curly, red, perm.

"If you don't start taking me seriously, I'm going to file a complaint!"

He groaned. Even if he convinced the Sexual Relations Arbitrator that he was innocent, he'd have to go through months of hearings and a probable suspension of publication. He couldn't afford that — but if he didn't sell his house and get a good lawyer, he'd never get another job. Of course, as a bankrupt . . . As worst case scenarios ran through his mind, he remembered that he had an illegal target pistol. Just stick the barrel in your mouth, slanted a little up, squeeze the trigger and no more problems. Fortunately, he'd kept clear of marriage and there were no children dependent on him. Comforted by knowing that he had at least one way out, he returned his attention to his copy editor, who was probably trying to figure out the reason for the manic grin on his face.

"But, I do take you seriously, Ms. Steinherz, very seriously. I just thought about this smog and hot air when you mentioned the word 'atmosphere.' Uh, just what did you mean?" What could he have possibly done to her? Did he appear to notice her cleavage at the last Christmas party? Did she think that he told a gender specific joke in her presence? Not fair! He constantly struggled to keep humor out of the work place. He knew there was no such thing as safe humor anymore.

"I mean," she said slowly and deliberately, emphasizing ever syllable, "the rampant sexism you expect me to copy-edit and dump to the factory every day."

"But the authors . . . " many of whom were women . . .

"Don't hide behind the authors, damn it! You buy the stories so they're yours. You can change any and every word. Don't you realize that forcing me to help publish references to MANkind, exploitive verbal pictures of naked women, stories that objectify women by calling us 'female,' and so on, is offensive? And there's all this scientific stuff. You men won't even *let* women be scientists and then you buy all this stuff that people can't understand unless they are scientists! That's sexist. Astrology and sympathetic magic are part of an organic, nurturing world view that is just as valid as all this male science. But not here, oh no. Must I help forge my own chains? Hell no!"

He almost said 'no one wants to chain you' but thought better of it, just in time. Desperately, he tried to think of something he could say that could not be taken amiss. It was useless to argue that some of their stories described naked men as well as naked women, or took scientific and alien points of view in which humans were reasonably described as male or female, or that, after all, the magazine was a science fiction magazine. No, that would just add fuel to the fire. The right thing to do was to lay on your back, wave your legs in the air, and wait for the tormenter to go away.

"I'm sorry," he finally said. "I didn't know you felt that way. I'll try to do better."

"I sure hope so, because if I see any more of that, you've got an SRA complaint on your record!"

"I hear you." George gestured to his computer. "Look, you don't want to see these submittals the way they are now, and there's nothing else to do. So, why don't you take the rest of the day off, Ms. Steinherz? I can finish up here."

"Oh. Why, thank you. Sears is having a going out of business sale, and I can get there early. I think my carburetor has been acting up, and

I need a set of metric tools to work on it."

"Of course. Good shopping, Ms. Steinherz."

He must have exhaled for a minute after she left the office. He had a finger of V.S.O.P from the flask in the bottom left drawer of his desk. Then he picked up the phone.

"Karen, this is Mike Prescott. . . . Fine, how are you? . . . Look, at the last con you were talking to me about some expert system software that could be trained to do editing. Do you think that could be trained to recognize and rewrite sexist language? . . . I'm in trouble with my copy editor and . . . Yeah, I know she is, but she comes to work on time. . . . A demo? Great! . . . Yes I have the time now; this day is shot anyway. I'll be right over."

★ ❋ ★

"You don't need to worry about me, Mike. I burned my NAW membership card ten years ago." Karen laughed heartily. A tall, thin, black woman with owlish silver rimmed glasses, her software company was always struggling and she was often short on funds, but on good nature, never.

"Thanks. It's getting so that every day in the office is a minefield. I get so tight, I have to wear a neck brace. Brenda Steinherz isn't that bad a copy editor, really. She gets the work out. I just need to diffuse this sexism thing and give myself a little breathing room. What I was looking for was some program she could train, so it would highlight and rewrite the stuff that sets her off."

"Whoa now. The rewrite part may take some doing. Is she consistent?"

"I'm not sure. I'm hoping that if I can just filter out most of the irritating stuff, what leaks through won't irritate her that much."

"Uh, huh. Well, first let me show you WordOut. California's been using it since 2028 to make sure their license plates don't have objectionable words. It checks homonyms, non-standard spellings and even missing letter variants."

"I need that, but It's not just words, Karen. Some complicated phrases can be objectionable, too — and contextual situations. Like with "ladies." It's okay for a story to mention someone in a Ladies' Professional Golf Association event, but a male character can't come up to them and say, 'hey ladies.' To Brenda, that's a condescending, white glove, stereotype."

"Good grief! What does she want? 'Hey you guys?'"

George smiled. "You're getting the picture."

"Hmm. Let's see what kind of data bases are available on line." Karen tapped the screen of her Granny Smith with the eraser end of her pencil a couple of times and the machine started searching.

★ ❋ ★

After a few minutes, they located the National Association of Women's *Monthly Dictionary of Sexist Words and Phrases*. The entry on 'female' made his eyes pop. There were twenty different situations alone in which "female" was considered sexist and only three in which it was politically acceptable: including when used by a woman or when used by anyone in a strictly biological context. The whole file would have taken five minutes to download, so he had it put on his cloud.

"Now," Karen told him, "we need a good political pattern-recognition word-eater. Like, REVISIONIST." She tapped her stylus on the menu screen a couple of times and a specialized desk-top appeared. I've got an old World War II era book on file. What we can do is: scan through, look for any references to 'disabled veterans' and change them to something like 'physically challenged victims of imperialist war policies.' It will consider passages as long as a paragraph, just in case."

Mike watched the program pull up: " . . . and other veterans of the Japanese attack on Pearl Harbor who were disabled as a result of injuries sustained . . . " and change it to " . . . and other victims of the reaction to U.S. imperialist interference in Asian affairs, who became physically challenged as a result of injuries sustained . . . "

"Not good," he said, "but not bad either. Looks like it could handle sexist language, all right, but I'd like it without the Marxist doublespeak."

"No problem: that's just a data function. Just think of the program as a black box. Text and data bases go in one end, politically correct language comes out the other. I'll let you have it on trial, for a week." Karen smiled. "There's even a weekly data base update service, linked to all the interest groups. We subscribe to the NAACP's for instance so you know whether to call me African-American, a black, person of color, or Negro, and when. By the way, you can spell out that acronym, NAACP, again. It's okay this month."

"Karen, I think I'll just call you beautiful."

"Any day, honey." She put her hand on his arm and gave him the best smile he had in a week.

He let himself dream for a moment, but she was a head taller than he was. It would never work. He patted her hand then got up to leave.

"Thanks for the help. I have to do something about this situation tomorrow, or I'll lose my mind."

"If you do, I'll sell you a new one," Karen laughed.

★ ❋ ★

"Ms. Steinherz," he said the next day. "We are going to have to cut expenses. I'm reducing both of our salaries ten percent."

"You can't do that! You're doing this just because I challenged your sexist editorial policies. I'll complain to the Arbitrator!"

"Just a minute," Mike smiled. "That's just to keep the accountants happy. The next thing I'm going to do is appoint you to our new associate editor position, with a ten percent salary increase!"

"Oh! I guess that cancels out, then. Well in that case . . . but what will I have to do?"

"You need to teach the new computer program I got how to recognize sexist language. Something at which I'm obviously no good at all. To make up for the time, I'll go ahead and send the submittals to the factory myself and answer the mail."

"Oh. Okay. I can do that. But what about the content? — All that science stuff?"

"I'm afraid I can't budge on that. After all, this is a *science* fiction magazine. That's what writers send me. I can't rewrite it well enough myself; if my stuff sold that well, I'd be writing best selling novels instead of doing this!" In fact, it was the royalties from his novels that let him do this job at all — but flattery never hurt a sales pitch. "I've seen your stuff and I think you can do it better."

"Well, we'll see." She actually smiled at him. Gold fillings. "See, I'm not unreasonable."

Mike sighed in relief. The transition period had its rough edges, but to give the devil her due, Brenda gave him a chance and didn't file her complaint. Both he and Brenda worked overtime at the start, but pretty soon the computer program was correcting submittals well enough to satisfy her. And the software was so fast she was going home early every day.

But happiness lasted just long enough for the March issue to be seen by its authors, who were livid. But more worrisome were the two hundred subscription cancellations that month. George polished up his resume, and stayed up nights doing a rewrite a long delayed novel with a state of the art Grammar checker. The thing still was pretty dumb about context, but . . . One morning, as he turned in for an hour's sleep before hitting the 405 the thought occurred to him that grammar was patterns. Learned patterns.

"Tell me one more thing, Ms. Steinherz," he said with forced cheerfulness after his commute.

"Yes, Mr. Prescott?"

"Do you ever read our magazine? I mean after it goes out?"

"Why should I? It's too expensive, and besides, I've already read it here."

"Just as I thought. You're a very intelligent la . . . ah, woman."

"What's so remarkable about a woman being intelligent, anyway?

Just watch it, buster."

"Didn't mean anything," Mike said quickly. "I was just trying to be nice."

She still frowned at him.

Mike started staying late. He built his own version of REVISIONIST, one that would keep a history of all the grammar and punctuation changes Brenda made as well as her political changes. He inserted deliberate errors and it remembered how she changed them. Then he created yet another version of REVISIONIST without Brenda's politically correct data. He ran back-up disks of the authors' submittals through this version, and what he got out was grammatically improved, but still what the authors sent him.

Then, when he was satisfied, he started dumping that version to the factory. The politically corrected stories which Brenda gave back to him showed up in file log, but that was a dummy. He just barely made the September issue on time, and so narrowly avoided being lynched at that year's Worldcon. But the next issue was a week early. And by December, subscriptions were up again.

Since he was staying late, he came in late, too. Soon he was down to seeing Brenda a couple hours a day, around noon. The tension level came way down, and in a couple of months he stopped wearing his neck brace. REVISIONIST got to be so good an editor that he even had time to do some writing of his own, and time to find out that Karen really didn't care that she was a head taller than he was.

Brenda, of course, was now spending her six hour or so a day at eight hours salary doing nothing that resulted in anything. This didn't bother him: the magazine was making enough money to support both of them, and since she thought she was getting her say about everything, she never complained.

Then one day she came in holding a copy of the magazine, jaw set, eyes flaming.

George held his breath.

She waved it at him.

"The cover price is up and my salary isn't. What are you going to do?"

Slowly he reached for the magazine. She held onto it.

"Maybe I can get another hundred a month for you."

She stared him in the eye in a way that told him, she knows, she knows. Then she looked around at the computer she only needed to use four hours a day, the clean office, the awards on the walls, and her name plaque with the "assistant editor" title on it. The pattern of her life.

"All right. Just make sure you get it for me." She gave him the magazine with a quick smile and waddled back into her comfortable lair to go through her comfortable motions.

The magazine was dog-eared and obviously read.

He never heard about the issue of sexism from Brenda again.

But, he thought one evening as he dumped an issue to the distribution factory, it wasn't true that she was doing nothing to earn her salary. Her copy editing expertise was fully resident on REVISIONIST, working for him every day. It was only fitting that she continued to be paid for a contribution, which, like that of a factory worker who taught a robot, or an author of a book, continued to produce value long after the original labor ceased. After all, her expertise was why he'd hired her in the first place, and if it now resided in an optical chip instead of gray jellyware, what difference did that make?

STORY NOTES

When I was in high school in Minnesota, many years ago, my mother did relocation assistance work for actors and professional athletes coming in and out of the Twin Cities area. As a result of this, we got to know Billy Martin, who was then managing the Minnesota Twins. The last time he was at our house, after an evening of raconteuring, he told us that if we ever got to a ballgame again that he was managing, just yell out "Hey, Dago" and he'd wave or come over. Needless to say, I never did that, but it did remind me of a bygone era in which skins were a little thicker and people less likely to jump down each other's throats. It was also an era of subconciously absorbed stereotypes that were taken for granted even by the objects of the stereotypes themselves and moving beyond that, to the extent we have, is a good thing. But there can be too much of a good thing.

This is a humor piece, of course, with the broad brush observations of humanity, and ridiculous exaggerations that go along with that. No, I don't seriously believe this, that, and the other thing, but if there's a grain of truth in there, somewhere, maybe it will stand out.

The story is also a look at the range of what even limited artificial intelligence might be capable of. It was originally drafted a quarter century ago and I've changed a couple of terms here and there to help readability for today's and future audiences. Some I didn't. For instance I like the name "Granny Smith" better than "iPad" so I kept it.

This sort of near-term science fiction becomes alternate history rather rapidly anyway. We progressed faster in some areas (mainly hardware), but not as fast in others. Programmers are struggling a bit more with getting machines to understanding context than I thought they would. Maybe things will be different by 2028. That's only 13 years from this writing, so I stand half a chance of living until proved wrong again.

HARPOON

Erikka Nilsdotter first spotted her prey on the radar, then swung her binoculars in its direction. There it was! Huge, low and gray on the horizon. She sucked in a breath and felt her heart race. *This*, she thought, *must be how Captain Ahab would have felt!* She punched the sonoblaster button, and felt, rather than heard, the ship vibrate with what they hoped signaled "danger." Near them, the huge sperm whale they'd been marking broached so high she could see the sucker scars on its jaw and then it sounded, its huge tail falling off to the right as it slid majestically below. A cheer broke out among the crew of the ESPS *Bardot*, and Erikka raised her fist and sang out, "Dive friend, dive!" in a voice that cut through the hiss of the sea and clatter of gear with operatic force. Round one to them.

Now for the dangerous, exciting part. She wiped the smile off her face; control was important. No one should see how stoked she was, lest their opponents accuse them of doing what they did for the fun of it. She turned to the tall, thin, blond-bearded, bare-chested eco-warrior beside her.

"Reef the sails and pull up the boards, Marc, then full ahead. We'll block them port if we can. The whale went off that way, bless'm, and more likely than not it'll surface in that direction, if it hasn't gone deep to feed."

Eager Earthsea Warriors jumped to their winches and, one by one, genoa, main and midden sails vanished into hollow booms. The turbine's hum became audible and slowly built into a scream; it had belonged to a tug once, but on the *Bardot*, it had a different gear train and a different prop. The port side board rotated up, out of the hissing foam.

The Bardot's stern sank, then began to rise again as its shallow draft began to spank the waves and wind of their passage set the sail rigging to song. Erikka wondered what the target whaler's crew thought as they saw their unlikely contraption heave itself out of the sea and crash and heave again.

"They're going for the whale, winding the props up," the soundman sang, clasping his headset to his ears with his hands in an apparent effort to keep out other noise.

Erikka hit the horn for one, two, short blasts and cranked the wheel counterclockwise. They would say the *Bardot* was technically overtaking and altering her course to avoid hitting the other boat's stern. This would put them technically in the right, though they knew damn well where the other ship wanted to go and that their maneuver was putting them in its way before it could even begin its turn. The thing to do was to make it look as if the whaler was turning into *them*; in an inquiry or public debate, people would believe what they saw. "Fenders out!" she shouted. "Dinghies! Cameras!"

Thirty old half-tires nailed to a fifteen-meter beam laminated from redwood planks jumped over the side at the urging of eager hands and thunked against their starboard side. Thrills were great, but they should be survivable thrills, and this would be the *Bardot's* thousand tons of displacement versus her opponent's twelve thousand. Erikka reached for the mike and flipped the other switches, too; what she said now would go out on PA and the recorders as well as channel 16.

"Whaling ship *Marianne*, you are hunting an endangered species and endangering us as well. Stand on to starboard."

The larger ship ponderously began to bear port, toward the whale. Erikka altered port to match, still heading for a spot between the whaler and where the whale had sounded. The *Bardot's* bow had been reinforced to take an impact, and her wide bottom would tend to slide rather than roll, but a glancing blow was still much less dangerous and would look just as good to the cameras.

She hung on as the *Bardot* crossed the whaler's stern wake and slid into the trough behind the bow wake, the power of her engines keeping her well in hand. The courses converged on a point between the whaler and the whale's last position. To make it look good, the *Bardot* had to get there first. She looked up and saw that Marie was out on the bowsprit with a camera, getting the best angle possible, her dramatically long hair flying and her t-shirt plastered against her figure in a way that she probably hoped would distract the other ship's crew.

Erikka smiled and shook her head. Marie laid it all on the line, everything, all the time. Then she frowned. Marie wasn't wearing her life jacket.

Erikka slapped the radio toggle off and keyed the mike. "Someone get a life jacket forward to Marie. Anyone who isn't wearing one, get one on, *now!*"

Someone touched her arm. A quick glance showed it was Marc, with her own life jacket. Without saying a word, or taking her eyes off the situation, she shrugged herself into it.

They came up on the whaler's bow wake and powered through it more than over it, spray flying so high it splattered the wheelhouse windows. "Prepare for collision!" she shouted. They were pulling ahead of the other ship.

They were close enough to the port side of the whaler to see some of its crew shaking fists at them. "Get the f . . . hell out of here," a big, black-bearded man boomed at them, "get the f . . . out of here you f . . . bitch!"

Erikka snapped the radio switch up again.

They were being hailed in English with a north European accent: "Approaching vessel, approaching vessel, this is the research ship *Marianne*. You are interfering with our work. Leave the area! Approaching vessel, approaching . . . "

Erikka keyed her mic. "Stand to your course, *Marianne*. We are overtaking on your port, giving you way starboard. Stand to."

"Get out of our way," came the response.

The words were for the record; it was too late for either vessel to do anything much. She grinned. Almost sexually aroused by the danger of the impending crash, a fantasy of martyrdom took hold of her mind. She could give herself to the cause now; a sharp turn starboard, and the *Marianne's* bow would cleave them in two, crushing the boat like kindling, hammer its way to the wheelhouse where she would meet its final fatal blow unafraid, oh, yes, unafraid . . . She shook herself. No, not now. Not everyone on her boat was so ready for a martyr's death. She wasn't, really. Duty called.

"Cut power, neutral as soon as it's safe," Erikka told Marc.

The turbine wound down and the *Bardot* started to settle down. The whaler finally started to turn starboard. At the last moment, Erikka wrenched her wheel port and the *Bardot* heeled starboard to take the hit with the flat side of the *Marianne's* bow, instead of the prow, against *Bardot's* mid beam. But the cameras would clearly show the *Bardot's* bow ahead of the *Marianne's*.

The impact happened almost in slow motion. The tires squished flat and the beam that supported them splintered with cracks sounding like gunshots. The hulls of both ships groaned under the enormous pressure. Marie screamed. Erikka's heart jumped as she saw the camerawoman fly from the bowsprit as the slow-motion impact accelerated the Bardot sideways, correcting its heel and them some, as the starboard side rose impossibly high. She caught a whiff of burning rubber as the tires scraped against the Marianne's hull. Water sprayed high over the port side, but, as it was designed to do, the flat-bottomed *Bardot* finally slipped sideways and the port safety lines did not go under.

But the boat groaned audibly with the tremendous pressure of water on the port side.

"Neutral, braked," Marc said, calmly. "Camera tethered," he added with a smile.

Sure enough, Marie's camera hung accusingly from the bowsprit lifeline. "Marie jumped clear?"

He nodded. "I think she made an act of it. But we still have to pull her out."

Erikka grabbed the mike and briefly considered a "*M'aidez,*" but settled for:

"This is motor barque *Bardot*, thirty degrees two point four minutes south, fifty-nine degrees seven point eight two minutes east. We have been struck by another ship, have one woman overboard, and as yet unknown damage. We have ten aboard, one overboard and unknown minor injuries. We are still afloat but hull integrity is not known yet. We are a twenty meter foot motor barque, black hull with white trim and two masts. We will be listening on cha . . . "

"*Selonce distress,*" a much stronger transmitter broke in. "This is Norwegian research vessel *Marianne. Bardot* is an Environmental Sea Posse protest boat that deliberately bumped us and is undamaged as near as we can tell. The girl overboard jumped and . . . yeah, well port of us, full ahead . . . and will climb back on after her little swim. There is no problem. *Marianne* out." The thrum of the its propellers echoed through the *Bardot* as it bumped along the side of the whaling ship.

Erikka's jaw tightened. Why is it that half truths always hurt more than boldfaced lies? Those greedy bastards were trying to kill intelligent beings; they had no right to try to appear in the right! She gripped the microphone as if it were a weapon. "This is *Bardot. Marianne* struck us by maneuvering into us while we were overtaking in an effort to chase a whale in violation of international law quotas. Anyone wishing to render assistance, meet us on channel 68. *Bardot* out." She turned to Marc. "How's Marie?"

"Don't know yet."

Erikka felt the beginnings of a hard, cold cramp in her gut. The adrenalin was wearing off now and the enormity of the risk beginning to sink in. "I don't care how good the cause was, that was a foolhardy stunt."

Marc scratched his beard. "Well, we know that territory."

They stared into each other's eyes. Marc was getting close to the forbidden topic. She and her number one both knew that the line between just playing brinkmanship with martyrdom and really going for it could get fuzzy when the adrenalin started flowing. Erikka had done her share of standing on the edge of a cliff wondering what that one final, cathartic experience might be like. She would not make that choice for others, but it would not surprise her if there was enough madness in her group to crew a genuine suicide mission. And what if she was asked to captain it?

Adrenalin did strange things to the head when moral certainty justified . . . anything. She shook her head, trying to banish such thoughts. She had a crewmember overboard. She had the microphone in her hand.

"Anyone on the port side. Do we have a visual on Marie Suarez?"

The bridge phone rang almost instantly. Marc answered it.

"She's waving to us from the water, about a kilometer astern," he said.

"Great, thanks."

Erikka watched the whaling ship plow on toward where they saw the whale dive. No sign of the whale yet, thank goodness. Should they try another blocking run? How long would Marie last in these waters? The antarctic currents swung well north in these longitudes and the water was not warm. Marie was only wearing a T shirt and shorts. Erikka turned the wheel. "Give me ten knots," she said.

"We're going back to get Marie," she responded to Marc's questioning look.

The turbines whined and the *Bardot* began to push itself forward again.

Getting Marie meant coming about with differential thrust, motoring back to within a few meters of the her, turning the bow into the light, choppy sea, launching the zodiac, pulling her aboard, getting them all back to the ship, getting them up the rope ladder, and hoisting the zodiac. It took half an hour. The crew cheered as Marie climbed up over the rail.

Erikka met her and asked if she was all right.

Marie straightened up to her full 160 centimeters. Her skin was blue. "You should have gone for another block! I can tread the water for hours, and if not," she shrugged, "it is good publicity."

She pointedly ignored the proffered towels and blankets and marched, dripping, back to the bowsprit to get her camera, to applause from the crew.

By the time they were done with all that, the sound of harpoon cannon fire reached their ears. It was the better part of a kilometer from where they thought their whale would come up.

"Damn!" was all Marc said. Erikka bit her lip. Maybe it was a different whale.

"We'd better go document the butchery," Erikka said. There was no urgency now; they could save their fuel. She checked the wind direction and speed; about seven meters per second thirty degrees east of the bearing to the whaler. She brought the bow around toward their target.

"Portside board down," she called out, "and hoist the main." In a few minutes they had everything up and were making progress. As a sailing ship, the *Bardot* was compromised and had a fair amount of leeway even with the sideboard down; by bearing directly for the whaler, Erikka figured her heading would bring them a hundred meters or so off its port side; just the right place to watch the slaughter. It would turn their stomachs, but that was probably due punishment for failing in their mission. Revenge would come later when the video hit the news.

They arrived all too soon. The dead whale lay next to the ship and men scrambled over it like ants, attaching the lines that would drag its carcass into the ship's stern. She brought the bow to the wind and lowered the sails; they would hold position with the turbine as they documented the horror.

Marie, still looking like a wet T-shirt contest entry, and Barry put their big gun on the operation. The thirty centimeter modified astronomical telescope could read a person's watch a kilometer away and hung from a actively compensated suspension fine enough to let it do just that, assisted by the fuzzy logic of the attached video camera. Erikka watched the monitor on the bridge.

"Can you believe that?" Marc said. "Those jerks have carved graffiti right into the whale's hide!"

Erikka looked. Sure enough, there was a very crude line drawing of a whale with something like a flower or a Japanese sun on its side.

"Probably meant for us," Erikka said. "But I don't get the symbolism. If it were a Japanese ship, it would be obvious, but the *Marianne* is about as far from being Japanese as you can get. Look, one of them is going over to it. Maybe to do some more."

But she saw the whaler motion to one of his comrades and point to the graffiti. The other man, hanging carefully onto the ropes that now crossed the carcass, came over and looked. Both of them were obviously surprised.

"They're just acting surprised," Marc said. "Like some of those farmers that discovered the crop circles in their fields that they made the night before."

Erikka grunted. This was a complication they didn't need. A "who's carving on the whales?" episode could take attention from the main fact of whale hunting. After a thirty-year ban, the "recovery" of sperm whale populations to mid-sixties levels and the "need" to monitor the population by taking samples had been used by whalers to allow resumption of limited hunting with research quotas. The fact that these were intelligent animals seemed not to matter.

Well, she thought, it was too late to do anything about the images from where she was; everything they were seeing was going out through the satellite dish on their stern in real time. The folks back at ESPS headquarters' 'Restore the Ban' campaign would have to take care of spinning it.

The *Bardot* took video until the whaling ship's rear door was raised high enough to block their view, then resumed their patrol of the area. The *Marianne* was unlikely to try to take two whales and there were two more ships in the area on the satellite imagery. Those were probably other whalers, as they were well out of the shipping lanes.

Erikka ran the *Bardot* north with the wind on her starboard rear quarter, toward the last position of one of the other whaling ships. Huntress again, she scanned the radar.

Marie, with the sharpest eyes of all of them, and the least fear of heights, spotted the sick whale before the radar. Her tiny, dark body was ferociously conditioned, as might be expected of the circus acrobat she was in the off season, and clinging to the top of the waving mast thirty meters above the deck was her kind of place.

"It's just kind of lolling around," she said over her wrist phone. "Hasn't broached or sounded or done much of anything in twenty minutes."

Erikka got the bearings and, half an hour later, the *Bardot* reached the whale. The seas were a bit heavy and with the *Bardot's* leeway, it took some tricky sailing to bring them alongside down wind of the whale. It was huge; over fifteen meters long, maybe eighteen, and clearly unhappy, dipping under and giving frequent, anemic blows from its lumpy, off-center blowhole.

"Fresh sucker scars," Marie noted. "Above the left jaw."

"I see," Erikka said. But she knew the wounds of such unequal contests were unlikely to be the cause of its distress.

"Cetacean B virus, I'll bet," Marc said. "I'll get the inoculator."

Erikka nodded. The ocean had epidemics of its own, and this one had been responsible for many whale beachings. They had a cure; an otherwise harmless bacterial infection that produced a substance toxic to the virus. The inoculator would shoot a tiny sliver full of the things deep into the whale's flesh. If it could survive another three or four days, and not be found by the whalers, it would recover.

"Jesus!" Marie, down from her perch, exclaimed, pointing to an area just behind the whale's eye. "Do you see that?"

"That" vanished beneath the waves just as Marie mentioned it, so they had to wait a few minutes before the whale rolled that part of its anatomy above the water again. When it did, Marie had her camera ready. The area was visible only for a moment and Erikka wasn't really sure she'd seen what she'd seen.

"A harpoon wound?" Marc asked, hesitating to fire the inoculation dart.

"Dunno," Erikka said. If the whale were both sick and wounded, it was a poor candidate for survival. But to Erikka, they were fellow beings. When a fellow being is on his or her last legs, you don't walk away; you try all the harder. "I'd proceed with the inoculation anyway."

Marc fired the inoculator and the prick of its dart must have stimulated the sick whale out of its lethargy. It sounded and left them staring at the waves.

"Hope it will be okay," he said.

She nodded. But what she thought she had seen unsettled her.

"Look! through the viewfinder," Marie said and offered the camera to Erikka, frame on pause.

In the viewfinder, there was no mistaking what had been carved into the whale's skin. The crude drawing again showed the outline of what had to be the whale; a crude sideways triangle with eyes, a tail, lines for flippers and a slit jaw. It had a flower-like thing on its side with several long "petals." But this time Erikka clearly saw a long torpedo shape below the "flower." Also, there was a line sticking straight out of the "whale" as if it had been harpooned. One of the petals of the flower seemed folded back against the harpoon where the others stuck out straight. Silently, Erikka handed the video camera to Marc.

He looked at the viewfinder screen replay, tight-lipped, for a minute or more. Then he lowered the camera and handed it back to Marie.

"Is there any way," he asked, "that another whale could have done that? Held a harpoon in its jaw, maybe?"

No one spoke. They all, she thought, knew whale behavior well enough to doubt that idea.

"Maybe pranksters in submarines?" Marie ventured.

"How would they get the whale to hold still for it?" Erikka asked

"Robot submarines made to look like giant squid?" Marc theorized.

"In secret? We have spies in every whaling company. We'd have heard."

In the following silence, the obvious explanation, the one that she'd been avoiding, buried itself like a cold dagger of ice in Erikka's gut. The same explanation, and its implications, must have reached each of them, she thought, because Marc put his arms around Marie and she buried her head in his chest to hide her tears. Moral certitude, she mused, is like a bright shiny mirror that reflects everything the universe throws at you so that you can proceed confidently about your oh-so-self-righteous business. But God help you when that mirror shatters.

★ ❄ ★

The *Bardot* approached the whaling ship the next evening. It was quiet; the night watch had probably taken over. They worked twelve hour shifts, Erikka figured, and the few men on deck were likely looking at stars or just getting air. A day ago she'd denounced them as murderers, but that ideology was clouded now. *Murderers*, she thought, *weren't we all?*

Erikka contacted the *Marianne* on channel 16 and moved to 68. She wasn't welcome, not hardly, but they'd let her come aboard to talk rather than clutter the airwaves with chit chat.

She was met at the top of the ladder by a dark, rail-thin woman who looked at her as though she were seeing the devil herself. Erikka stared for a moment, not realizing that such ships had women aboard. She nodded to the woman and made no effort to explain herself or make other small talk.

The Captain was a tall, white-bearded man who might have matched many images of the legendary captain Ahab, except for his New York Yankees baseball cap. He did not offer his hand and she did not offer hers. But he did nod to the weather display.

"Big low spinning off the circumpolar. Goin' ta be damn bit windy in a couple days."

His version of English tended to have long vowels and accents on every other syllable, but was generally understandable. That being the case, Erikka decided not to try her rusty Icelandic.

"I know," she said. "We'll be gone."

"Gone?" he asked, eyebrows raised.

She explained the markings on the whales and where they likely came from.

"Don't get me wrong," she concluded. "I'm still dead set against killing whales, at least by human beings. This isn't our fight and I don't think we do any good by getting involved and changing its rules and then changing them again."

"I just do my job, miss," he said, the Norse cadence of his voice growing stronger with feeling. "But if I think about it, we working human beings are just as much a part of nature as anything else. Those who set the rules say we can take some whales again and I have a family to feed. I have not exceeded any quota, and if some properly designated authority tells me to stop, well then I stop. But you are not a properly designated authority."

If you saw a child getting raped, she wanted to say, *would you seek a properly designated authority? Or would you do something?* The sea breeze did not totally annihilate the stomach turning stench from below. But for once, she kept her lecture to herself.

"I hear you," she said. "I didn't come over to debate. Do you have a harpoon on this boat that you can spare? The old fashioned hand-held kind?"

"Huh?" He stared at her. She stared back. Finally, he seemed to convince himself that she was serious. "We got the spikes we use to hold things to the carcass. Pretty much the same kind of thing, about two meters with barbs on the end. Don't tell me you're going to switch sides, now? But if you are, it's just a good way to get killed in a small boat. Those sperms *are* just smart enough to know what's goin' on and they *will* turn. That's no legend and besides, you have no permission to kill."

She shook her head. "Not me."

He looked down, as if he could see through the dozen steel floors in his floating castle to the depths below where, in the gloom, whale and squid fought their ancient battle.

"You're crazy," he said after a while. "You think they'll know what to do with it?"

"Probably. I'll pay for the spike," she said.

"You and your boat leave tonight, before the storm?"

"Yes."

"Payment enough, that, I think. Luck to you, then. Sonja will get the spike. And if a whale floats up, we'll send some more down."

Redress, Erikka thought. It would only be redress.

On the way back, she asked Marc to stop rowing midway between the boats. On the horizon to the left of brilliant Fomalhaut lay the constellation of Cetus. To some, it represented a whale, a fellow warm-blooded mammal that bore live young, lived in families and sang songs that humans could almost understand. But there was an older tradition.

She took the barbed spike in her hand and tried to imagine how she would grab it if she had a tentacle instead.

For in the beginning, Cetus was not the gentle giant, but a sea monster, devourer of anything in its path. For those solitary beings far below, it had always been that way. They were beings whose descent was so utterly alien from that of man and whose behavior and society — for that must be what they had — were so utterly unknown that they may as well have come from another planet. But they could see with eyes, manipulate with arms, and imagine with a brain that were, in function, even closer to hers than those of the whale. They had taken the initiative and contacted humanity.

What flowering of Architeuthis culture had happened when the attacks from above had lessened? What disaster had it been when the predation had built up again? She tried to think of the courage it would take to wrap one's tentacles around the monster eating you and continue, even as your arms are being severed and the sea darkened with your blood, to scratch out on the monster's skin with your beak or a shell in a free tentacle, a plea to the gods above who had deserted you.

Whatever else human and Architeuthis had in common, courage would be part of it. Did they, she wonder, dream of the ecstasy of martyrdom as well?

She took some cord and tied a plastic bag to the spike, by way of a crude speed brake.

She looked back at the whaler. What that and the sperm whale had in common was that they both killed and ate other thinking beings. The squid were predators too, so they might understand. Man and squid would send pictures to each other and, eventually, she imagined, the full story would be known. But the first message was clear enough. Loosely translated it might read:

"Help us. We are dying. Why did you stop hunting those who kill us?"

She tossed the spike and watched it fade in the depths below. "Luck to you," she whispered.

STORY NOTES

Whales are fellow mammals and squid are soft squishy tentacled things like Wells' Martians or Cthulhu, i.e., exemplars of horrible. Saving the whales, the point of Arthur Clarke's *Deep Range*, has been a moral *cause célebre* for decades. So the contrarian in me wanted to turn this phylum chauvinism on its head. The sperm whale, however magnificent its brain mass (the largest known), is a predator that acts pretty much like any other predator; it eats other things. It doesn't like being prey itself (with Moby Dick as a witness) and tales of its rage and cunning abound in the whaling world. We have no idea of how bright Archeteuthis is, but some large cephalopods are almost scary in their ability to manipulate their environment and anticipate the actions of other beings. The octopus is generally a solitary creature, but some large squid are social.

As a guess, I've transferred the latter to Archeteuthis. In the story their intentional creation of imagery to communicate with us (at great risk of being eaten!) is complete speculation, but that's what science fiction is for.

Some humans, of course, find it fairly easy to take sides and heap moral opprobrium on others. It also serves as a rationale in their minds, doing exciting stuff (meaning illegal, or really risky, for themselves and others. Being an ecological vigilante can be, in a word, fun. And, truth be told, in many cases, in particular that of wanton polluters, that is not necessarily a bad thing.

But here I wanted to trouble the morally comfortable. The question of what are the unintended consequences of our interference with preexisting ecological relationships (including those our ancestors established) is a real one, as is the question of what are the unintended consequences of changing such a pattern after we've established it. If humans keep something up long enough for biological adaptation to occur, there's little chance of going back. And if it involves another aware, sentient species (or two of such!) it could be an ethical mess. And both action and inaction can have consequences. So when science tells you it's all bad and you have to make a choice anyway, you make it with your heart.

It may not be that much a wonder, if true, that vastly more evolved (biologically and technologically) ETI, if they exist, leave us strictly alone.

GDN January 2016

THE OFF SWITCH

"Good Evening, Ed Miller. I hope I'm not bothering you, but we need to speak."

The voice outside my tent was low-pitched and smooth with perhaps a slight British or Canadian accent. I did not know the speaker. 1156 pm, though still technically evening, is deep into my sleep time. But I had a story to finish.

"Just a minute." I set my laptop aside, pulled myself out of my canvas camp chair, and opened the fly of my tent.

There in the glow of my camp light stood a Sasquatch or a Wookiee, or at least someone in a pretty good costume with elevator shoes; it had to be at least seven feet tall. I took a second or two to collect myself. I touched my wrist, but the Tracy phone lay back by the sleeping bag somewhere with my smart glasses.

"It is probably just as well to *not* create a digital record of our meeting." It looked around. There seemed to be a great dignity in its movements and a deepness in its eyes, but also some concern.

"It's not a costume?" I had to ask.

Sasquatch nodded, baring a little bit of tooth in what I took to be a smile. "It is not. My race evolved on a planet, now tens of thousands of light years from here with," it sighed, "somewhat lower gravity. The resemblance to Sasquatches, Yetis, or Wookies, is purely a coincidence, though a convenient one. I've come to ask your help in a matter of great concern. Could I come in and sit down?"

I think I could hear my heart thump. Was I really awake? Could some Three Buck Chuck from this evening's barbecue be coming back to haunt me? Assuming not, and this were real, if anything bad were going to happen, it would have already happened

"Sure. Okay. Come in."

It ducked in and flowed down to the floor, folding its legs somewhat more adroitly than a human could have. I sat in my chair. Thus positioned, our eyes were at about the same level above the Carbenon floor.

"Okay. Sasquatch?"

"That will do nicely."

"Ah, how may I help you?"

"I need to send a message, surreptitiously, and I am not built for surreptitiousness. May I give you some background?"

"Please do."

It nodded toward the Tracy and the smart glasses, lying innocently with a half eaten Mars bar on the foot of the sleeping bag. It had not occurred to their makers that some people would want to *not* avail themselves of constant contact with the internet, so they did not have actual off switches. I looked around and grabbed my lightweight aluminum pot, put a paper towel in it, put the Tracy and glasses inside on the paper towel and put the lid on by way of an improvised Faraday cage.

Sasquatch nodded and exhaled. "Put the pot out of audio range?" It asked, very softly.

So it could pull me apart for dinner without witnesses? No, there were a dozen other tents within a hundred meters and besides, those kinds of monsters wouldn't speak with British accents outside of movies. This one sounded deadly serious. I excused myself and put the pot in my car. When I came back, Sasquatch was noticeably more relaxed.

"Are you familiar with the term 'gray goo'?" it asked.

A knot formed in my stomach. "Self-reproducing nanotechnology, out of control?"

It nodded. "Yes. On the other side of the galaxy about 1.5 million years ago a war occurred between two roughly contemporaneous races that developed on different moons of a giant planet orbiting a star much smaller than this one."

"You couldn't stop it?"

"Uh, no." Sasquatch sighed, "I am now far removed in time and space from that event. Both races evolved fairly rapidly, going from stone and bone technology to nanotechnology in a mere 60,000 of your years or so. But even if one of the elder races had happened upon it, it is unlikely they would have intervened; the galaxy has a fairly firm noninterference directive."

I detected a hint of irritation in its voice as it said that.

"Eventually," it continued, "the conflict ended. However, it left an unintended consequence to its resolution. The losers were using self-reproducing nanotechnology to mine asteroids for their war effort."

"Risky."

Sasquatch nodded. "We are not far from the Hanford nuclear reservation?"

"Point taken."

"They did have an 'off switch,' but in a piece of extraordinary bad luck, a few hundred thousand years after the war, an asteroid with these nanobots got ejected from their planetary system. It drifted through space for hundreds of thousands of your years until it encountered another sun and a revival routine — a wartime exigency, understand — started some of them up again."

"But cosmic radiation . . . "

"Those whose business it is estimate that only one such nanite in a hundred million would survive to start up again, but, of course, with a couple trillion or so to start with, it was virtually certain that at least *one* would and since they were self-reproducing, one was all it would take.

"They reactivated far away from anyone who could use the off switch."

I began to get a very uneasy feeling. "What do these mining robots do?"

"Think of them as a kind of mechanical termite. Anything they encounter they turn into nice mounds of constituent elements, and, of course, more mining robots."

"What do they do for energy?"

"They are nearly perfect absorbers of any electromagnetic waves that reach them. If the intensity is low, they reproduce very slowly, but even in interstellar space, if they have some source of matter and enough time, they can do their thing."

"Do they work," I waved my arms around, "in an atmosphere?"

Sasquatch shook its head. "A few nanobars of gas will stop them — a safety feature — their makers were desperate, not stupid. However, your moon does not have an atmosphere. Their default program was to deliver their products to the nearest inhabited planet, so they shape them into tiny reentry vehicles and send them down."

"That seems innocuous, maybe even useful . . . oh."

"Your moon has more than one percent of your planet's mass. The surface of your planet would be buried under a few kilometers of such usefulness."

I suppressed an inappropriate chuckle at the ignominy of being buried under interstellar termite shit. "This 'off switch' . . . ?"

"It's a radio signal, their version of pulse code modulation. I have specs and the code," it tapped an outsized index finger on its skull. "What I need is some time on a large radio telescope, or radar system."

"But if you just contact the authorities . . . "

"That's not a good idea. Noninterference and all, you know."

"You aren't supposed to be doing this?"

"It's an ethical gray area, one of these things where it might be better to apologize afterward than ask permission. My view is that "letting nature take its course" doesn't really apply to this kind of thing, but others take a larger view. After all, a potentially intelligent race vanishes every day in this Galaxy, for one reason or another."

"Potentially intelligent?"

Sasquatch shrugged its shoulders, much as a human might have. "You have a ways to go."

I could understand that intellectually, but it still rankled. My face must have revealed my feelings.

"Sorry. What it means is that what I do constitutes interference by their standards, which means you'll need to proceed as if it were your own idea. It's conceivable you could hack the nanite's code and turn them off yourself."

"Conceivable?"

"But not very likely. They would recognize my interference and counteract it."

"Even if it meant destroying the Earth?"

Sasquatch sighed. "Nature would create a new one, reshuffling the deck with limitless possibilities. As I said, we have a disagreement."

"Why didn't you just turn these things off yourself before you came down here?"

"That would very clearly have revealed my presence and purpose. I am not suicidal and this might not be the only nanite cloud. I am doing this entirely without electromagnet emissions. Despite outward appearances, this body is the product of hundreds of millions of years of biological technology. My spacecraft are also emissions-free. They are also free of what you call "dark matter" and any nuclear emissions above background."

Sasquatch seemed much more cautious than seemed reasonable. Perhaps its opponents, if that was the right word, were not reasonable. Could I trust it? Could it have made me trust it in some biochemical way? I shook my head.

"You are, understandably, being very cautious. But this is really very urgent. Do you have a radio electronics laboratory?"

"No. But I can use a friend's." Dick Princeton's to be exact, a ways up the mountain.

Sasquatch smiled. "Ownership versus access, of course. If you give me a piece of paper, I will write down the carrier frequency and the bit structure, and draw a picture of the wave form; the last doesn't have to be exact but should be close. You will need to be able to make something that will generate that. Then you will need to find a large, powerful, communications or planetary radar dish to amplify it and send it to certain coordinates."

"You could type it into my phone."

It shook its head. "I need to avoid anything like that, particularly devices that have cameras in them."

"Someone is looking for you?"

It nodded. "Something would be more the case. Something that undoubtedly has access to terrestrial information networks."

"And that something wants Earth dead?"

"I wouldn't go that far; I don't think it would be much bothered if your civilization emerged of its own accord, but any notion of 'uplift' or 'assistance' is greatly frowned upon. It's a slippery slope that could lead to too much demand on the galaxy's resources. In about five billion years, galactic civilization will need to deal with the consequences of the merger between our Galaxy and M31 in Andromeda. A smaller population in both galaxies would make this less problematic, and over the course of the last few billion years, agreements have been reached. The rate of increase needs to be managed. My view, that some exceptions can be made, is somewhat in the minority, I'm afraid, and I haven't conformed. That is the short version, of course."

"Of course." A kind of knot developed in my gut. I knew too much, now. If this was true, I was a microbe, and my whole planet was a microbe, to beings whose extent through time and space so far exceeded any human intuitional capacity that I could only deal with it as numbers. "I'm kind of wishing you hadn't told me that much."

"A necessary cruelty, if your civilization is to survive."

I thought of Patty, my parents, my writing, the glass factory and everything in my life up to now. If only I could give the last five minutes back! If only this Sasquatch had chosen someone else!

"I am sorry, truly sorry. But your reaction tells me that the implications of this are not lost on you. But we must go on. I will write down . . . no, I will tell you and you will write down the message."

It took about half an hour to get it all down and I still didn't understand it, but I thought Dick would.

"Okay. We've got about a half-hour drive."

Sasquatch looked in my cluttered van with some obvious misgivings.

"Or a two-day hike," I said.

It nodded, but looked dubious. But after a little tetrisizing I cleared enough floor area for it to sit down with back support and its legs straight out, then off we went.

I didn't think I could outsmart a billions-of-years old civilization. But maybe I could land a sucker punch before they knew about me.

★ ❋ ★

Dick Princeton lived alone south of The Dalles, about a mile in and five-hundred feet up from Mill Creek road on the east side of the mountain. He had no close family; he was a nice enough guy, but shit happens. This quest, if real, was probably going to kill him — and me. But, again, if real, we were dead anyway. It just hadn't caught up with me yet.

I left Sasquatch near the driveway entrance munching on Salal leaves, which he seemed to think were a great delicacy, and headed up the two-rut drive.

Dick had a couple of single-wide mobile homes in a hundred-foot clearing on his land on the east slopes of Mount Hood, a reasonably radio-quiet area. He'd built a peaked roof covering the area between the single-wides, kind of a poor man's open, protected courtyard. He was sitting there in the shades in his shorts with what was likely a tall Long Island iced tea. He'd trimmed his usually full black beard to a summer heat minimum.

"Yo, Dick," I shouted as I got out of my van.

"Well, look what the cat brought in!"

Dick didn't have a phone; if you caught him at his computer and on line you could Skype him, but otherwise you emailed him or drove up there and took your chances. We hadn't had time for email.

"Nice to see you too. Is your twenty inch still in working order?"

"There's a glitch in the go-to system, so I'm back to using a Telrad, but the optics are just as good as the day I built them. You want to look at something tonight?"

Now I took his life and mine in my hands. "Yeah. I got a radio gizmo I need to make, then I want to look at something, at these coordinates."

"Coordinates. Ah, okay, I'll find a star on the charts in about the right direction and we'll offset a bit. Come on."

We marched up to the top of a mostly-bare small hill. I took my jacket; shadows stretched, and it got cool early on the east side of the mountain.

"Chain saw and Roundup," he said, gesturing at the clearing. "It would be awful if everyone did this, but everyone doesn't."

Here and there, scattered around like strange bushes of some sort, were old satellite dishes. Cables ran from them like a spider web, at the center of which sat a couple of prefab sheds. The small one was on wheels on tracks; it could be rolled off his telescopes. The larger one had his electronics shop and the back end of the radio telescope array. I hadn't told Sasquatch about that, so nothing tracking him could find out.

A turkey vulture soared overhead and glided down to a landing near one of the dishes. Then it froze, not moving a feather.

Dick laughed. "Come here," he said.

It waddled over to him and froze again.

I got it. "It's a drone. Very realistic, too. The way it rocked while it soared fooled me. I didn't catch on until it froze. But it's not legal, is it?"

"I'm sure the FAA would say 'hell no' in triplicate if I asked. So I haven't asked. He's fully autonomous. I got a friend at Channel 10; we send USB drives of stuff back and forth. Chocolates too."

Dick thought outside the box. I needed that.

Inside, he frowned at the notes, then pulled a crate out from under his work shelf and produced a circuit board with a number of small components on it. Cyrillic characters decorated the board — to someone they meant something. Dick grabbed a bunch of alligator clip leads from another open box and clipped a couple of them to wires coming from an old Sears Diehard sitting in a plastic pan on the shelf. Others he clipped to leads coming from an oscilloscope that had to be fifty years old. But it powered up and soon I saw a waveform on the green screen. He stuck a tiny screwdriver into a slot-head screw on one of the tiny boxes, and turned it this way and that. In about half an hour we had something looking like Sasquatch's waveform.

"Seventy-five point three megahertz," Dick said. "And that's the waveform you want?"

"Looks good to me. Can you build another one?"

"The boards are Russian surplus." He rummaged around. "I could build four or five."

"That would be good."

"Whatever you say, buddy. You *are* going to tell me what this is all about?"

"It's about active SETI, in a way. I'm going to write you a note while you build them. Don't look at it until I'm long gone."

"You want me to call the aliens again? They didn't answer last time." He laughed. An answer from Tau Ceti, of course, wouldn't get here for another couple of decades.

"Be careful of what you wish for." I grabbed a pencil from my shirt pocket and wrote below the modulator description: "In the note . . . later . . . they may be listening."

He looked at me and at what I'd written, pursed his lips and nodded. Dick catches on quick. He went back to the box of electronics and got busy, while I wrote the note. The first line was "Don't read this until we're gone. They read minds — not sure how or under what circumstances. But I think it's a case of they can read anybody's mind but not everybody's. Too much data." I folded it then wrote, under the fold. "Sasquatch and I will take a chip and head to northern Washington State, where there was a big dish. The rest is up to you. I can't know."

Evening had gone well past astronomical twilight when we rolled the smaller building off the telescope; the building rode on tracks, the telescope stayed put. Dick star-hopped to the target in Cetus without much difficulty.

"Whoever's out there, I hope they like TV. Gotta comsat passing through . . . WestStar Eight will be rotating through there in about six hours, that's my link. Well, I don't see much there. Take a look. The equatorial platform will hold it there about twenty minutes, then I'll need to repoint."

I looked into the eyepiece and saw the satellite exit the field of view, but nothing else. I shook my head.

"What are we looking for?" Dick asked

"A dust cloud, sort of."

"Hmmm." He stepped back into the rolled-away building and came back with another eyepiece, with something colored on the end that goes in the scope. "Filter," he said. "Bigger eyepiece. More contrast. Ahhh. Now take a look. Use averted vision, stare between the two stars on the right. It'll be in the corner of your eye, upper left."

I looked and saw a very dim patch, almost perfectly circular.

"It's not a comet." Dick said. "There's no coma. I should report it anyway. What am I looking at?"

"The end of the world."

★ ❄ ★

Sasquatch and I got back to my campsite by ten-thirty. I packed up and we headed for the nearest big astronomical dish, near Brewster, Washington, normally a five-hour drive. I didn't plan on driving normal.

A former dedicated Very Long Baseline Array dish, since 2020, the dish operated part-time as an individual radio telescope for SETI research and part time as a planetary radar for Washington State University. Such were the vagaries of funding. But now it had a transmitter, and a powerful one.

We got as far as a bit east of The Dalles before I was pulled over. The trooper shined the light in the van and his eyes got wide. I thought fast.

"Looks real, doesn't it?"

"I'm listening."

"I'm a science fiction fan; my convention starts tomorrow and I'm late. That's my costume."

"A Bigfoot?"

"A Wookiee. From Star Wars."

"Oh. I remember. Could I try it on?"

Fortunately, he probably hadn't passed a physical in the last decade.

"Waist's 40 inches."

"Darn. Well, we have speed limits around here."

"Understand. Sorry officer. Nobody else on the road."

He nodded. "Look, I don't want you driving tired. But watch it now, we've got your number and there won't be a second warning."

"Yes, sir."

I stayed under the limit until we hit Briggs Junction and crossed the Columbia on '97 into Washington State, where they fly low. If the galactics were as good as Sasquatch said, I thought, they were probably onto us — but we had to play this out to give Dick a chance. Sasquatch didn't know anything more about Dick than I'd told him. So, if the galactics caught him, I'm the only one he could give up. If they caught both of us, it would be up, unless Dick got a step ahead of all of us in the meantime. The longer we stayed out of their hands, the better.

I picked up a six-pack of Dr. Pepper and a couple corn dogs in Yakima, and that kept me going until the GPS led me to the well-lit big white dish at about four in the morning. But I was on the wrong side of the Okanogan River and watched as it went by. Siri kept me on '97 until the Monse Bridge; I'd asked for minimum time, of course. So we crossed and approached from the North, telephone poles flying past us. That might have given some time; we saw flashing lights before they saw us. I pulled over a couple of telephone poles before we got to the dish.

"This is bad," I said. "There must have been a copcam on the trooper that stopped us."

"Of course. My opponents would have recognized me as soon as the video hit their system. I should get out here; they seem to be waiting for us rather than coming after us." I got the grin with teeth again. "Overconfidence." It picked up one of Dick's modulators; I'd taken two. "There's always a chance," it said.

I shook my head. "I'll try to talk my way in. You need to hide your hide."

"I've been hiding for half a galaxy of travel, since your ancestors were in caves. I am getting very tired of it." It offered an oversized hand. "This is very probably the last time we will meet. May your road from here be a good one."

I shook it, and nodded. Then he slipped out of the van and into the night. Courtesy of a light breeze, I got a good whiff of the bovine bucolic before he shut the door. We were only two or three miles out of town, but it felt, looked and smelled about as rustic as anywhere I'd ever been.

I got out my cell phone and called WSU's phone tree. An agonizing forty minutes later, the robot transferred me to the Brewster facility; the dish had work early the next morning and was staffed tonight for preparation, thank whatever for small miracles.

I called the tech inside and a lady named Denley Clark answered. I introduced myself as Harry Phillips from the *Spokesman-Review* and asked for access and an interview.

"Sure, if you can get in," she said. "I don't have the foggiest what the cops are all about. We're going to try a bistatic radar experiment with a Near Earth asteroid that's passing by for a mining company. Maybe they don't want claim jumpers? You got me. Then we get an hour's worth of data on a SETI target about 0600. So sure, come on in, I've done the prep and I'm just watching TV. They're rebroadcasting *Universe* again, on PBS. I'll give you a tour."

"Thanks. See you soon," I said with more confidence than I felt.

Then I rolled up to the cop convention, very slowly.

Because I live in Vancouver, I have a Washington State driver's license. I positioned my thumb over the address, and got set to wave it as if it were a press credential.

One of the officers approached and I rolled down the window. His name badge said "Grav."

I put on a big smile. "Hello, Officer Grav, I'm Harry Phillips, from the Spokesman. I have an appointment with Ms. Clark inside."

The officer drew his gun and pointed it at me. "Where's the Sasquatch?"

I shook like a leaf. "I gave the costume to someone in Yakima to take . . . "

"No, you didn't. " He grabbed my hand. I felt a tingle at the point of contact that spread up my arm. When he let it down, he had a rueful smile on his face and reholstered his gun "We aren't monsters. You won't remember any of this in an hour, and won't worry about it. Your Sasquatch friend explained things truthfully. We have a difference of opinion. Should your people ever evolve to be part of the galaxy, they will understand fully."

It doesn't seem very likely, now. I thought.

"No, but one cannot anticipate everything."

As soon as I thought something, the "cop" knew.

"We stopped a transmission from Mr. Princeton's telescope, but he was nowhere to be found. He will be found. You can save him some embarrassment by telling us where you think he might have gone."

There was a moment's pause as I tried to think of anything else.

"We'll check all of those places. You're a very creative individual."

Dick had escaped! They couldn't read his mind. Maybe there was still hope.

"No, we can't read his mind until we find him. But he will not be believe We have your 'Wookiee' in custody, we caught her going through the fence. " He smiled like a shark. "Do you have any idea why she was so obsessed with stopping the nanite cloud?"

She?

"They're sexually dimorphic and her form hosts the cub. No doubt she didn't tell you because you would have taken a male bigfoot more seriously. You had suspicions of her motives, but didn't take them far enough."

Officer Grav looked at me quizzically. Was he a human being controlled by aliens or an alien in human form? I couldn't tell. It occurred to me that I was having an intelligence test. If not philosophical altruism, why would Sasquatch be so concerned . . . did it, er she, have something to do with the dust cloud. Guilt?

The cop nodded. "They're her children, in a way."

His expression froze. He stood up away from the window.

Then he turned back to me with a quizzical expression on his face. "Well, It seems you, Sasquatch, or someone, succeeded. Something sent the deactivation command. Well played."

My diversion had worked! Dick had gotten through!

"I would like to keep my memories. What harm could it do now?"

He nodded. "Too little harm to deny your request. But you are advised to be quiet about this. You won't be believed. An alien Wookiee bigfoot? People would only laugh at you."

Sasquatch?

"Her mission is also over." The cop smiled. "She is very tired of this; we will return her to her part of this galaxy."

Mission over?

"She helped make the cloud," the cop said. "That is why she knew the off switch."

It's the only one?

"The only one left, as far as we know. She's been busy."

They must have tracked her across the galaxy.

"We tracked the clouds. She followed. It's over now."

With that and a nod, he turned and walked away.

As he did, the lights died around the station faded, all the officers returned to their cars and drove off soundlessly. The air became filled with a mist, made ghostly by the half moon high overhead. As the mist swallowed the police cars I watched their tail lights fade out, two by two.

Then the mist lifted and the tops of the distant hills shone pink with dawn. A rooster crowed. It was as if they were never there.

An eagle soared over the river, making me think of Dick's drone vulture. Of course! He'd sent the message to someone he trusted with a dish pointed in the right direction. Three of them, as it eventually turned out, including that PBS station sending out *Universe*.

As if on cue, my Tracy beeped — a text from Dick. "Finished yr story, hope u don't mind. Coast Clear? Need ride home."

I laughed; he'd gone to my tent! I hadn't once thought of that.

"AOK," I sent back. "ETA 6 hrs."

I had a long conversation with Denley, a slim, intense woman of fifty by her face, but only thirty by her body, who looked interested and listened patiently. She was curious about the signal device, so we went ahead and sent the signal anyway — everything worked and redundancy always helps — there is that one-in-a-trillion-survival thing. But I don't think she believed a word I said. After an hour, she condescendingly ushered me out into the daylight; she had to begin her work of looking for intelligent life among the stars.

STORY NOTES

This story was written, mostly, on the slopes of Mt. Hood south of Hood River Oregon at a very informal annual writer's retreat we call "Campcon" where one sleeps in tents and writes with the laptop on a picnic table. Somehow, stuff gets done. This not entirely serious story is my contribution to the "gray goo" genre, a chance to explore an unlikely, though not physically impossible, answer to Fermi's Question, and an invitation to think about just how far the prime directive might get taken. And if you notice a certain resemblance to the ending of this story and that of the movie *Arrival*, it is, I think, sheer coincidence. But for what it matters, this story was written and submitted well before the movie came out.

GDN February 2017

FLIGHT OF THE STEAM DRAGON

Let me first admit that I don't make a living as a writer. I earn at least three times as much from my Air Force pension, twice as much from investment appreciation, and a bit more from selling books and stuff at conventions, county fairs, swap meets, and so on. So I do well overall, but in no sense, at age fifty, can I afford to retire or even slow down.

So there I was one Memorial Day at the fair on the banks of the Willamette, amid Ferris Wheels and corn dogs, vending my books when a rather tall thin man, presumably of African heritage, with thick curly black-and-gray hair stopped to look. He passed by my *The Tractor that Ate Ashland*, a steam punk yarn about an automaton logging and pulping steam tractor run amuck in the 1880s state of Jefferson, picked up one of Luna Lindsey's books about cult indoctrination and started to read it.

After about five minutes of that, I cleared my throat and asked the question. "Interested?"

He looked up. "Uh, oh, sorry. I'm DeSam Darren. Is this for real? You know the author?"

He sounded pure Northwest, not even a hint of anything else in his voice.

"It is and I do. She had a rough time. My name's Ed Miller. These," I gestured to the titles at the center of the table, "are mine." Never hurts to try.

He clutched the Lindsey book. I sure hoped he was buying because it was beginning to look like a used book.

He shook his head. "Maybe later. A cult's kidnapped my daughter."

"Jeez. Sorry to hear that. Have you talked to the cops?"

He shook his head. "She went there of her own free will. Except she didn't, she was conned. Or at least her mother was. But they don't listen to that. Her mother has custody."

"What cult got her?" I was getting in too deep; I knew that. But that didn't stop me. It never has; I consider such episodes to be research.

"McGrud. The New People. My ex joined a couple of years back and took Cindy with her."

I vaguely recalled some mention in the news.

"Mormon offshoot of some kind?"

"Nah. More like he's doing his own thing of some kind. Lots of charisma, lots of women, lots of girls, lots of kids. Lots of money, too."

I started tapping my phone. In seconds, the whole sorry mess was in front of me. "Your wife?"

"Not any more. She's made her own bed and she can sleep in it. I just want to get my little girl out of there, at least talk to her, try to make sense." DeSam's voice, and he might mean make sense to her as well as make sense of the situation but he doesn't finish the thought which is what people sometimes do in conversations with me.

"How old?"

"Twelve."

"Ouch. You sure she's there?"

DeSam nodded.

"No phone?"

He shook his head. "They don't allow them."

"You think she wants out?"

"If the tales they tell of that place are true, I'm sure *hoping* she wants out. I mean I want to be a grandpa some day, but not that way. If I could only get a phone to her, talk to her."

"Hmm." Okay, some imagination goes along with the science fiction writer occupation. I gave DeSam a card with my home address on it. "I might know someone who could do something for you."

"Really?"

I shrugged. "Not certain. But drop by about 8 p.m or so. And, yes, read that book. If they've had her a while, it might not be as simple as you hope."

He nodded and left. It was at least ten minutes before I realized he hadn't paid for the book.

★ ❋ ★

That evening I got a knock on the door about 7 p.m. Darren was early, I thought. I opened the door. It wasn't Darren.

"Mr. Miller." There stood a six-foot-two man, athletically built, but just past the competitive years with a slight paunch. He wore a black windbreaker, black jeans, and black New Balance trail shoes. There was a hint of iron in his hair. A shiny clean black four-door sedan sat in the drive behind him.

"Yes?"

"You've been meeting with DeSam Darren." He might have been from Brooklyn or somewhere back east.

"Who are you?"

"I'll ask the questions."

"No, you'll tell me who you are and what this is about or I'll shut the door in your face."

"That wouldn't be wise." He put a shoe on the threshold.

I shut the door. It's a power-assisted door.

The knocking resumed and continued.

I grabbed my phone, hit the home intercom app, and watched the door cam on the screen. "Get out of here before the cops get here. This is your only warning."

"Look, I work for a guy that owns the cops around here. Stay away from Darren. We're tailing him and he's more trouble than you want to get into. Drugs. I'll leave."

"Then leave."

"My shoe's caught."

I stood well aside and told the house to open the door a crack. I heard a grunt and with some uneven steps down the walk, he got in the car and left. The door cam would have got the plate if there'd been one.

Drugs, BS, I thought. This guy wasn't from law enforcement of any sort. No ID. He was probably from that cult, I thought.

I live in a heavily modified thousand-square-foot seventy-year-old one-time starter home on a hill halfway to Gresham with a bunch of other ticky-tacky houses. Claire's diner was is at the bottom of the hill; and that was the only way up. I got out a clean pair of sweats, put a note on the door and went down to Claire's.

Claire was a seventy-something escapee from one of the cults that used to have a compound south of Portland, so as soon as I explained the issue, she was up for a little adventure. I asked her to pull the security footage from around ten to seven and dupe it to my stick — nothing wireless. I watched it on my tablet, and found what I was looking for just before Darren came in about a quarter after eight.

Like I asked in the note on the door, he sat as far from me as he could. However, it's a small diner, and Clare delivered another note with his coffee.

By 9 pm, he was out the back door wearing my sweats, I'd swapped wheels with Claire, and we were in her van on our way to the backside of Mount Hood to visit Dick Princeton.

★ ❈ ★

For a mad scientist type, Dick is kind of hard to get in touch with. He has no cell coverage to speak of, no landline, and hardly ever looks at his email. He can Skype or Zoom via satellite when that's arranged.

But he hardly ever goes anywhere, either. You pretty much have to plan way ahead or drive up there and hope.

We got up there about midnight. I saw a low amber glow, so I put the lights down to park about half a mile from his house.

"We're sneaking up on him?" Darren asked, surprised.

"No moon tonight," I said. "He's probably got a telescope up and running. I don't want to blind him."

That proved to be the case; Dick was showing off his homebuilt "F4, 13 inch aperture, apochromatic, variable density Fresnel-zone, refractor" to a lady friend, a thin, sharp-faced type with graying shoulder length hair. After introductions — her name was Sarah and she was a paleontologist — and an explanation of our mission, Dick put us up for the night on the notion that plans of attack are best made after a good breakfast.

★ ❈ ★

We ate sausage and pancakes in the wide roofed-over area between the two single-wides Dick called home.

"Just where is this place?" Dick asked while chewing his sausage.

DeSam grunted. "Ye' follow Steens Highway past Princeton to Dunce's Farm, take the cutoff and head south on the west side of Ramshead Ridge, maybe five miles east of One-Bit Lake. It's dry as all get out there but McGrud bought the land in '23, sank a well and struck water. There's maybe a couple hundred people there now, all answering to Angus McGrud and his cronies. Some say they may have found gold as well as water. I think he just takes the savings of everyone who drinks his Kool-Aid. But he's smart; made half a billion in high tech before all this and he's got robots, all sorts of surveillance stuff, high voltage electric fences, and those antidrone blasters, you know, the kind that knockout all the electronics."

"Hmm," Dick said and pulled out his tablet. After a little road following, a reasonably good resolution picture opened on his screen.

"Took the cell phones?" Dick asked.

"Yeah, not that they had to. Hardly any coverage out that way. Cindy got a few letters out at first, but that stopped a year ago."

Dick pointed to a fuzzy pile of junk near the northeast corner. One could make out some wings sticking out of the pile.

"Dead drones, I suspect."

"Yeah. Some outside relatives tried that. The drones got blasted, then the FAA jumped on their operators. The buildings to the left," DeSam said, "have private rooms, where the leaders can "regenerate" the cults word, they call it, the younger ones. McGrud has his own special place somewhere, though. You'd think he'd be slowing down some with a pacemaker and all, but not the way the insiders tell it."

"Ugh!" Sarah exclaimed. "DeSam, do you think your daughter's being . . . used?"

DeSam's stare told me the story. He couldn't put it in words. I didn't know what I would do in his position. Nobody said anything for a while.

Dick pulled on his beard the way he does when his mind is engaged to the point where he doesn't care about anything but what he is thinking about.

"I've got something to show you," he said at length. "After I finish my pancakes."

So nourished, he led us over to the shed that served as his workshop and pushed aside the rattly metal sliding door.

Once inside, he picked up a box about the size of a deck of playing cards. It had various orifices and couplers like those you might see on a high-pressure gas line. The lower side was all deep wide grooves, or high thin ridges depending on how one looked at it.

"Okay . . . " I was flummoxed. "Uh, what is it?" . . . and what did it have to do with DeSam's problem?

"It's a miniature steam engine — runs on propane." He pointed to a nipple protruding from the box. "Everything's fluid controlled; no electricity. Control signals in here, air in here, clean high-pressure air out here, vapors out here. The back side is the radiator-condenser. Puts out about ten watts of mechanical energy."

He picked up another box, about the size of a domino. "This is an altimeter with a memory; it can provide rate of change info, too. All fluidic." He grabbed another card-box sized gizmo. "This is a fluidic analog computer."

"That must be incredibly . . . intricate," DeSam said.

Dick nodded. "That's why I print 'em. It would be darn near impossible to make this any other way." He picked up something that looked like a plastic suction cup on a Lego. "This is my sonic range finder. Almost as good as a bat's."

I felt bewildered. "Okay, but what . . . "

"That!" he said, and pointed to the strangest bird I'd ever seen standing at the end of the cluttered room. It was huge, as tall as I was. The head looked something like a pelican's, but with a huge narrow crest pointed backward. It had little stumpy legs and rested on its wing claws. The wings seemed very thin and bat-like, covered with gray velvet instead of feathers. The body was blue-gray on the back and white on the belly. I'd seen something like that somewhere.

"A dragon?" DeSam guessed. "A miniature Rodan?"

It finally clicked. "A pteranodon, an old flying reptile. You've made a steam powered model pteranodon," I said.

"Both right in a way," Sarah said with a smile. "It's related but it's a Dawndragon. Dawndraco *kanzai*. It's a near perfect reconstruction; its flight can tell us a lot about how these critters lived. I've been working on the outside while Dick's been working on the inside."

"Yup," Dick said. "She'll takeoff, fly, turn, soar and land in a variety of profiles without any electronics. Everything's pneumatic, fluidic or sonic. I even have an ancient film camera. That fits in where the breastbone would be."

"McGrud's drone blaster . . . " DeSam started.

"Can't touch it. Nor can anyone else's; we have too much work in this."

"Ten watts doesn't seem like much," I said. "Can it take off on its own?"

"Not only that, but she's got a compressed air reservoir that can go up to fifteen hundred psi; it's laminated graphene — hardly weighs anything. The ten watts is good enough for soaring and topping off the reservoir. We could use Dizzy to take some video, then use Dawn to get a close-up and deliver a message, or maybe even a cell phone, inside the compound."

"Dizzy?" DeSam and I said simultaneously.

"His robot vulture," Sarah said. "A bit modern for my Cretaceous tastes, but also a nearly perfect replica."

"You named him!" I noticed she didn't say "drone."

"He earned it, don't you think?"

"What did he do?" DeSam asked.

"Pretty much saved the planet," I said. "It's a long story," I replied to DeSam's incredulous look, "but he delivered some important messages."

"Jeez," DeSam said. "This is happening so fast."

Dick nodded. "We need to stay ahead of their power curve now that they know you've talked to Ed and neither of you is under surveillance. Lady and Gentlemen, I think its time for a little recce."

"Now?" I asked.

"It will take us most of the day to get down there — New Princeton or Rome should be close enough. Dawn doesn't have the range Dizzy has.

Dizzy can't get close—the drone blaster would work on him—so we'll keep him far up and away, acting very vulture-like. But he'll be our eyes and our cell phone tower. Also my control relay. He can screech really loud, in the ultrasonic range, of course."

"I should drive there, too," Sarah announced. "We might need room for one more coming back."

"Sounds like a plan," I said. "We find Cindy, see if she wants to get out, then get her out."

"I'll get Dizzy up and test his cams and links," Dick added.

The robot took a couple of very lifelike strides and a jump to get airborne. In seconds he was over the treetops.

"I've got video," Dick said almost immediately from behind his pad, and frowned. "I think we have company. Do you recognize these guys?"

He showed me Dizzy's view of the road to his place, with two black late-model cars on their way up.

"Ohhhh-kayyy. We should get going, now!" I said. As an ex-military guy, I recognized a tactical situation when I saw one.

"Ed, they must have tracked your van, somehow," Dick said.

"That's Claire's," I said. "They couldn't have known I'd take it beforehand."

"Maybe me," DeSam said, looking mortified. "Maybe they got a chip on me."

"Okay, you come with me," I said. "We'll lead them away. Dick and Sarah, you've got the mission."

"Where are you going?" Sarah asked.

"Well," I thought. "First, the Black Bear Diner in Madras for lunch, then maybe the Wal-Mart in Bend. By this evening, we ought to be at the Half-Moon Bookstore in Burns that sometimes carries my stuff. I know the owner, anyway. Then we'll have dinner at the Highlander, maybe a block north of State."

"Haggis?" Dick asked with a smile.

"Angus Steak. It's just a block or so north of the Police station. We'll try to lose them there."

Dick laughed. "Might work. We'll plan the op for about 1000 tomorrow. Dizzy should be fully charged and high overhead. We'll overnight in Rome Station. I'll need to stay there with the controls."

"Do you have anything to deal with bugs or trackers?" I asked, nodding toward DeSam.

Dick pulled on his beard. "Hmm. Not on hand. I could rig something in an hour or two, but . . . "

"I'll see if I can give you that time. Drop it off for me at the Half-Moon Bookstore in Burns. Ask for Celeste."

He grinned. "You've got it."

"We'll make the pick up, if there is one," I said.

"Uh . . . " DeSam's eyes were wide.

"I'll go down there, too," Sarah said. "It gives us two chances."

"I couldn't ask . . . " DeSam started.

Sarah held up a hand. "I don't like these goons already. Besides, I don't want to see Dawn in the Drone dump. She's my baby, too." She gave Dick a quick peck on the cheek, making him look embarrassed for the first time since I'd known him. "She may need my help."

Dick recovered himself. "We do need to get Dawn out of there; I'd rather people didn't know about some of this stuff just yet." He glanced at his screen. "Ed, you need to get outta here. Sarah, let's get Dawn airborne and drive your van out back a way, then take a walk. I'll grab some things from the shed. Ed, bring Dawn out front. Igor, lock it down in five."

The last was to his computer. Dick didn't like leaving the lights on accidentally, but was usually too busy or absent minded to think of it. So Igor locked the doors and powered down everything that needed to be powered down.

I picked up Dawn easily, considering that she was bigger than I was, even with her wings folded. Her velvety "fuselage" dimpled where I grabbed it, but sprang back quickly. I put her down in the big bare spot in front of Dick's sheds. By the time I had that done, Dick was outside with a big black bag and a couple of cheap cell phones with bubble wrap around them that he put in a hinged compartment in her nether end. Then he reached in the bag for a couple of things that looked like miniature organs with labeled keys and a tube. He pressed one and blew in the tube.

At first, I didn't hear anything. Then Dawn made a low sound, something between a hum and a hiss. He pressed another key, and Dawn unfolded its wings, each one much longer than I was tall. It flapped them a couple times slowly as if warming up.

"Go, baby, go!" Sarah shouted.

As if hearing her, the Dawndragon's hum and hiss got louder. It spread its wings and held them high, then took a couple of hops and jumped, brought the wing-claw knuckles down and leapt into the air. With two or three big flaps it was up over the treetops.

"No batteries?" DeSam asked.

"No batteries," Dick answered with big grin. He handed one of the pipe organs to me. "Back-up," he said.

I hoped it had an instruction book.

"The goons are about two minutes out," Dick said, looking at his tablet. "Better get going."

We all got in our respective cars; Dick headed out back while a still wide-eyed DeSam and I headed east to face the music.

There's a wide spot in Dick's access road near a blind curve. I got there first and waited. The two black sedans rounded the curb, going fast. They stopped quickly, but not quickly enough; they'd overshot me. I was out from behind them and down the drive, hoping it would take them a while to get turned around. My cell rang; I handed it to DeSam. "Speaker on," I told it.

"Good move, Ed," Dick's voice said. "We're pretty well hidden and circling out of sight. It looks like the second goon car got stuck trying to turn around and is blocking the other."

"Thanks much. See you later."

★ ❋ ★

DeSam sat silent, maybe in a state of shock, for the two-hour trip down to Madras. The Black Bear menu disguised itself as a 1976 newspaper with stories about fusion reactors and landings on Mars — robotic, back then. People have been working on some things all my life. The Black Bear hamburgers have more calories than a steak dinner. No bear on the menu, though. I got a trout; DeSam got a burger. I checked in with Dick. He and Sarah were on the road with Dizzy's camera overhead. Our faux vulture had locked in on one black car about 30 miles north of us from twelve thousand feet. The other car had headed east — out of sight now.

We had our food by the time I'd signed off with Dick.

"You're pretty quiet," I observed between sips of coffee.

"Yeah."

"What's your girl's name again?"

"Cindy. She calls herself Cindy Birdsong now."

There was something in his voice. That and the fact she wasn't using his last name.

"Issues?"

"Her momma accused me of doing stuff to her when she was too young to remember, to get custody."

I almost dropped my fork. What the hell was I getting into? What was I getting Dick and Sarah into? I almost said that he should have said something about that earlier, but things had been going bang, bang, bang . . . Then I remembered the book on cults. If they could reprogram an adult's mind, what could they do to a child's? I was not imagining those black cars.

"I didn't do nothing."

Of course he would say that. He sounded believable. Of course he would.

"Any judgments? Police record? Paper trail? Anything like that we need to know about?" I kept my voice neutral, friendly. After all, DeSam and I had been buddies, sort of, up until a minute ago or so.

He shook his head. "He said, she said. Cindy didn't remember anything like that so the referee just strongly suggested I let her live with Sonja or it might come up again. I couldn't afford to fight it, so I did what they said and never heard any more about it. Nothing I could do about it, I thought. I couldn't afford a lawyer. I think the referee could tell Sonja was lying, but she had to cover her rear end and clear her case.

"Now, Cindy's older and has been hearing this crap for a half dozen years. I don't know what she thinks about it, but the last time I was allowed to talk to her, she was kindof guarded. But she didn't like the cult. That was, uh, a couple years ago."

I checked the phone. Time to go. I needed a private conversation with Dick.

"DeSam, better take a pit stop. See if you can find that bug again. Then head for the car."

As soon as he was gone, I called Dick. He wasn't happy but reckoned he could do the background check we should have done earlier on his pad. I clicked off and moved to the diner's window. No. A couple of late model black sedans went through, but didn't look like my guy. My guy would probably stop. Or not, thinking that I would think that, so drive through and double back to try to surprise me. But anticipating that I would anticipate that, they might come back on foot instead of in the car. No, if we were in a car we'd get away too quickly. But not if he knew we weren't in the car . . .

The server came with the bill and I gave her my card. She looked at the name and did a double take.

"Something wrong?" I asked.

"Uh, you've got the same name as an author I've read. "

A coincidence, I hoped.

"The Tractor that Ate Seattle?"

Why now? I smiled, professionally. "Ashland, not Seattle. Yeah, that's me and I'm glad you liked it, but we've gotta get going here."

"Something big and steamy chasing you?" She giggled.

At that point, DeSam arrived.

"Something like that. Could you just process the bill? Wait a minute, maybe I have enough cash." I grabbed my wallet and started fumbling through it. I should have hit an ATM before zooming out.

"Maybe I can help?" DeSam said, and pulled out a couple of 20s.

The goons came in the door and started looking around. I was in front of DeSam and had a baseball cap on.

"You keep the change ma'am," DeSam said, quickly. "They's after us. Gotta back door?"

She nodded and ushered us out through the kitchen. We sprinted for the van. It started; I momentarily wondered what the trade was between taking the time to disable the car versus coming after us right away like they apparently did as I pulled out of the parking lot and onto

US 97 North for a couple of blocks. I'd have to come back south, but that's the way the car was pointed when I parked it in back of the diner, and maybe I'd confuse them. In doing so, I passed a barbershop.

DeSam was wearing my clothes, riding in a borrowed car. Where the heck could they hide a microtag on him? I glanced over at that afro haircut of his leaking out from under the ball cap. Hmmm. I now knew exactly what I'd look for in the Wal-Mart in Bend!

We were down there in forty-five minutes with no sign of the goons.

I got a set of barber's clippers at Wal-Mart in about fifteen minutes.

A couple hours later we were in Burn at the Half Moon Bookstore, about ten minutes before closing. Celeste greeted me with one of her all encompassing hugs, the package from Dick, and $12.65 for my share of a year's worth of sales. That was actually very good; writers, don't quit your day job. Dick had explained the mission, and Celeste offered us the back room.

Dick's gadget, which he'd mounted in an old smart phone shell, showed the tracker bug was on DeSam, but its Good catch! sensor saturated near him, so we couldn't pin down just where.

Celeste offered to search his hair, and there seemed something vaguely erotic about that that had them both smiling, but, as I feared, she didn't find the chip; those things are down to the size of a baby aspirin tablet.

"Dick thinks this gadget will zap the thing, but it's likely to zap you as well. I'm not sure there would be any long term effects, but it's several orders of magnitudes more RF than people worry about from cell phones."

DeSam frowned. "Well, if sacrifices have to be made . . . I don't want it on me, lettin' those people follow me around."

"I have an alternative sacrifice in mind." I pulled out the barber's clippers I'd gotten at Wal-Mart.

"The George Foreman look," he groaned.

"You're dating yourself," Celeste said.

"Jeez, just when afros were getting back in style."

There was a knock on the door out front. Celeste hit a monitor on her desk, which sprung to life and showed a goon at the door, black car on the street outside.

"You play barber," Celeste, not a small woman, told me. "I'll deal with this." She opened the desk drawer and pulled out a Glock.

DeSam's eyes got wide.

"Don't worry, that's just normal out here," I said.

"You just get buzzing, okay?"

I did. I put the hair in a plastic bag as it came off. We could see the front on another cam — Celeste had three views up on her display. She opened the door a crack. It had a chain, so it stayed that way when the goon tried to push his way in.

"I'm closed." Celeste shouted.

"Open up, or I'll break down . . . oh."

I couldn't see much from where I was, but I guessed "oh" meant that he'd seen the Glock. Anyway, "break down" sounded like a violent threat to me so I called 911.

"Look," the goon said. "You don't want trouble with us. We're after a" — he used the n-word — "and an old hippie type. They're in here."

I don't resemble that remark; he must have me confused with Dick. Which meant they were after him, too. Not good.

"Maybe and maybe not," Celeste said, stalling. "Just what do you intend to do?"

"Ya know, I don't think you have the guts to use that thing, so just get out of the way . . . "

He didn't get to find out, because of sound of sirens coming up the street interrupted his line of inquiry."

"It's all recorded," Celeste said, helpfully.

Somebody yelled from the car, and the goon vanished.

Celeste returned to the back room with a box in hand. In it was a copy of *The Tractor that Ate Ashland*.

Responding to my look, she said. "I figured you might want to donate that to the State Police down the street. We'll use that," she gestured to bag with DeSam's hair in it, "for packing. If somewhere in there is a GPS locater chip, the goons might think DeSam is a guest of the State Police. They might have a hard time explaining why they thought that." She turned to DeSam, "More like Kareem, I'd say."

That broke up DeSam and we joined in. It took a couple of minutes for us to stop laughing. Then I used Dick's gadget to verify the microchip was in the bag.

Then there was a knock on the door.

The State Police we'd called wanted in. They'd pursued, but lost the goon car and wanted explanations. Explaining was a calculated risk, but most of these guys were straight. After we showed them Celeste's security recording, one of them allowed as much as they wouldn't mind an excuse to stick it to the cult — apparently there had been other run-ins. There usually were, with an operation like that.

Somewhere in all of this, I'd totally forgotten about the allegations of DeSam being a child abuser. It came back in a rush; now was the time to say something about that to the police.

I didn't. I had to think it through, first.

After the police left with their donated, autographed copy of my book in its box, I spent about double my share of the Half Moon book sales on dinner at the Highlander.

★ ❋ ★

Oh-dark-30 the next morning found Dick and his equipment in Rome and DeSam and I bound for the west side of the Ram's Head ridge. Dunce Farm Road was paved so no problem there. The good news was that the cutoff road was paved, too, all the way past the compound and past the butte and over to US 95. The cult had money. The bad news was that none of the trails around it were packed down — when the cult put in the roads, people stopped driving on the sand trails and loose sand accumulates where they aren't packed down by repeated use. The road was it, and the goons had ID'd at least one of our vehicles.

We would stay in shadow on this side of the ridge until nine or so. I found a wash about the right size that looked pretty smooth and got DeSam out with a walking stick to probe the sand. Solid crust anyway, maybe hardpan. I backed in gingerly until we'd be pretty hard to spot, and waited.

Dizzy ran on batteries, and had a few watts of photovoltaic feathers for endurance, but it would be a couple hours before the sun was high enough to keep him in the air continuously. We'd need him for com, so we'd have to wait to start the op. I probably should have spent the time probing DeSam, getting to know him better. But what I did, and he did, was to put the seats back and catch up on our sleep.

Dick's call woke me up. Dizzy was overhead and doing recce. The cult's kitchen had started smoking, and he thought we'd locate Cindy coming or going from breakfast. I nudged DeSam.

"Dizzy cam is live," I said. "Dawn is on her way in. Time to start looking."

"Okay. What am I looking at?"

"It's the compound from about two thousand feet and a mile off to the side. Highly processed to take out the motion and improve resolution, but it will jump a bit."

"Okay. That building with the steam coming out . . . "

"It's the kitchen and dining facility."

"Got it. I think the dorms are east of that, closer to the ridge."

"Still kind of dark there."

"Yeah. Hold on. Here comes someone. Seen him before, one of cult staff. Big feller. In the shadow now."

I looked. The shadow line was about halfway from the dining area to where the dorms were. People going out of it were facing right into the Sun. It would, I thought, be really hard to see a vulture in that direction. Dick thought so too, and brought Dizzy closer as people started filing out of the dining room.

"That's my ex, I think," DeSam said. "In the blue hood. Cindy's not with her."

We kept watching, and watching. No Cindy. Finally, people

stopped coming out. Dick said he'd start scanning other places. The main road in the compound ran roughly north-south. Their fields were south, towards the Ram's Head butte; five big green circles. The north was all packed sand and tin-roof sheds. There was a big church in the middle.

"Some activity there," DeSam said.

A big silver-haired man in a monkish robe, hood down, was coming out holding the hand of a young woman. I recognized him.

"It's McGrud himself," I said.

"That could be Cindy" DeSam said.

"Could be?"

"It's been a couple years; she's growing, my eyes aren't as good as they used to be."

"If I bring Dizzy any closer," Dick said, "they might get suspicious and I'll lose line of sight from where I am." He was on the other side of the Ramshead ridge, of course. "I can tell Dizzy to record, then reascend."

"You talk to him? I mean it," DeSam asked.

"It's just a figure of speech," I said

"No, Ed," Dick laughed. "DeSam's right. I talk to him — natural language voice interface. I installed it a couple months ago."

It occurred to me that Dizzy was looking north, up the central road of the compound. McGrud was dragging the girl toward a white gate that crossed the road before the maintenance area. I looked out the window to the south and laughed.

"Dick, I wouldn't worry about Dizzy's cover; he's got company."

At least five other vultures circled with him, looking for the food they thought Dizzy'd found.

The Dizzy cam shifted view, and Dick laughed. "I need to do that more often."

"We call it situation awareness."

"Guys, Cindy's in the situation right now," DeSam said.

"Sorry, DeSam," Dick said and shifted the view back.

"Jeez," DeSam said.

It was apparent, even from a mile away, that McGrud was wearing nothing under that monk's robe."

"Ed, can you break out that ultrasound controller for Dawn?"

"Uh, sure." I found the backpack and got it out.

"I'm sending Dawn in on a low pass. She might distract McGrud. You may need to control."

"Huh?"

"Someone's knocking on my door," he said hurriedly. "Buttons. Right, left, up, down, fast and slow in the center. Dizzy's going to do the recce pass then go back up. Everything will be off line for a while, but it will come back. He'll respond to your voice . . . gotta go now!"

"Jeez," DeSam said again as everything went black.

I grabbed the binoculars and scrambled out of the car and looked up in sky over the compound to the south. One of the circling vultures was headed down. That must be Dizzy. Another bird was heading to the circle of vultures, significantly bigger, with bat like wings. I took the controller and tapped "right" and it began to circle with them. Okay, that was Dawn.

Dizzy flew back up enough to reestablish the link.

"That's Cindy," DeSam said. "They's going through that gate; Lord knows what gonna happen on the other side!"

"Dick?"

No answer. I tapped another link.

"Sarah?"

"On the road, I should be there in ten."

McGrud and Cindy were through the gate, and he was on a cell, or radiophone. Different rules for those in charge.

Drone blasters?

"Dizzy can you hear me?"

"I can."

"Go back up and join the other birds, quickly."

"You want me to ascend. You want me to circle with other vultures."

"Yes, quickly."

"I have to do this like a vulture to avoid suspicion."

Trust Dick Princeton, that robot vulture was smart.

"We already have suspicion. Quickly. Quickly."

"I understand, quickly. I am ascending at maximum rate."

He was.

"The picture's getting fuzzier," DeSam complained.

"Yeah, they might be onto Dizzy somehow. We're going to have to watch from further away. Far enough, away, I hoped. Time for a distraction.

When Dawn was headed the right direction, I blew into the device and hit the left key button until she straightened out. Tap right, tap left, tap, tap and she was headed more or less toward us over the main compound street. I tapped down, then up, and studied the controller a bit more. I had six other buttons; off, on, take off, land, emergency land, dispense, and squawk/flame. Dawn wasn't as bright a bird as Dizzy, but what do you expect from a Cretaceous critter? I tapped "up" until she leveled off at about thirty feet. Dawn might be dumb, but she obeyed instantly and didn't give me any backtalk.

"Dizzy, can you zoom out your camera? I need to see more."

"I can zoom out."

"Zoom out . . . okay stop zoom."

I tapped right and left until I got Dawn headed right toward

McGrud. When I was about fifty feet from him, I hit "squawk." I could hear it from where we were.

He looked up, then started yelling into his mobile. Drone blaster, I figured, and smiled.

Cindy used the opportunity to break free and start running away. That answered a whole bunch of questions.

I flew Dawn lower to the point where McGrud hit the dirt, flew past Cindy, and hit "dispense." From Dizzy's cam, I could see something hit the dust in the road ahead of Cindy. I tapped up before Dawn hit the fence at the north of the compound and kept her ascending to a couple hundred feet.

We started seeing dropouts and missing lines on the feed from Dizzy's camera. Lots of electromagnetic interference, I thought. Drone blasters. But they had the wrong drone.

Cindy stood over the bubble-wrapped package. Come on, girl, I thought. It has your name on it. Finally she bent down and picked it up.

DeSam's phone rang; some notes from "The Entertainer."

"Yes baby, we're just outside," he answered. "You wanna get out?"

"Jeez, okay, just try to stay calm. Ed, he's coming back."

Blow. Tap, tap, tap, tap . . . . Dawn straightened out again and descended, right at McGrud. I hit the squawk/flame key.

McGrud pulled a gun out of the pocket of his robe.

Maybe if I held the squawk button down?

A beautiful yellow flame shot out of Dawn's mouth, and McGrud hit the dirt.

I tapped up, up, up; a gun would definitely damage Dawn. I leveled her out at about a thousand feet. A light on the controller came on: "fuel." That flame had been costly.

McGrud got himself up and started after Cindy. She wasn't looking, head in the phone.

"DeSam!" I yelled. "He's going after her; she should run!" Run where, was my next thought.

DeSam yelled into the phone. It all took too long; we watched McGrud grab Cindy, rip the cell from her hands and stomp it.

Black cars showed up on the cutoff extension, headed for our position. A tan sedan, Sarah's, was on the road, too, ahead of them — -a veritable traffic jam for this part of the country.

I tapped Sarah's number. "Watch out, goon cars."

"Right. Nice and slow, minding my own business. I'm a paleontologist doing field work," she said. "I'm alone, I've got my hair up and am wearing dark glasses. No worries."

She was right. The goons might have seen her with Dick, but they'd have no idea who she was.

"Time to call the State Police," I told DeSam

"Done. Take 'em half an hour to get down here, though, and those guys are probably monitoring Police comm. McGrud's got her robe off," he said coldly. "She's wearing a long gray shirt underneath . . . " Completely helpless, he was going to have to watch his daughter get assaulted. "Damn, damn, damn . . . ."

The black cars had pulled Sarah over and were talking to her.

Dick Princeton was out of com, out the picture.

"Let's pull out of here," I said, scrambling back into the car.

"Too late," DeSam said.

There was a black car blocking our way out of our hiding place.

The fuel light on the controller was steady on. Sorry, Dick, I thought.

What Dawn did next was under control of its simpleminded fluidic flight controller. As its air pressure reservoir was below a critical value, it had to land. It used its echo locator to locate the sheds on one side of the street and the fence on the other, banked right to put itself between them, straightened out, and descended with its beak pointed right at McGrud and Cindy, who were standing in the middle of the street. Dawn hooted a programmed warning.

McGrud looked up, brought his gun up, shot, and missed badly. Dawn kept coming.

Cindy broke away and ran for a nearby shed.

McGrud tried another shot, then looked away at Cindy and brought his gun around.

Dawn, almost on top of McGrud, hooted again. McGrud lurched away from the seven-meter wings, tripped over the side of the road, stumbled backward down its embankment and into his own electric fence.

There he stayed and twitched. The twitching was probably not of his own volition; there was smoke.

"Pacemaker," DeSam said with a kind of wicked smile.

In the meantime, Dawn executed a perfect landing and stood motionless in the middle of the street about 20 feet from the gate, out of fuel. The goons in the car in front of us were staying in the car, maybe talking on their phones. It looked like there might be just enough room in front of them before the roadbed got too steep to climb.

"Buckle up, DeSam. I think we got room, but . . . "

He clicked as I gunned it. We made it by inches bottoming on the curb with a scary bang but kept going and had a quarter mile lead before the goons in the car blocking us woke up. The goons with Sarah abruptly jumped in their cars and started after us, too. She jumped in her car and followed discreetly behind.

"Back on line," Dick Princeton said, into all of this.

DeSam gave him the situation report.

"We've got to fly her out of there quick," Dick said.

"The drone or Cindy?" DeSam asked.

"Dawn. Cindy's too heavy. Sorry. Sarah's almost there, if we can get Cindy through that fence. DeSam, call her back, there's a second phone inside Dawn. Lets see if we can get her to it."

There had to be some air left in the reservoir. "DeSam, the controller's in the back seat. Blow in it and try the Squawk button."

He found it. "I'll try an SOS."

"Does she know Morse code?"

He shook his head. "Nah, just that much. That's all I taught her anyway."

We didn't hear anything, of course, but Cindy came out of the shed.

DeSam saw her and did the SOS again. She came over to Dawn.

"Try 'dispense'" Dick suggested. "Then call her. Same number as the other phone."

DeSam gave me the controller and I hit "dispense" as DeSam pecked away at his phone.

After an agonizing minute: "Hello?" came out of the phone.

"Cindy, can you hear me?" DeSam asked

"Daddy?"

"Yeah, Cindy. Are you okay?"

"Just fine for now."

"Ask her if they have some propane cans in those sheds," Dick said.

"I heard that," Cindy said.

"Yeah, that's Mr. Princeton," DeSam said.

"They've got tractors and stuff in there, gas cans too," Cindy said.

"Any propane canisters?"

"Like for camp stoves? Yeah, they got those too. Why?"

"We've got to try to get Dawn flying again. She's the . . . uh . . . . big bird that squawked at McGrud."

"She's a Pteranodon, Daddy, not a bird."

"Okay, okay. Anyone likely to come by?"

"No. He takes me out here because nobody else is out here to see what he does. I think he's got a special lock to the gate; nobody else ever comes in when he's here."

Dick told her where Dawn's canister was, and in ten minutes, Cindy got it out, found a replacement in the shed and had the canisters swapped.

"She's purring," Cindy said.

"The engine's running. Dawn needs a couple of minutes, then she'll be okay."

"I think they're trying to break the gate down."

The crashes were audible in the cell phone."

"Okay, Cindy, turn Dawn around and point her down the road.

Then head for the fence."

"The body's down there," I said.

"Don't bother me *one bit*," Cindy said.

Sarah called in. "I'm here on the other side of the road. The coast is clear for now."

"Any long two-by-fours or anything like that in the shed?" I asked

"Yeah . . . "

"If you take that down to the fence and shove it under, Sarah can hold the bottom of the fence up enough for you to crawl out."

"Sarah?"

"She's a thin woman with dark glasses and a big cowboy hat."

"Okay."

We heard a significant bang at the gate.

"Run, Cindy!" DeSam said.

We watched on the screen as a jeep hit the gate and made it buckle, backed off, then rammed it again.

Cindy found a two-by-four propped up against the building, grabbed it, and headed for the fence.

On the third try, the gate broke down and the Jeep started crawling over it.

"Now or never," Dick said. "At least it's downhill a bit. Dawn took a step and a hop, spread her wings, hit ground with her knuckles on the first flap, but that pushed her up and into the air. The second flap just missed the ground as she gathered speed, then altitude. The jeep rode over the broken gate and chased her with a blown tire.

Sarah got the fence up and Cindy was out. They got in the car, turned around, then pulled over to the side as the goons zipped by going the other way followed by the Oregon State Police, flashing lights and sounding their C-G-C sirens.

We gave them some space, then followed Sarah in the opposite direction.

"Keep going to New Princeton," Dick sent. "It's my something times great Granddaddy's town — re NO re, the town was actually moved; that's why it's now called "New Princeton" moved some. We'll meet at the Post Office.

Meanwhile, Dawn beat the Jeep with the flat tires to the compound fence, soared over it and kept flying over our heads.

In the New Princeton Post Office parking lot, Cindy exploded out of Sarah's car and leapt into DeSam's arms. What remained of the pit of uncertainty in my stomach went away in an instant.

"Ed," Sarah asked, "you okay?"

I nodded weakly, totally drained and leaning on Claire's van. "Yeah. I just bet the farm and won. But that was way too close." I was an okay judge of people, but I was going to be a bit more careful next time.

★ ❋ ★

Time has passed.

Sarah and Dick are still an item. "Experimental Flight Mechanics of a Full Scale Model Dawndraco *kanzai*," appeared in Paleontology last fall. They described ten minute flights with the pressure reservoir — Dick's printed steam-powered compressor is still under cover.

DeSam has full custody of Cindy; his ex having vanished along with a number of other now-wanted people just before the State Police arrived.

The New People of God dissolved within the year. Some of its former members told tales of God, or Satan, sending a fire breathing Dragon from the sky to punish Mr. McGrud. Others told tales of what he was punished for. The latter were believed.

STORY NOTES

This was my second anthology contribution for the Northwest group of Campcon writers. The anthology title, Steam and Dragons in fact suggested the title, and I went from there. I used the set of characters as in "The Off Switch." It was great fun playing with characters Ed Miller and his backwoods inventor friend Dick Princeton again, but the story also involves a couple of serious issues. One is electronics-free UAVs invulnerable to electronic countermeasures (i.e. drone blasters) and very hard to distinguish from actual flying animals--non threatening in our protagonists hands but keep in mind that technology is a word, not an actor, and has no moral sense. The other is the horrific damage done to people by some authoritarian religious cults; these did not vanish in the seventies and eighties, but keep recurring.

GDN October 2021

RUN, LAGOMORPH

The creek gurgled with white water and white noise. Orion winked through the pine trees while Leo, with Mars, shone brilliantly from just over the treetops. John Williams conducted memories through my ear buds, and my second Black Butte Porter was almost gone. A three-beer night? I'd done twenty pages today and felt uncommonly good, and the ears on the glowing rabbit by the picnic table seemed to twitch in approval. I lifted my mug to my lips and finished the draught.

Yeah, it took about that long for the glowing bunny's presence to sink into my critical awareness.

I shut my eyes as Wallace and Washington's "Pink Elephants on Parade" began to crowd the "Imperial March" out of my head. I shook my head, opened my eyes and the glowing rabbit was still there. Experimentally, I shut one eye, then the other. Still there. I paused the "Imperial March." Still there. Most definitely not a pachyderm. Wallace and Washington began to fade from my mind, as I contemplated the glowing rabbit.

On the slopes of Mount Hood, I was a fair distance from the Hanford nuclear reservation where such things were rumored to exist, courtesy of World War II and cold war expediency combined with ignorance and budget problems. Well, rabbits run. Maybe a rabbit, I thought, raised on a diet of grass grown in tritium-contaminated water, then painted with a phosphor encapsulated in nanobeads . . .

"Mr. Miller, will you help me?" the rabbit asked in a high pitched and raspy whisper that was just barely audible. "Pink Elephants" made a second appearance in my head, to be banished by a vigorous headshake.

"Sorry to bother you," the rabbit said.

"No, no," I said before it could jump away. "I'm just trying to clear my head. This is very, ah, unexpected."

"I can understand that."

"How did you know my name?"

"It's on the reservation sign at the front of your campsite."

"Of course. You can read."

"One has plenty of spare time in a cage lined with newspaper in a lab with closed captioned monitor television shows."

"Uh, do you have a name?"

"Yes, but since I'm being sought, I'd rather not burden you with it. I'm a *Lepus townsendi*, obviously GM. I guess you can call me Jack."

"Jack Rabbit," I said.

"Well, Jack Hare would be more precise, but we have more pressing matters. Is it possible to go some place where I am less visible?"

"In the tent. I'll turn the light on." I was going to need that third Black Butte anyway, I thought.

At age 53, to save my back, I'd gotten myself a tent I could stand up in. I grabbed another Porter out of the cooler, plopped down on the steel folding chair — the back again — and waved my arm around. "Make yourself at home."

Jack settled in off my left side, where he could see both me and the entrance.

I was forgetting my manners. "Do you want some beer?"

"That would be an interesting experiment for some other time. We're about to have company." Jack hopped under my cot, hidden by a towel hanging over the edge.

Huh? "Jack?"

A confused minute later, I heard voices outside the tent.

"Miller? Ed Miller," someone with a gruff basso voice inquired.

I got up, pushed the flap aside, exited to find two six-foot-plus men, one heavy, one rangy, suited in camou with rifles. I zipped the screen flap back in place. "Bugs," I explained. "What can I do for you?"

"This is going to seem a bit strange."

"Try me. I'm a science fiction writer."

"There's a mutant rabbit on the loose. It glows kind of a lime green if it's really dark. We need to bring it back."

I nodded to the rifles. "Safe?"

"Uh," They looked at each other.

I patted my right crew pants pocket as if there were something other than a cell phone in it.

"Okay," Heavy said. Rangy shrugged and satisfying clicks ensued.

That would give Jack maybe another second if he bolted — might be enough.

"I don't know of any mutation that would make a rabbit glow."

"That's what they . . . " Heavy started before Rangy jabbed him with an elbow. Too late.

"Who's "they?" I asked.

"Nobody. We're just hunting rabbits."

"Glowing rabbits?"

"From Hanford. All sorts of weird stuff up there."

"Why?"

"Damn it, have you seen a glowing rabbit or not?"

I raised my Porter bottle. "Working on it."

"Look," Rangy said. "It's not funny. Radiation. Isotopes. Mutations. Can't have that stuff running around loose. We can't say who we're working for and they didn't tell us much. Classified, understand? Now, if you say anything we'll have to shoot you . . . "

I started to reach for my cell phone . . . .

"Or have you picked up or something," Heavy added, quickly.

"My guess, gentlemen, and it's just a guess, is that the authorities would be much more interested in you than me. I'm retired Air Force and still have some connections. Now . . . " I summoned a command voice I hadn't used since Officer's Training School, "Just what is going on here?"

They actually backed up two steps. Heavy's mouth was a line, his eyes wide and looking from side to side. He might be anticipating action nobody else should see.

Rangy sighed. "We work part time for a guy who has a contract with Halfast Biotech Science who have leased buildings on Hanford. I told him that we'd run into people who wouldn't buy the B.S. cover story, I just didn't think it would be the first one. We'll likely be let go if you blab about this . . . " He sighed. " . . . but I have to start somewhere. Something got out that hops and glows in the dark. I dunno what makes it glow in the dark. Maybe not radiation, because we didn't get any radiation hazard briefing, equipment, or anything. But they really want it back."

"Dead or alive?" I asked.

"We aren't really equipped for 'alive,'" Heavy growled.

"Yeah, I can see that. You have a card with a phone number?"

Rangy shrugged, reached in his pocket, and showed me a card. "It's some doctor at the lab we're supposed to notify. Can you take a picture? It's the only card I have."

I did, and sent them off into the woods.

Once I was inside the tent with the flap zipped closed, Jack nosed slowly out from under the cot, quivering like it was already down to the thirties.

"Th . . . th . . . th . . . thank you."

"You heard every thing?"

He twitched his ears. "They're much better than yours."

"Were you intentional or a mistake?"

"Both. It's complicated; I don't know the whole history, but what I do know would take hours to relate. Some of my litter mates share some of my traits, but not all. We're all supposed to be sterile. But they aren't taking chances."

"Do they know you can talk?"

"Only one, Dr. Janet Jones, and she disappeared. That's one reason I escaped. I wanted to vanish on my own terms. How long until morning?"

"About eight hours. Why?"

He trembled. "I can rest during the day. At night I have to keep moving."

"You should be safe here. I have a cardboard box that would keep your light in."

"That was well meant, but I'm a hare, not a rabbit. I have to be able to see and hear around me, otherwise I get very nervous."

"Don't you sleep?"

"A few minutes at a time, during the day. That's instinctual but also necessary, if you glow. But I find I have to forage during the day, too. I haven't been able to stop moving at night long enough to eat."

"Okay. Do you know who this is?" I showed him the card picture. He shivered harder. "Craig. Dr. Craig Morton. He's the one who said I should be terminated. Janet argued about that and he told her that she might not be around much longer, either. I assume he meant fired; I haven't seen any humans killed except on TV. But Janet was gone the next day and her desk in the lab corner was still full of stuff."

Dr. Craig Morton was the name on the card.

So, I had a missing scientist, an illegal or at least protocol-skirting gene lab, and an intelligent hare in jeopardy for its life and needing a refuge. It was, I figured, time to visit Dick Princeton. First, though, I had a bag of those bite-sized carrots in my cooler. I got it out and offered one to Jack. "Rabbit food, I know. But it's all I've got." I ate one myself.

"It will do. I'm very hungry."

★ ✻ ★

I sent an email Dick's way, packed up the next morning, was on my way east with Jack. Dick lives on a ridge on a private road uphill west of Mill Creek Road, just outside the Park. He's got a couple single-wides with a roof between them and a couple of prefab storage buildings in a clearing on the hilltop — home to a home-built radio telescope, an optical telescope, and all manner of electronic experiments.

Halfway up the road, Jack shuddered and jumped down to the van's floor.

A minute later a turkey vulture buzzed us and rocked its wings. We were expected. Once again, I marveled at Jack's sight and hearing.

"That's not a real vulture, Jack. It's, Dizzy, a drone Dick made to look like one."

"A vulture? I can see it now, but my instincts said 'eagle.' Do vultures ever attack like that?"

"Hmm. We'll have to talk to Dick about that; could be a giveaway. People aren't supposed to know about Dizzy."

"Can Dizzy, see as well as a real eagle or vulture?"

"Better. His optical resolution is only a little better, but it covers everything from UV to near infrared."

"Could . . . he find Dr. Janet?"

"That's what I'm going to ask Dick."

★ ※ ★

Dick and Sarah came out to greet us. Sarah and Jack seemed to hit it off immediately. She bent down to shake Jack's right front foot, which he offered by standing as tall as he could, which was about four feet, ear tips to toes.

Dick's summer dining room was a picnic table between the two single-wides. I'd brought the carrots. Jack told us about his genetic modifications.

"They were trying brain densification — more neurons per cubic centimeter — to see if it would increase hare intelligence. In the next lab, they were working on human brain structure replacement cores, grown in animal hosts, for treatment of stroke victims and some developmental disorders. What happened next was complicated . . . "

Jack related what he'd told me, in somewhat more detail.

" . . . so I have hundreds of times the number of synapses you have and in a millionth the volume — less communication distance, so faster."

Jack twitched his ears. "My hearing is as good as you might guess; once I figured out English, I could tune into any conversation in the building and to maybe a couple hundred meters around. To a first approximation, I've learned what a state-of-the-art genetically modified organism researcher knows and remember it better."

"Including a lot of human personal life," I guessed.

Jack sighed. "Inevitably. I also know that they want me back before anyone else finds out what they did. They intend to terminate me."

"Do they know you are, uh, aware?"

"Yes. But not how much aware. They think I'm about at the level of Koko the gorilla or Alex the parrot, who were much discussed in my presence. They thought about keeping me around, but publishing the research on me would involve admitting their mistake. I played dumb bunny until my caretaker vanished a couple of days ago. Then I took the first opportunity to escape that came along. Now there is a small army with night vision goggles looking for me. They don't really need the goggles. I'm terrified, and hungry."

"You're equipped to forage and shelter in the wild," Dick said. "We can do it, too, but it's uncomfortable, time consuming, and takes a lot of work." He looked at me, "Even for those who think it's fun."

I chuckled.

Jack's nose twitched. "Typical hares live for maybe two or three years in their natural habitat. We can live a dozen or so with humans. My problem is that, despite all of this brain power, I have no learned experience for being a hare in the wild. I don't know what all I can eat. Another problem is that I'm constantly driven by all the evolutionary fears and appetites of a male jackrabbit. I can resist them, but it requires constant and exhausting vigilance." He trembled as he spoke, with his eyes fixed on Sarah.

I couldn't read the expression on Sarah's face. Jack was soft, cuddly, lovable, and he glowed. You wouldn't think twice about putting him on your lap, stroking, scratching and tickling him. But he had a mind, a voice, and was male to an extent that I probably couldn't comprehend. Nor could I comprehend how that package might affect Sarah, or affect Dick watching it affect Sarah.

If any of this human drama were affecting Jack (and why should it?) he gave no sign but just kept quivering and talking.

"My modifications were before differentiation; they affect my sperm; my offspring might not be as smart as I am, but they would be quite effective at evading predators and denuding the landscape. So it would be very irresponsible for me to mate with other lagomorphs. But mating with another species with the right chemistry could be exciting and might not be so dangerous."

"Who took care of you at the lab?"

Jack's ears twitched. "Jessica . . . no, Janet. Dr. Janet Jones. She made me a nice yard outside the lab that they kept planted with grass and bushes and a deep warm soft nest. I'm pretty sure it had a camera on it, but I couldn't figure out where it was."

"How did you get books," I asked, "and light to read them?" Everyone, including Jack stared at me. "Oops. Sorry."

"I can't turn that off, either," Jack said. "I did my reading surreptitiously, on a monitor, or cage papers, or from Janet's lap. I miss her."

"Poor bunny," Sarah said, her voice full of compassion. She picked him up and cradled him in her arms. Something passed between Dick and Sarah.

Dick shrugged and smiled. "Ed, let's see about getting some intel on the GMO compound. We'll get Dizzy and Bizzy both on it."

Dizzy was his ornithopter drone turkey vulture. "Bizzy?" I asked

"Dizzy Mark Two, with bigger batteries and a faster brain. It looks less suspicious if there are two of them, acting like buzzards. Come on. We should be back in a couple of hours or so, Sarah."

She smiled, stroking Jack. "No problems. Jack and I have something to do. We'll be back about 8 pm."

I imagined I could see his glow even in the day lit room. I gave them a quick smile and followed Dick out the door.

"She started out as a bio major and added the geology later," Dick said as we hoofed it up to the baseball-diamond sized hilltop clearing where Dick's equipment sheds were. The robot vultures stood like gargoyle statues beside a shed under its overhang.

"Igor?" Igor was Dick's home-built computer system that ran his single-wides, sheds, and anything else Dick wanted it to do.

"Yes, Dick?"

"Open the shed door and also check the Tri-City police departments for missing person reports for a Dr. Janet Jones. "

"There are none."

It took only milliseconds. I was impressed.

"Hmm, Igor, find her home address and give it to Dizzy and Bizzy and have them make video. Off you go, guys."

The vultures walked over to the center of the green and, with a few soft flaps, they were on their way.

★ ※ ★

Dizzy and Bizzy got back a couple of hours later. We went over the video. There was no sign of Dr. Jones, but . . . I hit the pause icon.

"Dick, that's the rangy guy, one of the hunters that questioned me."

"Who's that with him? I've seen him, somewhere. Let's get a face recognition window over him."

In less than a minute, we had our answer. "It's Dr. Craig Morton, the guy on the card Rangy gave me."

"To the right with the gun," I added, "that's Heavy."

Dick grunted. "So all that talk about just being a low on the totem pole hunter under a contract to middlemen, etcetera, was B.S. He's working directly for Morton."

"Looks like," I said.

Dick and I kept at the vulture's video until Sarah and Jack showed up.

"Find something?" Sarah asked.

Dick explained and played back the video.

"Stop!" Sarah said. "She pointed to a sunlit face in an open door on the north side of the largest building. "Is that Dr. Jones? It looks like she's taking a smoke break."

Some of the smoke happened to drift out the door into the sunlight.

"Missed that," Jack said. "Let me try to get a spectrum on that." Dick said. A couple minutes later, he stroked his beard and said, "Ayup, not tobacco. Face recognition time."

It was indeed Dr. Janet Jones. She was smoking pot.

"Nervous, maybe?" I asked.

Dick laughed. He looked the classic sixties hippie. But to the best of my knowledge, he didn't drink, shoot, smoke or gamble, and never had. "Boots on the ground time," he said. "Ed, Think could you get in there?"

I'm a sometime science journalist, and was already part of this. It could be perfectly reasonable for me to show up on their doorstep.

"Maybe. Could Dizzy take Jack in and out?" I asked.

"Jacks a big, well-fed hare," Sarah said, "maybe four kilos. I think all Dizzy can lift is two or maybe three."

Dick nodded, but with that far off look that said his head was elsewhere.

"Okay. Jack," I asked, "are you willing to go in with me? You're much better built for snooping."

Jack shook like a leaf.

"Janet may need you," Sarah said.

"I can do it." Jack said. "Let's show them what we did."

"First we need to turn the lights out," she said.

With the lights out, Jack glowed. But then Sarah covered Jack with something that blocked the glow, except for maybe a trickle of light where the covering touched the floor.

"Its a bunny suit!" Dick said.

"More like a hare suit," Jack said, emitting a slight glow as he talked.

"Okay, Jack, jump!" Sarah commanded, when our eyes had night-adapted to the point where we could see what was happening, however dimly.

Jack jumped almost to the ceiling. His glowing hind legs flashed briefly on the way down

"Laminated graphene," Sarah said. "I just printed it an hour ago; it's very thin. The eye holes and mouth holes were tricky. I had to leave the hind legs unencumbered; it's like the rabbit . . . er hare, equivalent of a hooded bathrobe, but it should work."

"I can go out to dinner!" Jack exclaimed. "Sarah showed me what I can eat."

"Okay," Dick said. "But stay around the clearing. I'll have Dizzy and Bizzy on the shed roofs as lookouts. As long as they don't have to fly, they can stay there all night on batteries."

While Jack foraged, we made plans for the next day.

★ ❊ ★

I contacted the lab. I'd done a Popular Aerospace article on bioengineered birds about a decade ago and used that, and Dr. Morton's card image, as "credentials" and got an appointment with a Halfast information officer, an appropriately named Miss Twitter. I'd get a sanitized tour and maybe a few minutes with Dr. William Koglitz, Halfast's COO, if he had time, and Dr. Morton. They said they normally wouldn't do this on such short notice, but, as I hoped, Dr. Morton had recognized the name and wanted to talk to me.

Sarah came with me as my assistant. Her story, if they asked, was that she was moonlighting — learning the trade. In reality, I had more to learn from her.

We rode in her car, a clean, shiny, respectable late model Ford — one of a paleontologist's jobs these days was putting the bite on wealthy donors. Jack rode in the back seat, in a white version of the hare suit, with a pink ribbon around his neck next to a toy piano and a Nerf ball, equipped with an audiovisual collar that communicated, spread spectrum, with the robot vultures in KVVK's frequency slot. If you tuned into Las Amazonas, you'd be getting slightly more than you tuned in for, but wouldn't know it. Probably illegal, I thought, but Dick's philosophy was what the feds didn't know wouldn't hurt him.

The plan was to park on the far side of the lot on the south side of the admin building with the right door facing south, away from the surveillance camera. Jack would ditch the white hare suit in the back seat, slip under the driver's seat and, when Dizzy said the coast was clear, push the door open — Sarah would leave it ajar when she left with me — and hide until we left. Then he would find Janet, determine and record her status, and meet us in the lot; I would leave one of Dick's cell surplus phones 'accidentally' and need to return their retrieve it.

It worked like clockwork up through the interview with Dr. Koglitz, a very nice elderly European gentleman, who was enthusiastic about the prospects of genetic engineering to cure all sorts of things, but spoke in generalities with a lot of we'll-need-to-get-back-to-yous on details. At the end of our short talk, I asked how they make their test subjects glow.

"I've never asked, actually. Putting bioluminescent genes in to show that something is actually there and replicating has been done for many years now, all over. It's standard technology that doesn't hurt the subject animal. That we do, and we also do this to help recover any escaped animals — we don't want them to breed with the outside population. That would make difficulties with patented genes, you see. But the details on how we make them glow I do not know. We will get back to you. I'm sure it is harmless."

Harmless unless you're are a nocturnal critter outside the fence that need to eat and not be eaten.

"Have there been other escapes?"

"Other than LLc 924? *Ja.* We have recovered them all. And It we will recover. We do not endanger the natural gene pool, that would not be in our interest or nature's, *ja*?"

I nodded.

"Oh, Dr. Molton has had to cancel. Perhaps you can come another day?"

"Certainly," I said, feigning slight disappointment. I was not surprised Molton canceled; I had no information on glowing rabbits and was taking info rather than giving.

He smiled broadly and looked at his watch. "It has been so nice talking to you, Herr Miller. Have a good evening."

✶ ❋ ✶

The look on Sarah's face as I exited Koglitz' office told me something had gone wrong. She pointed, to a company picture in the sitting area in the wide hall outside Dr. Koglitz office. It showed Dr. Morton with Dr. Jones' arm around him and a big smile on her face. She texted it to Dick with the one word title "Trap!!" and showed the text.

"Get out of there!" Dick texted back. "I verified Jones and Morton are a couple; they're working together to get Jack She's bait. Plan B on extracting Jack."

Plan B?

Sarah froze and didn't seem to want to move.

"Let's work on having only two captives instead of four," I whispered. "We can always call the cops."

"Terrible coverage out here," someone said, noting our consternation and not knowing the cause. "You need to get halfway to Kiona before you get more than two bars."

"Thanks much," I said, and tugged on Sarah's hand, as the someone talked urgently on his phone.

She seemed to snap out of it and came along. My heart pounding, and my eyes looking this way and that for Heavy or Rangy and instant death, we walked to the car. This was a look into Jack's life, I realized, and it wasn't pretty. I'd hoped Jack would be there in the car — he should have gotten Sarah's warning, too. But the empty white bunny suit and lack or response to our calls said he wasn't there.

I put a sweaty palm on the passenger side door handle. "We can't wait," I told Sarah. "Dick has a Plan B. We need to get out of here and trust that."

She nodded and drove. I happened to glance in the back seat and look at the collapsed white toy bunny suit. If the same guys checked us on the way out . . . I pulled off my shirt and my undershirt, put the shirt back on, and wadded the undershirt into the white bunny suit as Sarah rigorously followed the fifteen mph speed limit of the parking lot all the way to the exit gate.

We were searched. The bunny suit was squeezed, but not opened, or sniffed, and we were allowed out the gate. One turn down the road, out of view of Halfast, Sarah pulled the car over.

"You need to drive, Ed," she said, got out, and sat in back next to the empty bunny suit. I think she was trying hard not to cry.

I drove down to our rendezvous with Dick's van. Dick was in the cabin in front of a monitor, typing furiously.

"He doesn't respond to me. There doesn't seem to be anything wrong with the link. The feed's on DP734. You can watch with your cells. Sarah, did he tell you anything, any big secret, anything at all that might help?"

Sarah climbed in and put her hands on Dick's shoulders.

"Nothing that meant anything to me. Jones' name for Jack was "Roger," and she had him call her "Jessica." Why would he want to keep that secret?"

Sarah was born about 1992.

Dick could take care of that, I thought; I watched the feed. The hare cam showed the outside of the building we'd seen Dr. Jones in. Jack was stationary.

Dick sighed. "Sarah, google 'Jessica Rabbit.'"

She did so. "Oh . . . Interspecies . . . She couldn't let that be known. Even if it means Jack's death, I guess. Dick, he's not a legal human being, not a person; he has no rights. The worst they could get for shooting him is cruelty to animals, or hunting without a license, or destroying evidence, or something."

"Yeah," I said. "Hold on, something's happening."

The building door opened. Jack covered the distance very quickly, then stopped by a jackrabbit-colored tarp and froze. If he just stayed there, he would be pretty much invisible.

"Sarah, Dr. Jones is the bait of the trap and Jack's rabbit reproductive instincts are fully engaged. I bet they've got the right pheromones wafting out that door too; it is a GMO lab. What we've got against that is Jack's mind and his instinctive caution. We need to tip the balance. Call him. Say it's you or Dr. Jones."

Sarah nodded. "Dick, what do I tell him besides 'don't go in'? What's plan B."

"Run for the fence and jump as high as he can. About forty feet before the fence should do it."

Jack started to move toward the open door.

"Jack, it's Sarah. You're going into a trap. Janet isn't who you think she is."

"It's the only home I've ever known. She loves me . . . "

"No, she used you. You need to come to me. Run to the fence and jump high, to spoil their aim. Come to me," Sarah said. "Not her, me."

A tentative move toward the door, then a freeze.

"Rangy, with a shot gun, to the left," Dick said, watching Dizzy's feed. "Listen, Jack."

"Come to me," Sarah said

Suddenly, Jack turned and started bounding down the lane between the buildings.

"Bizzy, eagle mode," Dick said. "Catch Jack on the the way up. Toss him over the fence. Dizzy, defend Jack. Jack, Jump! High as you can Jump!."

No, it wouldn't work. "Dick, Jack's too heavy. Bizzy won't be able to lift him."

"Doesn't have to. He just has to push his apogee up a bit."

The blast of a shotgun echoed from our phones and dust kicked up well ahead of Jack. Jack kept running, bouncing side to side now.

"I'm above to the left," a new voice said. It must by Bizzy, I realized. "Dodge to your left toward the fence and jump as high as you can."

There was another blast, dust far to the right of Jack, and then a human scream. "Help, get this thing off of me!"

"That would be Dizzy," Dick said.

The fence came in view. Jack dodged toward it, jumped, and kept on soaring. Later, we figured he and Bizzy cleared the fence by twenty-two feet, three and one half inches.

★ ❄ ★

Back at Dick's place that evening, Jack performed his experiment with a bit of Black Butte Porter in a bowl.

"It tastes awful," he said

"I could make some chamomile tea," Sarah offered.

Jack took another sip of Porter. "Maybe I'll learn to like it. As I like my new home."

We all laughed and cheered.

"I've got good news for you, Jack, from Halfast Lab. They actually got back to me; the reason you glow is GM bioluminescent bacteria in your epidermal biome. We need to kill all the bugs on your skin hair and replace them with the normal variety. Then you won't glow."

Igor interrupted us with a KVVK report, from FAUX news, that

" . . . a pair of eagles had interrupted a rabbit hunt on the grounds of Hanford. Their expert said that wasn't usual eagle behavior — they would more likely to fight each other for the prey than cooperate — but that strange biological things had been reported at Hanford. Jackrabbits eat contaminated plants, glow in the dark and so on. This was all unconfirmed of course, but you heard it first on . . . "

Sarah laughed, Jack secure on her lap. "You won't find one person in ten that can tell the difference between a turkey vulture and a golden eagle in flight at a quick glance. Most people go by behavior; eagles don't rock their wings or gather in big groups over road kill. Casual observers don't get a good look at the head, nor, of course, inside it. Dizzy and Bizzy flew like eagles today."

Yes, I thought. And everyone else around me got "up where they belong," too.

STORY NOTES

This was my third CampCon anthology story and the last one before the pandemic. By this time, our aging group had relocated from the DEET woods to the comforts of a resort hotel. Our leader, Bob Brown, has a day job of dealing with radiation safety issues of the DOE Hanford Reservation, and at one point there were reports that some of the wildlife had been contaminated by waste leakage. This became exaggerated to the point that, at conventions, Bob became the target of good-natured tales of glowing bunnies. I took that as an inspiration, and imagined a somewhat tongue-in-cheek science-fictional realization of that squared and cubed. Ed and his vulture drones come into play, the Hare is now one of my favorite characters, and one is asked to contemplate the same kinds of questions asked of Asimovian AI "beings" now applied to genetically uplifted beings.

GDN October 2021

A HUNDRED MILES FROM RENO

Some things are timeless, Lohni thought, as she stepped from the shower of her double-wide. The two ranchers had been polite enough, and, warmed up by the first, she'd been able to let nature have its way with the second to the point where the soreness didn't matter much. Anyway, it should hurt, a little, she thought. Now she had a couple of hours. Besides there was light at the end of her tunnel; there was only twenty to twenty-five grand to go until she was done.

"Let's have the news, Madame," she told her computer. "BBC audio."

" . . . latest border incident," some talking head on her sound system noted, "has been smoothed over. Both Presidents expressed hope that the family planning aspects of the UNATE treaty will soon bring an end to birthrate and climate change migratory pressures. Meanwhile, the unemployment rate fell below twenty-five percent for the first time in eight years as baby boomers in their nineties are increasingly opting for full time retirement. Elonia, Mars celebrated its silver anniversary of continuous . . . "

"Cut the news." She didn't need that. Not yet.

"You have an unscheduled customer, Lohni," Madame interrupted, replacing the news with a picture of a somewhat nervous man, average height and not noticeably overweight, appearing to be in his late thirties, wearing simple dark brown slacks and a plain light blue shirt. His hair was thinning slightly, but that added character to what was an otherwise handsome, though world-weary, visage. "We have two hours before your next appointment."

A drop in! With time enough to make a hundred or two before Number 72 showed up for his regular. But someone that young and passable shouldn't have to pay for it. She frowned a bit. What was wrong? she wondered. "Take a sweat sample, Madame, run his prints, DNA and retina and show him a holo, and I'll be out front in five minutes."

After the shower, she inspected her merchandise on the room cam, looking for any immediate maintenance needs. She smiled — a side benefit of becoming fully bisexual was that she could appreciate her own body in ways she hadn't before; not bad for her early forties. She flicked her right pec and watched her breast swell and undulate sensually as its muscle-culture implant followed suit. She'd gotten just enough to hold 'em up better and fill out the skin; nothing stretchy or bizarre. But her skin was getting a little weathered in places; she liked the sun and there was only so much lotion could do. The effect was healthy and vigorous, and the clients didn't seem to mind. Especially the lack of tan lines. But she'd need epidermal gene therapy in a year or two.

She stepped out the bathroom rear door, threw her towel on the still-warm redwood, and did a couple quick pushups to get her blood flowing. Then sprung up and took a quick look around the deck and the little pool behind her trailer. Her last clients had stayed inside, so everything was neat, and clean. The deck was almost classically simple. The only concessions to her profession were a half scale fiberglass David, weighted with sand, watching the door to her working bedroom with electronic eyes, and a plastic Venus di Milo, flanked by potted plants, hiding her satellite dish.

The setting sun and the cool, clear evening sky lent a slightly magic air to the simple setting. The real Venus was high and bright. Well, all right! she thought. It would be a good performance, if she could get him outside. She liked to show Venus what she did, and the rest of the universe.

She gave the David an intimate pat as she left the pool deck and started looking through her closet of flimsy things. The waiting guy's hair was very basic medium length and he wore gray shorts and a light cotton shirt that wouldn't have been much out of place any time since Fremont came west through these parts. Not one for a lot of decoration? Okay by her. She grabbed a long T shirt that said "My body belongs to me" on the front with "inquire about rental" on the back. It clung to her softly, outlining her breasts in a healthy, natural way. No rings, no earrings; a smile would be her only makeup.

"You'll like this," Madame announced as Lohni ran a brush through her hair, parting it in the middle like a pioneer wife of two centuries ago, or a flower child of one century ago. It needed cutting. Next week would do. "He's a poet with a degree in economics. He's got a few flu virus antibodies still mopping up after a complete victory — probably never knew he had it. Other than that he's medically clean. Legally, he's married to an actress who's living with someone else now. Only one kid, a boy whose address is the same as hers."

Lohni's eyes widened. An unused basic allocation! The thought of children opened a memory door she tried to keep shut during work. But the Mars news had cracked it open and it all came came rushing back at her: the flashing red lights, the screams . . .

"Lohni?"

"Flashback, Madame, I'm okay now. Is this john any good as a poet? I mean does he sell?"

"Three paid publications last year. Nothing so far this year. It's not his day job."

Hmmm, she thought. Probably no wonder, with his home life falling apart. Well, she could be his inspiration! At any rate, he was earning a bit above his automation dividend — not much, but anything at all was better than most these days. An allocation board would like that.

She put the hairbrush down and headed for the living room. He got up, blushing, as she walked in. Madame had been screening one of her sample holos.

"Hi, I'm Lohni." She offered her hand.

"Greg," he said, and shook it nervously. When she didn't let go, he grinned a bit.

She tilted her head toward the holoscreen. "Don't you think that's disgusting?

"Uh, well, yes, I do."

She laughed. "So do I. That's why I charge more for it. But I know how to do it so I don't get hurt." Much. "Want to try it?"

He turned crimson. "Not really." Too bad. With him, it might be fun.

"Do you record everyone?" he asked.

"Sure do. Give you a copy of the disk for another C-note. Don't worry — you've got half the copyright. It's technically performance art — and you're automatically the co-author of the script-in-fact. I can't do anything with it without your permission, except maybe watch it an' masturbate." She laughed at his expression.

"Uh, what about him?" The holoviewer was still frozen in the middle of the 'disgusting' act.

Lohni laughed. "I've got his digital permission. If you're game, we can act a little and put ours in the Love Bank. If you're good, you might earn my fee back in a couple of years, and no one will know you did it; Madame morphs the heads so they can't be recognized."

"I can sure recognize you. You're pretty."

"Thanks. I work at it, and I want people to know it's me. Good for business." And it serves me right, she thought. "Speaking of which, I usually work by appointment and I've got one in about ninety minutes." She nodded her head toward the door, "Sooo . . . " Greg came docilely as she pulled him into the working bedroom.

"Did Madame explain everything to you?" She glanced at the screen, blue for basic lovemaking.

"Pretty much. Do you want me to use a condom? That wasn't clear."

"No, you checked out clean and I've got a fresh vagiguard film." That was a little white lie. She had a film, okay, but it was more than a guard.

"Huh?"

She laughed, sat him down on the side of the queen sized bubble bed and jumped in the middle herself. Sitting cross legged, she let her T shirt ride up to her hips so he could not see what she was talking about.

"It's invisible. Just a ten ply monomolecular film. You'll never feel it, and neither do I." She gave him a big inviting grin. "But I'm safe. We just do what comes naturally, feel our way through it, like on a heavy date. No extra charges as long as I go along. And I'll go along with things that'll cost you another C-note down the road."

He grinned back, embarrassed. "My information must be out of date. You've got me believing you're looking forward to this, but, like, I've read enough to know what a grind this kind of work is. I'll try to be as nice as I can. I don't normally . . . well, I'm in a very awkward situation, not knowing whether I'm married or not any more and it's been almost a year . . . " he trailed off.

She giggled, then nodded seriously. "Its okay. Granted, for me the sex itself isn't necessarily fireworks and rockets every time. But I really like to make people happy." She caressed his arm. "Especially nice people. I put on a good show, and I take pride in it, and sometimes, like, its not just a show. You just let me worry about my feelings.

"Say, tell you what — it's beautiful out there. The stars are just coming out, and the pool is warm. How about a little skinny dip to break the ice? Who knows, I might just get turned on for real."

"Uh, is it, well, private enough?"

"Not really. There are a couple of cabins on that mountain behind us where you could see everything we do pretty well through a pair of high powered binoculars." She gave him the evilest grin she could. "So, how about we go out there and put on a show?"

He blushed.

She circled around behind him, massaged his neck, and then pulled his shirt off, pressing herself into his back, the thin cotton of her shirt only making it more sensual as she let her hands go to his belt and below. He didn't turn and grab her, but let himself be teased, be stroked. Good, she thought, so much better for both of them. This had possibilities.

He turned and pulled her shirt up over her head while they felt each other out with their hips. His jockeys had holes below the waistband and she stuck her middle finger through one, wiggled it and giggled. He blushed again.

She knelt to remove his socks and carefully inspected his lower regions as she did so. No visible problems there.

When they were both naked, she gently pushed him out toward the pool. He hesitated a bit at the door, then shrugged his shoulders and marched out onto the deck. Good man. She sprung out after him, lifted her hands to the stars, yelled "Yippee!" spun around and fell into the pool with a big splash. He laughed, quietly at first, then louder, and dove in after her.

Soon, the esthetic eroticism of the pool gave way to a more practical position on the cushions of the deck. She gave an orgasm a real try, but she was too sore. So she faked it, and enjoyed his reaction almost as much. His orgasm, fortunately, wasn't fake and he gave her a lot of himself, oh, yes, he gave her just what she wanted.

★ ✳ ★

They lay side by side in starlit afterglow, holding hands.

"That was really, really nice." Greg murmured.

"Complements like that will get you a discount on the next visit." She squeezed his hand. "For the next fifteen minutes, I'm a woman who enjoys her job. Then I get back to reality."

"Another customer."

"A weirdo. For the money." Well, they were all for the money, but especially so this case. And for other, darker reasons, reasons which she might tell a truly compassionate man, some day. But how could a decent man understand a rituals of self mortification that let her tolerate her existence, and work toward fulfilling her promise?

Greg turned toward her, looking worried. She smiled back.

"I can take care of myself, and Madame is on line with the county Sheriff."

He smiled cynically. "A customer of yours, no doubt."

"Grrr." Lohni nipped him playfully on the arm. "She's straight as a ruler, but I vote for her anyway. So, like, don't worry. Customer Number 72 isn't dangerous. He's just disgusting."

"I'm sorry you have to do that."

"No, no! Get this straight. I *don't* have to do anything. It's my own free choice. Look, when an editor tells you to change something in your poem, or you won't get paid, you don't have to, do you? Like you could send it somewhere else, right?

"Yeah, but . . . "

"So I don't *have* to do this either. But I *can*. Without flinching. I'm not scared of that stuff, and I have enough power over myself to make myself do some really wild things, things that some people need because of what's happened to them sometime, I guess. And I'm making money in a legal job. So I don't want any pity and I don't need it."

She saw a satellite moving overhead, and suddenly she was back up there hearing the screams of her children on the other side of the door that wouldn't open. The door that kept her alive while they died within inches of her. They'd been going to Mars, but a hundred miles overhead was as far as they'd gone.

"Lohni," Ted had shouted, "stay in there. You've got to live for us. Don't lose everything. Get it back. Promise? For us. I love you."

She'd had enough control to promise and tell each of them she loved them, over and over as the sound faded. The last thing she'd heard was little Cindy screaming "Mommy!" Then there was no more sound. By the time the rescuers cut the door open, they'd taken the bodies away.

"Lohni, are you okay?"

"Sorry. Memories. All gone now." She smiled the professional smile.

"All right, all right, then. I . . . admire . . . you for being able to do all that."

She grinned and punched him in the arm. "Right on! But penance first, and now I've got to get ready for it. Time's up." She threw herself up to her feet in one smooth athletic motion, reached down and pulled him up.

"You're strong!"

Lohni laughed. She punished her body for that strength. "Yup. *That* has come in handy a couple of times, too."

As they went to the door, Lohni turned and waved. *He was okay, Ted*, she thought, *he was okay. But I'd rather be doing it with you.* The mountain behind her trailer was a dark shadow against the last trace of twilight in the sky. There was a light shining about half way up.

"You weren't kidding about the cabin!" Greg choked. "Was someone really watching us?"

She laughed and spun around, holding her arms out. "Who knows? Who cares? We weren't breakin' any laws." Then she led him into the bedroom, where she dressed him, first with kisses then with clothes. As she buckled his belt, she watched him scan the picture, look away, then look back.

"The guy in the picture, with the babies . . . "

"Mine. They all died in a blowout up on the low end of the big space station, fifteen years ago. I lived 'cause I was in the john at the time. The door wouldn't open, because of the pressure."

He looked at her skeptically.

She shook her head. "I know that sounds like a made-up-for-sympathy story. But you can check it out if you want. Lohni Johnson is my real name. I'm not ashamed of what I do." I'm just ashamed to be alive, she added silently.

"Geeze, I didn't mean to . . . your allocations . . . "

She shrugged. Yes, the allocations. People could have put the brakes on gently, fifty years ago. "Gone. That's life. Or death. Look, Greg, we've got six hundred million people in this country, and we're spread out compared to Mexico down there. If the boards let us replace accidental deaths, the population would never come down." If we'd only gotten to Mars, Ted.

"So," she sighed, "two's all you get and if you aren't a genius or rich enough to buy more, well, that's the way it is. It's a tough world, I'm doing okay, and don't let it bother you. Greg, I've had this conversation so many times it doesn't even bother *me* anymore."

"Eventually, you'll need to forgive yourself for surviving."

She'd said too much. Again. She softened her voice a bit, then. "You know what? It's only the decent guys that ask. That's why the picture's there — I kind of like to know who maybe cares a little. Makes it easier."

He snorted. "Okay. I care a little."

She looked at him seriously. She was asking for a heartache every time she did this. But she did it, anyway. Again and again. Because the only way to keep her promise was to ask. "Look, if I need to talk to you about something, in the future. Would you mind if I called?"

He was silent for a couple of seconds, like he was thinking of saying something he really meant. Then he cleared his throat and said, "I really do like you, but, well, life goes on, I guess. Uh, if it's a long time before you call, well, can you be discreet?"

"I can handle that. She doesn't have to be involved." Sigh. Maybe there will be enough money before there is a she. Then, Lohni thought, I might make another offer. "So, come back again, then, will you? I'm just a hundred miles from Reno and I'll even throw in something disgusting, free."

"Uh, what we did tonight was just fine," he muttered, "and I don't think I could . . . "

She interrupted him with the biggest belly laugh she'd had in a month. Greg joined in and they kept laughing together as she went, still bare and glowing, arm and arm with him to the front door. She kissed him good-bye on the lips and stood in the door as he waved and drove off. The coyotes could think what they want.

"Ten minutes," Madame reminded her.

"I know, I know."

She scurried back to her private bedroom and went right to the bathroom. There she removed her precious semen sample, placed it in its preservative vial, then opened the small refrigerator beside her real bed.

"What do you think, Madame. Was he a keeper?"

"How do you define a keeper today?"

Lohni laughed. "Intuition. Think he'll share an allocation with me, if I pay for it?"

"My psychological profile software indicates that he might be willing to share more than an allocation, if you play it right. I could give you more data; however, customer number 72 is . . . "

"You don't say. Before I make myself do that again, remind me of what my balance is."

"One million, four hundred and seventy-five thousand, three hundred and twelve dollars."

"Yeah!" With five hundred, if Greg were willing to use his share, she could have two babies. "Think he cares enough to come back?"

"You know better than to ask that, Lohni."

"Yeah, Madame, damn your psyche program. But I think I'm going to want to pretend he's coming back for the next couple of hours, if you don't mind."

"I never mind. And I think you have a better chance with him than most."

She went back into the business bedroom and opened the bottom drawer of the dresser there. She stared at the picture on her dresser as she laid out, with hardly a glance, the familiar black garters, the whips, the black glow-in-ultraviolet condoms, and the big, odd shaped vibrators.

After the blowout, the company shrink had mentioned dealing with survivor guilt. Well, she was dealing with it. Some days she wished someone like Customer number 72 would just not hold back and beat it out of her permanently. But she had another obligation; she'd made a promise.

Then she looked at the picture on top of her dresser. Another twenty-five grand, Ted, she thought. I'm no rocket scientist and this is the best I can do, so don't knock it. There just aren't any jobs anymore. With the money I get for this, with my own sperm bank full of scientists, lawyers, and poets to choose the genetically right father, I'll convince the allocation board, I can have my two kids. Maybe even a husband, too, if someone like Greg pans out. Nowhere near as good as you, but close. Close will have to do. I'll get it back, I will. Much as I can. Promised you that.

"Is that bitch ready yet?" Customer number 72's gravelly bass voice rumbled through the trailer.

Lohni adjusted her black bimbo-profile bra, slapped herself hard in the face to get in the mood, then squared her shoulders and marched off to absolution.

STORY NOTES

In 1994, I had already written and sold a number of off-Earth stories and was challenged to do something different. This was different and in many ways, more of a work of imagination than the others. I wasn't sure what to do with it, and it sat around for decades. Then my writers group had an opportunity to get a dealer table. But to get seats, we had to be the actual authors of a work for sale, not friends or guests. So we devised an anthology, tossed in what works we had available, and the multitalented and enterprising Valerie Frankel took charge — editing and publishing *Uncertain Stars*.

This story is set in a version of my future history, which is a bit darker than the usual; I was very concerned about overpopulation and environmental impact and wondered what if, like China, the U. S. had to control its birth rate. In 2017, it doesn't look like one will need an allocation to have children any time soon, but things can change. Meanwhile, private space stations and colonizing Mars, thanks to Elon Musk, actually do seem to be on their way in the very loose time frame allocated to this story, which I would put circa 2070 today. "Madame," Lohni's AI 1-woman brothel manager, seems right on schedule as well, and marks yet another occupation that can be replaced by a computer.

I have relied entirely on other writers and my imagination for the Lohni's interactions with her customers. I imagine them to be individuals, not types, and each with their own back story and reasons for doing what they do.

As a retired military officer, I have seen survival guilt and what it can do. Frequent refuges include drugs and alcohol; but sometimes the survivor becomes a driven person with a singular goal to his or her life. What happens after that goal is achieved is another story. But not this one.

GDN February 2017

THE KUBOTA EFFECT

"Eureka!" Hiro "Jack" Kubota shouted and a thousand echoes answered from the empty halls of the deserted underground lab. He jumped, maybe half a meter off the ground — there was no one to watch him. With a trembling hand he selected "print" from the menu of his Granny Smith. Eight years in this surplus would-be superconducting supercollider tunnel, and, finally, he had done it.

The equipment sat there just like it had five minutes ago. But then it had just been an experiment. Now it was a compact antiproton factory, a prototype for something that could change the course of history.

It's going to belong to the Smithsonian someday, he thought dizzily; I'd better be careful with it. The power could go down, the data could be lost, he might be unable to replicate the experiment and there would be only his word — the nightmare of being the participant in another cold fusion fiasco paralyzed his hand. Print it! Now! he told himself, and shaking himself willfully out of that train of morbid thoughts, he tapped the key.

In moments, the pictures of the particle paths slipped into his printer tray. Hard copy. Permanent. Real. With trembling hands he picked up the sheets — it was beautiful, elegant, as something of such significance should be. The particle traces looked like a perfect symmetrical flower, positive pions curling left, negative pions right, protons curving left, a thin trace of fluorescence down the center where the neutral particles accidentally disturbed an electron or two, and *there*, to the right, a firm, thick trace of antiprotons. Antimatter. Electricity in, antimatter out. He'd done it!

"Banzai!" Jack jumped high again, feeling for a moment he could sail through the dozen meters of rock and prairie above him like a neutrino. The old tunnels could not contain his joy. Still shaking, he sat down. He should make more measurements, file an email note, tell Dr. Grimski. Take radiation readings — he hadn't really expected it to work so *well* and that stream of antiprotons represented several joules of hard radiation. He'd have to be careful not to endanger his and Gina's future children!

A tear of joy dropped on the printout — careful, that's going to the Smithsonian too. The pion traces were thin, delicate. They were the noise — careful tuning should eliminate them, and the neutrons and antineutrons as well. The protons couldn't be helped — but, he chuckled — so what! He had proof of principle that antiprotons could be made at efficiencies approaching fifty percent of their energy cost. That was revolutionary; antihydrogen made by solar power satellites could replace uranium and plutonium in power plants. Antihydrogen-powered rockets could fly to orbit like airliners, with airliner payloads. Doctors could attack cancer with a tenth of the normal radiation side affects . . .

At least it ought to get him his doctorate!

Gina! He had to call Gina. He looked at his watch — she should be at the neutrino observatory, three kilometers down the curved tunnel.

"Artoo," he told his computer, "call . . . "

"Hold it!" a loud voice announced. It sounded as cold and solid as the concrete walls from which it echoed, and dripped with condensed authority.

Jack spun around in his ancient surplus swivel chair. "Who the . . . " The sight of the gun in the man's hand shocked Jack into silence; he knew next to nothing about guns. This was large, smooth and squarish — nothing like a cowboy revolver, and no gadgets on it that he could see. The mean looking hole in the end of it might have been almost a centimeter across. With the light from his desk lamp behind him, he could almost see into the barrel. "Who are *you*?"

"Don't even think of trying to find out, if you want to live." The speaker was wearing a black trench coat, as if out of a spy novel.

The face was very ordinary, though a little hard. Jack studied the face, trying to note details, but he knew he probably wouldn't recognize it in another context. He even had problems with Japanese faces, and he was raised there. Nonetheless, he noted that the hair was straight and black, with a touch of gray at the temples. The man was big, just under two meters and probably over a hundred kilos — twice Jack's mass. He could have been anywhere from forty to seventy.

The gunman carried himself as if he were used to moving. Jack saw no sign of softness or flab — but no sign of malnourishment either. The hand that held the gun was very steady.

"Sit down and keep your hands on your lap where I can see them."

As he backed into the ancient swivel chair, Jack's life passed in front of him — not the life he'd lived, but the one he hoped to have with Gina. A small college somewhere, a low pressure place where they could teach and do research. A child or two, a book written the way a textbook ought to be written. It could all be gone in the next millisecond. It wasn't fair.

"What. . . what do you want?"

"That." The gun pointed briefly to the apparatus, then returned to a boresight that must have been between Jack's eyes. "I've been waiting. Thought you might make it last week. That's what I'm after."

"But, but it's big. It's all over the place. It would take days to take it out, especially if you ever wanted it to work again. And it only produces a few picograms — nothing of any practical use. Unless you have a brain tumor?"

Was that it? They'd been treating people experimentally at Fermilab for years, shooting antiprotons into brain tumors that couldn't be touched otherwise. It worked, but it was very expensive. Jack felt a moment of pity — a desperate man, his thinking perhaps already impaired, taking a wild risk when he had nothing else to lose.

"I'm not a doctor," Jack continued, calming now that he imagined he had a handle on the situation. "But it's not out of the question that we could try something like that. It would take a couple weeks to get ready, but if you're really hurting I'm sure there are people who . . ."

A brief smile cracked the hard face. "I'm sure the people I work for will find ways of making money off this. Now, do you have some electrical tape?"

Jack nodded to a work bench across the tunnel from his desk. It was covered by a mass of miscellaneous equipment; flanges, meters, pliers, strangely shaped pieces of metal and plastic, and yes, no less than three rolls of colored electrical tape. Jack color-tagged his wiring, whenever he thought of it.

"Good. I want you to take a piece and cover up the infrared phone port before either of us says anything more. Don't even think of trying to do anything else." He motioned with his gun to the workbench.

Jack got up slowly, went to the bench and cut off a piece of tape. The phone box was on the utility pole next to the light switch a few meters down the tunnel. He walked to it slowly, thinking furiously. If he could leave just a little part of the dime-sized infrared pickup uncovered, he might get through by pointing his computer's transmitter window directly at the light box.

"Don't even think about it, or you'll lose everything," the man with the gun said, as if he were reading Jack's mind.

He was right. As long as Jack got out of this alive, they could put it all back together again. All he had to do was to keep cool and do exactly what this thug told him to do. He put the tape over the infrared window. No calls, no internet. He was suddenly aware of the utter isolation of this section of tunnel. The cleaning staff came by weekly and Gina occasionally, but other than that, he could — and had — spent weeks without a visitor. The gunman could have been watching him for days, and no one would have noticed.

Gina! With the phone out of order, she might come looking for him. And it came to him how important it was to have, in the world, at least one other person who cared about you on a daily basis.

"I, I should call my fiancee. She might come to find out what's wrong."

"Hah! Nice try, but I'll take that chance. Now, I have no intention of trying to cart the device itself away. You are going to explain how it works, give me copies of your equipment lists, layout plans, progress reports and anything else my clients might be able to use to duplicate your results."

Jack lowered his head, shut his eyes, and bit his lip. As he walked back to his desk, the gunman walked over to the phone box to check his work. He never came within two meters of Jack. Very careful, confident. As if he had been doing this successfully for a while. Jack's grandfather had been a policeman and often entertained the family with stories about how stupid most criminals were. But this man did not seem stupid.

"Come on. I know it makes antiprotons and I know it makes them more efficiently than anything else. What's the theory and how do you make it work?"

Commercial espionage? Who was he working for?

"Now!" the voice commanded.

"Do . . . do you know about the Benton-Kubota effect?" Gina Benton had given him the idea. Her graduate student neutrino observations of Supernova SN 2012A, ten years ago, indicated that the insides of white dwarf stars behaved as if they had more particles than were accounted for by standard theory. He had done a brute-force numerical simulation as a senior that supported the idea.

"Nano-scale quasi-singularities? You pinch a field to a point where it can scatter things like it was a particle?"

Jack nodded his head slowly. The gunman had given him a crude description that bypassed volumes of controversy. He and Gina had finally published in 2017, when some of his early experimental data had come out of the noise level.

"I . . . I see it like this. The collision between particle and quasi-singularity momentarily dissects the proton and blows it up into a quark-gluon plasma bubble, we call it quagma — " Jack looked at the gunman, who nodded, indicating, Jack supposed, that he understood and that Jack should go on.

"But my quagma bubbles are constrained, predictable. Each . . . "

"Keep your hands *down!*"

Jack froze — he had started to gesture as if he were talking to a graduate student, forgetting the situation. He was notorious for his one track mind — his ability, or disability — to concentrate on one thing to the exclusion of everything else. Gina called it the Kubota effect. Slowly he lowered his hands and continued his lecture, concentrating this time on the gun barrel.

"Uh, the, each of the three quarks in the proton hits the maximum field gradient in turn and produces quark — antiquark pair, which are separated inside the quagma by the imposed fields — the six positive quarks one way, the six negative the other. A field twist affecting the one-third-charge quarks more than the ones with two-thirds charge mixes the up and down quarks beams of opposite sign.

"As the quagma bubble collapses, the six quarks glue together to form two protons and the three antiquarks form an antiproton. That's the tricky part — the triplets are energetically more stable, but if the bubble collapses too fast, they don't all have time to form and you get a lot of mesons too. Each collision is as exactly the same as I can make it, except for a small time uncertainty so they emerge in controlled directions. Instead of spraying a variety of particles all over the place, I get pure beams of protons and antiprotons. That's the idea."

The gunman nodded again. "I surmised something like that. Your incident protons hit an electromagnetic wall and split — viewed in the proton's frame of reference, it's just high energy gamma scattering. How can you control it?"

"I, uh, prefer to think of the pinch nexus as a very special captive virtual particle, but the electrodynamic description is equivalent. Anyway, I get a big long quagma bubble."

"Okay, the net result is that you control what happens on a subnuclear level deterministically so you make an antiproton for five times its annihilation energy instead of five hundred. How?"

"Well, almost deterministicary." Jack winced at his own accent as he wondered, who was this? What could a man in a trench coat and a gun know about twenty-first century subnuclear physics? "I need control over the quantum numbers for 1.3 picoseconds. The main innovation is a Bell-effect probability filter. It, uh, cheats the uncertainty principle by defining the spin phase of the incident proton in exchange for a tolerable momentum spread. The theoretical basis for the experiment is in my proposal."

"That's classified. Do you have a copy here?"

Jack shook his head. What was his responsibility here? Would anyone punish him for giving up the document at gunpoint? There were people who thought antimatter bombs were a possibility. That was nonsense, but you almost had to be a weapons physicist to understand *why* it was nonsense — and some professional technophobe-baiters took advantage of that to bask in a phony world-saving glory at the expense of researchers' livelihoods.

Was that what he was up to? Was he going to try to create a scandal that would convince the world that Jack's research was too dangerous to be allowed — and free up Jack's measly thirty grand a year for something else?

"Come, on, come on." The gunman waved the gun at Jack's filing cabinets. "You must have at least a draft here."

Jack trembled but didn't move.

The shot was the loudest thing he ever heard in his life. In the closed space, the shock wave rattling off the curved concrete sounded, incongruously, like a ping-pong game. When the echoes died down, Jack opened his eyes. The gunman waved the gun toward the filing cabinets again.

There was a slightly burnt odor about, with a sharpness to it. Gunpowder? Jack had never smelled it before.

"I, I'll look."

He found himself in front of the file cabinet without remembering how he'd gotten himself out of the chair and over to it. There was a bullet hole in the bottom drawer of the first cabinet. Jack did a quick mental inventory — his diploma probably had a hole in it now. There was a picture of Gina in there — maybe too far back. His late father's Ph.d thesis might have protected it. His college physics department chairman's "Retter of Recommendation," as the kindly, but mischievous, old man had called it in good natured mimicry of Jack's accent, was in front of the thesis. So that had a hole in it too, now.

This was a lesson to him for something. Of course. His display of pride at his success had been immediately punished, a load of karma to teach him the humility he had not shown before the powers of the universe. He frowned deeply. Did he really believe that?

The proposal was in the top drawer. Jack's thumb print released the lock, he pulled the drawer open, found the section, and put his hand on the document.

Why stretch it out, he thought? Just give him what he wants now. Maybe he'll choke on it. Jack pulled out three thick file folders.

"The proposal, eight years of progress reports and three journal articles. There are other copies."

The gunman gave him that quizzical smile again. "That's nice." He waved the gun barrel again, toward the experiment bench.

It was like the gun was a "mouse" and Jack was the little arrow on a computer screen. He had to go where the hand willed. He felt powerless, like a woman in the hands of a rapist.

"Now let's see the business end."

"It's . . . in this vacuum chamber. I just finished a run. Perhaps you could look just through the observation window?"

Now the gunman laughed. "You may have thirty seconds left to live, but you don't want to waste a good pump-down. Ha! Fine. I want to see this mother work and I don't have time for another pump down either. So, talk me through a diagram."

Jack did so, with the gun so close to his head that he could still smell the shot. But his picture of his tormenter was filling in. The man had to have worked in a lab at some time — it was in his language. He knew things.

"Finally," Jack concluded, "the three beams emerge into the mass spectrometer separated by about a microradian. That's tunable — the momentum detector port is fixed and I change the magnetic field until the beam I want to measure is bent by the correct angle."

"Yeah, that's basic. Okay, now, show me how you do this. Every step. You won't be around to help when I . . . when my clients do this again."

That sounded pretty final. Of course — Jack's usefulness would end when the gunman had what he wanted. But the gunman wanted cooperation, and so allowed hope.

If one had to die, Jack thought, one should do it with dignity. That was the way it had been in the land of his ancestors.

Gina, I love you, I don't want to go. Not now, not this way.

"Let's get on with it." The man waved the gun back to the control station. "Boot it up."

Jack nodded quickly. "The software is still on. Artoo, activate program . . . no, just a minute."

If one had to die, one might as well see what one's apparatus could really do first. Radiation was beside the point, now. Gammas, neutrons, pions shooting right through the chamber walls, the pions decaying into the tightest beam of neutrinos this world had ever seen. He chuckled, inanely, to himself about seeing neutrinos — then stopped.

There were places where you *could* see neutrinos, and one of them was just a few kilometers around the bend of this tunnel — where Gina worked.

"Please excuse me," Jack said in a trembling voice. "I should not run that program again because of the radiation. We would both be sterile, I think. I need to be more careful."

"No shit! Okay, you have ten minutes — after which you'll be trying to do this on one leg. Understand?" The gunman grinned frostily at him again. But there was something eager in the grin, something beneath that hardened exterior that understood. The man must have been a physicist at one time, or at least a physics student. Where? Here? Before they canceled the supercollider? It would explain how he'd gotten in and out, and been able to hide in the tunnels until Jack's experiment had succeeded. The gunman would have been a very young man then, Jack's age — full of dreams. Then they'd let everyone go.

Jack nodded and fumbled through the papers on the desk beneath the computer. There it was! The main evacuation diagram. It showed the neutrino observatory around the curve of the tunnel — sixteen kilometers of solid Texas rock. Sixteen kilometers of near vacuum, to a neutrino. He had to eyeball the angle and be very careful to disguise his purpose — the man watching him would know about the neutrinos.

He brought up the mass spectrometer control simulator and adjusted the magnetic field controls until the negative pion beam was headed in about the right direction.

"We're just about ready. I'm going to up the output a bit, enough to get some secondary fluorescence out of the annihilation gammas. That way you can see that it's really working."

"Okay." The gunman was staring at the computer screen instead of Jack. Maybe if he was distracted enough . . . "You know we . . . they were going to make antiprotons here back before . . . "

Jack snuck a look at him; the man's eyes seemed to glisten for a moment. Thenthe moment had passed and the gun was leveled at Jack's head again. "Let's get on with it."

Jack nodded. Would just a steady neutrino signal be enough, he wondered? They might not look at their data for days. He should modulate it.

"Pulse mode," he said as he made the changes. Explain everything correctly, he told himself, but disguise purpose. "Keyed to the mouse, okay? Less radiation that way. I'm ready to start. If we turn the lights down, you should see flashes at the window."

"I'll take my chances with this light."

"Okay. Artoo, activate program nine point three."

There was a slight snap, and the screen display showed only a slight signal. That was because the beam wasn't hitting the detector, deliberately.

"I didn't get the, the beam aligned quite right, so we're not seeing it on the screen as much as it should — "

"You're misaligned a bit for the detector, but I saw the flash! Hit it again. Enough antimatter to make a reaction I can see! That will show them. Thirty bloody years, damnit! and they told us it wasn't worth anything. You didn't hear that, kid."

Jack barely *had* heard him. He was thinking furiously, trying to imagine a message, oblivious to everything outside his own head. What kind of signal would Gina recognize? Jack didn't know any code — was "SOS" three dashes and three dots or three dots and three dashes? His finger was poised over the mouse key when he spotted a cheat sheet with the physical constants he'd taped to the shelf next to the computer.

Ah — so. He started tapping the key. Six times, wait, six times more, wait, two, wait, six, wait, one, wait, seven, wait, six. That was "h," Planck's constant.

"I see it, I see it," The gunman said, his voice exited, not threatening. "Not too efficient, yet — you're getting some glow from the positron beam too, aren't you — on the left?"

Actually, it was the positive pion beam, but Jack didn't feel like correcting him. "Yes, but only a few. This is just an experiment; it — "

"I understand. Let's see some more. This is interesting, if it's this reliable already. You lucky son of a . . . Hit the key again."

Trembling, his finger tapped twice, then seven, then once, then eight, two, eight again. That was enough for "e," the base of natural logarithms. There was no "L" on his cheat sheet, but Jack had an answer to that, one that Gina would be sure to get. The universal gas constant: eight, three, one, six . . . Finally, P? Ah, standard atmosphere pressure, in Pascals.

Then back to Planck's constant. He tapped slowly, as if at random, looking at the flashes of annihilation energy. He did not have to fake worry about the radiation.

"That's enough," the gunman said by the time Jack had tapped his way back to "e" again. "Now, the most critical part of this set up has to be the collision chip, right?"

Jack nodded. "Yes, that was the hardest to make." Except for the software. There were eight months of work — trial and error nanolithography — in that millimeter-thin, square centimeter chip. It was unique in the universe — the first and only one that had worked.

"Not hot, is it?"

Jack thought about saying yes, but he'd explained the beam line too carefully. The gunman knew that the meson and baryon beams emerged into the steering magnets without hitting anything.

"No. But it will take a few minutes to dump the vacuum — non-destructively."

The gunman smiled wryly and waved at him again. "Get with it. You've got a briefcase here? With a security tag."

The bastard had thought of everything, Jack realized. With a cleared case, he could take anything he wanted out of the lab, provided it would fit. Who the hell was he?

Jack told the computer to open the pressure valve, and found his briefcase for the gunman. Brown, pseudoleather, D.O.E. issue — at least that had no sentimental value.

It took ten minutes for the pressure to equalize in the collider chamber, and another ten to unbolt the flange. The liquid helium had already drained and evaporated, but the gold plated box with the nano-channel chip and the field effect needles was still burning cold to the touch.

Jack ignored the pain, taking a perverse pride in his ability to do so. His ancestors would approve. Pain meant nothing now. He handed the precious device to the gunman and allowed himself a momentary pleasure in the scowl on his tormenter's face as his fingers closed on his frozen booty. They would both leave skin on it.

"Be careful," Jack said, with cold irony, "It has not warmed to room temperature yet."

"Ouch! Now you tell me!" It was like giving away a child. He'd used the scanning tunneling microscope needle as his waldo to placed the last ten thousand atoms on the chip with a precision that he could not yet be sure a machine would match. There were no little bumps and clusters in those final layers — it was a perfect geometric arrangement — a continuous superconducting layer with deliberately asynchronous flux pins to prevent resonant quenching. He had bound it against its titanic magnetic pressure with a monomolecular fullerene belt. That had taken him a six months to get right.

The man produced a small paper bag and dropped the device in it.

Jack shut his eyes. An end, he told himself, came to all things.

The man put the bag in the briefcase, with all of Jack's documents.

"There is no way I can talk you out of this?" Jack ventured.

The man shook his head and gestured with the gun again. "Move over there and face the wall."

There was about a meter of unused wall between the vacuum pump and the computer rack. Two-centimeter aluminum utility conduit tubes ran along it in a bundle at about waist level. Otherwise it was bare concrete. The last thing, Jack thought, that I will see in my life. "May I leave a note for my fiance?"

"We've been at this for three hours. If you haven't figured out how to do that, it's too late now. I let you play with your apparatus longer than I should. Once upon a time, I . . . " The man shook his head. "You've already done more than most people in a lifetime. Take that thought with you — but it's reality time now. Face the wall!"

"I could do more," Jack said, with as much dignity as he could muster as he turned. "If this science once meant something to you, let me live. Let me continue my research." There were a million undignified things he could do to try to rush the man and struggle with him. But they would all be ineffective — the man was at least twice his size and armed. Jack would not give him the excuse of self defense.

He stared at the wall for what must have been a minute. Get it over with, he thought. Finally, he started to turn back.

"Don't! I don't owe this idiot world and its idiot people a goddamn thing!"

The man was so close, Jack could smell his breath and thought he could feel the cold of the gun. What was taking him so long? He almost felt like shouting "get it over with." But no. The man was clearly troubled — Jack's words must have had an effect. He was an intelligent man, who once had thought to dedicate his life to acquiring knowledge instead of money. The thing to do, Jack thought, was to let the gunman's conscience work for him, a kind of psychological jujitsu.

If Jack gave him no excuse, perhaps he would not shoot. He had to take his mind away — to do nothing as hard as he could. He sought refuge in "the Kubota effect" and concentrated on the wall. He tried to imagine himself so small that he could climb inside the block, between the grains of concrete, and win his way through, then up through the soil into the bright sunshine above. The smell of the gunman faded from his mind.

He imagined doing this hand in hand with Gina — exploring the inside of the concrete block the way they were going to explore the universe together, cataloging passages like neutron stars, doing papers on the stochastic properties of molecular bonding in Portland cement and the topological similarities between cement and the large scale structure of the universe.

The bullet, when it came, would interrupt some very important work.

Sounds made their way to him. Somewhere, in the distance, or above him, he heard the whine of one of the electric carts they used to traverse the unused tunnel. Perhaps he and Gina could lay tracks for such carts through the pores of their concrete block.

An interesting endeavor; he thought. On the microscopic level there was a universe of passages in this one block — it would take a lifetime. Perhaps the way to approach it was with many machines, Von Neumann machines could do it, but they would have to be very tiny. Like his chip. He could use the same apparatus, with some modifications.

★ ❄ ★

"Jack! Jack!"

"Gina?" For a crazy confused moment, Jack thought the voice came from the cement, but no, no. He snapped back to reality. How had Gina come so soon? She'd get shot! He yelled right at the block, sure that it would reflect the sound, and heedless of the consequences. "Gina! Get away! He's got a gun!"

Then Jack spun around, hoping to draw the gunman's fire to himself. But there was no one there.

Dark-haired Gina drove into his laboratory's light pool from around the bend of the tunnel, left her cart in the center, and threw herself into his waiting arms. "Oh, thank God you're all right! What happened?"

"Oh. Oh, Gina. Oh Gina." That was all Jack could say. "Someone stole my plans and my chip, and our papers. I thought he would shoot me."

"It's okay, Jack. Whoever it was is gone. There's no one here. It's been half an hour since you signaled me."

They held each other for long minutes. Finally Jack let out a long sigh and caressed her arms as he released his embrace. "He knew what he was doing. There was something about him, as if he were, for a moment, involved, again, in something he cared about. He was one of us once, I think, a scientist or an engineer, on the supercollider. But he'd fallen to this. And he was bitter about. I made him wrestle with his conscience. I didn't give him any more reason to shoot. But he stood there forever — it was like he couldn't make up his mind about which world should live. Mine or his."

"You'd never fall that far."

"I think he was supposed to kill me." Jack shook his head. Entropy was gaining on the world above tunnels, these relics of an era when people could do things collectively. The dogs were eating dogs, and people had to carefully avoid dogfights. Finally, he managed a smile. "When I am too old to fall in such a way, then I will judge him. What took you so long?"

"When we realized those were physical constants coming through, one of the grad students grabbed a C.R.C. and sat down with it for what seemed like forever." Gina giggled. "Finally he turns around an asks 'why would anyone send h . . . e . . . R . . . P?'"

"It must have taken me a minute to figure it out. But then I knew it was you, where you were, and that you needed help! I called security and headed for your lab."

There were other footsteps in the tunnel. Uniformed security guards appeared around the bend.

Gina put up an hand. "It's all right now — he's gone."

A lean, dark haired security officer nodded. He was carrying Jack's briefcase. "We took this off of someone without a valid badge; he had a thirty year old key that still worked. Unauthorized, of course. Yours?"

With a trembling hand, Jack reached for the briefcase and thumbed the combination lock. Inside was the paper bag with the small, gold plated box that contained his life's work He shut his eyes and bowed his head briefly. He knew now that he could leave that life with dignity. But, fortunately, not just yet.

Jack nodded to the officer. "The man who was carrying this?" he asked.

"He surrendered and asked for protective custody. Says he's doing 'research' for the Myanmar government and wants to quit." The guard looked Jack in the eye. "He had a Berretta nine millimeter on him — fired recently."

Jack gestured to the punctured file cabinet. Then tension of the last hours escaped him and he collapsed into his chair with an audible groan. Gina rushed to help him.

"Mr. Kubota, are you all right?" the security officer asked.

"Just tired." Jack put his right arm around Gina and gave the man a big grin. "As rong.. *long* as this lady loves me, I am just fine."

STORY NOTES

I was once deeply involved in an Air Force effort to find out whether antimatter might be useful in lowering the cost of getting into space. It turned out, essentially, that while you probably *could* make and store antimatter and use it for propulsion, though with much more difficulty than it might first seem, it was far too expensive, and there wasn't really any prospect for making it less so. But we can always dream. In this story, my deeply sheltered (in more ways than one) character is on the verge of succeeding when the external world breaks in on him.

The abandoned Superconducting Super Collider (SSC) buildings and tunnels are, sadly, all too real (and for sale). My story's use of some of the tunnels for neutrino and antimatter experiments is imaginary, but not really implausible. The Kubota effect itself is highly unlikely but a reminder that something of that nature could pop up somewhere at any time and change everything.

The transmission of neutrinos through solid rock to a distant detector was real; Fermilab (near Chicago) sent neutrinos to a detector at the Soudan Mine in northern Minnesota, though I don't know if anyone has ever tried to modulate the beam with a message. The cliche of adventure fiction in such circumstances is to use Morse code. But what if your protagonist doesn't know Morse code?

This is the second anthologization of this story. The first one was for *Healing Waves*, edited by Phyllis Irene Radford a few years ago, a charity anthology for victims of the horrendous Earthquake and tsunami disaster in Japan. I have a Japanese sister-in-law; I was happy to contribute something.

GDN January 2016

TIN ANGEL

G. DAVID NORDLEY & HENRY STRATMANN

They both heard the sirens.

Angel's eyes went wide. "Automobile accident, drunk driver uninjured in custody, man dead at the scene, pregnant woman, coming here, possible internal injuries, unconscious."

Dr. C. Thornhart Benson looked sharply at his new protégée, momentarily surprised. She grinned and pointed a finger to her eyes. He smiled in spite of himself. Her eyes were infrared as well as optical receivers, and she was, of course, linked into every digital device in the hospital, including the comm net. He wouldn't have to wait for the call. Too bad about whoever it was, but this was an opportunity to see what Angel could do.

"Let's do it," he said. They had been about to leave his stuffy, cluttered third-floor office at the medical center after a few minutes of paperwork and decompression following evening rounds on his patients. Instead, he put down his journal, Angel put down a half finished stocking cap she was knitting, and they headed back toward the emergency room.

He wanted to be there when the patient came in, not only to do what he could to help, but also to see how Angel would handle the situation. If the experiment called Angel was to work, she'd have to learn this side of the business.

The wail of the sirens faded as the ambulance approached the hospital. Why, he wondered, did they still let people drive precybernetic cars? Inevitably, some of them did it drunk.

"That ambulance knows its business, Angel," he remarked as they left the elevator at the first subfloor. "No need to wake everyone; the siren's done its job once the ambulance hits the emergency room driveway."

Angel nodded with such a human look of concern on her face that he had to remind himself that she wasn't even alive in the usual sense. Her repertoire of appropriate verbal and non-verbal patterns of communication was extensive, but, he knew, required only an insignificant part of the optical core memory stored in her chest.

Approximately where her heart would be, he realized.

They could "can" diagnostics, anatomy, and pharmacology in a database and drop it into her brain, but experience was something else; a collection of someone else's anecdotes just wasn't good enough; too much missing. So the Artificial Intelligence Consortium that made her decided she should have an internship just like any other doctor. Of course, one of his long-time patients was part of the consortium, and when they'd needed an advisor to teach their creation the human side of medicine, they'd talked him into it.

They'd made her bright, cheerful, tireless and innocent. He was a childless widower. It had been pretty much a case of love at first sight. Hell, he thought, he'd fallen in love with cars, an airplane, even the great old oak desk his grandfather had left him. So, his attachment to Angel had been completely predictable.

They reached the entrance to the emergency room, and he held one of the heavy swinging doors open for her.

"Well, let's go."

"I'll follow you, Dr. Benson." She winked and tossed her head, sun-touched platinum polymer threads cascading around perfect shoulders. "Age before beauty."

"Hrrmph!" He went through the door first, grinning in spite of himself.

★ ※ ★

He nodded to the ER physician, a moonlighting dermatology resident who'd been only too happy to let Benson take over a major trauma case as he and Angel charged into to the prep room, stripped to shorts and T-shirts and shrugged into scrub suits. Then it was out to the ambulance entrance to wait for the stretcher. The woman's vitals were already displayed on the high-res overhead. Shock.

"Probably hypovolemic," Angel said, her voice full of concern. "Nearly two liters of Ringer's lactate in her ... starting to stabilize." She frowned. "Thorny, I'd better tell you this now. It's Linda Coombs."

"Oh, God!" Thorny winced and shut his eyes. He'd saved her life once before, twenty five years ago, when she'd almost strangled on her own umbilical cord in one of the more difficult deliveries a G.P. ever got to do these days — by virtue of his being in her parents' living room when she made her somewhat early entrance into this world. This meant Terry was dead, he realized. He'd been at their wedding just last year. Good kid, ran his own security service . . .

Angel's hand was on his arm. "Are you . . . ?"

"I'll be fine. Thanks for telling me now. Better than recognizing her on the stretcher."

As he spoke the doors slid open and things became a blur. He and Angel followed behind as the stretcher drove itself into the trauma room with its silent burden paced paramedics hovering around like ghostly bees around a red flower. Linda's nose and mouth were covered by an oxygen mask, and a cervical collar encircled her neck. A blood-stained white sheet partially covered her limp body, which was connected at multiple puncture sites to bags of intravenous fluids hung on tall poles. The portable heart monitor, connected by multicolored wires to electrode patches stuck onto her exposed chest, beeped in a disturbingly fast and irregular rhythm. Thorny motioned to the scanning table, and they slid her onto it, tubes and poles following in an orderly ritual that only looked like mass confusion.

Thorny still found it hard to believe this was the same exuberant, vivacious young woman he'd last seen in his office not quite a week ago.

Forcing himself into objectivity, he watched Angel do a quick visual examination for external injuries. Linda's chest was bruised, with some swelling above her left breast, and she had a golf-ball sized lump in the middle of her forehead.

"Beginning scan." Angel said, and the bistatic resonance sensor head beneath the table glided to the top of Linda's head and began to move slowly down the length of her body. As the imager started its examination, Angel resumed hers.

"Pupils equal, round, and reactive. No blood in the ears or nose." She continued while one of the ER nurses — Sarah Miles, a robust, almost angrily competent black woman who Thorny knew slightly — draw blood for the analyzer.

"Type AB negative," Angel announced. "The blood bank has it — it's on its way."

The nurse shot a quick look a Thorny as she prepared to do a twelve-lead electrocardiogram, and her eyes widened a bit when he nodded. "How the . . . ?"

Thorny held up a hand. "Later. Let's get those electrodes on." He'd been assured that the medical center staff had been briefed about Angel, but seeing her in action was, it seemed, something else.

The imaging camera stopped abruptly at the level of Linda's shoulders. "No fractures or bleeding," Angel declared. "We can take off the collar."

Now it was Thorny's turn to stare. Angel smiled and the holoscreen monitor above the table snapped on. Thorny noted the image was blue tinged — probably the blue laser power setting, since the ultra-high res screen with the interference patterns was digital. The unit was a bargain when the center got it ten years ago and was bulky and hard to maintain by current standards, but it beat the hell out of what he'd had when he started practice. In rapid sequence standard views of the skull and cervical spine appeared, rotated 360 degrees, and were replaced by images of the brain. Of course, he realized, Angel controlled its operation through her optical interface. For that matter, the images she showed would be strictly for the benefit of the human staff.

The imager resumed its slow path down Linda's body and Angel moved her hands quickly over Linda's pregnancy. The tiny sensors and transducers in her fingers and palms could, Thorny remembered, could sense pressure through ultrasound and electrical fields through microwaves.

"No fractures or bleeding," she repeated, "except — ". Her hands caressed the abdomen once more. "The placenta has partially separated, and there's some intrauterine bleeding. The size of the fetus is consistent with a gestation period of 34 weeks." She paused, then looked at Thorny. "I'm sorry. No fetal heart beat or cerebral activity."

Thorny felt a brief pressure in his own chest. Even though they were too late to save her baby, Linda still had a chance. Needing to do something to restore his clinical detachment, he glanced up at the overhead monitor. "Her blood pressure is . . ."

". . . 85 over 50." Angel completed his sentence without looking up. Thorny winced; he'd forgotten.

Angel fingers brushed across Linda's chest. "No pneumothorax or any significant bleeding — mildly depressed sternal fracture — the left fifth, sixth, and seventh ribs are broken. The aorta seems intact. Her heart — " Suddenly Angel froze; utterly, inhumanly, motionless.

For a heart-rending second, Thorny thought she had malfunctioned, and realized that he might have to lift her out of the way, somehow, and take over.

But she started speaking again, her mouth moving while the rest of her body remained eerily rigid. "Her left ventricular function is very poor. I'm not sure how to explain that."

Thorny sighed in relief, and remembered how often he'd told her; "When in doubt, don't just do something, stand there." Apparently, she'd taken that literally. He shook his head, pushed his attention back to the patient, and wrinkled his forehead.

"I'm not sure either. Her grandmother died of heart failure at sixty, and her mother at forty two — though that was complicated by smoking. But Linda never had any signs of a heart problem. I . . . "

Suddenly, Angel was a blur of motion.

"She's in v-fib!" Nurse Miles shouted. "No pulse!"

Even before the sentence was completed Angel had grabbed the defibrillator paddles, and charged the machine.

"Clear!" Angel ordered, and everyone obeyed instantly. Chalk up one for a humanoid robot, Thorny thought; people might have hesitated if something that was obviously a machine had issued that order.

Angel delivered the electrical shock to Linda's chest. Thorny peered anxiously at the heart monitor — and exhaled thankfully as it started beeping again. Nurse Miles pressed her index and middle fingers against Linda's neck, and smiled slightly. "Good pulse."

Speaking for their benefit, Angel ordered an intravenous bolus and drip of Cardiopax. The IV unit chimed in response before she finished saying "bolus."

As Angel still held the defibrillator paddles, Thorny placed a tube down Linda's throat to help her breath and made sure it was positioned properly. He started to ask Nurse Miles to connect it to the ventilator when . . .

"Clear!" Angel shouted, signifying that Linda's heart had stopped again.

Once, twice, three times — finally her heart started beating again, but now her blood pressure was dangerously low. They were losing her, Thorny thought, there was no time to . . .

But before he had a chance to speak, Angel brushed the nurse aside as the cart containing the cardiopulmonary support pump scooted over to the table. Moving so fast her hands seemed blurred, Angel prepped Linda's right groin and then, more deliberately, threaded the catheters.

"Right atrium," Angel announced, then "proximal aorta". As Thorny nodded, there was another blur of motion and Angel hooked the pump up and primed it.

They waited a minute in silence, then two.

Come on, Linda, Thorny silently pleaded.

Linda's vital signs stabilized as the pump assisted Linda's heart and brought oxygen to her body. Thorny allowed himself a breath. The nurse stood there wide eyed, shaking her head.

"I never . . . I never . . ."

"Sorry," Angel said. "I had to move very fast."

"No, dear, don' be sorry," the woman chuckled as she recovered her composure. "If you can do that, you've got to do that. Jus' happy I didn't get in your way. Look, blood pressure up to 100 over 60; heart rate's only 90. I'm Sarah Miles. You?"

"Angel S. R. X. It means surgical robot, experimental."

The dermatologist, who'd stayed well out of the way during all of this, cleared his throat nervously. So much, Thorny thought, for staff briefings.

"You ain't human!?" Nurse Miles exclaimed.

"No," Angel giggled, "But I'm a pretty good simulation, trying to get better. I'd like to be your friend."

Nurse Miles just stood there with her mouth open.

Thorny cleared his throat, "Angel, that might be too much of the direct approach. Meanwhile, we'd better finish the whole body scan, and then get her to the OR so we can . . . take care of that bleeding placenta. Also, we need to get cardiology and surgery involved. We still don't know why Linda's heart isn't working."

If the tests and all Angel's tricks didn't tell them, they'd have to go in and find out.

Angel nodded. "I called them while I was talking to Nurse Miles. Dr. Bruk Tunman is on for cardiology, but he hasn't answered yet. Dr. Elvis Creighton is on for surgery, and he just said that he's on his way. I hope you don't mind."

Thorny shook his head. "No, that's fine. They're both good." But to himself he added, Damn. It would have to be their chief surgeon. No one with that high an opinion of himself should ever have been made chief of anything.

Nurse Miles looked at him, "You in charge of her, or it, or . . . whatever?" she wanted to know.

"I'm her instructor. And, yes, she's supposed to be a she."

The nurse gave a wide grin. "Then as far as I'm concerned, she it is. Never been friends with a robot before, though we've got a bunch of them around. They're kind of standoffish. Not like you, Dr. Angel."

Angel laughed. "Thanks, Sarah. That makes me feel good. I'm really look forward to meeting Dr. Tunman and Dr. Creighton too, and I hope they're as nice to work with as you are."

Thorny cleared his throat. "Well, we can always hope." he said slowly and deliberately.

Angel picked up on it. Good pattern recognition algorithms, of course. She looked a question.

"Tunman will probably be thrilled to meet you, but I'm a little concerned about how Creighton will react."

"Amen to that," Nurse Miles added with no hint of humor in her voice.

★ ❋ ★

Within the next hour, they were in the operating room. Linda's blood pressure had dropped a little with induction of general anesthesia but then, to Thorny's relief, held steady. If her body could take the stress of surgery, he thought, there was a good chance she could still make a full recovery. Before the accident Linda's health had been excellent — she'd been a vigorous swimmer and runner until her figure had gotten too awkward a month or so back.

Angel's hands moved deftly and quickly during the Caesarean section. This would be the sixth one she'd performed under his supervision. She had seemed a little hesitant and unsure of herself the first time — while she was full of simulations of exactly how it should be, but every real body is a bit different, and her neural net processors still had to fit her body's motor responses and pattern recognition subroutines to the variances in real patients. He'd imagined, absurdly, little gears turning and slipping in her head — but after she oriented, her skill and speed far exceeded that of any human he had ever seen.

Linda's fetus turned out to be male — stillborn, of course. Despite himself, Thorny thought back to that last office visit. No, she and Tom didn't want to know what its sex was. "We don't care if it's a boy or a girl. Just as long as it's healthy."

I'm sorry, Linda. Sometimes there's nothing anyone can do.

An hour later, as they closed the incision, a voice came over the intercom. "Dr. Creighton is here."

The tall, boyish, good-looking Dr. Creighton raised an eyebrow at Angel when they walked into the recovery area, but spoke to Thorny.

"I saw your patient's tests. Her aorta looks good, but her cardiac enzymes are sky-high. I suspect she had a bad myocardial contusion, or maybe a blocked coronary artery . . . so . . . I should open her up and make sure nothing needs repair. She might need a ventricular assist device." He scrutinized Angel more closely. "I've been working with voice interface surgical robots for years, Benson. They do a good job of holding clamps, microcams, lasealers, and so on. First time I've seen one do anything as sophisticated as that support pump hook-up, though."

"Thank you, Dr. Creighton," Angel beamed.

"I'd prefer your machine didn't speak to me unless spoken to, however. It is your instrument and under your control. Agreed, Benson?"

Angel looked confused and said nothing. Legally, of course, Dr. Creighton was right. Thorny touched Angel on the arm to indicate his approval of her conduct in the circumstances.

"Agreed, Dr. Creighton," Thorny rasped, struggling to keep his irritation out of his voice. "It might be interesting to the board for her to perform the exploratory — the AI Consortium provided funding to cover this sort of thing."

Creighton's mouth twitched at the corners. He was, of course, aware of the arrangement.

"At your direction, of course," Thorny continued. "Angel can handle the standard teleoperated mechanical assistants through her data link much more expeditiously than a human doctor. She's really something special."

"She?" Creighton grinned and wiped a shock of jet-black hair back to his youthful hairline. His jug ears and toothy smile, Thorny thought, completely misrepresented his internal nature, and he wondered if Angel would pick up on that. "So it's Hoffmann and Olympia is it?" Creighton laughed, exploiting a fondness for opera which was their only mutual interest outside of medicine. In Offenbach's opera, the hero, Hoffman, fell tragically in love a life-like spring-powered mechanical doll. "Does she, then, have a cunt, too?"

Ouch, Thorny grimaced, but nodded to Angel. She, he had been briefed, should exhibit a studied, Miss Manners sort of coolness when confronted with repeated and unfair hostility. This, her design team maintained, would be usually less dangerous in most circumstances than a complete servility that would handicap her ability to help others. Part of what the hospital board had asked him to do was to evaluate her ability to handle real world stress of this kind. It occurred to him that it was just possible, however unlikely, that Creighton's crude remark was a conscious test of both Thorny and Angel.

"I haven't been equipped with simulated reproductive organs." she responded with a prim academic inflection, "However, there are anatomically correct designs which could be incorporated in a few days time to allow me to function in an educational role. May I ask what your interest is?"

"Benson," Dr. Creighton hissed, incongruously maintaining his boyish smile all the time, "one more smart-ass remark like that and your 'Doctor Olympia' doesn't step foot in this hospital again. Now, it doesn't say a goddamn thing in my presence except when I tell it to. And then it says yes, no, or provides data. Or I'll take it's wind up key away. Clear?"

Thorny shot a look at Angel, but she maintained a poised, expressionless, silence. She recognized a legitimate human order when she heard one.

"Very clear, Dr. Creighton," Thorny answered, with just a hint of senior to junior condescension in his voice. Creighton caught that and a brief cloud passed over his face.

"We'll start in ten minutes," he humpfed. "If we have to, we'll implant a temp and put her on the donor list. Agreed?"

"Agreed."

"See you then, Benson. Piece of cake." Creighton grinned and sauntered out of the room.

"Damned idiot jerk!" Thorny grumbled, too softly to be heard in the next room.

"Dr. Benson?" Sarah Miles entered through the main door. "I just finished my shift in the ER, and I came up to see if I could help out with our patient." She winked at him. "Never heard you speak like that 'bout anyone!"

"Nurse Miles, Angel, when someone's ego and stupidity puts others at risk, it's worse not to say something. He's a good surgeon, maybe a great one. But that kind of attitude about the kind of advance that Angel represents could keep people from getting the care they should get."

"I'm a robot," Angel stated with a shrug of her shoulders, "so I shouldn't care if he insults me. But I don't like it if what he says about me keeps me from helping people. Not at all. So I do care."

"Don' let it worry you, Angel," Sarah Miles. "He got more nerve tissue in his fingertips than his skull. He talks about me like that when I'm not around. I've heard him on the intercom."

"But he doesn't to your face?" Angel inquired.

"If he tried that just once, I'd have the union burn his ass so bad he'd never sit down. Notice he didn't say boo to me? Too bad they made you a doctor instead of a nurse. You'd get more respect."

A smile flickered on Thorny's face, despite his concern for Linda Coombs. "Perhaps they didn't," he said, with an arched eyebrow, "want to overreach themselves on the first demo."

Nurse Miles grinned and Angel grinned too. Pattern recognition and response, Thorny thought.

"Appropriate?" Angel asked with a wink that said she knew she'd used just the right pattern.

"Very," Thorny nodded.

"Uh," Sarah Miles asked. "If I'm too nosy, jus' say so. But do you have feelin's like people?"

"No, you're not too nosy. I'm supposed to be a demonstration so I'm designed to be very comfortable with that kind of question. I have a very human pattern of social behavior," Angel shrugged her shoulders, "because it's pretty much copied from what humans do.

"I'm always evaluating a large number of randomly generated possible behaviors and assigning preference values, on the basis of my programmed priorities, to the futures those behaviors are likely to help create. By definition, the higher the preference value, the better I feel. I know that's a mouthful, Sarah, but it means when something's going my way, I say I feel good about it and show it the way people do. Expressions and inflections are part of your language. I know a lot of it and I'm learning more all the time."

Angel beamed at the nurse, "And, Sarah, when you ask questions about me, well, that's going my way, and I feel good about that! So don't be shy."

Sarah laughed heartily and rolled her head from side to side. "Oh, you' sure not the first lady who likes to talk about herself! Well, I' seen a lot of doctors in my day and you're not the worst by a long shot. Now how 'bout helping me get our patient prepped? We're kinda short on staff."

Thorny pursed his lips. Would a nurse ask a doctor who wasn't a robot to do that? But Angel was going to need every friend she could get. She looked at him, and he gave her a wink and a nod. So she turned and followed Sarah back to the operating room.

"Sarah," Angel asked as they left, "do you knit?"

★ ❋ ★

Thorny was tense in the OR. The "textbook" sternotomy technique had to be changed to take into account Linda's fractured breastbone and ribs and was a severe test of Angel's ability to adapt — to use the general information and images stored in her database and modify her approach to fit this specific situation. Angel didn't move as quickly as she had in the ER, or when she did the C-section; she froze at times, then moved in spurts.

"Benson, where's that key?" Creighton griped once when she was motionless for a particularly long time.

Thorny, worried himself, shot a cold look at the surgeon. The non-standard chest opening was a good test, but he didn't want to see Linda open like that any longer than absolutely necessary. But when the heart was finally exposed, he snuck a look at the time and relaxed a bit. Actually, they were right on schedule; it had only seemed longer because of the uneven pace.

"Well, let's take a look here," Creighton said. His gloved hands disappeared inside Linda's chest. "It's just as I thought. Everything else looks OK, but her left ventricle is shot. Well, we knew that. Looks like she's going to need a new heart." He glanced up at Thorny. "We'll put her on full cardiopulmonary bypass, and then start." Without a glance at Angel, he added, "Robot, cannulate the superior vena cava."

Angel didn't move.

"What's the problem, Angel?" Thorny asked.

"I only see a small contusion involving the anterior wall. The rest of the left ventricle may just be stunned. If we can use an assist device, we might be able to tide her over until her heart recovers on its own. There have been several good review articles in the past year on the management of myocardial contusion in the Journal of the American College of Cardiology and . . ."

"Is," Creighton hissed, "this machine questioning my judgment?"

"Angel," Thorny said as smoothly as he could, "is providing data. She has up-to-the-minute access to the literature . . ."

"And so does a freshman medical student with a computer, but that doesn't make him qualified to give an expert opinion on something like this." Creighton's pupils flared above his surgical mask. "I've never seen any patient like this survive without a transplant, and, Old Boy, no pseudo-gynecological toy is going to tell me otherwise. Now either program this thing to follow my instructions, or get it and yourself out of here and I'll finish the operation!"

Angel turned to him, and reality set in. Thorny wasn't an expert in this area. He couldn't tell if a heart needed to be replaced by looking at it. Dr. Tunman, the cardiologist, was qualified to argue with Creighton — but they never had been able to reach him. And a decision had to be made now.

Linda Coombs was precious to him. He didn't want her to become one of Creighton's statistics if her heart wasn't replaced. Still, he wondered whether they would really be doing her a favor by giving her a mechanical heart. That choice had the potential of saving her life, if a donor heart could be transplanted later. But in the meantime she would have to live with the constant threat of a crippling stroke from a blood clot, or dying suddenly — or, worse, perhaps a lingering, painful death on life support — if the device malfunctioned.

He thought Angel might be right about the lack of serious damage, but there was no way for him to enforce that. If he told her not to do it, she wouldn't; — but Creighton would; and Angel would probably never get another chance. That wouldn't help Linda at all. Damn!

"Angel, we'll talk later. Right now, I think the best thing for Linda is for you to follow Dr. Creighton's direction to the best of your ability."

"I feel bad about this. Very well."

Once decided, her fingers, and those of her teleoperated assistants moved quickly and surely. Linda Coombs' heart was on a tray and the latest Rockwell in her chest in minutes. Thorny checked the telemetry to see that its glucose/hemoglobin fuel cells were up to full voltage, and nodded to the two surgeons. A charade for Creighton's benefit — Angel, of course, already knew the device was ready.

The rest of the operation was anticlimactic. Angel disconnected the heart-lung bypass, and the new heart took over. Both she and Creighton seemed satisfied by the readings. A special-purpose telop, bristling with microwaldos descended from the OR ceiling like a spider, and Angel used it to identify and ligate a few small bleeding vessels. Creighton seemed to lose interest about that time, mumbling something about the rest of the operation being routine and that he would check Linda again when she reached Recovery. Thorny, however, took a mild stimulant and stayed, fascinated with the repair work despite the hour.

Tireless Angel continued to work, closing Linda's chest. She applied a coral-based cement to the sternum and rib fractures that set in minutes and would be stronger than the adjoining bone until it was replaced by regeneration.

They finished at four A.M, and Angel bounced out to the Recovery

Room as bright and cheery as always. Thorny followed her, considerably less energetically.

"Except for her heart, Linda will be just as good as new in a few weeks!"

"Except for her heart, her baby, and her husband." Thorny reminded Angel. "And she doesn't know she's lost any of that yet, except maybe that she got a look at her husband before she lost consciousness."

"Post-trauma depression candidate, then?" Angel replied, her voice full of serious concern intonations.

"Angel, I've known Linda all her life. She's sensitive, passionate, drives herself had and takes things hard. I'm not sure how much she's going to take all this; everything she was living for is gone."

"That could be serious." Angel agreed. "The reason isn't known, but depression has been associated with an increased risk of implant clotting. We could reduce that risk by 50% with a tetracyclic antidepressant. At least, that's what Withers, Yung, and Zegrov reported in last month's *Archives of* . . . "

Thorny held up a hand. "First, it's too late for me to think like that. Let's just get her to the ICU and keep her asleep for another twenty four hours at least so we, I mean I, will be ready for her. Second, antidepressants can have some nasty side effects, like dropping her blood pressure. Her Rockwell won't help very much with that."

"You're right. Why didn't I think of that? The data's there. I just don't always create the right question."

"You can't anticipate everything, Angel. Look, Creighton's right about some things. There's a hell of a lot more to practicing medicine than just quoting articles. Every patient is unique. 'Cookbook' medicine works most of the time, but it takes judgment and experience to know when the usual rules don't apply — and those are the kinds of things you can't program. That's why you're doing this residency." Thorny winced at what he had to say next, but he had to be fair. "And we can't judge Creighton just on his phony personality. Many people actually like that style, and he really is an outstanding surgeon." He was trying to convince himself as much as Angel.

She nodded, seriously.

"I'm awfully tired." Thorny sighed. "These are late hours for a sixty-seven year old. I'll be back in the office about eleven, I suspect. I hope you don't mind answering phones."

"Not at all, Thorny." This time he got a hug that was a little scary in its intensity. "I never forget a message. Good night."

"Yeah. Night."

He left the recovery room and called his car, which met him by the time he'd walked down the stairs and out of the lobby. The east was already gray. Talk about the lullaby of Broadway! Looked like another snowstorm on its way, too. Suited his mood.

Angel's performance, he thought as he dozed off on the freeway, was the only saving grace in a very bad day, but it had only gotten her a fifty-fifty acceptance with the hospital staff, in his estimation. And that was equating Nurse Miles with the Chief of Surgery. And God help Linda Coombs when she finally woke up. And what would pathology say about her heart in the clear light of twenty-twenty hindsight?

The care woke him up in his driveway, and he staggered up the icy steps and into the house.

That morning he dreamed he was on Wheel of Fortune; never mind that the last show had been twenty years ago and Vanna White was now getting senior citizen discounts. Somehow he kept getting "bankrupt" and selecting letters anyway. Then he realized that it wasn't Vanna turning the letters, it was Angel. And she wasn't turning letters, she was turning over tombstones, all bright and smiley.

Late the next day, Thorny's home cybersystem informed him that the pathology report on Linda Coombs heart was available, and he pulled it up on his wall screen.

Good news and bad news; good news that they hadn't removed the patient's heart without cause. Bad news in that, apparently, Angel and he had been wrong.

"Angel?" he called, not loudly because the cybersystem would contact her wherever she was.

"Yes, Thorny?" her voice came instantly.

"Are you busy?"

"I'm assisting Dr. Tunman and Nurse Miles with a coronary endoscopy and ultrasonic atherectomy. He told me he felt bad really he wasn't available the other night — he knew Dr. Creighton was around, he was tied up with a very sick patient over in Coronary Care, and he just never noticed that his link wasn't working. He felt sorry about that, so he volunteered to teach me the procedure."

Thorny wondered if there was any correlation between the times Creighton was on call and the times other people's personal data links stopped working, but put the uncharitable thought from his mind.

"We're working on a seventy-two year old black male," Angel continued, "mildly obese, apparently healthy until he started having severe chest pains with exertion about two weeks ago. He had a strongly positive stress test, and Dr. Tunman thinks he probably has three-vessel or left main coronary disease. The patient was really nervous about having the procedure, so we had to sedate him pretty heavily. So, yes, I'm busy, but I can talk to you, or as many as ten other people, in parallel, without affecting what I'm doing because I have to do things at about one tenth the speed I could do them — so that I can be supervised. That leaves a lot of me available for side conversation. I like it when you ask questions about me." Her voice smiled.

"Glad to hear it, Angel." Thorny laughed: the comment was pure Angel as he'd come to know her. All he'd asked was if she'd been busy. Listening carefully, Thorny could hear the man snoring in a deep bass in the background.

"Thorny, I've got emergency in C-12." Bruk Tunman said, his light Balkan accent somewhat more evident than usual. A prominent, but ethnically mixed, cardiologist before the troubles, he'd had to learn a new language and repeat much of his medical schooling at age fifty-three just to get licensed here. Little things didn't bother Bruk, and, while he never said so in so many words, he had way of shrugging off complaints with a look off into space that seemed to shout, loudly and clearly, "You think you have problems?"

"There is nothing more I have to teach Angel here. You can watch her this way, Thorny yes?"

Thorny hesitated a moment. It was a stretch; if something went wrong with Angel and a doctor wasn't physically present . . . But Bruk didn't use the word emergency lightly. And Sarah Miles was there — someone who knew Angel and someone he could trust.

"Probably better than if I were there. I've got her, Bruk."

"Thank you," he said, and was gone.

"Well, Angel, how is it going?" Thorny asked

"It's fascinating; we'll have those arteries good as new in less than an hour."

"Good. Ah, Angel, have you checked the pathology report on Linda Coombs?"

"Yes. Looks like I was wrong. There was a lot more damage to her heart than I recognized. Thorny, I know what's in the literature, but I'm afraid it's biased toward the interesting, unusual, and successful. Dr. Tunman says he's seen patients whose hearts were in that condition as well, and that none of those who didn't get a mechanical heart or an immediate transplant survived. So I owe Dr. Creighton an apology — but he probably wouldn't take one from a machine, would he?"

"No, Angel, he probably wouldn't."

"I think we might need his advice, though."

"Huh?"

"I'm having a little trouble here. Just now. I don't know why, but I can't find the ostium of the left coronary artery. I didn't have any difficulty with any of the other patients, and I don't know what I'm doing wrong."

"You can't find the opening for the artery?" What kind of problem had Angel got into now? He couldn't supervise her twenty-four hours a day, and she never slept, so it was inevitable that something would come up when someone else was "using" her.

As he thought about it a few seconds more, Thorny became even more worried. The procedure Angel was doing now was similar to what she'd done when she'd catheterized Linda's femoral artery to connect her to the assist pump. Both involved puncturing the artery and threading a long, thin, plastic-coated tube up to the heart. The only difference was the kind of catheter she was using. This one had a fiber-optic network inside it, and a combined sensor-transducer at its tip. By threading it into a coronary artery, blockages limiting how much blood was getting through could be seen, and then broken up.

If Angel could do a procedure under emergency conditions, why couldn't she do something like it again under less hectic conditions? Her programming was supposed to let her "learn by experience". What if that ability was more limited than what he'd come to believe?

Angel's voice came back on line.

"No, I can't find the artery. Here, I'll send you video." Thorny's wall screen flicked on to an endoscope-eye view of the inside of the patient's aorta. There was no pathology Thorny could see.

But no sign of the tiny opening to the left coronary artery either.

"I've done everything just right," Angel continued, "the endoscope control unit checks out fine and I can't find anything wrong through the hospital computer either. My ultrasonic imaging tells me the catheter tip is within a few millimeters of the right place. Maybe Dr. Creighton could tell me what I'm doing wrong. Could you talk to him? He's not likely to respond to me."

"Right away, Angel." Well, maybe Creighton would respond to the "humble seeker of wisdom at the feet of the master" approach. Maybe.

But not likely.

"Benson?" Creighton's voice came on line, and his face smirked from Thorny's screen. Of course, Angel had placed the call.

"I'm on, Creighton." Thorny explained the problem.

"Your machine's in over its head again. I've got video, and it's obvious what the problem is. Ask if it did a high-res scan of the heart before it started. Or was this Nurse Miles' project?"

Ask her yourself! Thorny started to say, but thought better of it. Diplomacy, diplomacy . . .

"Dr. Tunman didn't require it, Dr. Creighton, but it sounds like a good idea now . . ." to everyone but the taxpayers who were going to pay for it, he added silently. "Angel — "

"I can't get enough resolution with my own sensors. The machine's on its way." Within a minutes, the imaging table drove through the door and Nurse Miles and Angel had eased the three hundred pound patient from one table to another. Thorny had to smile; no two ordinary women could have done that without an orderly's help. But Angel and Nurse Miles were, each in her own way, most un-ordinary.

"Well, those two are good for something, I see," Creighton chuckled in what he must have thought was humor. Sarah Miles raised her head, jaw clenched — but she couldn't stare at a disembodied voice. Thorny counted to ten. But soon, a tri-D view of the patient's heart appeared on the screen.

"You see?" Creighton said triumphantly. "This patient only has a single large coronary artery, coming off the right aortic sinus. That's why your machine couldn't find the left coronary — there isn't one! Any experienced cardiologist would have recognized what was going on and done a scan right away, without freezing up! It makes you wonder what else they left out of its programming."

Angel's voice returned. "I was focused on the procedure, and it didn't occur to me that his heart might just be different. I won't make that mistake again. But I do know about coronary anomalies. They occur in 1% of the population . . . "

"Benson . . . " Creighton started, ice in his voice.

"Angel, let's try to get Dr. Tunman back on the line as soon as he's free." Thorny interrupted. This was turning into another confrontation, and not reinforcing Angel's social matrix at all. "Until then, just do what Dr. Creighton says." Silently, Angel completed the procedure flawlessly at Creighton's direction, ignoring a sarcastic comment now and then with a robotic ease that Thorny envied.

"Benson," Creighton drawled as Angel was removing the last catheter, "I hope you're going to be honest to the hospital board about how dangerous a robot like that is."

"Dangerous, Elvis?" Thorny used the younger man's first name. He'd been in practice twenty years longer than Elvis Creighton, and in what most people now acknowledged to be a more demanding practice than any specialist's. "Elvis, whatever mistakes Angel has made are minor compared to the mistakes any intern makes, and she learns from them. She never forgets. And she has skills neither you nor I can ever hope to duplicate."

"Duplicate? Interesting choice of words, Benson. We can duplicate the skills without the bogus personality. This fraud of yours looks and acts too much like a person — so much so that someone can forget at times that it isn't a person. It doesn't have a person's judgment; it freezes up and consults when a real doctor would make a decision. Instead of doing what you tell it, it argues with you! I'll bet when Tunman finds out how your little wind-up toy endangered his patient, he'll be so mad we'll all learn some Croatian they don't put in dictionaries!"

"Benson, we can have the useful parts of her, of it, duplicated as we need them. We don't have to anthropomorphize it, and shouldn't."

"But I think," Thorny replied evenly, "that human simulation was the general idea. The AI Consortium hoped that packaging their technology as a compassionate young woman would lessen patient's psychological fear of advanced medical technology . . ."

"Patients! What about the doctors that have to use it? That thing is high end technology; it doesn't get used until the patients are unconscious or sedated! Has any patient even 'met' your machine yet? Have any of them known they were being worked on by some out-of-control robot?"

Thorny stared at him. The plan had been to get staff acceptance first, then start easing Angel into patient relations. But maybe that was all wrong.

"No, Angel hasn't interacted with patients, not yet. The trial still has months to go."

"Not if I have my way about it! Good day, Benson." He faded from the screen.

"Angel?"

"I heard. Maybe I should try harder to be friends with Dr. Creighton. Could he use a stocking cap? I know you don't think this is a good idea, but I've tried it twice, you and Sarah Miles, and it worked both times. No one else has wanted to be my friend."

Thorny shook his head. "Now you're questioning my judgment."

"Angel," Dr. Tunman's voice finally came on line. Thorny wondered how long he'd been monitoring them. "I would be your friend as well. Elvis is correct that I am upset. He is not correct concerning the reason for my displeasure. Instead of trying to impress you about how much he knows and you don't, he should be trying to help you learn. That is perhaps all I should say, other than I'm happy to work with you. I'm done here, not successfully I regret, but there is nothing more to do. We have another patient on the schedule in a half an hour. I'll meet you in the viewing room in about ten minutes and we go over the chart. This is okay?"

"Just fine, Dr. Tunman. I'm sorry. I'll be there."

The link counter indicated that Angel was the only one left on line. Thorny shook his head, "Angel, your 'I want to be your friend' line is corny as hell. But maybe you're right. I don't see what harm it would do. You have my permission to try."

"Should I get the reproductive education package installed first? He seems to be interested in that."

Thorny opened his mouth, but words wouldn't come. It would serve Creighton right, but the repercussions . . . Finally, he choked out: "No, Angel. Bad idea. Very bad idea."

★ ❋ ★

Two days later under a bright sun in a crisp blue sky, the snow along the roads was dirty again and puddles were breaking out of their icy prisons. It was time, Thorny decided, influenced as much by the bright springy feeling of the day as much as anything else, for Linda Coombs to wake up. Creighton, busy, had given a perfunctory concurrence and excused himself, but with Angel and her instant knowledge, Thorny felt he could handle any technical questions. Those weren't the ones that worried him.

Linda's injuries were healing well and she had been weaned off all the external hardware except for a pair of IV's, but she remained in a sedative-induced sleep. Now, all her body needed was some exercise. And a donor.

Angel turned off the IV line containing the sedative. The Rockwell heart responded to the change in chemical environment and increased it's pumping rate. After a few minutes, Linda's eyes opened.

"Doctor Benson?"

"Good afternoon, young lady. How are you feeling?"

She squirmed and smiled. "Comfy . . . fuzzy . . ." She yawned, then her eyes went wide. "Ouch . . . I'm sore all over. Where am I? Where's Terry?"

"Linda, there was an accident. Do you remember?"

"Accident? . . . I'm in a hospital! . . . What happened? . . . What day is it?"

A tone signaled that the Rockwell had reached its peak pumping rate, unable to keep up with the demands her system was trying to put on it.

"Please try to calm down," Thorny told her. "I know this is a big shock, but it's very, very, important that you try to remain calm and not work yourself up. You and Terry were on your way to his folks' place and a drunk driver hit you. It happened very quickly and Terry didn't suffer. I'm sorry." Thorny couldn't think of anything to say, so didn't as a chaos of expressions raced across Linda's face. Finally, it occurred to him to fill the void by simply answering her question.

"Today is Wednesday, the twenty-fifth, and we're very happy you're back with us."

Suddenly Linda's hands jerked up toward her nearly flat, empty belly.

"The baby . . . ." It was partly a question, and partly a scream.

"I'm sorry."

"Terry . . .?" Tears began to form on Linda's face, and Thorny placed his hand on hers. Angel looked concerned, but, following Thorny's instructions, didn't try to say anything.

"We were going to . . . it's all gone." Sobbing, Linda shook her head. "Just like that, everything, all gone? This isn't happening! Dr. Thorny, No! No!"

"Linda, Linda," he shook his head. "It's awful, I know. I was a basket case for a week when my wife died, and I still miss her. But there will be a lot of people to help you, and don't worry about the time. You just take all you need. You'll just have to go on, now, and concentrate on getting well. That's what Terry would have wanted."

She sobbed and nodded, uncertainly. He gave her hand a slight squeeze.

"There's something more you have to know, then we'll leave you alone if you want. Your heart was badly damaged in the accident. We had to give you an artificial heart."

She looked at her chest, confused, then horrified. "I don't feel different . . . "

"It's a good one, but you'll have to be careful with it. The first rule is to try not to let yourself get too emotional, or exercise too strenuously. It can follow you a little way, but not what you were used to. The second rule is that you'll need to eat a fair amount of sugar. It isn't like the old ones, with wires and batteries; it pretty much runs off the same fuel the rest of your body uses. But it's not as efficient as a real one, so you'll need to eat and drink more. Except for salt — that's a no-no. The third rule is that you'll have to be very careful about cuts and things. You'll need to take blood thinning medication as long as you have it, because clots tend to form and break off inside it, and they can block the flow of blood to your brain."

"But that's the worst. Otherwise, you should be able to lead a fairly normal life until we find a donor. Then you'll get a brand new heart that will work just as well as your old one." He smiled reassuringly, but wondered how much of this was really getting through to her.

"After you get it, you'll have to take medicine for the rest of your life, but there's no reason you shouldn't live as long as you would have if this hadn't happened. Back in the Dark Ages, when I was a medical student, the only drugs they had to prevent the body from rejecting a new heart didn't work all the time, and weakened a person's resistance so much that a lot of them died from terrible infections even though the heart itself was still okay. The medicines we use now are 'customized' for each person's new heart. They're nearly perfect at fooling the body into thinking that you still have your original one, and they don't have any of the bad side effects like infections that the old ones . . ." He trailed off. He was babbling like an old fool, he realized, and Linda's mind was somewhere else.

Linda's eyes suddenly got wider. "I remember it now. We were coming home from his parents' place. Someone crossed over the median. I screamed, Terry hit the brakes, then we skidded and hit the rail and the airbags went off. We skidded around and around, it seemed like forever. Then the other car just slammed right into Terry's door. I slipped up over my belt and slammed into the windshield and dashboard. Terry's head . . . I . . ." She was sobbing again. "It's all over. Everything's gone."

Thorny put a hand on her shoulder, like he had when she was

twelve and had to convince her that acne was not the end of her life, either. "Not for you, Linda. With luck, you'll have a long full life ahead of you."

"Life? It's all gone." Linda's tear-streaked face hardened, and she took a breath and looked at her chest. "Doctor Thorny?"

"Yes?"

"Can you just turn it off? Please?"

No! he thought, Linda, don't do that to me.

"Please. I want to be with Terry and my baby. Not be some kind of ghoul or cyborg. I'm sorry to have been all this expense and trouble but I don't want to live this way. I shouldn't have survived. It's not fair. I don't want to have to deal with this. Please don't do this to me, Dr. Thorny, just put me back to sleep, forever." Linda shut her eyes and turned her head on the pillow and sobbed.

"Linda . . . Linda, I can't do that. You can go on. Everyone does, even though they feel like there's no point. And then they find something else. You'll do that. You have to." He motioned to Angel, and she re-started the intravenous sedative at its lowest dose.

Linda shook her head and didn't say anything. Thorny, you old idiot, he told himself, you've been down this road one way or another, often a dozen times a year, for forty years of practice. If you can't make it better, at least stop screwing it up!

"Look, Linda, I need to talk to the nurses taking care of you. Could you put off any drastic decisions until I get back? Give old Dr. Thorny that much?"

Linda nodded her head on the pillow. He blinked and she looked like she was five, not twenty five, when he'd helped get her through an ear ache and she'd told him he was called Thorny because he was always sticking people. He and Ellie had never had any children of their own; too poor, then too busy, then too old. But he'd had a thousand little girls and boys come through his offices. He patted her on the shoulder again, possibly as much for his own comfort as for hers.

"I'd like you to meet someone. This is Angel. She's a doctor, and a robot. The first. I'm her teacher. She knows just about everything, and she's been working with me. We were in the hospital when you came to the Emergency Room after the accident, and as part of her training she helped to treat you. I wish to God it hadn't been you, but we can't do anything about that now."

Linda's eyes opened and she turned to Angel as if looking at her for the first time.

"Hi." Angel said.

"Hello." Linda's voice was lifeless, but her eyes held a spark of wonder. "You're a robot?"

"Uh, huh. They finished me five weeks ago and I've . . . "

"Excuse me ladies," Thorny interrupted. "I should be back in a little while."

As he left the room, he heard Angel say; "I'd like to be your friend. Do you knit?"

He smiled. The folks at the consortium said they'd been going for independent judgment.

★ ❋ ★

"Well, how are we this morning!" Dr. Creighton beamed at Linda, throwing his not inconsiderable charisma at Thorny's patient, in for her bi-weekly. They stood amid the light wood of Dr. Creighton's spacious ninth floor Danish Revival anteroom, looking out over the fresh and flowered spring green of the medical center's spacious suburban grounds. Linda seemed to be reasonably cheerful for an outpatient waiting on a heart transplant, but Thorny felt rumpled, out of place, and out of sorts. He had asked Creighton if Angel could be present, but after the third sarcastically condescending demurral couched in elegantly gross innuendo concerning his relationship with Angel, Thorny got the point. Further argument would have only upset Linda.

"Oh, hmmm. That looks good!" Dr. Creighton continued, grinning at Linda.

"What looks good?" She asked, smiling back.

"I see you've been sticking to that high energy diet, maybe even a little too well? Heh, heh."

Linda blushed. She had, Thorny realized, put on a few pounds.

"Feeling good?"

Linda nodded, then hesitated. "I've been getting a little stomach ache every now and then. And I'm a little out of shape — ."

"Oh? Probably too much rich food. And according to the tests we did just before you left the hospital, your circulation's fine. Rockwell's making a good product these days, not to worry. But we can't keep it forever, can we? Well, no rush. You're moving up the donor list; I'd say in a month . . . "

"If this heart's doing so well, why can't I keep it?"

"Oh, everything wears out, eventually. We'll see you in another week. See that she gets some exercise, Thorny. I want her fit for the transplant. Speaking of exercise, I'm due for some of my own; a quick nine at Bellewood. Make yourselves at home!" With that, Creighton breezed out.

Thorny had to deliberately unclench his teeth before he could talk.

"Where's Angel?" Linda asked

"Children's wing, probably," he replied. "They aren't as prejudiced — a robot doctor doesn't bother them at all."

A cloud passed over Linda's face at the mention of children. She'd hadn't been able to keep up with her old job at the newspaper, but Thorny had been able to find a lot of free-lance editing work at the hospital and word of mouth had gotten her even more business. She could do that at home; that and the insurance settlement had given her an adequate, though not generous, income. But it seemed to him that she'd been a little morose and out of sorts lately. Maybe she could use a challenge.

"Linda, would you mind putting up with another little experiment?"

She sighed. "What now, Dr. Thorny?" Then she brightened. "Maybe you have an artificial ear for me that works off a remote control so I can turn off my hearing when certain people are talking at me!"

"Ha. I won't mention any names," he chuckled a bit, then sprung his idea. "Linda, what I'd like to try is to have Angel talk with you, as if she were going to do the surgery instead of Dr. Creighton. I'll just sit in a corner and watch. You don't mind me letting her practice on you, do you?"

"No. Angel and I are good friends. She's teaching me how to knit; I'm up to moss stitch now. I tell everyone she's the robot that cut my heart out, and they get this awful look on their faces, and we laugh and laugh. Yesterday, I asked how they made her look and act so human and she almost took herself apart in front of me. Said it was only fair since she'd seen most of my innards."

Thorny laughed. "I guess that's fair. Now, I've been too polite to ask that kind of question."

"She doesn't mind at all. She likes to show you everything. Her skin is thick and flexible, like ours. Her skeleton is just like yours or mine everywhere that counts for surface appearance, except it's plastic. Everything underneath is in some kind of padded composite. She has muscles that swell and contract just like ours when they get electricity, but they can do it a lot faster. She's got silicone implants for breasts — she says they're the same kind they used to use in flesh-and-blood women before fat cultures. But they didn't give her any nipples."

Thorny wondered how difficult it would be to have the programmers tone down Angel's cheerful exhibitionism; it wasn't always appropriate. But how small a cage does one make for a butterfly?

"Well, she's not likely to use them, is she now?" he said.

"Why not? She'd make a great nanny. I bet someone clever could figure out the plumbing. Then she'd look right in a T-shirt. And it would make her happier because she'd be able to make more people happy."

"Linda, she was designed to be that way, it's not like a she was a human being . . . "

"Hey, Dr. Thorny, she is what she is. Who cares how she got to be that way? And I can think of at least one person who could learn a lot about being a real human being from her: your great Dr. Creighton. That pompous, lecherous, phony can go take a flying you-know-what."

"Hey, yourself," Thorny chuckled — but it really wasn't funny. So Creighton had been up to his old tricks with Linda, just this side of doing anything that would generate a formal complaint. One couldn't really blame him; so many female patients went gaga over his looks and his natural charisma, the poor man probably thought that making a pass was a fail-safe way to cheer someone up.

"Linda, just because somebody has an 'M.D.' behind their name, doesn't mean they automatically qualify for a 'Saint' too. I'll grant his bedside manner stinks, but he's an outstanding surgeon, and by his own lights, a good person." Aren't we all? Thorny wondered. "He's still responsible for you, and when the time comes he's the one who's going to give you your new heart."

"I'm not going to let him cut me again. Or let him see me naked again."

"Linda, you have to have the transplant."

"Angel can do it."

"Maybe she will. But it has to be under a specialist's direction. As human as she seems, she's legally just a tool. Like a scalpel, or a stethoscope. She doesn't have her own malpractice insurance." Or her own anything. She wasn't a legal person, Thorny thought. Angel was a slave; property pure and simple. Maybe that had something to do with how protective Sarah Miles had been with her.

"Nuts. I want her to do it all alone."

"Linda, that's not possible."

Linda shrugged and looked him in the eye. "Then no operation and I die. I'm ready. Doesn't bother me at all. I shouldn't have survived in the first place. Just turn me off and save the trouble."

Thorny shook his head and tried to smile. "Please don't talk like that. I've got too much work invested in you. What if we talk to one of the other surgeons?"

"That's better, but not what I want. I want people to treat Angel like a real doctor. I've been trying to figure out why I didn't die with Terry and my baby, and maybe this is it. So I can help her. You keep saying you want me to live, Dr. Thorny. Give me something to live for. Make them let Angel do my transplant."

"Linda . . . " Thorny threw up his hands, then he thought of a way that she might accept. "I'll work on it. But I want something from you, too."

"Anything, Dr. Thorny, as long as Angel does the operation."

"Leave yourself a little room for compromise, okay? Even if Angel were a human doctor, she wouldn't be doing this alone."

"Okay. I understand there have to be others around. But I want Angel giving the orders, I want her cutting me, and I don't want Dr. Creighton anywhere near that operating room!"

"I'll do what I can," Thorny temporized.

"Please. My life depends on it."

Thorny shook his head. "Well, then, I guess you should talk to your other doctor too. Let's go find her." They left the opulence of Dr. Creighton's office for the elevator to the basement, the bustling lower floor corridors, and the children's ward with its bright painted anthropoid ducks and chickens shedding feathery chips of paint here and there. They found Angel helping a hairless young girl in a red stocking cap build a castle from red foam blocks.

"Hi, Linda." Angel beamed at them. "How are you doing today?" One wall of the castle started to collapse. Still smiling, Angel's hands moved in a blur, catching the foam blocks in mid-air and setting them back in place. The girl giggled.

"Oh, okay. Dr. Thorny thought I should talk to you."

"I'd really be happy to talk to you." Angel turned to the little girl. "Tippy, I have to go now."

The girl's forehead wrinkled. "Will you come back and play with me?"

"Sure. We're friends, aren't we?"

The girl giggled and turned to Thorny. "She can take her whole arm off!"

"Angel . . ." Thorny groaned.

Angel smiled and shrugged. "Bye, bye."

"Bye," Tippy said.

A few minutes later, they were in the cramped examining room of Thorny's office. Its narrow crack of a window looking out over a shaded parking lot filled with dirty snow left over from winter. True to his word, Thorny positioned himself in a corner and tried to make himself invisible, almost knocking his ancient analog scale over in the process.

"Are you comfortable?" Angel asked her patient, after she and Linda had sat down.

"Yes."

"How have you been feeling?"

"Oh, okay. Well, like I told Dr. Creighton, I've been getting a little stomach ache every now and then. And I'm a little out of shape. Terry's gone, but still . . ."

"You'd like to feel good about yourself, I understand. Why do you think you're out of shape?"

Linda shrugged, "I've put on some weight, so I guess that's why I get tired going up stairs. And if I try to do any work around the house, I have to stop and rest after a few minutes. I can't seem to swim full out for more than a couple of laps. Sometimes I wake up short of breath, like I had a bad dream or something. Maybe about the accident. But I'll sit up and read for a half hour or so, then get tired again and go back to sleep. Do you sleep?"

"Sometimes I shut down for a few milliseconds and reorganize my files. That's kind of what people do when they sleep, but I do it a lot faster. Hmm, Linda, have you had any swelling in your feet or ankles?"

"Sure, after I've been sitting in a chair or standing for a while. Isn't that normal? Maybe my body still thinks I'm pregnant?" There was more than a note of sadness in her voice, Thorny thought.

"Hmm, I wouldn't think so, those hormones should be out of your system by now. You said something about a stomach ache?"

"Yes, sometimes after I eat."

"Oh. Thank goodness I don't have to eat the food here!" Angel joked, and they all laughed.

"Can you show me where it hurts?" Angel continued to ask questions for the next five minutes. Finally, she finished with "any other problems, anything else you want to tell me?"

Linda squinted for a second. "Nothing that I can think of."

"If you do think of anything else, let me know. Right now, I'd like to do a physical examination. Is that OK?"

"Sure."

Thorny rose out of his chair. "Let me step out so you can put on a gown — "

Linda laughed. "That's OK, Dr. Thorny, you've seen everything before anyway."

Thorny watched Angel do a brief but thorough examination — one that was far more thorough, he reflected, with her built-in sensors than he could have done with only a stethoscope and the few basic instruments in the room. They fed A blood sample into the office wall terminal, ran a saliva slide under its microscope, and had Linda step up and down Thorny's battered old kiddie steps wearing a cellular cuff.

After Angel finished, she spoke to Linda.

"Linda, do you mind if we have you sit outside in the waiting area for a few minutes? I need to talk to Dr. Benson while we wait for the lab results."

For a second Thorny was afraid Linda was going to ask, "Why? What did you find wrong?" But instead she smiled back and said, "Sure. He walked her out and she settled down with a smile to a coverless magazine that looked like a relic from the twentieth century, and probably was.

Back in the examining room, Thorny asked. "What do you think?"

"I'm worried. Her symptoms suggested at least mild congestive heart failure, and my examination confirmed it. She's definitely retaining too much fluid — in her lungs, liver — everywhere. So I did a complete diagnostic check on her implant."

"Fortunately, there were no large blood clots inside the chambers, or on its valves. But it's still not working as well as it should. The Model 4 Rockwell is rated for a peak cardiac output of 4.9 liters per minute, but hers is down to 2.8. There have been some reports in the past few months that smaller units like the Models 4 and 5 may lose efficiency much sooner than they're supposed to owing to problems in the semipermeable membranes used for oxygen transfer. The recent article in . . . "

"I'll take your word for it, Angel."

They sat silently for a few minutes. Angel's programed knowledge of the pathophysiology of congestive heart failure, Thorny knew, was more exhaustive than his — but the basic points were simple. When a human heart began to fail, the body retained water. With a little extra fluid, the heart's reflexes made it work beat more forcefully, and for a while the person did better.

But if the body kept too much of it, the excess fluid actually made the heart work less efficiently. Then fluid leaked out into the lungs, replacing the air that was supposed to be there — and the person very gradually began to drown. When not enough blood and oxygen got to the rest of the body, the kidneys and other organs eventually failed too.

Linda's mechanical heart had none of a human one's reflexes. In her, any extra fluid was "too much" — and, if got worse, could kill her.

Angel's face became very serious and professional. "What did Dr. Creighton think?"

Thorny grunted. "Dr. Creighton thought everything was 'fine'".

Angel looked puzzled. "But what about her symptoms and . . . "

"Angel," Thorny snorted, "Dr. Creighton doesn't even know that there are any symptoms because he didn't listen to Linda. So he didn't bother to examine her, didn't check her unit, or even order blood tests. Why go to all that expense if everything's fine?

"I don't understand. Why didn't Dr. Creighton listen? Why didn't he want me to see her?"

Thorny sighed. "I don't know, Angel. For the first, you have to have a lot of self confidence to do what Elvis does; it's hard to absorb contrary data if you think you already know everything. Nor does it help to need to impress people so much that you can't admit you need any other input. For the second," Thorny shrugged, "maybe he sees himself as John Henry racing the steam hammer."

"Hell, I'm the one who should feel threatened. You'd make a great G.P., Angel. I may call myself a G.P., but really there's been no such thing as a general practitioner for almost two centuries." Actually, to be technical about it, he really hadn't been a "G.P." for a long time himself; he'd gone back and completed a Family Practice residency five years after he'd finished his internship, even done an extra two years of obstetrics — and a year with the army in Zaire back in oh seven had left him with a lot of surgical experience he'd rather not have had. But, as a slightly pugnacious "badge of honor" — especially around some of his more snobbish colleagues — Thorny still liked to call himself a "G.P."

"Back then, if a physician knew how to saw off a limb and deliver a baby — if they had a supply of morphine, calomel, foxglove, and maybe a few anemic leeches — they could do just about everything that could be done for patients. But as the 'science' part of medicine grew, no one doctor could know or do everything anymore — so some, and nowadays most, became 'specialists'.

Thorny exhaled deeply. "And now we've come full circle. With your programming, and a little more experience, you can be a 'general practitioner', in the literal sense. Potentially, not only will you be able to do everything I can, or Creighton can, or any other specialist can — but you'll be able to do it better. Someday, instead of you being my assistant, we poor human doctors will be assisting you!"

Angel looked concerned. "I don't want to threaten anyone. I just want to be their friend."

"Progress, Angel. As long as I've been around, there's been a kind of de facto hierarchy among doctors, with 'specialists' like Creighton at the top of the pyramid, and 'generalists' like me a lot closer to the base. I think Creighton knows that, if you succeed, his prestige is going to suffer. The bottom line, though, is that the kind of advance you represent is going to help patients — and that's a lot more important than bruised egos."

"Don't worry, Dr. Benson. As long as I'm around, you'll always have a job with me."

"That," he laughed, "makes me feel so much better."

Angel started to laugh too, then froze for a second. "Linda's test results are in the hospital computer." She recited a long list of lab values.

"Well?" Thorny knew all too well what they meant, and it wasn't good. But he wanted to hear Angel's interpretation; diagnostics were one of the first and most successful uses of cybernetics in medicine, providing everything was in the database.

"The low serum sodium and elevated liver enzymes are worrisome, but her BUN of 83 and her creatinine of 4.1 are very alarming. They were only 20 and 1.2 when she was discharged from the hospital." Angel paused. "If this goes on, she going to lose her kidneys — and that won't help her implant either. I think she's going to need a real heart much sooner than we expected."

Thorny thought it through. As long as Linda's kidneys worked reasonably well, they could use medications to stimulate them and get rid of some of the excess fluid. But if her kidney function got too bad, her body would retain fluid even faster. Before too long the artificial heart itself would get starved for fuel and oxygen, and work even less efficiently. Then the kidneys and lungs would get worse, which would make the implant's function deteriorate more — and the whole vicious cycle would keep on repeating itself, until her lungs filled up, or a blood clot from her failing heart caused a stroke. He remembered what he had thought when they implanted the heart — about a lingering death.

Thorny imagined Linda lying bloated, in a constantly dirty bed pan, connected to a ventilator, and surrounded by a metallic forest of IV poles. He had seen her in similar surroundings once — and he didn't want to see her to end that way. For the first time he thought seriously about her request to turn the Rockwell off. And what they might do to him if he did. Hell of a consideration, that.

"Angel, we'd better tell Linda. And then we're going to have to talk to Dr. Creighton."

✦ ✳ ✦

Things went even worse than he'd expected. Linda's response had been bad: ". . .thanks for the extra months, but I guess I'm really not supposed to be here. You can turn me off any time. Thanks anyway, Angel." Angel and Thorny had had to convince her all over again that her life had a purpose.

But Creighton's reaction was even worse.

When he found out that Thorny had ordered the tests Angel wanted and that she had made the diagnosis, he turned so red that Thorny thought Creighton would either have a heart attack himself, or resort to physical violence. Actually, either event would have simplified things — Elvis in Intensive Care, or in jail, would be Elvis out of the loop, unable to screw things up with Linda. And Thorny derived a little guilty pleasure from imagining what the AI Consortium's lawyers would do to the wealthy Dr. Creighton if he damaged Angel.

It soon became apparent that they had reached an impasse with Creighton, so, with the freedom of someone long retired from trying to climb greasy poles, Thorny went over Creighton's head.

Not unexpectedly, Creighton did not like the idea — but he didn't really have any choice in the matter and whatever revenge he might arrange would have to be delayed, and very circumspect.

✦ ✳ ✦

It was the next day when they all sat in the office of the Director of the medical center. Dr. Tunman and several other physicians involved in the transplant program had also been asked to attend. So far, Tunman and the others had said relatively little — apparently trying to stay out of the line of fire of all the verbal bullets that were flying around them.

The Director, a tall, serious obstetrician of such poise and patrician bearing that she could usually silence an interloper by raising an eyebrow, frowned severely at Dr. Elvis Creighton. The surgeon had been in fine form — earnest, sincere, at ease, never stumbling or hesitating. But the facts were a little too much, and if the Director was frowning, Thorny and some of the others were doing a slow burn.

"No one's disputing that the patient has a problem," Creighton concluded, flashing his disarming grin. "I just don't think we should exaggerate it. There are desperate patients ahead of her, and while I agree that her Rockwell's function might deteriorate further, there's also a reasonably good chance it won't. Besides, we all know any nephrologist would tell us that a moderate amount of renal failure might help for a while; it could actually reduce the risk of blood clots and . . . "

Thorny interrupted. "Elvis, whether you think so or not, the next thing in line is a stroke — and we don't have a brain machine." Or you'd be first on that list, he added silently.

Creighton shrugged. "We all know the risks. She could go on a kidney machine."

"Ma'am," Thorny bristled, "for reasons which some of us find obvious, Linda wants Dr. Creighton off her case and out of the loop." Thorny took a breath, the next wasn't going to help, but he had to be truthful. "She's not going to tolerate being rooted to tubes the rest of her life; if you as her now she'd say she'd rather be dead. She's already asked us to turn the Rockwell off rather than face some of what she has to endure." No point in trying to hide that, it was on the record. "And, frankly, I'm not into raising human vegetables no matter how profitable they might be."

The Director raised the other eyebrow at Thorny. "That makes me wonder how good a candidate she really is for a transplant. Patient will-to-live and compliance is very important. What if she decides after she gets her transplant that she's also not going to take her antirejection medications? We can't 'waste' a heart on someone who's not going to take her doctor's advice, and die anyway."

"Exactly!" Creighton interjected, waving a hand dramatically. "And these calls should be made by experienced specialists." He glared at Thorny. "Not by a generalist who sees these kind of things once in a, blue moon, however well-meaning he may be." His eyes barely moved toward Angel. "And certainly not by an experimental robot, no matter how superficially sophisticated it may seem."

Angel gave Creighton as cold a look as Thorny had ever seen from her. "Ma'am, may I defend myself?" she asked.

"That does it," Creighton hissed. "Benson, get that, that thing out of here!"

"Dr. Creighton . . ." the Director murmured, followed by an embarrassed silence; Elvis didn't run this meeting.

He appeared to calm down instantly, and flashed his boyish, charismatic smile in her direction. "Pardon me ma'am."

"No." The smile disappeared from Creighton's face.

"Angel," the Director continued, "Thorny tells me you've followed the patient since her accident, and I'm very interested in what you have to say about all this."

"Thank you." Angel stood up so she could be seen by everyone. "Although Linda Coombs is 'competent' in the medical sense of the word, she's depressed. You all know the 'facts' about her — how she lost everything she was living for. Is it any wonder that she might be ambivalent about living? Is it any wonder that she might speak impulsively and say things that might seem noncompliant — things that a critical person might use to make her look like a bad risk?"

"I know what the 'rules' say to do in this kind of situation. I literally can't forget them. But we have to think about how to apply them, and do what's best for the particular person we're caring for.

"Linda is not non-compliant in general. She's followed Dr. Benson's instructions exactly, even though she knew it would compromise her figure, which had always been important to her. Linda doesn't want to die, but her life has to have more of a purpose than just existing and she does have a reason to live which has become very important to her. That reason happens to be me, and what I and others like me can do to help people . . ."

"This self serving egotism is hardly an objective analysis," Creighton sneered.

"Dr. Creighton, are you suggesting our robot is not being objective?" the Director inquired mildly. "How very interesting. Do continue, Angel."

Angel's face was most hard set and un-Angelic. Where, Thorny wondered, had she got that?

"I have to make a point. I, and future robots like me, can help many people — if we are allowed to do it. I'm an artificial intelligence, yes. But I have likes, dislikes, and a full range of human emotional expression. I don't want to hurt anyone, but when someone's insecurity and stupidity . . ."

"Damn it!" Creighton growled. "Put a lid on that machine, Benson! Or I . . . ."

"Stuff it, Creighton!" Angel snapped back in a voice that dripped with authority, at a volume that surprised the hell out of Thorny.

A shocked silence gripped the room. Creighton appealed to the Director with a look of gaping-mouthed outrage, and got a stony stare in response.

"When," Angel continued sharply, "someone's insecurity and stupidity puts other people at risk, I think it's better to say the situation and the idiot responsible stink to high hell than not. I won't risk peoples lives just to be nice!"

The Director gave her a ghost of a tight-lipped smile. "We do have to keep priorities clear. But, Angel, the language of a crusty old family practitioner doesn't quite fit you." She looked at Thorny, who coughed in embarrassment. There was a scattering soft laughter around the room as other people realized just who's language had inspired Angel.

"Ma'am, the words fit. Not only has Dr. Creighton's behavior threatened to deny Linda Coombs and others the benefit of the speed and accuracy with which I can perform surgery, but the patient has asked that I, specifically, perform the surgery. I regret hurting Dr. Creighton's feelings but those must be secondary considerations. . ."

There was more laughter, including from Angel. Thorny realized that one way of interpreting the laughter around the room was that the other doctors had reached a conclusion similar to Angel's. Creighton, for once, sat in shocked silence.

"Ma'am," Angel added, "Linda happened to latch on to me, but someday she'll latch on to other things, and other people. Another husband, a child. She's young, she's a fighter and a very determined person. She's not going to forget her medicine, sit around, mope, give up and die if we let her have a reason to live. And with respect to objectivity, one has to ask how much Dr. Creighton's dislike of what I represent has affected his treatment of Linda."

"I only suggest," Creighton huffed, "that putting one willful, non-compliant, patient ahead of others on the priority list not be dictated by the advertising needs, if you can call them that, of a robot."

"My patient, Dr. Creighton," Thorny interjected, "has not been non-compliant. And I don't make any claims to objective detachment here, I'm too old for that charade. I brought Linda into this world. I don't want her to rot waiting for a heart just because you don't put her into the right 'category' for reasons that I don't think have a gnats ass to do with her suitability!"

"Doctors," the Director interjected, at a volume and with an inflection that brought instant silence. "We were listening to Angel."

"Thank you, Ma'am. Physically, Linda's a good candidate for a transplant, and if I do it, she'll be an excellent candidate psychologically. And I can help those unnamed other patients if I can help Linda. She's a real person, who needs help. Please let me help her."

A deep hush filled the office. Corny, but effective, Thorny reflected. On second thought, maybe it wasn't so corny.

The Director leaned back and laced her fingers together. "I'll have Dr. Tunman do a thorough review of the case and discuss it with all of you" — she nodded to the other transplant people, pointedly ignoring the fuming Creighton, "and we'll follow your recommendations."

She paused. "Angel, Nurse Miles told me about Linda's feelings, and that she would be comfortable with you as lead surgeon on the transplant. From what I've seen today, you are a responsible, independently-thinking being, and highly motivated to help your patient — whether by feelings or programming doesn't seem to matter. But . . . you aren't a doctor and you aren't even a legally responsible person."

"I know, Ma'am. Dr. Benson could still supervise me, and a surgeon would have to be technically in charge of the operation. Whatever I may think about him as a person, I don't want to deprive Linda of Dr. Creighton's experience. Dr. Tunman has already agreed to help us from the cardiology side when the new heart is in, and I know I can do a very good job with the surgery itself. If Nurse Miles will take charge of support, I think that would make a very good team."

Creighton's face was now a stoic stone mask. "I have no current objection to, uh, her performing the surgery with whatever assistance is suitable. A heart transplant is, after all, fairly straight forward from a technical standpoint. I can concentrate on donor selection and postoperative care and monitor the operation itself from my office. But since I will still be legally responsible for the patient, I reserve the right to have the final say as to how the operation is done. I assure all of you I am as committed to this patient's survival as anyone. And, well, I'll try to be a good sport about it." He gave Thorny a wintry grin. "Then have your dance, Thorny."

But he'll call the tune, Thorny finished the line silently. Creighton saw himself as Figaro? Despite himself, he felt some sympathy for the humiliated man. Modified sympathy. Angel looked concerned as well. Perhaps, he thought, there was a greater distinction to be made between biological emotion and her emulated anger than her other emotions; it was more copied, more phony.

The Director looked around the room for any other comments, but there weren't any. "Very well. It's a risk, but clearly one the patient wants to take, and arguably one that will help her morale and increase her chance of survival. Dr. Benson, Angel is your project and . . . Linda is your patient. I'll look to you to organize everything. See me if you have problems; a lot is riding on this."

"That's fine with me, Ma'am," Thorny declared, forcibly putting aside any second thoughts.

"And with me." Angel added.

The Director nodded curtly, and the meeting was over.

★ ※ ★

At his home office the next evening, Thorny watched Angel handle one of his young football patients with a badly dislocated thumb. She had his forearm and hand strapped to a conformal imaging plate, so he could watch what was happening as she maneuvered the joint back into place.

Thorny's mind wandered to the advances he'd seen in four decades of practice. He remembered having to send patients to a hospital for a long wait to get a two-dimensional still photograph taken with radiation so hard it might cause cancer in its own right. And then waiting more hours, or sometimes a day or more for an "official" interpretation by an underworked, overpaid, "no weekends, 8-to-4 and off to the golf course" radiologist.

Nowadays, a three-hundred-dollar flat plate array of nanosensors could use a few photons that made it through soft tissue light by monochromatic light to reconstruct a real-time three dimensional image of anything thinner than a man's arm. Anyone who'd covered a bright flashlight with their hand could see that something like that was possible, and, about a decade ago someone had finally done it. In five years the price had dropped to the point where Thorny could afford one. Best of all, he didn't need an "expert" anymore — his eye and the computer's interpretation were just as good, if not better.

The young man, however, seemed to take it all for granted. He was clearly more interested in Angel's sculpted anatomy than his own — something which pleased Angel no end but, he worried, might be sending the wrong message to her patient. Young men these days, he thought testily, had to learn to suppress any outward evidence of such natural interests to protect themselves from harassment charges, so Angel wasn't doing the boy any long-term favor. Another thing to mention to her.

"I can't believe, uh, you're a robot," the boy said, manfully ignoring what must have been a fairly painful twist and pull from Angel. "You're so pretty. And you act so, so natural like."

"The people who made me had a lot of fun doing that, and I'm really happy that I please people. But most of that is just following examples. The hard part was my imaging processor and my future-modeling functions. The stuff that lets me predict what will happen when I do something like this."

"Ouch! Oh, that feels better now."

"It's back in place, so it should," Angel declared with what seemed motherly authority.

"See how the proximal phalanx — that's the short bone — fits on the metacarpal bone — that's the longer one — there now? That's how it's supposed to be. Your tendons — these ropy things here, and here — are going to be sore for a while and you might experience a little tenderness in the joint, here, off and on for a few weeks. Don't worry about it — just take it as a warning to take it easy in that area. Keep wearing this brace until the pain and swelling are pretty much gone. Call me in a couple of days, and let me look at it over the phone. Remember, the longer you can keep from re-injuring it the better. I'll give you some exercises to do, too."

"For my fingers?"

Angel laughed. "Just like any other part of you that plays football.

The stronger and bigger your finger muscles are, the less likely that something like this will happen again."

"You don't have to exercise do you?"

"Actually, I do. I have to move to pump lubricant to my joints; otherwise they'll dry out and get hard to move. So I knit for my finger joints and have some other exercises that make sure I move everything. I'm programmed to feel good when I do it, so I do it whenever I don't have anything better to do with my body and it isn't likely to bother anyone. My joints are really sophisticated; they can move in ways that yours can't so that all my fingers are opposable. I can take my skin off and show you what it looks like inside. Want to see?"

The boy shook his head, embarrassed, "Uh, no, that's okay."

"Angel," Thorny interrupted, "Our patient's mother is probably holding dinner for him."

"Oh, yeah." The boy said. "I'd better get going." He gathered up his things, clumsily with the thumb in its brace. Angel helped him. "See you, Doc, Angel."

The boy was out the door, and Angel turned to him, displaying joy at what must have been near the top of her scale. Not quite appropriate for her last patient, Thorny thought, so something else must be going on. "Well?" he asked.

"We did it!" Angel gushed. "They decided to move Linda up on the waiting list, and she should get a new heart as soon as they find a match! The hospital cybersystem just got the decision, and now it's going out on the national transplant network."

Thorny smiled. Angel's learned repertory of emotional display had grown over the last month to the point of near histrionics, and he'd had to caution her to tone it down a bit for some audiences because some people would react against that style of communication. But at home, she could let herself go. One of her programmed purposes in life was to display her abilities, and she got internal rewards for doing so. Was this, Thorny wondered, so very different from what went on inside his own biochemical machine?

"May I tell Linda?" Angel asked, with standard hopeful intonations.

"Sure," Thorny agreed.

★ ❋ ★

The operation started out uneventfully. Everything went by the book, quickly, smoothly, efficiently. Thorny glanced at Tunman, who stood silently in a corner of the operating suite, poised to take over when the new heart was in. Until the operation was completed, Creighton was officially in charge, and Tunman's authority was as limited as Thorny's. They all knew Elvis was on the line, monitoring everything from his office. But he said nothing.

Angel moved smoothly, accurately, tirelessly. She never paused, except to wait for one of her human assistants. They were ready for the donor heart in half the usual time.

The Rockwell unit came out and the connecting large blood vessels were trimmed carefully — too much and they would be stretched to reach the new heart, requiring a graft; not enough, and there would be tissue weakened by its prolonged contact with the prosthetic.

The new heart was that of a thirty year old woman from Alabama, brain-dead of a gunshot wound inflicted by a husband who'd complained of her laziness. It was the twenty first century, thought Thorny, but some things never change. The one saving grace was that the murderer would probably also wind up on the donor list — as soon as his appeals ran out. Dr. Creighton, in a rare display of personal concern, had personally flown to Montgomery to examine the potential donor, and brought the organ back in his own private jet. Perhaps, Thorny thought, the man had learned a lesson.

An overhead waldo descended to the carrier, cradled the new heart out in a basket of arms, and set it in place as Angel held the chest cavity open. The microwaldos began connecting blood vessels immediately, gluing the small ones, adding a few stitches for the main arteries.

"Any problems?" Angel asked. Everyone said no, so she started the heart, sending a slight current through one of the waldos. The heart began beating, and Thorny sighed with relief. Angel touched it gently, almost lovingly, and then let it take over fully from the heart-lung bypass. Nurse Miles shot a look at him.

"She can hear through her fingers. She's listening."

Angel froze. "Thorny, the heart's defective. Listen, I'll send it through the cybersystem."

Thorny heard the rhythmic swish of blood coursing through the heart from a nearby speaker. A few seconds later a tri-D view of the heart with animated false-color blood flow appeared on a monitor.

"Damn," he said. He wasn't entirely sure what he was seeing, but he knew it wasn't good.

Angel spoke, "This heart has a flail anterior leaflet and wide-open mitral regurgitation."

Tunman nodded in agreement, but Thorny didn't see him. Even a non-specialist like himself knew what "wide-open mitral regurgitation" meant — with every heart beat, much of her blood spurt back through the leaking mitral valve into her left atrium and lungs, and not enough went to the rest of her body. How could that happen? Every donor heart was supposed to be thoroughly checked before it was harvested!

Linda was as good as dead. She was weak already, and this heart would never sustain her. It wasn't Angel's fault, nor his, but there was no question in his mind where the blame would fall.

"I see it, too." Creighton's disembodied voice broke in, very quickly. "The heart will have to be removed and a new Rockwell implanted. And I don't want any argument from you, Benson! Stabilize her and I'll be in with the new unit in ten minutes." His link went off line.

"No, her kidneys won't take another wait on the donor list." Angel declared, "Let's fix the valve."

You can't do that, Thorny almost said. Angel "knew" the standard techniques — but she'd never actually done that kind of operation, and not even the best, most experienced human surgeons were always successful. If she ignored Creighton's order, and Linda died . . .

It was bad enough that Linda's life was at stake — but, potentially, the lives of so many other people that Angel and her successors could help were also.

She looked questioningly up at Thorny.

"Bruk?" he asked.

"You have ten minutes, I think," the cardiologist coolly replied.

Thorny's throat felt like it was on fire, and the pressure building in the center of his chest made him wonder if he might need a new heart soon too. But . . . heart, kidneys, the patient's mind, the whole patient. It was a 'general practice' decision if there ever was one. He nodded.

He could imagine Angel smiling through her surgical mask.

"Miles?" she said.

"I dunno . . . "

"Please . . . "

"If it were anyone else but you, and her, I wouldn't. Okay, Angel, my ass is on the line now too. Do it good, lady."

Angel glanced back at Thorny. "Looks like all our rears are uncovered," he said.

"Okay. I'm going to re-establish cardiopulmonary bypass and cardioplegia."

What happened next was a blur, like watching the operation on a fast forward. Unhindered by human reaction time, Angel showed her full range of talents. Much more now, Thorny realized, than what the consortium had built into her. Tools seemed to fly into her hands as she plucked them off their trays unerringly. Microwaldos buzzed like hummingbirds. Thorny could follow only the large scale details in real time. The heart was stopped and laid open, the valve repaired, and the entry closed in a matter of minutes. Angel re-started the heart as the doors to the OR flew open.

"You can't do that, Angel! Benson, make her stop!" Creighton shouted as he caught onto what was in progress. A first, Thorny realized — Creighton had addressed Angel directly, admitting, essentially, her personhood. However, Thorny thought grimly, it was too late, and he would choose to ignore Creighton's accidental trip to reality.

"No," Thorny responded, "Angel and I can do it. With Angel, I can do more than any specialist can do, and be a friend to my patients as well. You should consider retraining in family practice, Elvis — you might learn to like it."

"Do you want to close, Dr. Creighton?" Angel asked, surgically.

★ ❊ ★

Angel's next appearance before the Director was at a meeting of the full medical staff in the ground floor auditorium. Winter was in full cold bore again outside and the coat racks were full of greatcoats and stocking caps, not a few of which were hand-knit white with big red hearts on them; Thorny's yarn bill was beginning to get significant.

Linda Coombs was accounting for some of that; Thorny was helping finance her boutique by buying the raw material. Last he heard, she was getting friendly with a skier who'd bought a sweater from her. She was writing a book about her experience, with Angel's memory to help, of course.

The atmosphere in the meeting was much more friendly this time, now that Elvis Creighton no longer sat as a department head. The "official" line was that Creighton had resigned from the staff to pursue a better employment opportunity in another state. But word travels fast in a hospital, and everyone was talking of how the Director had invited him to review, in her presence, a huge folder filled with formal complaints filed against him by patients and staff — the last few from Linda and Nurse Miles. When he was done, the story went, she had smiled thinly and raised both eyebrows.

Thorny's report and recommendations concerning Angel had been accepted, unconditionally.

"Angel," the Director called. "Would you come up here?"

Angel smiled and walked up to the dais. The Director first handed her a large frame wrapped in brown paper, which Angel unwrapped. She read what was in the frame and gave a squeal of delight.

"What is it?" Nurse Miles called out.

"It says I've completed my internship!" Angel gushed. "Thank you! But how did you manage that without my being a person?"

There was a bit of a gleam in the Director's eyes as she answered, and a twitch upward at the corners of her normally severely straight, thin, lips. "Forgive me if I found an obstetrician's solution to that little problem. This," she produced a simple vanilla envelope and read it, "is for you, Dr. C. Thornhart Benson. Congratulations."

He went forward and accepted the envelope. Angel looked at them in confusion.

Thorny opened it and then laughed hard and long. "Well, assuming this holds up in court . . . "

An eyebrow went up and Thorny coughed a retreat. "Ahem. Angel, it appears I've finally become a father. It's a birth certificate. Yours."

STORY NOTES

Dr. Henry Stratmann and I did this collaboration in the early nineties by actual postal mail exchanges! resorting to email only later on. This was his first science fiction publication and he has gone on to much bigger and better things. See: http://www.hgstratmann.com/. I'll note that while our story is still set a bit ahead of 2021, the gap has lessened. Teleoperated robots are now able to do some surgeries, medical AIs are getting good at diagnoses, and Boston Robotics has shown that robots that can move even better, quicker and more smoothly than biology are here. It just needs to be finished and put together. (There is also, apparently, a market for medical personnel who can't get sick themselves!). The self-driving car is here, but not quite to the point where you can pass out in the seat and be confident of getting to your front door intact. But the biggest remaining challenge for our story may be programming the consciousness our Tin Angel displays, and, of course, her acceptance by the community. I optimistically imagine that before Henry passes, and maybe even before I do, this story may join "His Father's Voice" in not being science fiction any longer.

GDN October 2021

DEMOCRITUS' VIOLIN

"The whole is greater than the sum of its parts," Dr. Andre Stevens declaimed with sharp vertical movements of his hands punctuating every word. "There is an *ineffability* to some things, a spiritual content if you like, that laughs at the efforts of small minded reductionists to dissect and explain them away. Words like chaos simply hide the truth that there are things which cannot be known by their parts, but emerge from something greater and can, perhaps, be *felt* and be appreciated by those who open themselves to it."

His words were addressed to the class as a whole, but seemed aimed at me in particular. I shrank from view, as much as ever conscious of my six-foot-one ostensibly female body and my straight black hair. I hid my eyes in the paper on my desk as he spoke.

It was marked C- right next to the K. Kim. My name was my Korean-American parents' solution to multicultural sexual ambiguity–Kim Young Kim supposedly worked both anyway you cut it. How clever. Couldn't they have anticipated me being called "Kimykim!" for twelve torturous school years? Ever since I'd had a say in it, my name was "Kay" to anyone that was my friend.

Back to the paper. I had dared to dissect Bach, citing recent analysis of how the brain triggers endorphin release in response to acoustical harmonies as well as optical symmetries and reasoning that a healthy voice is tonal (because of the way healthy vocal chords are), so less indicative of a diseased person, and so more attractive.

Stevens' comment was that I'd researched irrelevant trivia and shown no feel for the subject at all. Bach's music, he said, is beautiful because of its whole, not its parts.

I probably should have cited some of Stevens' writings in my paper, but they were all just collages of quoted post modern generalities with nothing specific on which to reason, predict, or test. As a microtechnology engineering major, I was underwhelmed.

"The point of *holistic comprehension* in the arts," he continued with a pleased smug grin on his face, "is that reductionism has failed; things too complex for humans to understand must be appreciated at another level–a transcendent, holistic way of knowing that defies this nit-splitting analysis. The whole is more! In this music course, those who deny the ineffable are, most definitely, effable!"

A round of groans grew into general tittering. Stevens cleared his throat and continued.

For the thousandth time, I wondered why I hadn't signed up for the archeology course. Archeology always fascinated me because it was one area where culture and technology go hand in hand–indeed, before writing, culture and art are *defined* by technology–the stone age, the bronze age. While the "two cultures" are as old as the academic trivium and quadrivium, I saw the pathological split represented by Stevens as a modern invention; Jefferson and Franklin, for example, were both competent scientists of their age as well as competent writers and philosophers. And archeology used all sorts of hard science techniques to study things–dendrochronology, radioisotope dating, spectroscopy, radar imagery–it was much more my kind of thing. But that was the problem; at the time, it seemed too close to a hard science, and my advisor thought I needed broadening.

Dear Old Lloyd College was into anything Welsh, of course, and music in particular was supposed to stir the souls of the Men and Women of Harlech. Well, that and poetry and politics. If it came out of the mouth, it was us. Besides, I had a crush on Felix Mendelssohn– never mind that he died a couple of centuries ago at the age of thirty-eight.

"Come to my concert," Stevens droned on, "and I will show you, or," he gave a slight chuckle of phony self deprecation, "try anyway. And listen to my Stradivarius, if not to me or to Schoenberg. People have picked apart and tried to analyze his violins for over four centuries, and they can't duplicate them. No, they can't. Not all the analysis in the world will make another Stradivarius, and I'll give an A in this course to anyone who can prove otherwise!"

The bell released me from my music appreciation requirement to the more rational world of quantum mechanics. I bundled myself and books against the snow and the bitter Minnesota cold, stepped out into the tundra between the Fine Arts building and the Jobs Science Hall, and kicked the nearest ice chunk half way to Minneapolis. Just because I *knew* all about endorphins and evolutionary behavioralism didn't mean I didn't have them.

I didn't need a "C" in anything this semester. My scholarship was in jeopardy. Mom's back didn't let her work anymore and Dad–well, lugging boxes around was about Dad's speed these days. Therapy make-work that robots could do better and cheaper. It hadn't always been that way, Mom tells me. If they could just get in his head and fix what that kid's bullet had done. If they could just fix the head of the kid with the gun. Who's "they?" I'd asked myself. Then I'd looked at myself in the mirror and chosen a major.

Maybe it was more than I could do. C minus. I wanted a shoulder to cry on. Ted's.

As boyfriends went, Ted was about my speed. Charming, polite, and honest–about dating other girls and not being ready for an exclusive relationship. But we took classes together, hung out together, and it was pretty generally conceded that we were an item. I hoped. He was, at least, a full inch taller than me, and while not a football player, he'd lettered in Track and Field–throwing the discus.

He made me do weights to fill out my chest with something and taught me to throw the discus, I threw one sixty meters which was a mistake because he tried to get me to join the women's team. Doing the jock thing in public didn't fit my self image–I didn't like being reminded that I had failed to become the delicate Eurasian beauty Dad had wanted.

I found Ted sitting on cushioned bench in the hall just outside the nano lab with his head in a book.

"Hi, Teddy, got a moment?"

"Uh? Oh, Kay." He bushed a strand of jet black not-too-clean hair from his brow. Since all the adults were wearing short hair in reaction to the previous generation, we were growing ours long again to make a statement to *them*. Silly, but style is style.

He looked into my eyes and knew. "Stevens again?"

"It was just too much, Teddy. He was ridiculing me and my ideas, and he's wrong! This whole idea that you can't understand how things work except by some mystical . . . " I sang an approximation of the Twilight Zone theme. " . . . comprehension is complete maximum nonsense that really only amounts to people getting their content-free arguments published by force of personality and politics and no one seems to know that particular emperor's not wearing any clothes!"

"That's heavy, Kay," he said with a grin.

I grimaced. "Well, thanks for listening, anyway. I just want to *do* something. But you can't prove anything to these people because the only proof they accept is how they feel and you know how *that's* going to come out!"

"Hmm."

When Ted start's going "hmm," I perk up. Another thing I like about Ted is that he shows signs of being an okay provider. I mean, I intend to handle my own affairs and break through the glass ceiling and all that, but it's good to have back-up. And Ted is competent. When he says "hmm," things tend to happen. Excitement. Turn on.

"What are you thinking, Teddy?"

"We're just about ready to test our replicator on something with a little more structure than a stainless steel fork. I think something organic is next."

"Yeah?" I'd worked on the nanotech replicator two semesters ago–mostly on the software to extract the molecular structure from non-destructive scanning with soft x-rays. The "conga line" of molecular placers was only a few million atoms long then, and not working very well. I'd kind of tried to keep up with it, but when Ted and I were together, there were, well, other matters to occupy our time.

"Maybe we could arrange a demonstration–show that even organic things, anyway, are entirely determined by where their atoms are. Drive another nail in the coffin of vitalism, so to speak."

"Could you replicate a mouse?"

"Yeah, I think so. But we'd have to freeze it first. That would get the fuzzy mafia all over us and besides, what would it prove?"

"What if the duplicate mouse remembered what its original knew?"

"Hmm, Kay, you're bright. Hadn't thought of that one. Actually, I was thinking something else . . . "

Terri Maraschino came by just then, a petite girl with big blue eyes and golden locks down her ass.

"Hi, guys," she said, raising an eyebrow at me. "Doc Andre's got your number, Kay, huh?"

Lloyd College only has about thirteen hundred students and word gets around fast.

"It's nothing. I just made a sign-up day mistake and I'll get my C, get out of there and go on with my life."

"Gotta watch the GPA, kid. Sometimes, you know, you just gotta go with the flow, Kay. Give 'em what they want. Then they give back. He's not so bad, off duty, so to speak."

"Oh?" Teddy said, tensing. Why would he care? I mean, sure, he dated Terri occasionally, but so did the whole world. He couldn't be jealous about her; it would be like being jealous about air.

"Not too." Terri shrugged her shoulders.

"He's got a little surprise coming," Ted said with a grin.

I had no idea of what kind of surprise, but when Ted grins like that, good things happen.

"Oh?" Terri asked with maybe feigned indifference.

"Yeah. Kay, can you come by the lab tomorrow evening, about ten?"

I looked at Terri and grinned. "Sure, Ted."

★ ❈ ★

When I met Ted in the lab, he had two dishes of lime Jello waiting.

"Lime Jello for dinner? You're weird, Teddy. Nice, but weird."

He gave me a spoon. "Taste one and then the other."

I got it, and did so. They both tasted like lime Jello.

"We made one of these the usual way in about ten minutes. The other took ten hours and most of the big Opticor as well as all of our home-made parallel processor. Can you tell which is which?"

I savored the Jellos again. They both had fruity bouquet and a cool and rubbery start with just a little citric bite. Then syrupy sweetness melted in my mouth and slid down my throat. Damn it, they must have used real sugar. I pulled my stomach in, as if that would make any difference.

I shook my head in wonderment. "Can't tell the difference."

Ted grinned. "The replicated Jello is on the blue-bordered plate."

"Herr Doktor Professor Andre Stevens would, of course, claim there is some kind of ineffable difference to be elucidated by direct experience," I said.

"Let's call him on it."

"How would anyone get *him* to do a Jello taste test? Especially if he knew why? He's like any one of these hypocritical creeps with a made-up dogma—the last thing in the world he'd go for is an objective test of it. Teddy, we'd have to trick him, somehow."

Ted grinned. "Hmm. We could catch him in the cafeteria line. I know someone who works there—he could serve it to him—then we show up with cameras and say "surprise!"

"But he'd have to take the Jello, he'd have to eat it where we could get at him and he usually eats in the faculty lounge and we'd have to prove the Jello was replicated, and if we do it with Jello everyone's going to just laugh."

"I see. The Jello test is an interesting problem, but off target?"

"Yeah." It came to me just then what we had to duplicate. But it would be risky, risky as hell—not to mention illegal. "To prove it to him, we gotta get him where he lives," I said.

"Yeah. Hmm."

The look in Ted's eyes told me we'd had the same thought. I waited expectantly, hopefully. It would be a lot better if this were Ted's idea.

"It's complicated, but . . . do you know where he keeps his Stradivarius?"

That's my Ted.

★ ❋ ★

So there we were lying in the snow below Stevens' office window on a moonless night with the stars shining down about as bright as they ever do in the middle of a two-million-person megalopolis, our skin-tight "moon colony" suits turned white as the snow to help keep our heat in with a black bag hidden under Ted. They were high-tech smart fabric and super-insulated but it was one of those Minnesota January nights where the difference between Fahrenheit and Celsius starts to look academic. I was literally shaking in my boots.

As soon as the campus patrol car finished snow-crunching through the parking lot and headed toward the Broiler, we got up out of the snow and dusted ourselves off. While I admired my snow angel, Ted held his watch face up at the window and pressed a stud. We waited and shook.

Earlier, he'd put on a maintenance uniform and stuck a remote control bypass on the window crank motor–if the departmental admin support person had recognized him, she'd said nothing. Several students moonlighted in maintenance, so it was likely no big deal. He spent some time in the other offices too, for cover.

I'd unlocked the window today just before closing. I'd brought Stevens a cup of coffee on my way to plead for my grade, and he'd taken it. The coffee, not the plea. A couple of minutes later, when he excused himself to the bathroom, I'd flipped the latch up. We hoped he'd not noticed.

He hadn't. The window cranked itself open smoothly.

The rope ladder caught on the second try, and up we scurried.

"Less than three minutes," Ted said, obviously pleased. "Now, where's the violin?"

The best laid plans . . .

★ ❋ ★

Fast forward to the last Saturday of spring break after a 12 inch snowstorm. As a certified science nerd, I know why global warming means more snow and occasional cold records, too, but I still wonder at the paradox. Anyway, there'd been a concert that night at which Stevens had played, and we hoped against hope that, this time, he'd left the violin in his office. It was our seventh try.

I had not, however, made seven more appointments to see Stevens about my grades–even he would have suspected something was up if I'd done that. Fortunately, that had been unnecessary.

Now I know I could never sell this as fiction because no editor would believe that Stevens never checked the lock on his window for over two months. But that's knowing neither Stevens, who opens his office to fresh air about as often as he opens his mind to fresh ideas, nor Minnesota winters. Anyway, we checked with the remote every day before our attempts and the window always opened.

The last fourteen weeks had been Chinese water torture, but we'd gotten into a routine and it had become sort of part of our lives. Nothing like a dose of repetitive failure to keep your feet on the ground–as if I needed anything more than my first semester grades. But maybe the delay was a good thing–in the mean time they'd made some improvements to the scanner.

We had faculty help, of course. Hard science people are a minority at Lloyd who often have to eat it off the academic Trivium and Stevens' attitude wasn't that popular with them. It was unpopular in particular with Dr. Gustaf Molar–a fitting name for a chemist, I thought, and another reason you know this isn't fiction. Anyway, he had time on the replicator for designer molecule work, and was kind enough to front for Ted's experiment–billed as an effort to demonstrate assembly of complex objects.

But when we told him how much time we needed, though, he was taken aback, and asked, "What is it? That's huge–I hope it's not someone's cat!"

"It's a violin," Ted told him.

I watched Dr. Molar's face frown, then break into a grin. I think he realized just then *whose* violin would get duplicated and why.

"You know," he said, "Democritus told us it was all just atoms. Two and a half millennia ago he'd figured out more than some people today will ever concede! Eliminating the fairies gave him such a sense of inner peace that his contemporaries called him the laughing philosopher. So, yes, reproducing a so-called unique violin would be an appropriate jest. Quite appropriate." He laughed a little himself. "Yes, a very good joke–and *if* you don't make any bad mistakes, I don't think there will be too much retribution. The whole college knows *that* particular balloon needs to be pricked. But, of course, you will be very careful, and very discrete about my role in this?"

We'd both nodded.

Tonight, under cover of the blizzard, we didn't even have to lie in the snow. Everything went like clockwork. We had the violin in the scanner by midnight and back in Stevens' office by two a.m. And there was all day Sunday for the puddles of melted snow our boots left in his office to dry out.

★ ❈ ★

Dr. Molar got us time on the replicator the first weekend in May.

With exams and papers being written, there wasn't much demand. We started at 8 pm Friday evening, and took shifts. I know Ted saw Terri on his first off-shift because I smelled her perfume when he got back at five Sunday morning. One of those pheromone things, and they work because I got excited second hand. When the scanner is just sitting there going ka-chunk, ka-chunk, there's not much else to do.

But E. M. Forster was running things that night–like in his story, the machine we depended on stopped. There was a little, tinny, *thwack* and a pleasantly synthesized woman's voice announced that the program had terminated due to error code seven thirty two.

It broke the mood, kind of. I disengaged from Ted and went over to take a look in the reconstruction tube. There, encased in a block of clear matrix to be dissolved later, was a half-finished violin, done just about to the bridge. Except the matrix wasn't completely clear anymore. There were cracks. "Teddy, there's something wrong with the violin."

"Huh?" He got up, pulled his pants on and came over to inspect the repro. "What's code 732?"

"That," the system answered, "is for motion detected on the reconstruction stage by an accelerometer."

"Motion?" he asked. "Crap. The tension. It's unstable."

I realized what we were seeing. "The strings. We should have taken them off first."

"Yeah, they're under tension. As the rendering plane moves up, the strings get longer and just a little slippage anywhere along the string before they're complete . . . cascade . . . the matrix couldn't hold it any more."

I was silent for a bit. So near. Now we had to go through it all over again, maybe into next year! It had taken us fourteen weeks to get the Stradivarius long enough to replicate this time. We didn't have another fourteen weeks in the school year. Hell, we didn't have another fourteen *days*. I was furious and thought that way, coming up with nothing, of course.

"Maybe we could just continue and restring the replica." Ted said. But he didn't say "hmm" first, so I knew there had to be something wrong with that. It didn't take me long.

"It moved, Ted–that's why the program stopped. There was an acceleration. I don't care if it just moved a couple of nanometers–we'd end up with two halves of a Stradivarius."

He smiled and winced at once. "You're one bright lady, Kay. But just this once I wish you were wrong. I wish I could just reach into that scan pattern and . . . hmm."

"What, Ted? What is it?"

"If we rotate a virtual imaging plane so it's parallel with the strings– let's see, they bend at the bridge so there's eight string segments to worry about, but we could get two segments in each plane so that's four planes, maybe a few million molecules thick . . . If we make a software tool to erase just that part of those few million sections . . . "

He was going to do just that–reach in, and, in virtual reality, take the strings out of the pattern–*then* replicate what was left. "Wow, Ted, will it let you do that?"

"Let's ask it."

★ ※ ★

After half a day of very sophisticated machine language persuasion, it let us, and we got going again on the broken string violin about two Sunday morning. But now we were really short of time. At normal speed, it wouldn't finish until noon Monday and the lab would be full of students and it would be impossible to keep a secret. And it *had* to be kept secret.

"Any ideas?"

"I'm too tired, Kay."

I put a hand on his shoulder and sighed. "Me too. Maybe next year." If I had a next year.

"Hmm. Kay, why don't we just tell the truth? We're replicating a violin."

"But that would give it all away . . . oh!"

"Nobody's going to know *what* violin is in that tank. We'll just have some practice violin lying around and everyone will think *that* was the scan object."

Where would we get that? "I hate to say this; it's like a breach of security, but we need someone with a violin and an extra set of strings to put on the replica when it comes out."

"Terri plays the violin. And she's got a 1789 Figer–not a Stradivarius, but it looks old."

I had to ask, didn't I? The thought of her playing the Mendelssohn violin concerto made me want to puke. Couldn't she leave any of my men alone? "Don't you know some else? Any old fiddle will probably do."

"You can trust Terri."

He grinned at me, the jerk. I groaned.

"She'll help us; I know she will."

"You know she will? Ted, what did you tell her?"

"I didn't tell her everything, but I had to break a date."

I felt like a hundred-meter-long lobster had seized my stomach with his claw. Terri's pillow talk is legendary. I kept my cool, oh, yes. But I think I might have had some tears in my eyes, then.

He melted and put an arm around me, "Sure, Kay, sure. All I want from Terri right now is a violin and a tuning. She's just a violin object, okay?"

"A violin object. Right." Somehow I nodded.

★ ❄ ★

Two hours later, Terri looked at the stringless violin in the block of plastic matrix and laughed. "First, you don't just restring a violin like this. The bridge will fall down as soon as you wash that stuff off, and then the sound post will probably move."

"Fall down?" Ted said.

"Sound post?" I chimed in.

Terri held her instrument up with a superior smile on her face. "Look inside, through the F-holes. See that wood dowel standing between the front and back? The tone of the violin depends on that being in just the right place and it's not glued. It just sits there, held in place by the pressure the strings put on the bridge above it. You need a special tool to get it back in place and hours of fiddling around with it. And the bridge has to be put up at exactly the right angle too, or the violin won't sound the same."

"It hasn't moved yet," I observed.

"But I can't restring it inside that stuff." Terri folded her arms and raised her eyebrows.

"Suppose," Ted said, "I just wash the stuff off the top. You could restring it and set the bridge up, then I'll wash the rest out."

"What do you wash it with?" Terri asked. "Water would ruin it."

"It's not water–Dr. Molar designed something that turns the matrix into carbon dioxide, methane and something else. I forget what, but you just squirt the solvent over it and it vaporizes."

Terri took a deep breath. "Okay, Teddy. For you, I'll try it. But I don't think it will fool him."

It will if you keep your mouth shut, I thought. "We've got to try at this point," I said.

No, we didn't. I could give the whole thing up.

No, I couldn't.

Terri smiled at me. "It's going to take a while, Kay."

I wanted to tell Ted to wipe that silly grin off his face and smash the "1789 Figer" over its owner's head. But she was holding the violin and all the cards.

So I smiled back. "Okay. Gotta book. Thanks. See you." Outside it was dark, thank goodness. I didn't want anyone to see my face like that.

★ ❄ ★

I buried myself in books Monday night while Terri and Ted took

care of stringing the replicated violin, etc. Yeah, it was an abject
surrender, but I had a final Wednesday and classes Tuesday. I had
to sleep. Passion is one thing, the rest of your life is something else.
Grades were the rest of my life. Ted would be loyal or not, but I *had* to
book, had to.

That night, I dreamed of sleeping with Andre Stevens for a grade.
He took what he wanted, then laughed at me when I asked for the grade
and gave me an F. I was about to deck him when I realized his laugh
was my computer telling me it was time to get up and get going.

I didn't recognize the woman looking back at me from the mirror.
Three months of non-stop tension, climbing rope ladders in subzero
cold, and all nighters with nothing to eat and I looked like I was halfway
to that dreaded thirty. A touch of frost in the hair and I could be a prof.
Weight problem? What weight problem?

No time for breakfast, even. Throw something on, grab the books,
lock the door, and head for campus. Head back. I'd forgotten the
lights–fifty cents of electricity. Fifty cents a day was fifteen dollars a
month–a good part of my disposable budget. And it was raining. I
slogged back through the mud to turn them off, grabbed a raincoat,
locked the door again and started trotting for Calculus class. There
wouldn't, I realized, be time to see Ted and the violin replica. What
kind of girlfriend, I thought, leaves her squeeze all day with another
woman for a fifty-cent light bill?

On the other hand, with the violin project known, maybe I shouldn't
be around. Let's make my being late a strategic decision to maintain
the element of surprise. Strategic decision, hell, I thought as I pulled
the door to Jobs Hall open. You forgot to turn the lights off.

★ ※ ★

By the time the week was over, I was headed for B's in everything
but Music Appreciation, with an outside chance at an A in calculus. I'd
even managed to get Ted for a night–Wednesday–and saw the violin.
We talked and planned until two a.m..

★ ※ ★

A couple of days before the concert, I went downstairs in the science
building to see Ted to tell him what happened and saw Ted and Terri
making out down in the Physics lab assistant's room, said "'scuse me,"
and left. Ted had won the conference meet–damn near seventy meters,
and he was getting his reward, I guess. That giant lobster got hold of
my gut again. I kind of collapsed on that little bench outside the room.
I'd had such hopes and plans. Well, we still had the project. We could
at least finish that together.

They came out a little later and Terri waved a cheery goodbye, leaving me with Ted. He came over. I looked up into his eyes. He pulled me up and put his arms around me while I got a little wet-eyed but I clamped down on the cry. I wasn't going to fall that low.

"Kay, Kay," he murmured. "I wish I could be two people."

I thought of knocking him out and of using the replicator. I really did. Terri could have one Ted, and I'd have the other.

"Just give me a little room," my Ted said. "I need to sort this out. I still like you. I like you a lot. You're bright, you're competent. I'm just fighting my chemistry."

I just looked up at him and did something really stupid. "Ted," I said. "*I* love you—and *she* can't give you that." It was the first time either of us had ever said that word and it was most definitely uncool. But, again, I was feeling a little desperate. Terri just didn't *deserve* someone like Ted—she deserved a *real* jock, the dumb kind.

"Gee, I wish you hadn't said that, Kay."

"Yeah, me too. But there it is. Deal with it."

★ ❄ ★

The last concert was Friday night. Stevens would take the violin home to practice Wednesday and Thursday night, so our only chance to switch the violins was Tuesday night. Ted gave me the violin and the remote Tuesday, between my calc final and the final torture session in Stevens' class.

"Can you handle this alone?" he asked. "I've got other plans."

I could figure that one out. But I wasn't going to give up now. "No sweat," I said in my best competent, liberated tone of voice. "I have the drill down cold."

He smiled and looked a little guilty.

We taped a cardboard box into some semblance of a violin case, and soon I was trotting off down the quad with a stolen Stradivarius.

Except it wasn't a real Stradivarius. Or was it? How could one tell? And what was its value? I had a sudden glimpse of a future in which our little escapade would not be seen as a harmless student prank. There was a lot of money tied up in things that were supposedly unique. Maybe my folks should have named me Pandora.

In Minnesota, on daylight savings time, within a month of the longest day of the year, it stays light pretty late. I waited in an open practice room—they should have kicked me out, I guess, but no one did. Besides the practice stool, it had a nice comfortable chair. So, yup, with all the stress and lost sleep and everything I was out cold by the time my rear end got comfortable.

It was twilight when I woke up. I snuck out under the gray, got below the window and opened my bag, partly hidden by the bushes. It was still pretty light, I thought—better wait a little while longer. Then I noticed something funny–it was light in the wrong part of the sky.

I looked at my watch. 4:50 a.m. A jogger ran by and waved at me. No way was I going to cat burgle this morning–Stevens' office window faced east. I sat down in the grass and pounded my head and cried. The whole thing was over. One screw up, and it was all over.

★ ❈ ★

Determined to get the bad news over with and deal with it, I found Ted.

"I didn't make the switch," I said. "I fell asleep waiting for the coast to clear."

"Oh, oh." Ted said. He looked as miserable as I felt. "Then you've still got our replica?"

I nodded, miserably. I was deep into self loathing. I thought about how to end it all–it wasn't cold enough out to freeze anymore, but the Mississippi was just a few blocks away, and the fall from the Lake Street bridge would probably stun me enough to let me drown in peace.

"Hmm," Ted said. "Maybe it doesn't matter. If the violins are identical, atom for atom, there would be no way to prove that one you have isn't *his* violin. You could just go on with the plan as if you had made the switch."

I shook my head. "He'd just say I was lying. How could I prove otherwise? I should have taken archeology. Then I could go on a field trip down to the Yucatan and sift for shards of some ancient cannibal's chamber pot while being eaten alive by AIDS-bearing mosquitoes."

But even when I'm emoting nonsense, Ted's a stickler for accuracy– an engineering disease, they say. "I don't think," he said, "there were cannibals in the Yucatan, I've never heard of them using chamber pots, and I don't think you can get AIDS from mosquitoes. Malaria, maybe."

"That's not the point!" I said.

Ted smiled–he knew, he was just trying to break the tension a little.

My mind ran open loop. In the middle of this disaster, I imagined myself in the central American jungle up to my knees in chamber pot shards, trying to figure out what pot they belonged to and how old they were.

How old? A thin ray of light pierced my gloom, a faint twinkling candle of hope a million miles away.

"Ted," I said slowly, "how would you date a chamber pot, anyway?"

I looked at Ted–and suddenly his smile changed to a big grin.

"Kay you'll want to see Dr. Molar and tell him what's happened. And then you'll need to talk to Stephen's insurance company. We'll need a witness and certification."

Stephen's, it turned out, had insured his violin through Lloyd's of London, appropriately enough. And yes, they would be very interested in proof of which violin was the "real" Stradivarius. So interested that the fact that there was only a week until the concert was *no* problem.

★ ✳ ★

That evening before the concert, I put on my one long black dress, grabbed my "good" black jacket and headed for the physics building, just a short walk from the concert hall. Ted was there with the Replica. He gave me a kiss and we headed for the fine arts center.

We caught up with Terri in the foyer. She was was in a tight all-black pants suit with a turtleneck collar.

"Hi," I said. "I'm going to sit up front to give him the replica to try."

She got the strangest expression I've ever seen on her face. "But doesn't he already *have* the replica?"

"I didn't make the switch. Fell asleep."

Terri looked first at me then Ted, looking for everything like a cornered rat. "Oh," she said.

The first few notes of "Dear Old Lloyd's" sounded on the PA chimes and we headed for our seats.

The concert was beautiful despite the character of the performer. For an encore, Stevens took the violin to the podium and played his own arrangement of "All Through the Night" with soft voices in the background sounding like an organ. There was hardly a dry eye in the house, including mine. I felt just awful. I knew, right then, that this was the wrong time, wrong place, wrong situation. It would just have to wait until next year. I'd planned to run up and spring the replica on him before the applause stopped. But I shut my eyes and stayed right where I was.

"You have something for me, Ms. Kim, I believe," Stevens announced, in front of everyone.

The lobster got my stomach and and grabbed hard. All of a sudden Terri's expression made sense; Stephens knew, and there was only one person who could have told him. I shot a look back at her that would vaporize an elephant. She kind of shrugged her shoulders.

"Ms. Kim, and some of her deconstructionist pranksters," Stevens continued, "have thought to play a little joke on me, and you. They made, with their little atomistic reductionist gizmo over in the physics building, an alleged copy of my Stradivarius violin. Now, the violin you heard tonight was quite adequate, surprisingly so, I must admit, or we would have had *this* conversation a little earlier. So, in fact, I am quite impressed. But the fun is over, Ms. Kim, and I would like my violin back, for this is not, as you all will soon hear, a real Stradivarius. Let's have it back now."

I desperately wanted to bail out of the whole thing. But it was much too late. I took the replica out of its tacky cardboard box and with as much poise as I could manage went up onto the stage. If you're going to go down, I told myself, go down in style.

"Well?" he intoned.

"I didn't make the switch," I said, hoping my voice didn't waver too much. "I'm carrying the replica."

"Nonsense. Young lady, this has gone far enough. That violin is worth over a million dollars, and you must return it this instant!"

I scanned the audience for Dr. Molar. He was the only one that could verify that I was telling the truth, but I couldn't find him. Had the analysis gone wrong? My hands got sweaty.

I turned back to Stevens. "But . . . but you've got it wrong. This isn't . . . "

"I do *not* have it wrong. This is not a Stradivarius." In anger he raised his violin by by its neck over his head, threatening to smash it down on the very solid-looking conductor's music stand.

Suddenly, I realized he really *could* destroy it, destroy the original Stradivarius, destroy something made so carefully from ancient wood by the long dead master. My arms shot out toward him with the replica. "No! No! Don't break it. Here, take this then."

He frowned down on me and brought the violin down, but not on anything. Then he gave it to me. "So maybe I have taught you something after all. You would not see a beautiful instrument destroyed, even if it *wasn't* a Stradivarius. Very well. But now, you have to hear the difference," he beamed to the crowd, his voice and face full of confidence and triumph, "you and any curious folk who might wish to stay."

No one, absolutely no one, had left. My public humiliation was to be about as public as it could get. He turned to me. "You," he said ominously, but then smiled, "may sit down now."

The audience burst into laughter as I negotiated my way back across the stage. Why I didn't just run home, I don't know. Pride, I guess. Or maybe a death wish. At any rate, on my way back to my seat I saw Terri and Ted. Terri was laughing with everyone else. But Ted was sitting very quiet, with that "hmm" look on his face.

Stevens started tuning the replica. He frowned. Then he tuned it a little longer. It took a while, but finally he seemed satisfied.

The replica violin's performance of "All Through the Night" was, if anything, better. Stevens, subconsciously, no doubt, probably put more feeling into it. Or perhaps the tuning was slightly more fresh. At any rate, he proved my point exactly–but Ted, Terri and I were the *only* ones in the hall who knew it.

"I hope," Stevens said, "the superiority of the real instrument is obvious and the stupidity . . . "

"*Dr. Stevens,*" a deep base voice echoed from the back of the hall. A hundred heads turned. It was professor Molar standing there backlit like the stone statue in Don Giovanni, and with, I hoped, a similar purpose. I wilted in relief. "Stevens, a moment please."

Stevens, interrupted in his moment of triumph, looked down his nose. "What do *you* want?"

"Privately, please, before you say anything else."

"**Nonsense!** This is my concert and I'll damn well say what I please!"

You could have heard a pin drop.

"Very well," Molar said, calmly. "Have you ever heard of carbon 14 dating?"

A few whispers started.

"What?" Stevens said. "Of course I have! What of it?"

"The violin you hold in your hand is less than 50 years old. Perhaps as new as yesterday."

There were a few nervous chuckles.

"**Nonsense**!"

"I did the test myself. The one you described as the real Stradivarius is, in fact, the replica."

Titters began in the back and rolled forward to the stage in a wave of mirth.

Stevens looked at one violin, then the other, opened his mouth, shut it, then abruptly set the replica down, picked up the real Stradivarius, and held it for a long time. Then he laid it down again and shuffled out a side entrance. Some said there were tears in his eyes. The laughs died and the audience sat in shocked silence.

I went back up to the stage and took the new violin the old laughing philosopher had given me, and simply flowed down off the stage. The first claps started as I got halfway up the aisle and by the time I reached the back of the hall, I had to turn and wave. Ted was standing, leading the applause. Terri was nowhere to be seen. Ah, sweet, sweet vindication!

★ ❈ ★

Just to tie this off, the "Democritus Violin" as they're calling our replica–it's quite famous now–was deemed property of the college and is on display in the science building. The debate still rages as to whether it is a real Stradivarius, but we've been enjoined from making any more replicas until some legal dust settles.

Professor Molar, it turned out, was late to the concert because of a long meeting with the College President and Dean of the faculty. Dr. Molar had done more than analyze the violin. He'd compiled a list of grievances from over a hundred students and faculty. Andre Stevens didn't like people disagreeing with his views, it seemed, and expressed his dislike in grades, recommendations and various other ways. There are advantages to being a private, rather than a state institution, and Dear Old Lloyd released Stevens from his contract in time for the disgraced musicologist to take an appointment at Twin Cites A&I for the next semester. He conceded nothing in a bitter final letter to the school newspaper saying that as his talents had declined to the point where he could no longer tell a real Stradivarius from a copy, he would never play again.

While Stevens' promise of an "A" for proving him wrong was not considered an enforceable contract, I was allowed to withdraw, post facto, from his course, and as a result, my grade point was high enough for my scholarship to be renewed–with some help from the athletic department. My penance for all of this will be to throw an aluminum disk as far as I can for the Women of Harlech next spring. A small price to pay; and, in partial compensation, I now have exclusive possession of Ted.

But I carry a secret with me. There was an ambiguity in my victory that makes me fear that Stevens may have won after all, if only in my own mind. When he was about to smash the original Stradivarius, I stopped him.

Now why, if the replica was no different, did I do that?

STORY NOTES

The setting of this story is strongly inspired by my alma mater, Macalester College, in St. Paul Minnesota, though the serial numbers, as they say, have been filed off. Also, I assure you that none of the Macalester College faculty would display any of the pompousness shown here, nor would any Macalester students so cavalierly flaunt its rules and regulations, nor make use of its equipment in so personal an endeavor. But some of the buildings might be recognizable.

Though a prototypical liberal arts school through most of its existence, Macalester has always had a strong science faculty and is increasing its involvement with the "art" of data management and associated careers. It is thus not too far a stretch, I think, for such a college to host, in half a century or so, a one-of-a-kind first-generation replicator. In any event, for the purposes of the story, dear old Lloyd College has such a machine, and students willing to use it to challenge the notion of uniqueness.

Rather than scanning and placing atom by atom, as the machine in " Of Fire and Ice," this machine is organically smart and works with molecules and cell replica, achieving a much higher level of data compression.

This is one of a few stories which I have done from a first person female point of view. It is, I'll admit, somewhat cheeky for an old man of European descent to imagine himself as a young woman of mixed Korean-American ancestry. Spending a year in Korea courtesy of the US Air Force helped. Being married to a musically talented woman helped. And I should note here the contribution of Marion Sterns, who played violin at church services for many years at the UU church in Livermore, CA. In any event, whatever I did was successful enough that the story won the Analog reader's "An-Lab" award for the year 2000, my last such award as of this writing, and one very bright in my memory.

GDN January 2016

OF FIRE AND ICE

With a frozen deliberateness that was almost majestic, something was forming. Whether perfect or mishappen, only time would tell. But it was, indeed, forming. Lieutenant Shane Foster's pulse was up, and her mouth was dry. She tried to calm herself with the thought that anyone in her position who wasn't worried would be someone who didn't understand the situation. It was too soon to try this much, too tricky, not enough safeguards in the equipment, and too dangerous if things went wrong. But they needed the royal demo and the publicity to keep the project alive. So it had been scheduled and it was too late to back down now

So far, every thing was indeed working. The reconstruction plane was rising at its nominal rate, and a quick look at the data screens and the test article below the plane showed everything was still go.

She snapped her eyes back to the man standing next to her; Dr. Graff Frank, the Laboratory Director. Tricky as it was, the demonstration wasn't her biggest worry; one bad impression with him could start a trail of less than perfect performance reports leading to separation, unemployment, and worse. Her memories of childhood poverty — and a teenage suicide attempt that she hoped nobody knew about — came to the fore in these circumstances and sometimes she stuttered, trying too hard to please.

He was frowning. But his attention was still locked onto the fuzzy gray reconstruction plane, not her.

✳ ❀ ✳

From the shadowy rear of the auditorium, Brendon Kelly also stole a look at the gray, utilitarian, auditorium stage; surprisingly dull for a royal showcase. The Lieutenant in the hated uniform was a surprise as well, a slight, wiry, blond woman, unarmed. The tall pom in the gray suit next to her was fidgeting with impatience. They didn't seem to notice him; their attention was focused on the dense, fuzzy gray plane that hovered over a half completed piece of machinery in a transparent vertical tank.

He smiled grimly. This confirmed all the rumors and speculation; he was seeing the apparently successful demonstration of a matter transmitter. But Brendon had no interest in the wonder of it. What fired his imagination was that *this* was what his royal target would come to see; bait for his trap.

He took a painful deep breath. Wounded at 'Derry in '45, he'd gotten bad blood — contaminated by the bloody poms, somehow, he was sure. He had pulmonary neural necrosis now; he'd stop breathing altogether in about six months, they said. But before that, he'd return the favor.

An idea, and then a plan, formed. If the device worked as advertised, the tactic looked feasible; and if he could pull it off, the King would have a surprise indeed. Brendon tweaked his 'hearing aid,' bringing in their voices a little more clearly as he watched. The fuzzy layer they called "the reconstruction plane" stuck out of the side of what looked like an oversize white filing cabinet rising two meters above the stage floor. The plane seemed static if he stared at it, but when he looked away for a bit and then looked back, it revealed a little more of the object being transmitted. It was like watching the moon rise on its shallow slant over the arctic wastes outside, he thought, and looked away impatiently.

A glance a minute later, and he recognized the object being transmitted: a standard utility motile; roughly the size and shape of a human being. Yes, indeed, this might be the way.

The pom cleared his throat and happened to glance at Brendon.

Brendon wiped a hand on his stolen maintenance coveralls and turned back to disassembling the optic data port. Careful now, he thought. He didn't want to be noticed, no, not after walking three hundred kilometers through the Canadian arctic from Quebec to reach this secret research station. The French help had ended at their border, and he had invested too much in this chance to strike back at the very heart of the Anglo-American Commonwealth, and too little time left to make a botch of it now.

"This is about half our theoretical maximum speed," he heard the Lieutenant explain. The clear bell-like tone of her voice seemed out of place for Brendon's eternal enemy. "We can pack the nano-operators only so close because we can make them only so thin and still control placement accurately enough. That's the limiting factor, sir, that and thermal noise. We've got the placement frequency up to a megahertz: you're watching thirty trillion nanites each place a million atoms every second."

Technocratic gobbledygook, Brendon thought. Her gadget took something from "there" and sent it "here," however slowly. That's what he saw; it was all he needed to know. That's how he'd reach his target, he decided, if he could find only out where "there" was.

★ ❀ ★

"Can't it go any faster?" The director seemed impatient. He had been briefed by the contract scientists, and her boss with pretty charts, graphs, and pictures and apparently none of it had sunk in. So it was up to her. If she were too technical, he'd be irritated with her for breaking that unwritten rule that says that bosses must be allowed to think they know what they were doing. If she weren't technical enough, he'd think she was patronizing him. Maybe she could start by describing what they were looking at, again, in a little more detail.

She opened her mouth to speak, and nothing came out. She opened and closed it twice like a fish out of water. Then she dug her fingernails into her palms and choked out: "This is about half our theoretical maximum speed. It — it's limited by how many ops — operations — er, atom placing operations each nanite can do every second and by how close together we can get the nanites.

The director frowned. Angry? Frustrated, Just concentrating hard? She didn't know. She took a deep breath.

"We — we can pack them only so close, about half a nanometer center to center and still control their placement accurately. That's the limiting factor, that and thermal noise. We've got the placement frequency up to megahertz; you're watching thirty trillion nanites each place a million atoms every second."

"Okay, Foster, maybe what it does is amazing enough. Maybe the slowness won't matter." the director told Shane, nodding judiciously, thin lips pursed. It helped in a small way to realized that he was just as afraid of the people above him as she was of him. "If this is already halfway to its theoretical speed limit, I can understand why it won't replace assembly lines."

"Sir, it — it was never intended to replace assembly lines. But, in a year or so things like it could *build* an assembly plant — out of nothing but bare rock and sunlight. Without any human intervention. I mean if we get it working right." She winced. Col. Themis wouldn't be pleased if he heard that — never say anything negative to boss men, he'd told them all. Never. Find a positive way to say what you have to say, if you want to keep working. But the director didn't seem to react to her qualification.

"How," he asked, "are you going to keep His Royal Highness amused while this goes through its somewhat, um, *deliberate* routine?"

"We'll start the demo right away, sir, then explain what's going on while it's in progress. That's going to — to involve a brief review of basic physics for His Majesty, and by the time we're done talking, the replication should be done."

"Hmmpf. Is that," he indicated the half completed motile, "what you're going to reproduce? It seems a bit prosaic. We should make a more lasting impression — do something with some zing in it!"

A small laugh escaped unbidden from her throat, and she stifled it in terror. Control, she told herself, don't do or say *anything* around this guy without thinking carefully about impressions first. Noise suppression, she reflected, of several kinds was vital to this project. "We've pa — planned a surprise that we hope will amuse His Majesty."

"What? What kind of a surprise?" The question was sharp, challenging.

"The Disney people have donated a simulacron of, of him." Her hands were shaking and she hid them behind her back in a parade rest stance. She realized, too late, that that posture would push her bust out and perhaps sending an unintended signal to which the director might respond, might resent, or both. She slowly put her hands back by her side and willed them to be still.

The director seemed amused, and seemed to relax. "Ha! Well His Majesty should like that then; worth waiting for. But make sure you check with his people first. I'll expect a report in the morning."

"Yes, sir," Shane responded with a deliberate, tentative smile and, with her body frozen, let her mind escape briefly to thinking about what the presentation would be like. It would work, she thought. It had to.

"Will the motile work after going through?"

There was a part of her that recognized the absurdity of trying to pretend confidence when she was scared stiff — but perhaps the wryness in her smile would be taken as self assurance.

"We have to wait a bit to find out, sir. This reconstructor is a three coordinate device and there are actually seven degrees of . . . "

He raised a hand to cut her off. "I have a fifteen hundred meeting, but this was plenty impressive. Good work. Just make sure there aren't any screw-ups. Thank you, Lieutenant."

She shook hands with him and watched him walk up the aisle and pass through the door. Then she sat down on the nearest front row chair, shuddered, and started taking deep breaths. There were many things she should have said and hadn't, but she didn't think she'd made any show-stopping gaffs. Col. Themis shouldn't be too unhappy.

Gradually, she let her mind go back to technical issues. The King's simulacron was just a fancy motile, of course. And she was pretty sure this one would work if the warm-up speed . . .

★ ❋ ★

Brendon watched the man in the suit leave and the Lieutenant collapse in a seat. No one else was around and he'd disabled the auditorium's IR data port. She was preoccupied and unarmed. This was his chance.

He had the hypo in her bare arm before she knew he was there. She did a half turn and registered a surprised look before she collapsed. He counted to thirty. Her eyes opened again, barely. Her apparent thinness disguised a well trained body; her shoulders were as wide as her hips. Fortunately for his failing lungs, he wouldn't have to fight her.

"If you understand me, raise your arm." Slowly, her arm went up. The amnesia instructions had to go in now, before her left brain functions recovered.

"You won't remember this when you wake up. You were dizzy for a bit and sat down, that's all."

"Uh, huh." Her jaw hung open, she looked very unhappy, confused perhaps. The drug was having just the effect it was supposed to have.

"Now why are you sitting down?"

"I got dizzy. That's all." Her speech was slow, but normally inflected.

Brendon smiled, nodded, and took her hand.

"Well, don't let that be botherin' you now." He hoped the stage-Irish blarney would be soothing. "Oh, now, can you tell me from what room you transmitted that object on the stage?"

"Transmit?" Her face contorted — a sign that some higher functions were coming back.

"Yes, transmit. You scan things somewhere else and reproduce them here. All I need to know is where the transmitter is. I've got to fix it a little, see?"

"Don' understan'" the woman slurred, right brain and left brain fighting each other.

Brendon frowned. She understood very well, he judged, in half her brain. He reached in his pocket, pulled out an army knife, and opened the blade. "Give me your hand."

She reached toward him with her right hand and he took it in his left.

He held the handle of the knife in it. "I could tell you to cut your own wrists and you'd do it."

She smiled, "Yes, I could do that. I understand that." The right side of her face twitched. "Do you want me to kill myself?"

"No, miss, I wouldn't be wanting you to do that. Just tell me where the transmitter is so I can fix it. You wouldn't be wantin' it broken when the King comes to visit, now would you?"

"Transmitter? Broken?"

If he could just tip the balance, plant doubt while she was still suggestible . . . "Yes, miss. The transmitter, from where you'll be sendin' the robot that just appeared on the stage."

She brightened at the word scanned. "Oh, you want to see the *scanner*. Not transmitter. Doesn't work that way." Her face twitched. "Can't tell you where. Classified. I'm supposed to die rather than reveal classified material. Do you want to kill me?"

"No, miss." She'd do anything he told her — if only he could tell her to walk to the transmitter. But he couldn't risk that. "Just tell me where the scanner is."

She looked very unhappy. "Can' do that. Classified. 'Sides, not broken. Works okay."

She was resisting. He'd taken the drug himself and knew what she was experiencing; an artificial schizophrenia. The right part of her brain wanted to help him, would do anything for him. The other part was perfectly well aware of what was going on, but was almost completely isolated from any voluntary control. Unfortunately, that was the part that had the technical knowledge. He hated himself for what he had to try now, but his mission depended on it. It was a war. They were both soldiers.

He took her hand and put the point of the knife in her palm.

"Now I *am* going to find the transmitter anyway," he told her, "and no one will blame you if you tell me. You don't want to hurt when this is over, so let's just go ahead and tell me. Please."

She just shook her head, but remained silent. Tears formed in her eyes, from the helpless part of her brain. "Don't care about me. But I have to please you, please Colonel Themis, please the King. please Everyone. But I can't make everyone happy, and it hurts," she pleaded.

"Don't move your hand." Brendon pushed the knife blade through between her finger bones, and blood dripped on the floor. Good clean blood.

He pulled the knife out slowly, to maximize pain. The part of her mind that controlled her voluntary muscles would obey him, gladly, dumbly. But the part that resisted him was fully conscious, and experiencing the pain fully. If pain could break her mental deadlock between conflicting duties in favor of him, to save herself, he'd get his information. Saints preserve me, he thought, what he was doing was drastic, but there wasn't much time.

"Now *that* hurts." He took another deep painful breath; he had six months, the doctors said, but at times like this it felt like two. "*Now, can you tell me where the transmitter is?*"

Her breathing was short, tears rolled freely, and her mouth gaped as part of her mind tried to obey him. But her intellect had a veto power over language. She chose duty over self, and stayed silent. He knew the tremendous effort that took, and was saddened. He'd known mollies like her, and it pained him to see one in that uniform.

Her pager started beeping. Time was up.

He nodded sadly. "You're a good soldier. I'll tell them that if I get the chance. But it has to end now, you know that? This is a war, and I can't have you ratting on me, can I?" He wiped his prints from the knife, put it in her left hand and guided it to the part of her right wrist where it would be most effective. "When I say now, cut there, slanting up the arm. Deeply and quickly." He hesitated, hating himself — but to leave her alive would be to warn them all. "Now."

There was no hesitation, and her bloody hand repeated the operation with the other wrist. She had solved her dilemma of making everyone happy, and looked to him for approval as her life flowed from her wrist, seeming relieved. He nodded and held her shoulder until she lost consciousness. No one well educated enough to be an officer in the Commonwealth service was really innocent of its crimes, he told himself. They knew about their government's oppression in Northern Ireland, and served it anyway. This was the price. He took her key badge — probably no way he could use it without her live thumbprint, but just having one to flash would make him fit in better.

As Brendon left the auditorium, they paged her again. He walked quickly down the hall and chanced by a maintenance area with its door left open. He slipped in and pretended to do something at the workbench.

An hour passed, then two. He waited.

Finally, amid the purposeful noise of a shift change, two other maintenance personnel entered, an older man and a plump, black haired woman.

If anyone was normally supposed to be at "his" workbench, they didn't show. He smiled to himself; it was his business to gamble, and he'd just won another. He stayed, hoping to pick up some information. He reached to his ear and adjusted his "hearing aid" to bring the conversation at the back of the room in clearly.

" . . . that this place is just to damn remote. That makes two suicide attempts in the last month."

"Eh? Out of ten thousand? It's not statistically significant, not out in this frozen hell. Still, who would have guessed Lt. Foster? She seemed right."

"Some of us put on a good act. She was getting pretty stressed out, with all the pressure, trying to please everyone. You could tell how she felt from the stuttering. Lucky you thought to check-out that white noise in the auditorium data circuit. That is, I guess it's lucky. They'll cashier her for this and she'll end up unemployable, out in the cold, and then dead just like she would have done anyway."

The Lieutenant wasn't dead already? By the saints, Brendon thought, he'd watched her die! But the authorities might be on to him and spreading disinformation for his benefit. He'd have to be extra watchful just in any case, because if she were alive her memory would start coming back in a few hours.

"Oh, really. That's a bit . . . " the overheard conversation continued.

"I'm not serious. But it's rough on a woman sometimes. Did you hear that they're going to put that P. R. officer, Rick Carpenter in charge of the demo. He's overseeing the tests now."

Carpenter? Brendon concentrated. There was a Captain Erik Carpenter in the base directory, with a little effort, he visualized the page. The office comm code was 745-372.

"Do okay I guess, if he listens to the techs. Cold fish — that suicide try won't faze him at all."

Brendon tuned out and concentrated on finding Captain Carpenter's room number . . . ah, 74b.

★ ※ ★

There was someone in Shane's room, someone who wanted to do things to her. She had to wake up and scare him away, but she couldn't move a muscle. She tried to breath faster, but couldn't, so she started to panic. If only she could move a toe, a finger, something. The person in the room was almost on her, she could hear his steps next to her bed. Finally, her breath came faster. She gasped aloud and shuddered, breaking through to reality.

She opened her eyes — the lights were on — brilliant. Where was her nightstand? What time was it?

She sat bolt upright in terror of the prospect of missing a morning meeting.

"Hold on there, Lieutenant," a man said. He was all in white, an orderly.

Forget meetings, she was in the clinic. Her arms were wrapped in bandages. She was on an IV! It started getting dark again, and she felt woozy.

"Just lie down for now, ma'am."

"What . . . who?" she croaked, as the room started to whirl around her. The man pushed her back down; she couldn't resist. Lying down, things started to clear.

"I'm Sam," the man said. "You tried to do yourself in."

"What? No, no I didn't."

"Those are some pretty mean self-inflicted wounds in your arms."

"God. No." She couldn't remember anything after getting up in the morning. She had been going to give a demonstration for the director — no, she'd given the demo. But her memory got hazy.

"I gave a presentation to the director. Something happened."

She felt an ache in her arm hurt above the bandages, and unconsciously moved a hand to the area. It was tender. She remembered noise, like someone talking. The wasn't clear, but the pain. . .

"Sam — someone gave me a shot."

"You've had a lot of them, I suspect."

"No, just after I talked to the director in the auditorium. A shot, a sting on the arm. I — I, was drugged. Look:" She showed him the hypo bruise on her arm. Things were beginning to come back, the soft Gaelic voice she wanted so very much to please and the things she tried so hard not to tell him.

The medic looked at her arm, then looked at her, comprehension seeming to dawn on his face.

"Oh. We certainly didn't do that here, ma'am. Shouldn't be doing that to yourself."

"I *didn't*. Uh, how long have I been under?"

"Just over a day ma'am. What do you mean you didn't?"

"Sam," she asked, "Is the demonstration still on? Is the King here?"

"Arrived this morning. Opened the Commonwealth Assembly at Victoria and flew right up here. Big to do, eh. They've got guards all over the auditorium, now."

"Oh, no! Sam, look. I've got to talk to someone in security. Whoever did this to me might have planted a bomb or something in the auditorium."

Sam's eyes narrowed. "Now just calm down, ma'am. I'll call someone."

★ ❋ ★

Brendon must have removed and installed the corridor ceiling panel fifteen times before the door to Captain Carpenter's quarters opened. Once the tension of that was over, it was child's play to follow him to the transmitter room. The officer waved a badge at the front of the door and it opened. Brendon followed, flashing his purloined badge and clipping it on backward with feigned confidence. Captain Carpenter looked a question at him.

"Problems with the optical ports, sir," he brazened.

The Captain nodded. "I heard about something like that in the auditorium yesterday. Let's get it fixed, we don't want any miscommunications with royal security all over the place."

"No that wouldn't look right, sir, would it?"

Brendon grinned, amazed at the lack of security. Of course, the primary security for the laboratory was its remote location, and he'd defeated that already. But they would surely have guards around the auditorium. He smiled to himself. Ye'd be forgettin' the back door now would ye? He located one of the outlets, turned up his hearing aid and set to his phony work, sneaking looks at the equipment in the middle of the stage.

The transmission tank looked pretty much the way the receiving tank looked — a rounded transparent half cylinder about two meters tall built into the end of a big cabinet. Cables as big as around as Brendon's thigh left the cabinet.

The lone technician, a plump, ruddy, type with a shock of white hair, nodded to the officer. "You'll be the O.I.C. for the demo now, I gather. Too bad about Foster. Well, It's all ready to go, sir. It will take about an hour to scan at one meg."

"Fine, Bellows. I wish the hell we could record this and play it back. Foster explained why we couldn't but I'm afraid I don't remember."

"Eh? Reason is too much data sir. Best we can store is a million sections, and the whole object will take over ten thousand million. So we have to do 'er in real time."

"Oh, I see — I think." The man's face was puzzled.

Brendon smiled: he'd probably learned as much about this device in two days of skulking as this Captain Blimp they'd just put in charge of the demo knew.

"Tell me, where is the scanner?"

The man pointed to the floor of the cylinder. "Gravity feed."

"I see how that works. So the replication goes from bottom up?"

"That cuts down the size of the buffer, sir. First in, first out."

"Oh. I see. You're all ready, then. Well," Captain Carpenter continued, "how's the family?"

Brendon looked at his wrist comp.

"Got the folks up to Santa Fé in time. Mom's too old to learn Spanish, so she traded houses with some Mexicans that wanted to move back to the other side of the line, now that Señor Diaz has taken Albuquerque. Cindy's a Lunie now — her application was approved three weeks ago and off she went. Just me and Evie left."

Serves the Poms right, Brendon thought, seein' what it was like being on the other side of arrogance for a bit. Fifteen million good Catholic Mexicans under arms should put the fear o' God in 'em. But he pulled his thoughts back to the task at hand. Let's get on with this.

"Oh, I see. Well, I hope its not too lonely for you." the Captain added as he looked at his wrist comp. "What's the schedule?"

"Flexible. When you're ready to start your talk, signal. I'll fix the subject and begin scanning."

Fix? Brendon frowned — of course it probably wouldn't do to be moving around while you were being scanned. He'd hate to try to hold still like people had to do for photographs a couple of centuries ago. Probably a stasis field. He'd read about stasis fields, and the people on the Galaxy Trek re-runs always stopped in mid-motion when the their transporter came on. He probably wouldn't feel a thing.

A tone sounded and a voice came from a speaker somewhere in the room. "Captain Carpenter, Captain Carpenter, you'll be needed at security at 1455."

"On my way," the officer replied. "That means the King's finally here. Good luck, Bellows."

Then Brendon was alone with the technician. He checked his weapon and its magazines. All was in readiness. The technician unsealed the cylinder and swung it open, then opened a crate.

"This better work," the man muttered. "Okay, your highness, up on the scanning stage."

Brendon's jaw dropped. As if out of a coffin, the King sat up. His fashionably long, iron gray hair and familiar craggy profile were instantly recognizable. He was dressed in a conservative black shirtcoat with the embroidered arms over the left breast — the same as he wore at the installation of the princess royal.

A ruse! Brendon realized. The security at the auditorium was a ruse to attract potential assassins while they slipped the King in the same back door he planned to use! A hell of a demo, but it made a sort of dramatic sense, and the fumbling old figurehead was known for his sense of humor. Brendon quickly fumbled around his gray coveralls for his weapon and, fingers shaking with anticipation, withdrew the trank magazine and put in the fatal charges. He would take care of this business right now.

★ ❀ ★

"Every . . . everybody is under stress here!" Shane snapped at the shrink. The situation was ridiculous. An enemy agent was roaming around a supposedly secure installation, and he was questioning her sanity. "This," she waved her bandaged arms, "was not my doing! I — I'm *sane*! There's an intruder on the loose here, a potential assassin. I was his first victim!"

The idiot psychologist, a blond blue-eyed young man named Dr. Poole, was watching her body moving under her ridiculously immodest hospital gown instead of listening to her. He was Navy and didn't outrank her, so she had no reason to kowtow to him. But her only hope of saving His Majesty's life, let alone her own career and dignity, was to convince this lecherous, condescending jerk that she was not paranoid.

The frustration threatened her self control.

"Now, Ms. Foster, we wouldn't want to be starting another bomb rumor today, would we? I strongly suggest you cooperate with therapy; at the very worst, you'll get a medical discharge. And if we cure you, who knows?"

Shane gritted her teeth. She would never be promoted with that in her file, but with a clean record otherwise, she might be continued. She tried to imagine herself as the gray-haired oldest lieutenant in the Commonwealth Forces. At least she would have a job. The shrink was giving her an out, a chance to save herself and let events unfold as they might. Did she really care that much about some pampered aristocrat?

"What do you want of me?" she asked.

"Let's try to be objective. Something inside us needs a lot of attention, and maybe takes control. Without really thinking about it. And then this story about assassins. It's just the thing someone would say if they were trying to deny a suicide attempt, which, according to your family, is not the first time."

"Attention?" she gasped. Shane's skin went cold and she stared pure hate at the shrink. They had no right, no damn right to dig that up. She left her family, all the abuse, and all the lies behind her when she got her commission out of Officer's school. This was crazy, Shane thought. Then another chilling idea occurred to her; the shrink could be in on it. Any number of people could be in on it. And she knew too much. But if she should even hint that she was thinking that, he'd have her dead to rights as a paranoid.

Rights? That was what this all came down to wasn't it, she thought. The government that the pampered monarch symbolized was, or tried to be, a government where people like her had rights and weren't just subject to the whim of the most greedy, powerful, corrupt, or fanatical. To maintain those rights, from time to time, there had to be sacrifices. She'd taken an obligation with her uniform that transcended obedience to authority, and she realized with a sudden clarity, it was time to make a payment on that obligation.

Shane had lost a lot of blood, but they'd pumped her up with glucose and by virtue of hard training, she was stronger than most men. She might gain temporary freedom, get to someone who would listen, of find the assassin . . . No, it wouldn't work. They'd just start hunting her instead of the assassin. She had to get through to the idiot doctor. A frontal attack with reason, she decided, with stealth, or seduction, as a back-up. She forced anger back and spoke in a quiet, tension filled, voice:

"First, I — I do not want attention. Not that way.

"Second, I don't remember how my wrists got cut, I was drugged. There's probably some of it still in my system. At least check it out, please.

"Third, notify security. You can't take the chance that I'm not telling the t — truth. With the King here, you have to err on the side of — of safety."

"Look," Dr. Poole said, still leering at her, "I'm sure you believe what you're saying. But I have to exercise some judgment here, and it doesn't look to me as if you're accepting reality."

Furious, but desperate, Shane changed her posture slightly, pushing her bust against the thin fabric of the hospital gown and tried to put something resembling a smile on her face.

"Please? If I'm just imagining this, I'll have to be convinced of that, won't I? Just a little test. I'll really be grateful."

"Well," he continued, grinning, "it would be useful to confront your conscious mind with the truth. For that reason, we'll go ahead and do the blood test."

Shane rolled her eyes to the ceiling. "Quickly," she pleaded breathlessly, "do the tests *quickly*." And honestly, she added silently. And, God help me, do them honestly.

★ ❋ ★

Brendon raised his gun in the shadows of the equipment. Incredibly, the technician still had not noticed him. The King got quietly out of his box smoothly and started walking toward the transmitter stage. Something was wrong. The King's movements were controlled, coordinated, consistent with his public demeanor, but still very smooth for someone who'd just spent hours inside a crate. Unnaturally smooth, and his face was . . . expressionless. A damned robot!

Oh, that was close, Brendon thought angrily as he changed his aim. A brief snap, and the technician collapsed. Too late, Brendon remembered he had the fatal magazine loaded.

So, he thought, the grim reaper would get three of them. The technician, the King, and, because he had no illusions of being able to escape after his deed, himself. How much easier it is to kill, he thought, when your own life is forfeit. At least the hell-and-be-damned virus wouldn't get him.

The simulacron of the King moved toward the transmitter stage. Brendon moved quickly after it, and when it halted in a regal pose, he reached in, grabbed it, and pulled it out and down with a resounding crash. It tried to get up, but Brendon swung his leg at its head with enough power to score a goal from fifty meters. He cursed the pain in his toe as the head bounded across the floor and the now-sightless motile body froze in place. Then he started removing the thing's royal clothes.

★ ❋ ★

An hour had gone by and Shane was getting desperate. There would be a comset in the hall of the dispensary. She'd only need a minute. Dr. Poole had gone, but the medic, Sam, was still watching her. Of course, officially, she was a risk.

"Sam," she said. "I need to visit the loo. Any chance you could disconnect the I.V. for me?"

"I have to keep you in sight." He grinned.

She grinned back, nastily. "I'd rather that than the bedpan. But don't get any ideas."

He shrugged, came over to her bedside, and disconnected the glucose. She swung her legs out of bed and got to her feet. She might have felt a little lightheadedness, but that soon passed and she stood steadily. "Where is my uniform?"

"Uh, it's in the closet, but you don't need it to go to the loo, that's right here." He motioned to another door in the tiny cubical.

"Supplies," she said, opened the closet door, and began feeling through her cloths. Thank God, her personal comset was still in her pants pocket. She palmed it.

"Bloody gone," she complained, "maybe some in the loo."

She went in and he followed to the door, probably getting an eyeful of her bare bottom. Never mind. She turned and matter-of-factly took off the rest of the hospital gown and started running the water and unwrapping soap. A quick look showed he was mortified with embarrassment. She smiled and slid the small door shut. He didn't do anything.

As soon as the door shut, she called the lab computer. "Locate royal security, emergency," she told it. It took less than a minute.

"R.S.," a thin, curly-haired civilian answered. "Talia Barnes speaking."

"Ms. Barnes, listen carefully. I'm Lieutenant Shane Foster, from the replicator program. I was drugged, questioned, and attacked last night by someone who tried to make it look like a suicide attempt. I'm in the clinic and they won't listen to me here. The person that attacked me is still at large."

"Shane, Talia will do. You say a possible assassin?"

"That or a particularly vicious attempt at espionage. I think it's an assassination attempt. He know's the King's here for the demo. Irish accent, if that means anything."

"God. You're at the lab clinic?"

"Yes."

"We'll send someone right over."

"Thanks." Shane exhaled and sat for a minute, head in hands. She'd done it. If things didn't happen to back her up, Col. Themis would have her at the bottom of his rating list. But that was in other people's hands now. She looked at the her bandaged left hand. A memory of pain came back. Vague.

Sometimes, she recalled, you can remember better if you are in the same state as when you got the memory. She took a breath and put pressure on the wound. Despite herself a tear rolled down her cheek at the burning pain. There had been a question, a persistent question. She had wanted so much to answer,but had struggled so hard not to answer. Something had been wrong with the question, and that had helped her not to answer directly. But what was the question?

She finished her toilet as best as she could with the bandage-encumbered forearms, shrugged into the hospital gown, and emerged just as Sam called her name. Dr. Poole was waiting, looking wistful and a bit frightened at the same time.

"Your turn?" she inquired innocently.

"Huh? No." Dr. Poole's attitude had changed completely. He was almost deferential. "You'll want to put your uniform on or get back under the covers. We've got a colonel and your surgeon on the way. It seems your blood test was positive. I, uh, I'm sorry."

Shane gave him a curt nod; apology noted but not accepted. With her luck, they'd bust her for a controlled substance. Or maybe they intercepted her call. Well, given the option of getting back in uniform, she would take it. By the time the knock came on the door, she was presentable.

There were three people: her commander, Col. Themis; a doctor she'd never met; and Talia, looking grim. Talia exchanged a look with the Dr. Poole that said "get out of our way." He excused himself with an embarrassed nod.

"The demonstration is underway, Lieutenant," Talia told her, "and everything looks as planned. Everyone in the auditorium is cleared and there's no way in that isn't guarded."

Of course, Shane thought. "He thinks there is one. Damn! We — we have to move fast."

"What?" Col. Themis asked, not about to be stampeded by a subordinate.

"My attacker wanted to know where the scanner was. I — I'll bet he thinks it's another way into the auditorium. One he can use."

"Oh, God. You think he's replicating a bomb?"

"I think he's sending himself with a gun but . . . " There was too much to explain and too little time. "You should get those people out of the auditorium and . . . "

"Wait a minute," Talia interrupted. "Shane, that may be just what he wants. He may have accomplices just waiting for us to be panicked into a breach of security. Is there anyway for you to stop this *without* sending His Majesty out of the planned security perimeter?"

Shane thought rapidly. "Yes. But please contact your people and tell them, whatever shows up on that stage, *don't do anything.* Don't react to it. Definitely *don't* shoot. Understand?"

"I should think, Lieutenant," Col. Themis intoned, condescendingly, "that they should do whatever they have to do to make sure whatever shows up doesn't injure the King!"

"Ye — yes sir." Shane bit her lip. Damned if she did, damned if she didn't. "I — I mean no, sir. In this case, I think safety means not doing anything until I change the cycle. Please. No pounding, no commotion, definitely no gunfire. B — best to not even talk if the cycle completes."

"Why not stop the replication immediately, why let it go to completion?" the Colonel asked.

Every second was precious. "Sir, he could explode!"

"Nonsense. The nanomanipulators place an atom exactly where its counterpart was in the object that was scanned. If it stops midway, the assassin will be cut in half or something. Tough on him, but that's all."

He didn't understand and there wasn't time to explain, or argue. She opened her mouth helplessly — nothing came out.

"We can talk about this later." Talia interrupted. "Let's go!"

Without trying to say another work, Shane was out the door and charging down the corridor.

★ ❊ ★

After experimenting a couple of times, Brendon found that the transmission chamber door would lock tight with a good shove. Getting it open again was a problem until he found the power switch. Then the display screen recycled and the start-up menu solved that problem.

The screen also confirmed what he had overheard — the scanning process was preprogrammed and ready to initialize. Dressed in the royal simulacron's finery, he stepped onto the stage and waited. And smiled. The would see just what they expected until it was too late.

"We are ready to receive," Captain Carpenter's voice said.

"Roger," Brendon risked, with his best imitation of the late technician's voice. Then he started the clear door on its way to closing shut, snaking his hand in at the last millisecond, and heard it thump and latch. His gun was primed, cocked and ready with its load of lethal darts. He raised it above his head, where it would be partly hidden by the small opaque dome over the chamber, and would, of course, be the last part of him they would see.

He would not have much time to think when he came out of stasis, and shot. No time at all before the inevitable reaction of the royal guards ended his thinking and his virus forever. So he composed his thoughts.

For you, Katie, my sister dead in a blaze the English authorities let burn. For you, Finn O'Grady, who let himself be executed for another's deed. For those like me who got the virus-tainted blood for their wounds. And for all of you gone in the glorious struggle.

There was a sound of opening valves and a hiss. His feet burned. He wanted to scream, jump and push himself out, but there was no way to open the door now. Instead, he held himself rigid as he cried with agony. Oh why, mother Mary, did they have to make it hurt so much? In his last thoughts, he recognized the source of his fiery pain. The so-called 'stasis field' was simply liquid gas.

★ ❋ ★

"Is this," His Majesty joked as Shane rushed into the auditorium, "someone's way of suggesting I need plastic surgery?"

The reconstruction was almost complete, Shane realized with a start. "That's not your simulacron, Your Highness," she shouted from the back of the auditorium, "Everyone please be still."

She pushed her way down toward the stage as fast as the people clogging the aisles would let her. The confused Captain Carpenter was staring, transfixed, at the object taking form in his tank. Of course, she thought, when two thirds of the atoms being placed are simple hydrogen, things had gone much more quickly. Two or three megahertz, some part of her brain estimated.

"Sir," she called, "please disable the warm up, and lower the thermal set as far as it will go, now!"

"Huh?" The public relations officer spread his hands. "I don't know how."

Damn! Shane thought. Of course he didn't. She pressed into the crowd, toward the stage.

"Help her get through!" Talia yelled at her security people. They pushed and pulled. Shane pushed and pulled. Finally people started getting out of her way. But the king's doppleganger was almost complete — and it was holding something above its head, something so simple in its materials that the replicator was finishing it off at about a centimeter a second. Something that would galvanize the security people Talia didn't have time to brief.

"Look," shouted one of the security people, "He's got a gun!"

"Don't shoot!" Talia's voice cracked out. "For the love of God, don't shoot."

Shane finally reached the stage, grabbed the stage lip and pulled herself up, feeling the fresh surgical glue tear under her bandages. She flopped onto the stage as the last of the nanite cloud swarmed back into the reservoir, pushed herself up, and sprinted for the equipment, trying to keep her body between the rigid assassin and the King's security men.

A low hum began, signifying the start of the warm-up cycle. Damn, she thought, they should have put a voice interface module on this thing. They should have hooked it into the lab cybersystem, they should have done a dozen things instead of pulling out all the stops to get something together for a royal dog and pony show.

She got to the screen. Shaking, it took her two tries to get the right menu.

Warm up cycle initiating, the screen flashed, preempting the menu. Damn! She forced herself to think. Carefully now. First the command display button. . . .

She got the menu on again and touched the cycle icon on. Trembling, she reset the temperature to minimum. Then she selected activate.

The screen asked her if she wanted to interrupt the warm up cycle.

Yes, damnit, yes! She stabbed at the accept icon.

Did she want to cancel the warm up cycle, or initiate at a later time?

Which choice would generate fewer menus? She couldn't remember. She hit cancel.

The hum vanished and the screen told her the warm up cycle had stopped.

Shane slumped against the panel and groaned with relief.

★ ❀ ★

On an arctic gray afternoon days later, Shane and the King faced their would-be killer in the snowfield, still holding his gun over his head, his face still a mask of hate and pain. Security was only a few yards away, but the mist and blowing show made them feel alone in a world of white.

"One quick blow would crack his frozen arms off, Your Majesty. He's just an ice statue, now." She absentmindedly dug in the snow with her boot. "It took three days to get him safely recombined."

"Three days? The King shook his head and put his arm around her shoulder. Perhaps she should object, but instead she turned her face up to him and grinned. She knew making people feel comfortable was part of his job, but he was the first person in her chain of command that didn't make her stutter, and that would be worth . . . whatever he wanted. Sure. Why not? She felt a bit giddy.

"Yes, your Majesty," she murmured. "When his body came through, it came through as, basically, a hundred kilograms of hydrogen and oxygen atoms plus impurities, all right next to each other a millikelvin above absolute zero."

"Oh, say no more," he raised his hand with a smile. "Newtonian physics describes the state of a particle by seven coordinates, as I remember. Three spatial, three more to tell you its velocity, and finally the time at which this is all measured. By placing every atom with zero velocity, which is absolute zero temperature for any ordinary purpose, you have vastly simplified your problem, eliminating in one fell swoop time and three velocity coordinates — but in the bargain creating the one of the most unstable energetic chemical explosives possible!"

"Hey, you know this stuff! Where did you . . . "

"Cambridge. My parents thought King's college would be appropriate. Ha."

 She laughed. "Yes. The recombination would have been very sudden, I'm afraid."

"He would have killed hundreds of people to get me."

"I don't think he understood that, Your Majesty. He must have thought he was going to materialize on that stage and shoot you. And one more thing; he was dying; PNN. If we ever improve this to the point that we can reproduce people, we might edit out such viruses."

The king shook his head. "So the instrument of his death might, in better times, have been the instrument of his continued life. Look at him. His face is the whole damned Irish thing; the fire of a hatred frozen in time."

Shane nodded and looked at the dead man's face. Then she looked at the scar in her hand.

The king raised his eyebrows and nodded. He took his arm from her shoulder, took her hand, and placed a ring in it, a plain silver band with a raised royal crest.

"My sincere thanks. Not just for my life, but for everyone else's. I suggest that if your superiors should ever make you nervous again, simply fondling the crest of this ring in their presence may have a calming influence."

Shane grinned like a child at Christmas, and let herself have a slight laugh. "Your Majesty . . . thanks." Hugging in parkas wasn't very sensual, but she found it to be emotionally satisfying.

"Time to go now, Lieutenant, before my people start looking like," the king tossed his head to indicate the ice man beside them, "him."

Shane nodded, and for some reason, maybe the freshening arctic wind, there were tears in her eyes. The King squeezed her hand, the one with the scars and the ring, one last time. Then, beneath the frigid stare of the would-be assassin, they trudged back to their respective duties through the crackling, glittering, snow.

STORY NOTES

This is a very early story about what we would now call an advanced 3D printer. It does not quite take place in the same future history as most of the rest of the stories, though perhaps the King here could have been one of Empress Marie's ancestors, with a bit of "retcon." In this alternative future, the "reconquista" has taken the southwest U.S., while the northern parts have joined with Canada as part of a more muscular Commonwealth of nations — not very likely, but look at the demographics and wonder. As I write this, the Northern Ireland question has settled into a low-level chronic ache while Islamic State terrorism is ruling the media. That could change back again in a couple hundred years; we are dealing with conflicts that have persisted on a millennial time frame.

Back to 3D printing. Todays machines are not really replicators. They are pretty much limited to one, or a very few "feed stocks" and the resolution is far too coarse for atom-scale work. But people with the replicator dream in mind are constantly working to improve the machines and in a couple hundred years or so, who knows?

To initiate a chemical reaction, the reactants first have to achive a certain activation energy, a little hump on the energy curve to get over before all hell can break loose. In rocket propellant work, we call that "metastable" and there are all sorts of extraordinarily explosive things that seem very stable at temperature near abolute zero. Every now and then, some rocket engineer proposes to store cryogenic hydrogen and oxygen in the same propellant tank, to save weight. Seriously. We even looked at suspending antihydrogen ice in electromagnetic bottles, containing a perfect vacuum, of course. A few milligrams would get you to the moon, maybe even when you wanted to go.

I once viewed the servicing of a Titan IIIc booster payload (a communications satellite) from the top of a launch tower, along with several higher ranking officers. Despite signs saying that all tools should be tethered, the worker was using an untethered wrench. The Titan's fuel is Aerozine, more stable than hydrazine alone, but still, the kinetic energy of a wrench falling several stories might well have set it off. Do I say anything? I decided the risk to my career was greater than the risk to my life and kept my mouth shut. It worked out.

GDN January 2016

LAST CALL

We gathered just outside the door of the White Horse in the crisp clear December air for a look at the end of it all. John Junior had informed us that one could see it now, with all the lights of London gone. The lights were indeed gone, except for the one that mattered.

"Ms. D." Harry said into his mobile. "Shut the porch light off so we can see the bloody thing. In fact, come out and take a look for yourself."

It was Mr. D.'s granddaughter, of course. But she'd inherited the name, tradition being what the White Horse was all about. Harry, at 140 years young, was the only original, though John Jr., at 98, got an honorable mention.

"Now first let's try this without the tech. Find the North Star," John Jr. said.

In a minute or so, everyone's heads were properly oriented.

"Now find the bowl of the Little Dipper."

"Not as easy as it used to be, with all these stars, is it?" Harry said.

Some ironic chuckling ensued.

"Ahem," John Jr. continued. "The two stars at the front of the bowl, Kochab and Gamma, are the brightest in the area. Use them as pointers, but go below the bowl instead of above it as you did with the Big Dipper to find the North Star. About three Little Dipper bowl widths in that direction, you'll see another bright star; that's Eta Draconis. Now halfway between the bowl and Eta Draconis . . . "

"I got it," Edward said, waving his smart glasses.

"Bloody hell," complained John Jr. "Where's the skill in that? What's the world coming to?"

Stony silence. We all knew what the world was coming to.

"Figure of speech. Anyway, what you're looking for is the little whitish pinprick to the right of the tip of that narrow triangle, not the orangish one at the tip of the triangle."

"Doesn't look like much," Harry said.

"It's only about as wide across as Earth, and it's as far away as Jupiter," John Jr. replied.

"If we can bloody see the thing, why do they call it a black dwarf?" Edward asked.

"Reflected light," John Jr. said. "It's called a black dwarf because It used to be a white dwarf, but cooled down into the infrared. It's still warm and if we were really close, we could probably see it glow like embers."

"Like hell you say," Harry said.

"Quite."

A shaft of light and the scent of recently consumed steak and kidney pies announced the opening door and Ms. D. joined us outside. She was a big, no nonsense lady, but with a smile that could melt the ice of your drink before it got to you. John Jr. pointed out the black dwarf to her with a pocket torch.

"Half the mass of the Sun, that?" Edward asked.

"And then some, unfortunately," Harry said. "Chandrasekhar's limit for making Supernovae is only 1.44 solar masses, about two tenths of a solar mass *less* than the mass of the combined star. Though some simulations have the shock of impact blowing everything away before any collapse."

"Others don't," John Jr. said. "Not that the passage of the black dwarf wouldn't be been pretty disruptive in any event, but a supernova kind of puts an exclamation point on things. Anyway, by any mechanism, there's no stopping it. When it merges with the Sun, boom."

"Last call," Ms. D. deadpanned.

"So to speak," John Jr. answered. "Now, over on the other side of the sky . . . " he turned and we followed him almost in unison, " . . . can you make out the W of Cassiopeia, high up?"

"We aren't entirely tyros, John," Edward said.

"Of course. Well, continue south from that past the left side of the Great Square until you're about the same height above the horizon as Rigel in Orion to your left. See the patch of light around a middling yellow star?"

Our heads turned to the direction at which every big communications dish on Earth was already pointed. The destruction of the planet would be well documented.

"The Pleiades," said Edward.

John Jr. sighed. "No, that's not the Pleiades; those are fainter and up to the left in Taurus.

"*That* patch of light is in Cetus and is the backscatter glow from the tens of thousands of starships being pushed away from here to Tau Ceti, the new home star for all of humanity." He looked pointedly at Harry. "Well, *almost* all."

Despite the lateness of the hour, we were here to give it one more try.

"I haven't changed my mind," Harry replied.

"*Last call*," Ms. D. said again. "No joking; I haven't changed my mind either and it's getting late."

We filed into the bar for the last time. Like most of the rest of us, she'd be on the last shuttle tomorrow, bound for the *Fred Clarke* and Tau Ceti in half a century or so, most of which we'd spend sleeping. Tonight she would lock the door, as always, and never return.

Harry sat at the bar, having given up competitive darts — the prosthetic exoskeleton he wore under his tweeds making it unfair competition — and ordered a Guinness — a black stout, to go with his mood.

"Harry, you're still not going?" John Jr. asked.

"Oh, I'll get there," he said. "As plasma. I've done my time. My planet's done and I'm done with it. But you know, this reminds me of old Joe Cavendish."

There was a last "thunk" of a dart into the dart board and we all gathered around the bar for Harry's last reminiscence.

"Joe worked for the RAE back in the 70's, when this place was still at the Embankment and they had an office up there somewhere near Westminster. He and this visiting Swiss engineer, Hans Hoffmann, got into an argument about evacuating the Earth in one of Arthur's stories."

"A silly story," Edward said, ironically. "The Sun can't become a nova."

"That wasn't funny, Edward," Ms. D. said.

"Er, it can't by itself, anyway."

"Quite. Back to Joe's story, perhaps, Harry?" John Jr. suggested.

"Er, oh, yes. Anyway, when this happened, Arthur had long since emigrated to Sri Lanka. It was about the time the pub moved and he got rid of that American . . . "

"Harry, Joe Cavendish . . . " John Jr. prompted, gently again.

"I was getting to that. Joe was thirsty and a little short on funds and the German was arguing that space could never absorb even a small fraction of Earth's population, let alone all of it. So Joe made a wager."

Harry stared off in the distance, perhaps remembering many wagers, long ago.

"A wager . . . "

"Oh, yes. Joe wagered a beer that the Earth could, indeed, be evacuated, with enough time and motivation. Well, they went back and forth, talking about World War II aircraft and ship production rates, limitations on capital resources, von Neumann machines, energy requirements, Dyson spheres and so on. Finally, after several beers, Hoffmann up and said that he simply could not believe that enough spaceships could ever be built in time."

Harry took a long pull on his stout and gazed around him.

"What?" Edward said. "He stooped to an argument of personal incredulity in a White Horse debate? I can't believe it!"

There were groans all around.

"How did Joe answer *that*?" John Jr. asked.

Harry nodded and took a breath. "He asked Hans that if a single given bacterium can replicate itself once a day, and it takes one of them a month to fill up half a Petri dish with its descendants, how long would it take to fill up the other half?

"Well, Hans replied automatically that it would take another month."

More groans were heard.

"Quite. Silence *descended* on the room as if someone had turned on a sonic inverter. Of course, if all the bacteria in a half full dish replicated in the next day, the dish would be full. But to Hans, who had consumed a half-dozen pints in an hour, that wasn't brilliantly clear. Joe, who had consumed only the wagered pint, for financial reasons, then made it clear . . . "

Harry trailed off and gazed around the room, possibly remembering people who had sat, well, if not exactly at this location, at this bar, on some of these often-reupholstered bar stools, surrounded by some of these furnishings, including the dart board.

"Gentlemen," Ms. D. Announced, "It really is *last call*. We have a vactube train to catch to the Kenya spaceport. Harry, old boy, can you sum it all up?"

"In a moment, Ms. D., in a moment. Now, Hans didn't concede immediately, but he had a troubled look on his face, as if a longstanding article of faith had just died inside him.

"There was more discussion about asteroids, O'Neill colonies and such, but in the end, he conceded that the numbers for evacuation worked out, in principle. Then he asked Joe just what these giant mechanical "bacteria" — this was pre-nanotechnology, you understand — were supposed to eat?

"Joe waved his hands, literally, and said it was a future engineering problem and that they were just discussing the possibilities. Hans said 'Ja, Ja.' and Ms. D.'s father declared that, if he heard no objections, he would consider the debate won by Joe.

"Hans seemed as if he were in a trance as he paid the bill and staggered off to find transportation. Fred, ever the gentleman, followed him and hailed a cab. According to Fred, who knew some German, as he was assisted into the cab by the driver — human driver back then, mind you — Hans muttered that if feeding mechanical bacteria was just an engineering problem, then he would solve it."

"Ha!" Edward shouted, waving his smart glasses. "*That* Hans Hoffman. It only took him half a century!"

"Just in time, I would say," John Jr. remarked.

Indeed, the robotic doubling time had only recently gotten down to three months, and that, along with some other issues, meant our starships had only just begun departing.

"For some, perhaps," Harry agreed. "But for me, well, an end is made to everything. I belong here, in England, under the Sun and not in some rotating can around some less brilliant star. As it happens, the event will occur on Christmas day . . . "

"*Another* of Arthur's stories," John Jr. noted.

"He's Swiss, not German," Edward remarked.

Harry shrugged his shoulders, "He was speaking German. As I was saying, on Christmas day in 2063, if I last that long, when London is turned away from the Sun toward Orion, I shall put on a warm pullover, sit down on a comfortable chair on my porch, and take one last look at the Universe. Then, before the moon becomes too bright to see the stars, I shall turn myself off. At 143 years old and half mechanical anyway, that should present no insurmountable problem."

Ms. D. started pouring into the ensuing silence, and had five and a half pints of stout drawn before the cask ran out with a kind of hissy bubbly sound. "There ye are, gentleman, the last pints of beer ever drawn on planet Earth — for I am sure that by now, you are the last human beings on Earth at anywhere other than a spaceport! Now, drink up and be on your way."

"Very well," Harry said, grabbing a pint. "We'll be going. I have told my last story at the White Horse and the world is ringed with starships to take you all away."

"Just one starship, now, Harry," Ms. D. said, "and to catch up before the event vaporizes its power source, it will have to depart at five gravities with all of us immersed in fluid for three months! *Last Call!*"

"With a couple dozen years to work on it, Harry, they'll be able to give you a new biological body by the time we get there," John Jr. said. "Everybody is supposed to go, Harry; that's the basic premise — no down selection, everybody goes. The whole world goes."

Edward coughed. "Now just a bloody minute. The world isn't going anywhere. It's getting fried. The pub's getting fried. We're leaving it."

"Not exactly," Ms. D. said. "I'm the proprietor here, and this pub is going where I'm going. I'll have these things printed when I get there — weight limitation, you know. The White Horse has been in a dozen different buildings since 1732, but the name, some of the furnishings, and an unbroken chain of ownership go back to then. It is to *keep* that chain of ownership unbroken at a new location around Tau Ceti that I will be on that shuttle. That is *if* I can get ye all on your way! A pub is not a building and if I may abuse my role a bit, a world is not a planet."

Harry laughed. "So a pint of beer your father drew over half of a century years ago saved the world? Then," he lifted his own pint, "to Joe Cavendish and his wager!"

"Hear, hear!" rang out around the bar.

"But all the world is not saved unless everyone goes, Harry," I said. "You are not the oldest cyborg on the planet, and even if they don't all make it to Tau Ceti, everyone goes. Will you come, Harry?"

He seemed to be somewhere else already.

"Harry?"

He shook his head and nodded slowly, then he rose and, wisps of gray hair flying about his head, strode across the room, shut the doors of the dart board cabinet, and with exoskeletal strength, ripped the cabinet from the soon-to-be-unneeded wall, and turned to our assembly with a smile, holding his trophy over his head.

"Very well. But if they want me, they'll have to make room for this!"

"I'll put it on the bill," Ms. D. said with that smile on her face. "Now, *out* of here all of you."

We obediently filed out beneath the sea of stars. Ms. D. was last, of course. She smiled as she walked out the door, and didn't bother to lock it.

STORY NOTES

Besides being set in a venue very similar to Arthur C. Clarke's *Tales of the White Hart*, the story contains homages to his stories "Silence, Please" and "The Star" as well as Larry Niven's "Inconstant Moon" It can, itself, be seen as a prequel to Clarke's "Rescue Party" in which an alien starship attempts to rescue some of humanity before a Nova, only to find the planet deserted. The situation may also remind you of Harry Truman, the elderly proprietor of the Mount Saint Helens Lodge at Spirit Lake, who refused to evacuate before Mr. St. Helens blew up and, presumably, lies buried under tons of volcanic debris, fully understanding and choosing his fate.

While the elderly Clarke, perhaps a victim of one of his own laws, was skeptical about the possibility of evacuating the Earth, the younger Clarke, who wrote "Rescue Party", would have been very much aware of the scale of production achieved — without robots — in the latter stages of World War II. For instance, Britain, Russia, and the U.S built over 150,000 aircraft in 1944. Another interesting fact is that over a billion people leave this planet for the edge of space every year. They come back down from the stratosphere of course, and a space ship like the one on top of Elon Musk's notional interplanetary transportation system is probably an order of magnitude more costly than a Dreamliner — but not two. It is, as they say, beyond the scope of this note to take the argument further, but you get the idea. Do the numbers and yes, our progeny could evacuate Earth if we needed to, build interstellar spacecraft to go to, and with tireless robots, build the hardware to push them to the stars.

We say a permanent goodbye to Planet Earth in this story, so it isn't part of the future history most of my other works use. But there was a point to be made. When Clarke's rescuers got to the Earth, nobody was home. And that is exactly what happens, with a little additional effort, in this story.

GDN February 2017

FUTURE HISTORY TIMELINE

Year	Major Events	Tech. Notes	Stories (Unpublished Works) *Characters*
1930	**Quasi Historical Period**		
1936			**Voice of Ages**
1940	WWII	Multistage rockets	
	Cold War	Digital computers	*Lisa Reynolds 1958-2062*
1960	Moon landing/ASTP	Lasers/Moore's Law	*Halvorsen 1960-2060*
	Budget interregnum	Primitive space stations	**Karl's Marine & Spacecraft Repair**
		Cell phones, Internet	*George Samios 1982-2071*
2000	Russian revival	"Soft" AI: receptionists, etc.	*I. Karlsdotter b. 2000*
	Non-gov. made rocket in orbit	Self-driving cars legal	**P.C. Software**
		Robotics take off	**Harpoon**
2020	Orbital hotel	Fuel and Fly space access	**The Kubota Effect** (alt. history)
	Coriolis founded as a robot lunar farside mining camp 2026	Dustoff (nano coating repels dust)	**His Father's Voice**
		EML launch of lunar resources	**Hunting the Space Whale** (alt. history by 2010)
	Coriolis settlement	Gekro & other nanotech apps	
2030	**Interplanetary Era 2030-2150**		
	NEA mining begins	Benchtop refining	*Sally Duluth 2030-2128*
	China expansion wars	Antiproton scanners	*Somjet Turner b. 2041*
2040	UN/ISA Established, first Mars landing	Room temp superconductors	(Between Earth and Moon)
	Space resources become economically significant	O'Neill colonies, Main Belt mining	**Democritus' Violin**
		Nanotech refiner-printers	**Burdens The Moon House**
2050	Lunar weightlifter wins Olympic silver medal		(Hollow Moon) (Golden Wings) (Walls of Space)
		Fullerene cable (finally!)	**Tin Angel**
	Permanent Mars base	Spin batteries	(HM: A Time of Firsts) (HM:At Hyperbolic Excess)

Year	Major Events	Tech. Notes	**Stories** (Unpublished Works) *Characters*
	Cislunar Republic formed	Antonymous factories	(HM: Under the Gray Flag) (HM: In the Old Forrest)
	Ceres base established		(HM: The Last Rocket from Vittoria)
2060	Tension between ISA & CLR	Compact fission reactor	**The Fire and the Wind**
	Lisa Reynolds, First Cislunar President		(Himalia)
2065		Mars/Venus terraforming begins	*Hartigan O'Reilly 2081-2182*
	First Mercury Landing		**Haumea**
2070	Uranus, Neptune missions	Nuclear electric and beamed-microwave propulsion	*Wojciech Bubka b. 2072*
	Pluto, Eris missions		**Mustardseed**
2080	Jovian magnetic field reversal	Deimos-Mars elevator	*Miranda Lotati b. 2082*
	Trilateral tension between ISA, CLR & New Reformation on Mars	Efforts to replicate living organisms	**This Old Rock**
		Martian dome colonies	**Of Fire and Ice**
		Space colonies in Asteroid Belt	**Alice's Asteroid**
2095		Saturn, Kuiper Belt	*Gwen Chryse b. 2084*
	Makemake, Haumea visited	Saturn stations established	**Out of the Quiet Years**
2100			**Messengers of Chaos Haumea**
		Mass beam propulsion	**A Life on Mars Comet Gypsies**
2110		Interstellar probes	**Crossing Chao Meng Fu** (Down the Tubes)
	Proxima belt mission	P-B11 nuclear reactors	(Seas of Titan) **Into the Miranda Rift**
2120	Galactic Library Node found		**The Protean Solution A Calendar of Chaos Titan of Chaos**
2150	**Early Interstellar Era 2150-2250 — Humans Inhabit the Nearest Stars**		
	New Israel established at Proxima		**Barriers**

Year	Major Events	Tech. Notes	Stories (Unpublished Works) *Characters*
2175	First Kleth visit	Mars outdoor agriculture	**The Day of Their Coming**
	New Antarctica reached	Bioradio, biological immortality	**The Snows of Venus** **In HIS Image**
2200		Personality up/downloading	**Relic of Chaos**
	Earthmind and the Mind of Mars		*Hilda Kremer b. 2205 (N.A.)*
			Empress of Starlight (starts)
2250	**Later Interstellar Era 2250-2500 —** **Interstellar Commerce and Civilization**		
			The Black Hole Project
			Kremer's Limit **Small Pond**
2300	Nearby star systems settled	Terraforming as an art form	**Imperfect Gods** **Loki's Realm**
2350	After a political meltdown, an A.I. mediated monarchy established	Galactic technology adopted	*Empress Marie*
			To Climb a Flat Mountain (backstory)
			Democracy of Cannibals
2400	36 Ophiuchi intervention		**The Fountain** (backstory)
2500	**Post-Singularity Era 2500-5000 — S-Curves** **Have Approached Their Upper Limits**		
2550			**Empress of Starlight** (arrival)
2600			*Drinnl'Ib, Mary, Do-Tor & Go Tan*
			The Fountain
2700	Kleth, Do'utia, Earth form Trimus		**Fugue on a Sunken Continent**
2800			**Poles Apart** **Network** **Final Review**
2900	Epona encountered		(Broken Egg)
3000			*To Climb a Flat Mountain* (arrival)
3200			**Hell Orbit**
3400			**War, Ice, Egg, Universe**
3600			**Dawn Venus**

Year	Major Events	Tech. Notes	Stories (Unpublished Works) *Characters*
3800		Human-built Dyson spheres	**From Every Opening Flower**
4000	Resolution III home from Antares		**The Forest Between the Worlds**
4200	Venus terraformed		
5000	**Transhuman Era — Stories of Living Fossils and Allegories of Infinity**		
5200	Iota Cephi becomes North Star	Most people exist as programs	**Morning on Mars**
14 Ma	(1 Ma = 1 Mega annum/ one million years)	Intergalactic travel	**The Touch**
100 Ma	Nanocell beings		
5 Ga	The Sun becomes a red giant, Earth relocated		**Around an Ancient Star** (*After the Vikings* framing story)
6 Ga	The Sun becomes a white dwarf		
??????	A time of only slightly constrained imagination	Anything that's possible and worth doing has been done	**Attraction**
	Struggle against the dissipation of the Universe		

Printed in Great Britain
by Amazon

87814389R00162